PRAISE FOR BECOMING HUMAN

"*The Giver* meets *A Wrinkle in Time* in this twisty, sci-fi adventure."
~D.J. Butler, award-winning author of *Witchy Eye*

"Human and alien, complex and sweetly personal, Carpenter's thoughtful world blends sci-fi with coming of age as three unique worlds collide. This book will make you laugh, make you fall in love, and then make you re-evaluate what it means to be human."
~McKelle George, HarperCollins author of *Speak Easy, Speak Love*

"Packed with lively characters and amazing world-building, *Becoming Human* drew me right in and didn't let me go until the end."
~Molly Zenk, USA Today Bestselling author

"I was blown away by this hilarious, heartfelt story of two alien teenage girls and a human boy trying to save the world."
~Ruth Mitchell, award-winning author of *Deleted*

"I loved it. I seriously loved it. I can't wait for the paperback. I'm going to be first in line to preorder it. I must have it on my shelf!!"

~Samantha Rose, science-fiction author of *The Very Real World of Emily Adams*

"*Becoming Human* is an amazing read for sci-fi readers who love adventure with quirky aliens!"

~Celeste Harte, author of Buzzfeed's featured *Conquest*

"Engaging from page one, I fell in love with the tone and depth, the many voices of the many stories and how it came together in this beautiful and very relevant book."

~Pete Fanning, author of Amazon's top new release *Runaway Blues*

Becoming
HUMAN

AMY MICHELLE CARPENTER

Immortal Works LLC
1505 Glenrose Drive
Salt Lake City, Utah 84104
Tel: (385) 202-0116

Cover Art by Ashley Literski
http://strangedevotion.wixsite.com/strangedesigns

ISBN 978-1-953491-96-1 (Paperback)
ASIN B08N45KNNK (Kindle Edition)

To Mom, Carol, and Jesus. The ones who give and only ask my happiness in return.

Chapter 1

CARTER

I don't believe anymore. Don't get me wrong. I believe in plenty of *possible* things. Like Jesus. Hallelujah. Praise Him! Ghosts (they're another word for spirits, really). I even believe that we could get a snow day in Georgia. It's unlikely but still *possible*. But the aliens playing on the movie over Drew's pool are *impossible* things. They're straight-up fiction. And, when I was a kid, opening my mouth to defend their existence ruined my life.

So WHEN DREW settles in front of my comfy lawn chair in his speedo, I'm not too surprised when it leads to more ruining. He jabs his finger toward the projection screen by his pool and says, "So, Carter, does the alien your dad met look more like those ones—or Yoda?" I groan and skim the crowd to see if anyone notices. The chair's not so comfy once he starts to howl with laughter.

Everyone else is busy enjoying Drew's end-of-the-summer pool party. A group lingers by the snack table, munching on fresh empanadas from Antonio's mom. Some guys dunk each other in the water while others flirt with girls in the hot tub. The country music's amped to high volume, so maybe nobody heard him.

"Funny," I say, trying to stay cool. "Aliens aren't real." I sip my Sprite, running out of everything but ice cubes.

Ten dollars says he picked *Space Explosions II* on purpose.

"Really?" he asks. "I hear your dad still talks about aliens nonstop. Didn't you believe in them too?"

A few girls giggle, and Drew grins like he's so clever. I'm glad it's dark enough that they won't see my face burn as red as my hair. I dump the ice cubes into my mouth and chew. It's been years since I said I believed in them. *Years.*

Antonio shoves his way past the growing crowd around my chair. "Have you tried the empanadas?" he asks, cheese oozing from his mouth. He plops into a seat beside me. "Seriously, Carter, if Saturdays had a flavor, they'd taste like these empanadas."

I take a few from his overfilled plate and try to ignore everybody. "Real good," I say.

Drew turns his attention from me to flirt with some girls and leaps into the water. He flip-turns and swims butterfly stroke, probably in an attempt to show the ladies how much better he is than us regular swimmers.

Antonio leans in toward me. "You know, you don't have to be so defensive. Who knows? Maybe your dad did meet an alien." He runs his fingers over his shaved head. "With maybe ten trillion planets in the universe, there's got to be some life forms out there, right?"

I glance at him, and he shuts his mouth. I get that Antonio loves the universe as much as he loves swimming and MMA. His love for the planets is how we became best friends. But he's wrong. Aliens are a joke.

I'm not going to wait for Drew to make his next move. I get up, head to the snack table, and hope life returns to the way it was ten seconds ago. But there are still two aliens up on the screen, making funny noises. Now that I'm bigger than most other guys, people don't mess with me much, but it's hard to forget the past. *Why now, Drew?* Maybe because Anna rejected his invitation to come to his party, and he thinks it's 'cause she still likes me.

"So, is it true?" says a girl in a white t-shirt, filling her plate with chips. "Does your dad really say aliens are real? Oh, you poor thang."

Eesh, I can't take this. I'm not even a party kind of guy anyway. I just came because I thought it'd be good for building swim team camaraderie, and I love Antonio's mom's empanadas. Too bad I didn't get to enjoy them.

I'm outta here. I slip through the gate and stride across the front yard of Drew's parents' mansion. I climb into my truck, exhaling, and start the engine. *Going home. Save me some* 🍤, I text Antonio and then speed away.

A few miles down the street, I pull into our cracked driveway. Sputnik's tail wags under the bright porch lights. She barks and dashes over to me, slipping between my legs.

"Hey, girl," I say. I already feel better. "Want to join me?"

I pass the family swing set toward our woods. But then, Jason's tired voice comes from the back door. He holds a jar of lightning bugs. "Can I come, too?" he says.

Mama's probably tired of babysitting him and the twins all weekend for my big sister, Margi. Errgh. "Okay," I say. I trudge through the woods, trying to ignore the insane humidity. Jason weaves between maple trees and snatches lightning bugs, shoving them into his mason jar.

A blinking bug hovers above a higher branch of a tree. "Betcha can't catch that one."

"You're on, Uncle Carter." Jason sets his mason jar on a fallen log. It casts a yellow glow and makes his grin almost devilish against his identical-to-mine fire curls. He rushes forward with his arms out to snatch the lightning bug and misses.

"Here, lemme show you how it's done," I say, happy to distract him and myself. I whip out my flashlight, flipping it up and down to look like a bug like it says to do online.

The lightning bug hovers over us, and I reach for it but accidentally trip over the log and fall face-down in the mud. The jar spirals to Jason's feet. He cracks up, picks up the container, and taps it, while I moan in pain. "Yep. Showed me."

He mocks me by dancing around, pretending to fall.

I roll my eyes as he continues to howl with laughter. "Haha, funny. Don't laugh at me, or I'll tell your mama about all the dozens of cookies you swiped from our cupboard."

Jason frowns, and I swat him on the back to let him know I'm joking.

I relax against a fallen log and rub Sputnik's back. Being in the woods makes it easy to forget all the nonsense and drama.

"Think it's past your bedtime," I tell Jason. "And I gotta let Mama know I made it home safe. So, we should probably go inside."

"I'm seven. Basically a man. Men don't have bedtimes," he says and puts his arms over his chest just like his dad. Then, he jumps to a branch and swings from it.

I cave. I see a small light blink past a cluster of trees and I point it out to Jason. He dashes toward it, disappearing from view. It's silent except for the quiet crunch of leaves beneath my boots and the occasional chirp of crickets. I tuck one hand into my jeans and suck on a honeysuckle with the other.

And then, a single scream cuts through the air. I tear toward Jason as he continues hollering. Twigs break. Sputnik barks as I jet around a tree and spot him.

Hovering above Jason's head is a circular, metallic object the size of our beat-up ATV. It whirs quietly in the wind. Lights flash across it almost as if in a rhythmic dance.

If I didn't know better, I'd think the thing was a UFO. But, of course, I know better.

KOKAB

I SHOULD NOT *FEEL* THINGS.

Regardless, the first stirring of the day comes at 76:05, a slight painful sensation in my mind. I push it away. I must be as blank internally as the room is externally. White walls. White desk. White entrance door. Sterilized.

The only disruption to this blankness is the floor. Silver, indicative of perfection, lines run down the halls to indicate the government status of the building.

An Office Worker stands beside me and takes notes on a slim screen. As she types, her second pinkie twitches, ever so slightly. Her black eyes shift toward me.

She is practically identical to every other female, including myself. Her skin is transparent, head an exact sphere, lips square, eyes parallel to both noses—but her shoulders are too broad. They are more like male shoulders.

Mine are perfect.

"Name?" she says.

"Abedhakokab Trielldegerata. Kokab, for convenience."

"Age?"

"Two-hundred-seven."

A single strand of her metallic hair falls from the knot behind her shoulder. A piece of dust drops to the ground on the other side of the vast room.

It distracts my focus.

These details are easy for me to detect, not only because of my perfect hearing and sight, but because I have been trained to catch any errors. I keep my long hair knotted exactly at the back of my head and do not make her mistakes.

But even though I am superior in my actions, it does not change my classification. Actions are not enough. She is an Almost, and so am I. We are not Perfects like the elite in our society, but we are not Differents either.

The worker examines her screen and then motions for me to follow. I march behind her. My steps quietly drum the ground to the exact beat of hers. We move our arms in sync with one another. We pass a group of Younglings, all dressed in white with a bronze-wear medallion across their chest, which means they are here to be tested.

I should be a Youngling, but I completed my testing early. It is unusual for anyone who has already been classified to come to the

Elder Ones' Office since a summons often means reprimand or reward. It's unlikely that I will be rewarded, so I run through possible scenarios for reproof. I ate once more than commanded last week. I also fell asleep a few edes late last night. If they tapped into my brain waves, they would see that the flickers are occurring more often. The flickers, these abnormal emotional responses, are what keep me from being a Perfect.

She stops at a tall, rectangular door. "They are ready for you," she says.

I enter. The Elder Ones sit in silver chairs in a circle around me. They turn their clear faces immediately to mine. I remain quiet, standing there. Though the actions are correct, the flickers shift through me. A brief ache. They continue to examine me, and I shove the feeling away. I force myself to nothingness.

Emptiness.

The Elder Ones remain still, fingers tucked into their distinguishably colored suits: brown, orange, tan, and red. Each suit is lined with silver to indicate their status as Perfects. One, however, taps his chin. His entire suit is silver. He's older than anyone I have ever seen. His face is creased, not smooth like it should be. His body bends slightly. I have never seen someone so different looking before. Yet he is not a Different.

The leader of the Elder Ones? I have heard that he does not look like the rest of us.

Stop. I should not wonder unless I am asked to.

He rises and addresses me. "Abedhakokab Trielldegerata, daughter of Deandona Trielldegerata, we welcome you. I am the Eldest One." He confirms my suspicion, though I should not have had it. His eyes move rapidly across my face. "You have been chosen."

I blink. My sorting has already taken place. I am an Almost and Judger. We are not re-classified. I understand that only the Elder Ones have the agency to make choices for our people. What does he mean when he says I am chosen? But I should not—I cannot—

question *him*. He is the Eldest One, the one who should never be questioned. I push away my thoughts, listening, accepting his statement. I do not understand, but I must always follow.

The one in red rises. He blinks, and his mouth twitches but returns to blankness. He runs his fingers across a screen similar to the one the Office Worker used.

"I am uploading information to the nanochip in your mind," he says.

I close my eyes in order to focus. Planet Foxia appears, but it is different than what it is now. A male and female stroll across a dark green plain. Gray mountains hover behind them, covered in something white. Animals roam the peaks. A reddish creature with three ears jets between the two.

The two Foxians are not transparent-skinned. I cannot see their hearts, but I can hear them pumping. Only one heart each. They rest below a tree, hand in hand. Vines twist around them. Bright fruit hangs from it. We do not hold hands anymore.

"This is our world shortly after it began," the Eldest One says. "This is before Abaddon's War."

The images shift forward in time, passing over the Great War, where emotions were eradicated. The sky darkens, the animals disappear; only shades of gray remain. Then, it alters once more. An asteroid crashes into the ground and rips the surface into thousands of pieces. Some pieces hurtle quickly back into the atmosphere where they rain on Foxia and its inhabitants. Blackness sweeps across the planet as the dark debris of the burning asteroid blocks out the sunlight.

I cannot see anything now, but the screams of millions of Foxians pierce the usual silence. They should not scream, although death can invoke some feeling. Without the sun, they will die. Everything will die. I flinch but only briefly and quickly urge down the pain that enters my body as all our people die. I force myself to numbness.

"Is this real?" I pinch my lips. I should not ask.

"No. But it is what will happen. We made an error. Our ground-based telescopes and radars discover thousands of asteroids per year. But there is no known radar capable of sweeping all of space, even close to Foxia. We missed one," the Eldest One says. "It will hit us in thirty-two days. If we'd known sooner, we might have terraformed an uninhabited planet or tried to build temporary shelters somewhere. As it is, the most viable option we see for survival is to seek cohabitation with an already inhabited planet."

I nod my head, forcing myself not to consider how Perfects could make an error. This should not be. Perfects never make mistakes.

"It will take us twenty-nine days to build a ship large enough to fit two billion Foxians. One planet is most viable for our survival, but it is not an ideal fit. Through various studies and patterns, we discovered who among us will most easily adjust to that world. We will send that Foxian there as a scout to persuade leaders that our arrival is essential and to learn how to help us adjust. We don't want to incite a war—death and machinery are unnecessary expenses for them and us. However, we must evacuate and travel to this planet no matter what. It is our only option."

He pauses, an out of sync behavior. His eyes slip to the Foxian in red. "Some in our council do not agree that we should try to maintain peace."

Council members do not always agree?

"We chose you, Kokab. Our survival depends on you. You are different, but for this, you are also useful."

My eyes widen. Different is not my labeling. More visions are transmitted to me. A planet covered in green and a large amount of blue appears. Water? Creatures move through it. A small animal with fins jets to a green underwater plant, its movements not in sync with the others around it. A large group of beings parade across cement streets with movements so out of sync, it makes my head spin. Their voices grate my ears, and their clothing encompasses thousands of colors. Distorted buildings reach into the sky.

I swallow, no longer aware of the room around me. I attempt to stand still as the planet swirls in front of me. My senses are overloaded with the uncorrelated details of this world.

"It's called Earth. The intelligent lifeforms on Earth are titled 'humans.' They are nothing like us. They have emotions and freedom. Their world is filled with opposition, love, hate, joy, sorrow, doubt, faith. We've watched them from afar, but we have trouble comprehending them."

I remain silent. Elders are meant to comprehend everything. Understanding is their calling.

"We selected you to go to Earth because you may be able to experience those feelings. You feel in a way that most Foxians do not. You can become like a human, and try to understand how best to persuade those on Earth to let us come. There are other Foxians like you. But they are not as perfect in their obedience and physical actions as you are. We trust you with this important task."

The Eldest One pauses. "Your mother would have been a better candidate, as she seemed to understand these emotions better, but unfortunately, she is gone."

I flinch. We never mention dead ones. He notices the movement and nods as if achieving his goal.

"We will meet you at a later time with further instruction. Do you accept this calling?"

I remain still. Though they asked, I have no choice. We never choose, only obey. I must go, and I must succeed.

"Yes."

AGS

I wrap my fingers around the sleek, golden throttle and shift modes like I've been taught. Mom yelps as our two-person spacecraft jerks into speed-of-light mode and yanks the brake. "Ags! What are you doing?" she screams. "You didn't put up any shields. You're lucky those few seconds were empty space, or we'd be dead. Dead. Dead. Dead. Dead."

Mom shrieks as I nearly smash into an asteroid.

"Don't hurt your daughter. Just smile and support her. Smile and support her." Mom's been muttering to herself about me ever since I started learning to pilot.

Am I really that horrible? We're alive. For now.

Gods of the universe, please don't let me kill us.

"You're making me nervous," I say.

"I'm making *you* nervous?" Mom grabs a handful of her naturally pink hair and wrenches it around her manicured nails like a human child winding up a jack-in-the-box. Her hair makes me jealous. I hate that mine matches my orange skin and is the same shade as almost every other Yadian.

"Sorry," I say. "Do you want to drive? I'm too distracted to try to learn this impossible skill."

Mom stops attacking her hair and wiggles her thin nose up and down in agreement. She settles into the plush driver seat. The ship glides past asteroids, comfortable with her touch. Once we're out of the asteroid belt, she switches the craft into autonomous mode and moves to the bedroom in the back to get ready.

Rather than sitting, I pace and run through my required lines of acceptance. The thick fabric of my green dress chafes my legs. I'm not putting on the wooden shoes until the actual ceremony.

Usually, I like to wear human clothes. American blue jeans. French berets. Hand-stitched hijabs. Pieces of unique art and culture. Mom says it's good to embrace humanity, and I'm obsessed with all things Earth-related anyway. But I'm so excited to graduate the Academy, I don't mind the traditional garb too much.

Finally. Finally. I get to be an official Guardian of Earth. *I can't wait to rub my feet in your green grass for the first time EVER.*

WE LAND outside the Academy in the ship docks, and I dash through the craft doors ahead of Mom.

The buildings in Fis City glow, stacked so tightly against each other and reaching so far into the distance it almost seems like there's no room for air. Orange, purple, and pink lights swirl overhead in the sky, a backdrop to the massive school itself. People climb from their ships and hustle past me, donned in bright and dull colors, foliage and gemstone and plastic, all signs of the planets they protect. They grin as they nod their noses toward me.

I weave through the dock and stand in front of the Academy. It stretches up toward the heavens, twisting and reaching as if grasping at the universe to cuddle it in its arms. The bright building shifts from deep burgundy to light orange to blue. If I'd been in class more, I'd be used to the towering piece of architectural genius. I've been observing Earth for so long from an interstellar study with Mom that Yadia hardly feels like home.

That's why I don't notice it when Yas taps me on the shoulder.

"Stop gaping, Ags," he tells me. "You look like a visitor."

"I can't help it." It's weird to speak Yadian again, foreign on my tongue. I'm so used to human languages. I toss my arms around his neck. He's taller and has finally grown orange scruff on his cheeks, but he's just as gangly as ever. "It's just so beautiful. And I love art."

"I know," he says. "Why else would you want to be a guardian of Earth?"

"Just because Earth doesn't have a *lot* of alien risks—"

"Any alien risks."

"Doesn't mean it isn't interesting." I gesture to the pink bow in my hair. We may have to wear traditional clothes, but I *had* to get something human as a token of my soon-to-be new position.

"Sure, but it's not going to be like Artian. With all the planets wanting to jump in and take its untapped reserve of energy stones, I'll have to be a political genius to convince others not to attack. And you'll just be...taking notes."

He's told me this a few times. In his own awkward way, I know he's just excited to be a guardian too. Besides, it doesn't bother me. Artian may have energy rocks, an important fuel source for spaceships. But the creatures living there are as dull as the rocks.

Yes, I'm sure it'll be so exciting to watch the inhabitants sleep all day. Not interested.

Though guarding Earth is less esteemed, being a guardian is still considered the most honorable job title in Yadia. It takes a lot of years of schooling, and most families have at least one protector to boost their value in society. We're altruistic, or, at least, we consider ourselves to be. So, for hundreds of years, we've been helping out the planets that can't help themselves. Planets that aren't as technologically advanced. If anything bad were to happen on an interstellar scale, I'd step in.

I also get to collect data on the planet, which is what fascinates me.

"Gaining knowledge." I correct him. "Earth is incredibly fascinating. And entertaining. People— they're amazing, weird, and so, so gorgeous."

Yas rolls his eyes at my enthusiasm and yanks me forward, so we can make it to our own graduation in time. "So, like you, then."

I follow his lead, still focused on the masterpiece in front of us. Yas says humans are like me, but they are a lot more like Yas than he realizes—our species are as close as they come. Humans look like us but with different skin tones and hair colors, though we have a few extra quirks like really flexible noses. We are both emotionally-based species, unlike others who don't feel at all, and we even have similar rituals and practices.

But Earth is the baby, new and excited about life, still trying to figure things out. And we're a bit duller and less fun like grown-ups.

The noisy chatter of others engulfs me before I see them. Beaming young graduates roll through the huge seashell-like door in mass numbers dressed in the same glowing green material as me.

It hits me, what I'm about to do, the responsibility I will take on.

Can I really do it? Protect all those human beings from

interstellar harm if anything were to happen? Am I more than just a crazy art and cultural fanatic? Could I fight for them if I had to? I love my humans. I can't let them down.

Yas notices my deep frown and nudges my shoulder.

"Don't worry," he says. "Nothing ever happens on Earth. And you'd do great if something did."

He reaches for me and hooks his green shrouded arm around mine. "For the betterment of the universe," he says, stating the guardian motto.

Yas is probably right. Other than a few curious researchers or vacationers, no one's ever tried to invade Earth before. Why worry?

"For the betterment of the universe," I repeat, striding through the radiating front doors of the Academy to grasp hold of my future.

Chapter 2

KOKAB

The group of Younglings performs the test in their own individual rooms inside the Office of the Elder Ones. I examine their data from a screen in my personal office.

They step as they should, elbows bent at a ninety-degree angle, in sync even though they cannot see one another. Most of them answer questions correctly and refrain from emotional reactions.

One individual is off. I glance at his file: Bredrion Ahgraama Hoxia.

I recognize him from school, but I never learned his name. He was always the Youngling with a leg one-eighth ede longer than the other.

He steps left when he should, but his knees bend too far. The computer registers his movement as only 87 percent in sync. He must average 99.5 percent to gain status as an Almost.

The scan of his brainwaves indicates a few flickers. He feels something like me.

No. He is not like me. My behaviors are Perfect. I would have been Perfect if not for the occasional flickers. The Eldest One may have called me a Different, but I am not like this Youngling.

I am not.

The computer sorts him into the category of "Different." I shove aside the slight tinge in my stomach. I have never had to assign someone as a Different, but it is my job to relay his position.

I call him to my office. When he arrives, he sits in front of my desk. His lip quivers slightly, but then it returns to normal.

"You are a Different," I tell the Youngling. Usually, I hand out clothing, gray for Almosts, and silver for Perfects, but Differents do not have a color. They wear whatever they can find. "I will assign you a job after reviewing your file, and I will work with you to improve any inconsistencies."

Being Different prevents individuals from getting intellectually demanding jobs. His options will be limited, but he will be treated well.

He nods. His lip trembles again, and he exits. His steps echo down the hall, and the missteps make it difficult to concentrate. I return to my screen. I have three more appointments today, and then I am scheduled to go home and eat.

An Office Worker enters. "Kokab, the Elders have instruction to give you," she says. "You are to be surgically altered to appear more human, so you can acclimate mankind to us. Follow me to the medical center."

I leave my work. Someone will be put in my place to review the tests.

An order from the Elder Ones always trumps any other appointment. We take an airbus to a Perfect hospital. The Office Worker's steps echo carefully on the metal walkway. Her organs shift in rhythm to her steps and my own. They are almost exactly in sync. Based on her actions, she might have missed the mark to be a Perfect by .01 percent.

She leads me through a back entrance and ushers me into a small private room. A medical expert stands in a plain silver uniform. A Perfect.

"We have been preparing for you." He gestures toward an exam table. "It is requisite that you remove your clothing for the operation. It requires skin to skin contact to transfer the nanorobots in my skin cells to your skin cells."

I remove my clothes and lay naked on the metallic table. He ties me down using sixteen metal belts. *Is it possible that this may hurt?*

It is rare to feel pain as I only have little touch sensation, but intense enough pressure can be unpleasant. Lights flash into my eyes. Repetitively. The brightness blinds me, but I force myself not to blink. He shifts around the table and takes notes as he examines my eyes. Then the lights shift down my body. He continues taking notes.

He slides his index finger from my navel to my clavicle. My skin eases open as if I am being unzipped. His command to the nanorobots in my bloodstream to deconstruct is silent, but I know the codes to use. I have never utilized this command before, but I could if it was necessary. I could also repair myself and others with the nanobots in my bloodstream, but I have never needed to. It is rare for a Foxian to be injured.

I feel nothing, but green liquid oozes from me. My blood. It has been a long time since I have seen something organic with color.

He makes a neat slice into my arm and eases out one of my hearts. His fingers dash to clamp down on my veins. He closes his eyes, healing me, using a reverse command. He moves to the slice on my arm, doing the same. It disappears.

"Humans only have one heart," he says. "One heart will make you more fragile. We are still calculating how much."

He continues to give slice commands, pulling out organs and relocating other body parts. He removes both of my noses, and he places one in the middle of my face. A male in a gray uniform steps into the room. He carries a long needle to the table, injecting something over and over into my skin.

There is no pain, but I do get a stirring as my body transforms. Long thin hairs sprout and cover my bare legs, my arms. They take another needle, full of a light blue liquid.

"This will dye your skin," the male tells me, sticking the needle in me before I even respond. My skin shifts from translucent to tan. He uses another needle to dye my blood.

They pull me from the metal table and force me to stand. A tub of my blood floats to the left of the room, and I look away. My stomach churns, and it is now harder to control.

I am weak. I glance down at my arms. The inconsistent hairs. Small creases scattered across my fingers. Looking at myself causes stirrings, so I stare forward.

They order me to remain standing, so I do. I will not stop, no matter how long they require it. If they are testing my capability, I will prove that I am still able to obey.

After only hours, I find it difficult to maintain my posture. The doctor stands silently beside me with a timer. I realize he is waiting for me to falter, checking to see if I will fail. I do not move. I maintain composure, but too quickly, more quickly than I have experienced prior, my body begins to tremble.

I keep standing because he does not ask me to stop. I try to obey. I try to stay still. I stand all morning and all evening. The process continues. After only a full day, my legs shake independently of each other as if they're not attached to the same body.

Then, I fall.

I collapse to the ground in a balled-up heap, my body giving way. Unacceptable.

The medical expert lifts me as I continue to tremble and carries me to the table, and I prepare for it to be over, but it does not end. He uploads information based on the Eldest Ones' studies of the human species, quadrupling the information previously existing on my brain chip.

"We have been watching humankind via a satellite for thousands of years," he tells me. "They have recognized it, labeled it the Black Knight, but it is a conspiracy theory among their sort.

"State the capital of the United States of America," he says, speaking in a human language I have never heard before but somehow understand. It must have been downloaded into my chip. The language is less precise than ours, broken, and it sounds faulty. English? A metal machine records information at his side.

"Washington, District of Columbia."

"Correct. Label this." He points to an image of a small brown creature with pointed ears on the large 3D screen. His translucent finger stays perfectly rigid, not moving. It is difficult now for me to stay still.

"Species is dog. The common name for it is chihuahua."

"And the scientific name?"

"Canis Familiaris."

"Correct. Label this sandwich type."

"Meatball."

He does a few more tests and then stands. "The learning chip was effective. You will know as much about Earth as we understand and deem important to your mission."

He tilts his head. "Define *teenager*."

"A human between the age of a child and an adult. Some races distinguish them as a separate group, but others classify teenagers as adult," I say, staring at my colorful hands, trying to stay as composed as possible.

"Unfortunately, you will only know the facts. We cannot configure anything beyond the logic. Your senses may be a bit overwhelmed at first, causing dizziness and misinterpretation of info. But it is up to you to sort through all the information you learn to understand how human emotions work."

Our world may be four times larger than Earth, but Foxians do not function in the distinct ways humans do. We are the same. From the information I have stored in my chip, they are all different from one another, impossible to understand. But, understanding is my job now, and I must perform it perfectly. The Eldest One I previously met steps into the room, and the medical expert bends his head in recognition of authority, exiting without a word.

He hands me my clothes. "I see they have been working on you," he says, looking down at me. I am much shorter than him now. "But still tall. Six feet two inches is a very large human female."

The Eldest One holds a small mirror in his hands. The only times I used mirrors before were during posture practices to check the perfection of my movements. We do not use mirrors for any other reason.

"Do you wish to see yourself?" he asks.

"If that is your desire."

"But what do *you* want?"

"I have no preference."

He sets the mirror down and instead shows me a digital image. A group of people strides through a busy city street. They are covered in flaws and inconsistencies. Their bodies are different sizes, their skin tones differ, and they have various hair colors. Not even their eye colors or body parts are the same among their own species.

My fingers instinctively reach for the mirror, but I yank them backward. I have not been ordered to look.

"Take it," the Eldest One tells me. His lips curve up to the side in what, according to my chip, almost looks like a smile.

I snatch the mirror up, my motions not in sync at all, and stare.

My copper hair is gone, replaced with uneven strands that drop from my scalp in 203 shades of brown. 102,101 follicles dot my head. An odd number. The top half of my lips are inconsistent with the bottom, no longer square, but bright red. It is a color I have never seen as part of a living creature's coloring. Only the pupils of my eyes are still black. Blue tinges the irises. I press my finger to my cheek, and my skin indents against the pressure. So weak and malleable. My stomach drops.

I am changed, no longer an Almost. Not even a Different.

I am human.

My grip on the mirror loosens, but I stop myself before I drop it. I attempt to hand the mirror over to the Elder One with preciseness as always.

He holds the mirror in his hand, running his finger across the smooth, silver frame.

"A mirror should be an ornate, beautiful thing. But we use it to learn tasks. So exact. Useful. Like everything else. It wasn't always like that," he says. "Back before the war. I was there, you know."

I nod. I am aware. The Elder Ones were there several thousand years back before the world transformed. This is why they are in charge now. They tell us what to do because they are the ones with the most knowledge.

He sets the mirror facedown and says quietly, "Not all the Elder Ones wanted Abaddon to win."

I shove away the questions because we do not question Elder Ones, but the thought comes anyway.

How is that possible? We all have been taught that Abaddon's plan is superior.

The Eldest One shakes his head and moves on. "We have invited a man named Joe Turner to supervise you, help you understand Earth's customs. He will get you in contact with the right people. You must not tell anyone your identity or where you came from. This order trumps all. Do you understand?"

I nod.

He continues. "You will not be just like them. It is not possible. We, as a kind, are essentially Perfect, and they are full of imperfections. You will be stronger, faster, more attractive than any of them. You will have abilities that they cannot have. But this is the best we can do with the technology we have. You are fortunate to become like them, really. Humans are both better and worse than they seem."

I accept, though it makes little sense he'd call me fortunate. My body is no longer capable or even close to Perfect.

CARTER

I CAN'T UNSTICK my feet from the grass as the weird device speeds away. Jason stops hollering and turns to me.

"A UFO. Uncle Carter. A UFO."

When I was in fifth grade, I saw a real UFO in our backyard. It gave me hope that my dad wasn't crazy after all. But in the morning, I found the painted cardboard boxes with glued-in LED lights shoved behind our trash can. My hope was snatched away.

People can mess with me. But not my family.

I grab Jason by the shoulders. "It's a drone or something. A funny joke. Haha, got it?"

He rolls his eyes, so I repeat myself.

"Okay. Okay," he mutters.

I exhale. Didn't even know I was holding it all in.

A guy can't even find peace out in the woods anymore.

We trod back through the trees, past the falling-apart playset I made with Dad when I was younger.

The kitchen light's still on, probably 'cause Mama's up late working again. "Hey," I say, as Jason darts inside. I follow behind him and turn to shut the creaky door. "If Granny's still up, don't mention—"

"Papaw!" Jason says and plops his jar of lightning bugs on the floor.

I flip around, and there he stands. Dad's by the table.

I tense. Seeing him is almost as surprising as seeing a UFO would be. If it was real.

Jason dashes forward and throws his arms around Dad's neck. I stay by the chickpeas Mama left out for us on the stovetop.

"It's been two weeks," I say, not trying to hide the coolness in my voice. "Glad you didn't run off and leave us or something."

He glances at me with his dark eyes and skin bag of a body, thinner than even the last time I saw him. He's not the dad I knew— the strong hero I grew up with.

Through the window, his truck sits idly by mine. I missed it somehow. I guess I wasn't paying attention, the same way he stopped paying attention to our family years ago.

Dad hiccups and rearranges his blue glasses so that they are even more crooked over his nose than before. He does it again a few times and stays focused on the petunias in the window. He doesn't act this nervous around other people. How come one teenager's so threatening?

"I'm sorry," he says. "There was some important business to attend to. And Brian said there might be a job open in D.C. But it didn't pan out."

"Papaw, did you bring me any presents?" Jason asks. Right, he's here still too. Shoot. *Please, don't talk about the aliens.*

I send a zipped-face emoji to his phone, which his dad, Cody, thinks he's old enough to have. He giggles when he gets it and sends me a series of random emojis, so I don't think he understood me.

"I have to get Jason to bed," I say, "It's really late." Then, I try to lift Jason up onto my shoulders like he loves, but he pushes away.

"Where's my present?" Jason demands.

Dad pulls out a toy spaceship, and Jason's eyes get as round as a brown butter cheesecake. "Papaw, there was a—"

I quickly clamp my hands over his mouth. "Come on. It's past your bedtime," I say.

Jason thrusts it off. "Papaw, I don't think you're crazy like the hobo at Hickory Creek!"

Dad's so silent I can hear the grasshoppers creaking outside. He pushes his glasses to his eyes again and grimaces.

Finally, he speaks in a shaky little voice. "Who said I was crazy like a hobo?"

Jason glances at me with a naughty grin on his face, and I study the tiles hard.

Dad grips the kitchen chair, and he studies the ground too, frowning like a rejected hound.

I hurt him. Ersh, I don't want to hurt him. He's already been hurt enough for claiming aliens exist. The community laughed. The experts laughed. The world laughed.

I'm not laughing. But I don't believe in Dad, the astronomical genius, the grand inventor anymore either. Not again. Never again since the day he claimed aliens were real on national TV.

At least I stopped Jason from mentioning the UFO.

"Okay, you got your present. Bedtime," I haul Jason toward the stairs as he giggles, insisting that men don't have bedtimes.

"I wish you saw the UFO. It was so cool, Papaw," he calls down the stairs, before sprinting toward my former room and laughing as he runs in. Errssshhh. Gaaah.

I hurry the rest of the way up the stairs, but Dad's behind me. "UFO? Carter, you saw it? That's wonderful." His eyes dance. He tugs on the leather jacket he carried all the way up. "Let's go look for it. What you saw was a communication device to talk to—"

"Dad, stop," I say as I hightail it toward Jason's door and make it there before he catches me. I don't want to deal with this, but I don't want to crush him again, either.

"Carter, you don't understand. I know what I put you through, but aliens *are* real," he tells me. "You saw it yourself. You can't just—"

He reaches out for my shoulder, but I spin away. The words tumble over the carpet before I can take them back. "No, you're crazy. So just stop already."

I squeeze my fists open. And closed. I'm tired of it. All of it. "It's not real. None of it. And you ruined our family."

I slam the door and tuck Jason into the old pirate ship bed that Dad made for me when I was five. Jason stares at me. *Meanie,* he mouths.

"Yeah, I know. I know," I mutter. I have a quick pillow fight with him, but I'm tired from all this alien nonsense.

When I exit, Dad hasn't budged an inch. He stands in the hall with his shoulders slumped, shell-shocked.

The guilt hits as I enter my room. I shouldn't have said that. He hasn't actually ruined our lives. He's just made things harder. To pay the bills. To make friends. It's getting better with Mama's new job, but it took a lot of effort. And pain.

I close my door and fall into my futon. I crank the country to full blast to distract myself.

Jason would tell me that men don't cry.

AGS

"I am a protector, a diplomat, a warrior, and a seeker of knowledge. I will strive to watch over my designated planet and protect it from any interstellar harm. I will learn all I can about the inhabitants therein, so I can share my knowledge with the beings of the universe. I dedicate all of my heart, intellect, soul, wit, and strength to this great position. May the gods of the universe forever strike me down if I break this oath."

We all stand on the large radiating stage, hands clasped, as we recite our graduation pledges. I can't resist belting the last few sentences. Yas elbows me after I thrust my arms into the air.

I'm sure I'm embarrassing him. But today, who cares?

A professor works his way down the line, slowly shaking each individual's finger, handing us brass certificates of achievement.

"For the betterment of the universe," he says to me, giving me mine. I repeat the words back to him, bowing my head. Then, I cling to my certificate. Hold it to my chest, appreciating its solidness—its realness. I did it.

I am a guardian. As the humans say, pinch me. Eeeh!

I exit with a mass of green-gowned students, Yas behind me. We merge together as one large glob of bright, earthy light. Outside the Academy doors, families find their graduates, embracing them and overwhelming them with gifts.

"I'm so proud of you," my mom says. She throws her arms around my neck and rubs her nose against my cheek. "You did it. But don't forget everything I taught you. You'll do a great job of replacing me."

With my mom retiring as the head guardian of Earth, there'll only be two of us. Not too many guardians are interested in protecting a planet with such little threat. Still, she has a little time left to help me learn how to guard properly before she abandons the best planet in existence for a spot on the council.

I don't understand why she's doing it. With all the lessons she's taught me about loving the planet I guard, it doesn't make sense to me.

I quickly thank her, but then find my way to Yas, dragging him through the crowd past the Academy lawn to the city's main street.

The post-graduation celebration has started, and I don't want to miss a single second of it.

The edges of the streets brim with vendors selling the best meals from across the universe; a chocolatey scent embraces a hint of exotic fruit and edible linens. Dancers coated in rainbow paints twirl in front of me, and well-dressed diplomats ride on dogs as large as elephants.

Lights dance in the sky, like aurora borealis but in neon shades, and then a message explodes across it in Yadian: CONGRATULATIONS GRADUATES. The message is repeated in the dozens of different languages that are spoken in the worlds the new guardians will protect.

I twist through stalls, touching everything, breathing in the yumminess.

"Look!" I say to Yas. I giggle and bounce up and down on some kind of hovering trampoline. The vendor growls and shakes his nose at me, so I quickly move to a new cart.

Fis City is always a melting pot of cultures, where individuals (and their families) who've guarded the same planets move into the same neighborhood. I can turn one street lined with pyramid-structured homes to another one of metal tepees.

But here, after graduation, it's all lumped together in one beautiful mesh.

I linger at a booth with strange glowing balls. "What are they?" I ask the breathtaking female at the stand. She has pink hair like my mom, but hers has even rarer natural blue tips.

"ChemPods. They explode and release a chemical when dropped. Each does something different." She prods, lifting up one and pointing to its translucent swirls. "Good and evil."

Yas leans in. "I've made tons of these in the elective chemistry classes," he says. "Really fascinating. Each has a different chemical composition to do something—some induce hormones to make individuals happy, and others cause you to forget unpleasant memories. Some are even used for warfare."

I poke the ball, gently 'cause I don't want something crazy exploding. Yas goes to look around at other vendors. We make our way toward the purple-dyed hill, settling on the ground near other students, celebratory lights decorating the sky. A blue one sparkles over our heads, and I lean back, kicking off the annoying wooden graduation shoes. I bite down on some spiky, cherry-sized fruits I purchased. I'm not sure what they are, but they taste like the gods' paradise in my mouth.

"Congratulations," I say, sprawling out on the lawn, holding a finger to Yas. He grasps it, blushing.

"I got you a present." He holds out a package wrapped in shimmering fur. I untie the grass-sewn string, discovering a little polka dot bow tie.

"I know it's supposed to be for males," he says. "But, it's the only thing human I could find. I got it at a street market from a vendor who said he vacationed on Earth once."

Based on the high-quality of the fabric, it isn't from Earth, but I don't tell Yas. I wrap the bow tie around my arm.

"I love it. I'm so sorry. Should have gotten you something."

He shakes his head, wiggling his nose.

Yas is such a great friend. Even after not seeing each other for a few months, he still thought of *me*.

"Whoa, that one looks like a twirling ballerina," I say, pointing to a pink trail of color twisting and swirling above us. "She's very advanced. Her pirouettes and échappés are perfect. She must be performing at the St. Petersburg Ballet Theatre."

Yas chuckles. "I have no idea what a ballerina is, but that's great."

We grow silent as we watch the show. Soon, we'll be headed in separate directions. He'll deal with all the politics and warfare threatening Artian, and I'll be studying Earth.

We won't see each other for a long time. I wonder how Yas feels about that. He hasn't said anything. But he didn't last time, either. I figured we'd be distant now since I was only at the Academy for a few years. Doing an independent study track just seemed easier since Mom was always on Earth, and I already knew I wanted to learn about humans anyway. I loved watching humans from video feeds. Mom would bring me food to sample and music to listen to and art to look at, and I'd collect all the data. Even if I wasn't allowed to step on Earth because I wasn't a guardian yet, it was fascinating.

Still, it wasn't great for keeping up relationships.

Except with Yas. Somehow, amazingly, we stayed best friends.

I lay my head on his broad shoulder, our friendship as comfortable as always, the moment perfect. Until it no longer is. In the distance, a figure runs toward us. As an orange circular light expands, brightening the sky, I see her face. It's Mom, and she looks more scared than I've ever seen her in my life.

"Ags," she says as the orange light turns red. "We think Earth might be in trouble."

Chapter

3

KOKAB

The spherical space vehicle hovers just above the concrete ground behind the hospital. A few Elders stand beside it, gazing at me.

"It is time," one says, then motions toward the craft.

"We apologize that no one else could see you off," another states, his face unchanged. "You are too different, and it would be difficult for many of us to look at you. The possibility of a stirring is high."

I accept his answer. Alone and altered, I take my last steps on Foxia's dry surface.

My gut clenches, but I force the feeling away. When I arrive on Earth, I must accept these flickers. Today, I will leave as perfectly as I can.

The Eldest One moves forward, walking next to me, moving up the stairs of the spacecraft as I go. He turns to me after I reach the squared opening. "You can do this, Kokab," he says. His words are unclear, and his voice shifts. It is not normal for a Perfect. Or any Foxian. He turns so that he is shifted away from the others. He leans in, and in words so low even a Foxian couldn't hear from a distance, he whispers, "The others have different desires than me. But, I want more than simply avoiding war. You must embrace humanity. You must learn to feel. There is more at play here than you realize."

His words confuse me, but I agree to the last order given to me while on my home planet.

The door closes, and I am alone in the empty white craft. I settle into the long, thin stasis pod. My temperature drops one degree at a time. Even with the changes to my body, I can tell the difference in such major increments.

My breathing slows. My heartbeat quiets. And then, blackness engulfs me. I dream of the past.

It is a few moments after the designated time to get in bed. I lie in a metal bed with a small sheet for warmth. I'm quiet, obedient, my heart exactly in sync with my breathing. I need to be exact if I am to be a future Perfect.

Earlier, I wiped any dust from the room, sterilizing it with liquid sanitation. Besides the heavy bed, the rest of the room is empty, except for the small clothes slot where I put my outfit every day for cleaning.

I close my eyes and allow myself to go into sleep register mode.

The door opens with an erring creak; doors should be opened without noise. It must be my mother disrupting the schedule again.

She comes toward me. Her steps seem straight but not quite right. Her bronze hair is cut again. It's above her shoulders, much shorter than required, and isn't tied back.

She should not be here. She's being disobedient, yet I do not stop my mother's actions. As she speaks quietly, I listen and try not to move or acknowledge her presence.

"Kokab," she says. "I want to tell you a story about Abaddon's War."

My mother does this frequently. We only talk about the past in school, but she tells stories to me before I sleep. She talks about how our world was covered in an abundance of colors, more colors than any place in the universe. A plethora of foliage and animals ran wild. She often discusses the old world.

"There was once a strong king," she says, her eyes grasping onto something that isn't there. "He ruled over our planet fairly. But, as time passed, resources grew scarcer. He knew we needed more, and what the planet offered wasn't enough to save his people. So, he asked for all throughout the kingdom to suggest their ideas. Now, the king had many children, and one of his sons had a plan. Do you know his plan?"

"Yes, Mother." She has told me this particular story 126 times.

Mother stops talking, staring at the ground. Then, so quiet I can almost say the words aren't mine: "Keep going."

She starts again. "He suggested that if everyone didn't have a choice—if freedom was just taken away, there would be enough for all to survive on the limited resources. No one would be richer or better off than others. All could be saved. He suggested a medical implant—the chip in our brains—that would remove opposite emotions, and thus free will. However, the king did not like this idea. He wanted his people to choose for themselves, though he knew it would not allow all to be saved. He asked another child, his eldest daughter, to help the people learn to divide resources up equally. The younger son was angry, wanting the glory his idea could give him, and so a war ensued. The youngest son, Abaddon, triumphed, and so we survived. All of us. But at what cost is our survival?"

Even at the young age of 97, her question appears to contradict the world's stance.

My mother tucks my covers in, leaning over, and though she knows it is uncommon to touch without proper cause, she allows her hands to brush quickly against my arm. She leaves, the plodding of her steps not quite as correct as they ought to be. I adjust the covers to perfection.

I am completely still, my breathing in sync, but I can no longer sleep. A glimmer of something incorrect runs through me.

"Being Different is not bad, Abedhakokab," she says through the door. "We all were different once."

I shake my head.

"And some of us are different now," she says. "Some of us have built up a genetic resistance to our stifled ability to feel. The implant to the chip no longer works like it did."

Being different is unacceptable. We must be in sync. We must not think or feel for ourselves, or life would be challenging. It is easier if we all do what we are told without any emotions attached. If it were not the case, people would want more than bare minimum; others would consequently perish due to lack of options. War would rise again due to different opinions.

The time blinks rapidly on the wall. It's two minutes past the set time to go to sleep. I close my eyes, forcing myself to sleep.

In the morning, I awake. I prepare for the day quickly, efficiently. I pull my Youngling clothing over my head and allow the brown fabric to wrap perfectly around my body. I do not eat; I will not need food for at least two more days.

I step quietly on the airbus. My mother stands next to me. Perfects and Almosts surround us, their faces turned forward. Their positions are exact, meticulous. They do not question the perfection of our society. They know things must be this way. A world of opposition is painful. A world of opposition means somebody must lose.

The other riders don't look at us, except the occasional very young one, those whose lives have started just decades earlier. They are not trained enough to know to ignore a Different. Differents are not punished or harmed; they are ignored, forgotten. Still, the young ones' glances are quick. Then, they turn forward and stay still.

We hold to the rails. At 23:09, my mother glances down at me.

Her grasp on the silver rail is too tight. Her blood pumps too quickly through her clear skin. She screams, and her eyes glaze over.

She topples, improperly, into my arms.

"Hold on to the old ways," she whispers to me, "Kokab, I..."

She does not finish. I look into her pale stony face.

My mother is dead.

Something shivers inside my body, hurting my mind and stomach. I allow myself to hold my mother in my arms for 2.3

seconds. I stroke her face, the pose of my body out of sync. I push the shiver aside and set her correctly on the floor of the airbus. I return to erectness and touch my finger to the metal alert button. Collectors will come to pick up the body at the next stop.

No one on the bus moves. They do not acknowledge her death. They do not feel the pain that quickly enters my body.

They might not feel it, but I do. Today, I feel for the first time in my life.

AGS

I LOOP my finger around a few strands of blue grass and struggle to grasp Mom's words. They sink inside of me like a thick bowl of massaman curry.

Earth. My beautiful, wonderful planet. In...trouble?

"What?" I say, thinking I must have heard her wrong.

The brilliant lights in the sky fade as the show ends. The noisy chatter of graduate students continues as I pick up my clunky graduation shoes. Mom drags me barefoot toward our spaceship. I hate the shackle of shoes, but now the swishing of my feet through the grass seems to mock me.

Trouble. Trouble. Trouble, the grass whispers.

"Did you say Earth may be in trouble?" I repeat. Yas follows right behind me, and I'm grateful when he places his fingers in mine and squeezes before letting go. They may be thin and wimpy, but they are reassuring. Familiar. *Thank you.*

Yas turns to Mom, gesturing toward the ship, a silent question of if he can come. If it's regarding Earth, the guardians of Earth make all the calls, unless they need financial or other assistance from the council. He doesn't need to come, but I'm glad he's willing.

Mom quickly nods, opening the bright yellow door of our craft. We follow her inside. The screen over the dashboard is on. The glowing light illuminates our faces. A small white blip moves across it straight toward Earth.

"Spaceship's coming," I say, waiting for Mom to say more.

Trouble. Trouble. Trouble. The beeping of the monitor continues the mocking. Mom slowly wraps her hair around her finger.

"It's not just a spaceship, Ags. It's a *Foxian* ship with a Foxian girl inside," Mom says.

Yas yelps. His thick eyebrows furrow.

A Foxian ship? The same robot-like species that loathe the guardians? I learned at the Academy how we allied with Princess Elsimmona in Abaddon's War, and when she lost, they cut ties with Yadians and told us to steer clear of their solar system.

They killed millions of us in the war. Our politicians always fret about what they might do.

The Foxians think they're superior to every other race in the galaxy. They're like some sort of super robots, but pretty boring. I skimmed over everything else after that. They don't have any of the rich cultural arts that fascinate me. They're duller than the rock-like species Yas will protect. I have no clue why one Foxian might be journeying to Earth.

"So, I'm guessing she isn't vacationing?" I say, based on their reactions.

Mom shakes her head. "Foxians don't vacation. They don't do anything for fun."

"Well, what do you think she's doing?" I ask. My fingers tighten into fists.

Trouble.

"Don't know," Mom says. "But, even if her purposes aren't bad, she's dangerous. They obey every order they are given. If the wrong people got ahold of her..."

The monitor buzzes, making me leap. I knock over an empty cup next to the driver's seat, and it clatters to the ground. It's a video call from the governor's office.

"You saw the spaceship?" A mini hologram of Governor Ids floats up as the council room appears across our wide interface. Dozens of mini politicians sit at their desks while others dart across our skyboard in 3D. How big a deal is this?

"It hardly seemed worthy to note. What harm could one girl do," he says. "But then Hos had a source..."

He gazes at Mom's perfect hair, and I'm glad he's not here, or he'd be sneaking in sniffs with his extra-long nose. I know why the governor offered Mom a new job in the council with a shiny salary a single parent couldn't resist. But her choice to accept it after she proclaimed all of her infinite love for Earth? Now, that's a struggle.

Hos rises from his glistening award-covered desk. His purple cape drags across the interface. About a dozen officials cluster around him who basks in his ever-increasing fandom.

Some politicians point fingers at one another, yelling. One lounges in an intricate purple chair to the side of the room, barely watching. Like it's just another day dealing with another country's political issues. They deal with huge worlds-at-risk problems every day.

Not me. A few minutes ago, I sat enjoying a beautiful light show, grateful that Earth had no interstellar threats. Now, I don't know what will happen to my lovely planet. But I'm not going to overreact. Yadian politicians are crazy.

I unclench and inhale. It's okay. Just a girl.

Mom nods, and Governor Ids fiddles with his bright purple scarf. "I'm afraid it may be worse than you think," he says.

Hos shifts forward and sweeps his orange locks back. "A reliable source told me that Foxians plan to invade Earth. We think the girl is a scout, sent to evaluate the planet before an attack. Or perhaps she is bringing the weapon with her. My source believes it is their intent to attack and destroy Earth."

Mom's eyes grow wide. His words sound like the waves of the Pacific Ocean, beating against my ear.

Yas wraps his arms around my shoulders. His grip tightens as Yadian politicians start screaming again. Hos's words are difficult to understand, to grasp. Attack Earth? It's like I can't make the words real. No one attacks Earth. But the words continue to engulf me.

"Liar!" a portly fellow announces. "You won't even tell us the source, Hos. Everyone knows you think Earthlings are morally depraved. You're just trying to get us to cut ties with mankind. Stupid lies."

"It's not the people I'm worried about. But if they're planning to fight humans, imagine where they'll go next. We've got to stop this *now*," says another.

Another one speaks up. "Is it worth worrying? Earth is inconsequential. We have other wars and bigger concerns to deal with."

"Not worth protecting seven billion people? We always protect those who can't protect themselves," another states.

"What purpose would they have? They don't like to interact with anyone. They aren't the conquering type. They're happy with their planet," someone chimes in, but others yell that they always knew Foxians would start attacking.

"Tell us your source, Hos!"

The demand for Hos's source rumbles through the room.

"I can't," he says. "I promised the individual anonymity. And I always keep my word."

Hos is the most popular politician. Hos the *honorable*. Voters trust him.

The council usually trusts him, but now maybe because it's the Foxians, they're questioning him. So perhaps he made a mistake. I don't know. But I do know one thing. Some of the politicians are sailors ready to jump ship. And I can't have that. With Mom retiring, I'll have to be the captain, and I will protect my ship.

That's my job.

I grasp Mom's fingers as tightly as I can. I'm terrified. I'm terrified that Earth may suffer, and I'm terrified for what I am about to do.

You are a guardian. Be a guardian. Embrace the guardian. Your humans need you.

"Everyone can hear me, right?" I ask the governor, and he nods.

I open my mouth, leaping into the stormy seas of their fears. "I know I'm young—"

Hos scoffs and rubs his golden pin, indicative of his lofty career. "You'd be a teenager if you lived on Earth."

I try again, but stay focused on the Casio painting I decorated the flight deck with.

The blues and greens literally pirouette against the background. Seashells roll from the sea to the shore and calm me. Casio was a revolutionary artist who started a new art form, imbuing paints with a movement technology. Nobody believed he could do it, but he did. If he could stand up against the scorns of a whole galaxy for what he loved most, so can I.

"I know I'm young," I repeat. "But I just pledged to protect Earth at all costs."

They continue to fight with each other, but I speak louder, and they quiet down a bit. All I want is for them to find out if Hos's words are true. Earth is *not* inconsequential.

"'I dedicate all of my heart, intellect, soul, wit, and strength.' I don't know who the girl is or why she's going to Earth, but because of my pledge, I promise to find out."

My voice is clear by the end of it, wrapped up in my own rapture with Earth. "Humans are beautiful. And I love them. You all made a similar pledge when you became political leaders. Did you mean it? Will you help me find out if Earth is in trouble?"

I hope that they cheer; Yadian politicians love the dramatics, but they barely notice. Don't even acknowledge my existence. They start arguing again as if I said nothing.

I exhale, now realizing I was holding my breath. Yas said I could do this. But I don't know if he's right.

Mom stares at the ground. The governor glances at her, a look of concern on his face. Ugh. "Well, we politicians have too much to do to find out if there is a threat, but if there is an invasion, perhaps we can assist. I know you're about to finish, but can we trust you and your young daughter to get a more definite answer on whether Hos's source is valid?"

Mom agrees, and the governor plows forward. "After all, perhaps Hos's source is wrong. Or is lying. Foxians are very strict. They may be punishing the female Foxian by ejecting her from the community. Or she might have wanted to leave such a terrible society behind. Even if they are invading, it doesn't necessarily mean war. They might be peaceful—"

Hos cuts the governor off. "Ridiculous. My source says they intend to attack, and my sources are never wrong. Foxians are dangerous, strong, and domineering. And they win every battle they fight. Do you want to know what I think will happen? Human genocide. "

I squeeze my arms around myself.

And then the hurricane comes. The tsunami waves are a tumult of voices in my mind, slapping against Earth's large blue ocean. But, that one nasty, dirty word floods the place until I am sinking, drowning in it.

Genocide.

CARTER

I chow down on a pizza the size of a timber barn when the stench of athlete sweat punches me in the face.

"Gah!" I roll into my pillow, opening one eye, expecting Jason to be creepily hovering over my bed. Instead, the twins giggle as they shake their towheads back and forth. Lisa's holding one of my dirty socks next to my nose, which I haven't washed in about a month, a huge grin across her freckled face. I grab it, toss it across the room, then glance at my cell phone screen and groan. "It's Saturday and summer, and you decide to wake me before seven?"

I used to get up early and get projects done with Dad on

Saturday, but now he's not around. And when he is, I don't really feel like working with him.

"Sorry," Ellie says, automatically looking guilty. "But Jason said he'd give us Ben & Jerrys if we did it."

"And how is he planning to pay for that?" I pry my hair out of my eyes.

Lisa beams. Her lips pull over her gums, revealing a few missing teeth. "He said you'd buy it!"

Great. That little stinker is gonna pay. Big time. Ellie clears her throat, rubbing circles into the green carpet with her toes. "Besides, Papaw is still here and said he wants to talk to you."

Errgh. After last night's conversation, I don't wanna talk. I don't think it will end well.

"'Kay. Well, I'll meet you down there. Unless you two want to see a half-naked man stumbling out of bed."

Lisa giggles, and Ellie shoves her hands over her eyes. I wait for them to leave, and then I pull a shirt from the clean clothes pile on the floor. It's a little wrinkly, but it smells decent.

Dad's sitting at the large wooden table, smiling as Jason tries to balance a spoon on his nose, but when he sees me, he starts studying his grits hard.

"Look, Dad, 'bout last night..."

He shakes his head, finally making eye contact. "Actually—this isn't about that. A foreign exchange girl was supposed to stay with a host family down the street. Plans fell through, and she needs a place to stay. She's about your age, so I was wondering if you wanted to come with me to pick her up."

"Really?" I grab a bowl and load my grits with some thick slabs of bacon. It seems pretty odd that my die-hard Baptist family would let a girl sleep under the same roof as me. But I'm not complaining.

"Sure," I say, and add as a joke, "as long as she's not an alien."

Dad starts choking on a piece of sausage. "Well, great."

"I wanna come, too," Jason whines. "I want to show the new girl my karate kicks."

"Sure about that?" Mama says, winking at Jason. "It's the weekend. I wanted to do an outing with just my grandbabies. You'll miss out on good junk food."

The kids cheer, telling Mama how they want to go to Cheeseburger Bobby's for lunch.

I wish I was going on the outing. This is going to be awkward. And I really hope Dad doesn't try to talk to me about anything mental.

I climb into the old red 1989 Dodge Cummins truck and sit in the passenger seat.

The wide tangle of green trees encompasses the highway and taunts me, reminding me of the strange object floating in the sky in the middle of the woods. It was nothing. Some silly prank. That's all. I mean, what else can a couple of bored farmer kids do? Right? Right. It was probably Drew after his swim party. What a tool.

I flip on the radio to distract myself from craziness. Dad starts humming to the old David Bowie song while twisting one hand in the air, the other on the ripped steering wheel.

I glance at him, chuckling at his weird dance. "That the best you got?"

Despite my worries that'd we go to frustrating topics, we haven't. Using the hand crank, I open the windows and scream the song as loud as I can at the open highway. Pretty soon, he joins in, and it's like old times. Nice. Comfortable. Fantastic, actually.

I chuckle at Dad's strange chicken-head bob.

A girl darts into the street in front of us, a flash of pale white and gray; her somber eyes meet mine.

"Dad, wait!" I yell, as our massive truck plows right into her.

Chapter 4

AGS

"Don't let them see you panic," I whisper to myself, shutting the door to my small spacecraft bedroom. The bright yellow of the walls usually comforts me, brings joy. But now it just makes me sick. *"Do you want to know what I think will happen? Genocide."*

I grasp my stomach, retching, his words reverberating through my mind on repeat. I want to erase them. I *want* to pretend that nothing could ever happen to Earth.

Settling with my back to the wall, I try to force the words away, try to remind myself that nothing is for sure. Everything's fine. Maybe Yas is wrong.

Instead, I vomit onto my clean, bright blue floor.

I swing open my closet hatch, yanking some of my human belongings from it, seeking reassurance from the material possessions I love most. A Thai elephant statue. A photo of Brunei's Prince Mateen. Mickey Mouse ears from California. An Australian boomerang.

I spread the items around me on my sleeping pad, clinging to the decorated wooden boomerang, and sob.

In training, I watched the humans from our ship, surveying them, taking notes.

They hurt each other so often, but they love each other too. Holidays. Weddings. Family events. Innovation. Childbirth. Funerals. Hard work. First days of school. These are all some of my favorite things to watch and research.

Humanity, all its beauty, wonder, everything...gone? It can't happen. I won't let it. And yet, no one even took me seriously.

Protecting humans is my job, but I wasn't ready for this. Not on my first day. Maybe not ever.

I twist my arms more tightly around the boomerang and finally toss it aside.

No matter what happens, I need to be strong. I've got to be ready to serve mankind.

Slipping from my mattress, I do the only thing I can think of for now. I lift my arms to the air, bending my nose upward toward my yellow ceiling in prayer.

"Please. Gods of the universe. Please. Help me to help them," I plead, muttering over and over, my words weaving skyward, filling the galaxy. "Whether Hos is right or not. I need you. They need you."

After a few minutes, Mom comes in and then Yas. Each grasps onto my fingers, their arms lifted upward, nose high, hand in hand, the way group prayer always works. They don't speak. But they support me.

I pray until my mouth is dry, my voice too sore to talk. Then, I continue silently.

A few hours later, Yas heads off to start his own employment trillions of miles away on Planet Artian. I'm going to miss him, but I have more important things to think about. Mom sits with me in our cockpit, quickly making plans. I still feel horrified by Hos's words, but I am ready to help.

"Foxians are like North Koreans," Mom says. "They don't like to communicate with others. Won't even allow a satellite into their solar system. That's why we can't tell if something is wrong with their planet. But there is a device to communicate with the Elder Ones. Tricky to use, though. And Els has it."

Els is the third guardian of Earth. She's old, hard of hearing, and a bit senile, but she always speaks her mind.

I love her.

Mom's well-manicured fingers slide into my orange hair, her voice troubled. "I have to go to Earth. Be there when the girl arrives. Just in case. If she does have a world-detonating weapon, well, I just have to do what it takes."

Mom bumps my chin with her nose. "I need you to go to Els. The communication device to reach the Foxians requires two individuals. Someone needs to find out what the Foxians' intentions are, and like I say, it's always good to go to the source."

I want to be on Earth as soon as possible. I know Mom's more capable, qualified to protect it than I am. But if she's retiring soon, it's on me to take care of things.

"And what are you going to do if she's scouting it for takeover?" I say. "Pass on the info to me and then walk away?"

Mom nestles my hair. "If Hos is right about them attacking, I wouldn't leave you. But we don't know that's what's happening. I know this is hard for you—"

"Hard?" I say. "It doesn't make any sense. You helped me fall in love with Earth. And now, you're leaving, why? Just because of a better paycheck?"

She exhales slowly like this is a conversation she's been waiting for for a long time. "Because I trust you to do a good job protecting the planet. I love Earth, but I love Fis City, too. They need more dedicated council members. Ones who actually care about the 'small, insignificant planets.' Besides, you'll have Els to help you."

Els? I'm sure she'll be so helpful. Did I mention she's a bit senile? Oh, Earth, stay safe. I'll be with you in spirit.

"Mom, I need to come with you—"

"No," Mom stops me, examining the golden steering wheel. "If she has a weapon on her, I might have to kill her."

She glances at me, quickly looking away as if she is afraid of my reaction. "If so, I don't want you to see. Besides, I need you to find out what is going on. The girl's unlikely to tell us if she's been commanded not to by a higher up."

To be honest, I'm not sure how to react. I never thought I'd hear my mom say she might have to murder someone. Then again, I never thought any interstellar species would threaten Earth either. Or that Mom would change her mind about Earth.

She strokes my hair, untangling a few knotted strands. "Think you can handle this ship on your own? Get to Els? I'm going to take the emergency pod."

I grasp the bow tie wrapped around my wrist. "Of course," I say, inwardly pleading for the confidence to do this on my own.

Of course I can, can't I? For Earth. And for the seven billion beautiful people on it.

KOKAB

The ship hatch slides open, and I step out onto Earth's surface.

The first thing I notice is the warm breeze, shifting through the sky, causing leaves to shake and tremble out of sync, dirt to rise from the ground, and insects to change directions. I cannot feel it since I have little sense of touch, but I can see its impact.

There is no breeze on my world.

Then, I am bombarded—all the sights, sounds, smells that surround me, more than I have ever experienced on Foxia. There is a slight possibility it is more than my senses have dealt with cumulatively in the course of my existence.

There are thousands of colors. Each tree has at least seventeen shades of brown, thirteen shades of green, a few shades of orange, and other colors mingled in. Blue and yellow hues of Tradescantia subaspera. I have never seen many of these colors before in nature.

A fly hovers by a maple tree to my right, the whistling of its wings humming in the air, at least one hundred times a second. The scent of the dirt is a mixture of dead animal bodies and broken down vegetation, along with a stench of animal feces and moss.

My ears are filled with the loud, uncoordinated sounds of dozens of termites scuttling across bark, chewing wood, and regurgitating it from their mouths. Crickets chirp, high-pitched and out of tune. Far in the distance, approximately a mile away, there is the humming of an engine and a male voice yelling about someone named Tom. Is it singing? I have never heard music before, but my chip has information about the change in vocal cords required to sing.

The shapes are the most disorienting. They are not even, smooth, or round. They twist and bend, not quite in proportion. Every tree limb is distinct, every piece of bark a series of lines and patterns, hundreds of leaves, bumpy, varying in color, unfamiliar, and not perfect. One leaf spirals to the ground, erring in movement. There is a sound in the distance, some creature or person, stepping through the woods.

I would know more specifics if I was not altered, but it's still more data than I have experienced in one setting. My heartbeat quickens, and my stomach twists.

Stop. I command my body. *Stop reacting.*

It will not obey me.

I shiver. This must've been what the surgeon meant when he said my senses could become overwhelmed.

I'm dizzy. My surroundings begin spinning around me, transforming into one colorful mass. I recite the Elder One's order in my mind. *Joe will work with you.* I must obey and find him, so we can discuss plans to assist Foxians in a successful immigration.

I stumble through the trees, moving onto the black pavement, and the sun shines into my face. It's so bright. I blink as a truck moves toward me. The hum of the engine strikes my ears. The chip, inserted by the surgeon to understand humans, isn't registering what to do.

Do I greet it?

It slams into my body, and I fall, hitting the ground. The vehicle continues to move over me.

That is incorrect. Humans who get hit by cars may not survive. Being uninjured will appear out of sync. I should have allowed it to pass.

The sting is slight. I stand, wiping the black soot from my face. I turn toward the red truck, a large dent on the front fender in the shape of my body.

I have never broken anything before in my life. I cannot make mistakes like this. Even on Earth, damaging property is incorrect. It is unacceptable. I must fix their vehicle.

I press a finger to the vehicle. I send commands to the nanobots to repair it. The nanites force manipulation quickly before the humans see.

My stomach turns, and now, more accustomed to my surroundings, I can force the feeling away.

I must accept these feelings. Soon. But there is too much to process right now.

Two humans step out of the vehicle, running toward me, their faces distorted in an unusual way. Then, one starts screaming. The noise causes ringing in my ears.

He's a teenage boy, tall for humans, and redheaded. His slight gut hangs over his pants and is disproportionate to his back. The other one has darker hair tones and is so thin bones protrude through his shirt. Humans look so different from one another.

Water leaks from the teenage boy's eyes.

Tears, I correct myself after making a second mistake.

"I'm so sorry. I'm so sorry," the boy says over and over. "We could've killed you. Oh, where did the blood come from? I'm sorry. I'll call 9-1-1. 9-1-1."

His body shakes. His screechy voice is not a plain, even tone like I am used to. He pulls a cellular phone from his pocket.

Focus.

I blink, glancing down. Blood drips across the ground due to a slight slash on my arm. I gesture to it. This would not have happened to my body in the past in the case of such a small collision. The boy rips his plaid shirt and twists it around the laceration, though it is unnecessary. My arm will heal itself in a few edes.

He looks at me with some sort of emotion painted across his eyes. They're blue like Earth's ocean. I cannot stop looking at the unusual color, and I get dizzy all over again. Why would a stranger assist me?

The thinner one whispers to me, "I'm Joe Turner, the scientist. Are you the alien girl?"

I nod. In this world, I am the alien.

The man turns toward the larger, younger one and snatches the phone from his hands. "Stop," he says. "You can't call 9-1-1."

Chapter 5

AGS

"Fascinating, isn't he?" Els leans forward, typing furiously on her data recording screen. I nod. Quite, but this is urgent.

I told Mom I'd help Els communicate with Foxia. And the more I learn about the place, the more urgent it seems.

Before coming to meet Els, I had the ship teach me more about the planet. During the Abaddon War, we intervened to aid the king's cause. After the king died, we fought alongside the princess because we agreed with her views on free choice.

But they still won, and we weren't happy about it. We didn't like having such powerful beings as threats. Plus, they had a depth of knowledge we no longer would have access to.

Figures. We really do consider ourselves altruistic, but we are a bit like Americans who try to step in and aid other countries. Sometimes it's helpful. Sometimes, we have other motives. Sometimes we think we are helping.

But I'm not going to be like that. I'll always do right by Earth.

"Yes, but Els...we need your help. Right now, please."

Els shakes her wrinkled nose at me and places her hands on her thin golden dress, which is way too revealing for someone as ancient as her. She's also wearing bright red lipstick and glittery eyeshadow.

"So pushy," she mutters. "Kids these days. Always in a hurry. Just watch for a few seconds, girly."

I sigh and slip into the seat beside her. She's one of those types. If she wants me to do something, I just got to do it.

I glance at the mountain man on the screen, and I can't help it. Just like humans always do to me, he draws me in. I admire his calculated steps. He winds his way up the sheer cliff of the alps, a monstrous beast rising like an old tarnished European sword and piercing the bloodied, dying sunset. Wind and snow blare against his chapped face.

The man understands what it means to face adversity without giving up. I should be like him.

"What's on his back?" I point toward the tight leather bundle.

"Huh?" Els says, and I repeat the question louder. She claps her hands, delighted. "A newborn baby. His wife just had her two weeks ago. So cute." She sighs.

Els's notes shine on the screen.

I have been studying the couple in the Himalayas for the past few days. Every night, the mountain man pulls his wife out under the undiluted stars, and on the ledge of a fierce cliff, they cling to each other and rock back and forth to a beat that only they can hear. Then, in their fur-covered attire, they lay down in the snow, and gaze at the sky, mitten in mitten. This is one of the few places modern technology has not touched.

Romantic. Wonderful.

Watching humans like this is how I've spent most of my life. Before I even started at the Academy, I kept inside our little ship and watched humans speak, and laugh, and learn while Mom went out on adventures.

In fact, I've probably spent double the time watching Earth from a distance than I have on Yadia.

Since I was three years old probably, I've dreamed of the day I could step on it, but now I have to wait a little longer.

"Els, you need to listen to me—"

"I know. I know. Hos is worried about Earth's safety. The stupid boy called me earlier. Come with me," she says. Her back bends as she trudges down the hall. I try to help her, but she peels my hand off her glittering gold sleeve. "Let me decide when I need your assistance, girly."

We step into a side room generally used for storage. A person-sized cube so white it's startling sits in the center, but the room is otherwise empty. A steady whirring comes from the box, a neat rhythm. Seems creepy, to be honest.

"It's a strange device." Els places her hand to it, a bit of fear in her eyes. "Only used it once. The Eldest One gave it to me."

"You knew him?" I ask. Els has been alive for centuries, but it's still surprising that anyone would know a Foxian since they are so closed off to outsiders.

The woman chuckles and then looks a bit sad. "One of my oldest friends before Abaddon's War. But that war kept us apart. Lay down on the box, dearie."

"What's going to happen?" I ask.

"It's the device your mom said would help us to communicate."

I swallow. The object is so sterile.

I'm strong. I'm a guardian of Earth, and I can do hard things.

I slip onto the odd object and squeeze my eyes shut.

"We can't have you travel through their solar system in a ship, or they'll just shoot you straight down. This machine will copy your mind and soul and download it straight into an unused Foxian body. No big deal."

No big deal? I'm going inside another person's body! This is a very huge deal. I grasp the edges of the machine with my fingernails and almost stand. But, I stop myself.

You got this, girl. Didn't you just say you could do hard things?

Els chuckles again like this is all a joke to her. "Make sure you find the Eldest One before anyone suspects you. He'll let you know what's happening. I believe he wants something good for the Foxians."

"Well, what does he look like? How can I find him?"

Els explains a few things about how far the Office of the Elders is, what Foxians are like, and how to blend in. "Don't mess up. Foxians have a long, poor history with Yadians. We always like to stick our noses in other people's business," she says. She wriggles her nose around in circles and winks.

Before I have time to protest or ask more questions, Els flips a switch. The machine whirs louder and begins twirling me in a high-speed circle. My brain sears like it's melting. A hot wildfire rains across my arms and legs and fingers.

I can't breathe.

Am I a tortured soul in Dante's *Inferno*?

I grasp on to the author's words, trying something, anything, to distract me from the pain.

> "O'er all the sand-waste, with a gradual fall,
> Were raining down dilated flakes of fire,
> as of the snow on Alp without a wind."

CARTER

I've gotten stuck in the snow, and I've driven over an unlucky Diamondback or two. But this is nothing like that.

My arms shake, and I can't stop muttering. "I'm sorry. I'm sorry."

Dad ran into a pedestrian, and I was the one messing around with him while he drove. *He* might have killed someone. Her. He coulda killed *her*.

Blood gushes from a three-inch gash in her arm.

But she stands straight and unfazed. And I know I shouldn't be noticing this right now, but I can't help it—she's beautiful.

Long, silverish blonde hair. Tall with lean muscle. Great toned legs.

Okay, I know. It's horrible timing to think about the girl's legs. She's injured. And by her blank stare, she may be in shock.

"Give me back my phone, Dad." I clench my fists. Why won't he let me call 9-1-1? That's human decency. The golden rule.

Oh right, he won't let me because he's crazy.

Dad quickly runs his fingers through his dark hair, as if trying to figure out what to do. "I can't, Carter. It's dangerous."

I shake my head. Since when is it dangerous to call for help? Since never.

I want to punch him in the face right now for being a menace to this girl's safety, but I exhale slowly and reach for my phone.

"What are you doing?" Dad jerks backward.

"I have to do what's right. I. Need. To. Call. 9-11."

He slips the phone into his pocket, so I do what I need to.

Sorry, Dad. I leap forward and shove him to the hard pavement. Gravel grinds against my elbows. Dad moans and writhes against my grasp. A car drives by, and the driver honks and screams profanities as the vehicle swerves to avoid us.

I snatch the phone, holding Dad off with my elbows, and start dialing the number.

But he leans forward. I watch in slow motions as he thrusts my brand new iPhone hard against the road. I yelp. The phone rips in two, and glass pieces of my sweet possession scatter across the highway. Months of working at Kroger disappear down the drain.

What in the what? Really, what are you thinking?

The girl still stands there next to us. She hasn't moved, so now I know she's in shock.

If we can't call for an ambulance, I'll take her to the hospital myself. I jerk open our truck door with keys in hand. The stereo still blares from our short moment of fun.

This is ridiculous. I thought we were bonding. And then you pull this. A hit and run? Why? Why did you have to lose your mind?

Dad stands up and grabs my shoulder, wiping the black soot smeared across his nose. "Look, Carter. Sorry about the phone. I'll get you a new one. It's just—she's the foreign exchange student we were on our way to get."

"So?" I whisper in defeat. Not just in my desire to help the girl but in my desire to help him as well.

"She's—" He pauses. "She's not really an exchange student. Actually, she's...umm...not supposed to be here. If she goes to the hospital, and they find out her identity, they might try to send her back where she came from, or they might hurt her."

"So, she's illegal or something?"

Dad's done a lot of weird things while working as a scientist. Made a lot of high-up friends in different countries. It wouldn't surprise me if he'd gotten entangled in some weird plan to help a refugee or illegal. Even if he is crazy, I'd hate to get her in bigger trouble.

"Yes, and she's in a lot of danger."

I glance at the girl, who turns to look at me. Her eyes change. They look less empty. "Is that true?" I ask.

She nods.

"Do you feel okay?" She definitely looks okay. She's potentially the most beautiful person I've seen in my entire life. In a weird, pale angel or demon spirit-like way.

"Everything is under control," she says in a monotone voice. "There are some minor issues, but I am completely repairable without medical assistance."

Weird response. Definitely not American.

"I dunno," I say.

Dad grasps my shoulders and gives me a look with his sad, dark eyes. "Trust me."

My one year of driving experience is enough to know that this is not what you do when you pummel into a pedestrian with a massive truck. But he is my dad...and he's serious. Who is she? One of those slaves kidnapped from her home and abused? A crazy spy? A terrorist escapee? It must be a big deal if we can't go to the hospital.

"Fine," I say. "But the first sign that anything is wrong, and we head for some kind of help."

It's funny. This whole situation is ironic.

I'm usually the one with a finger dangling by only a few inches of skin, insisting that it's all good. There's no need to seek medical attention. What is this? I help babysit for a weekend and become the responsible one?

We hustle to the car, and I open the door for the girl and then sit beside her. For a few minutes, we're quiet. I need time to get over the shock of slamming into someone and the bizarre reality that followed.

I breathe in and out. *Don't think about Dad.* I need to stay light for her. If she's in trouble, she needs a friend.

"Hey," I nudge her knee with mine. "Don't think I told you my name. It's Carter, but some people just call me 'you crazy kid.'"

My goal's to get her to laugh. It doesn't work, so I try giving her a sample of my drumming skills on the back of the seat to the music playing. That doesn't work either.

Must not be as funny as I think I am.

"What's your name?" I ask.

"Abedhakokab Trielldegerata. The abbreviated version is Kokab. That version is simpler and more efficient to use."

"So Kokab. Where are you from?"

"I am not allowed to say."

"What brought you to Georgia?"

"I am not allowed to say."

Okay, Dad. What have you gotten us into?

KOKAB

I KEEP my back as straight as possible during the bumpy ride.

We drive up to a flimsy, two-story house in the middle of the woods. Pieces of paint peel from the walls. People laugh and converse inside. A high squeaky voice asks for cookies multiple times.

"Beauty, huh?" Carter smiles at me as we walk up the cracked driveway. Bugs move about in the woods around us. The buzzing of flies, humming of crickets, and movements of creatures in the trees continue to crowd my ears. "I helped my dad fix this place up."

I say nothing. I have never considered whether or not something is beautiful. Things need to be exact, and this house has many mistakes. It is broken. The structure is not ideal in case of an emergency, and the appearance is not clean. I do not understand what he meant when he suggested he fixed it.

"We're home!" He yells as he steps inside the dusty house. Joe comes in behind me to the front room. *Entry? That's correct. It is an entryway.*

A redheaded male child runs in, and he holds his hand up in front of my face. "Give me five, new girl," he says.

I wait until he explains what to give him five of, and he lowers it.

"What's wrong with her?" he says, staring at me.

"She's not used to our culture," Joe tells him. "She's adjusting."

The child continues to look at me. "You're scary," he says. "You don't look normal. Are you a dead person? You look like a dead person."

He jabs me with his finger and a high-pitched sound comes from his throat.

Laughter.

"I am not dead. I am alive," I say.

A woman walks into the room. She has disorganized curls and slight creases on her face. Two short girls cling to her pants. They look more similar than most humans but not as identical as Foxians.

"Jason." She shakes her finger at the boy, but the movements are out of sync. There is nothing for them to be in sync with. "You rotten stinker. Want me to tell your mama on you?"

What is rotten about him? He does smell a little unclean.

She tuts when she sees the blood around Joe's shirt, which is still wrapped around my arm. She grabs me and drags me into the kitchen. "I'm Sue." She has substantially more fat on her thighs and waist than Carter. "But, you can call me Mama if you'd like, honey. Best to get that wound tended to."

"It is not necessary," I say.

She pulls back the shirt, revealing the clean, perfectly healed skin.

"Oh," she says. Her jaw drops 1.2 centimeters in human-size measurements, which I must adjust to. "Well, that's different, isn't it?"

Joe steps in the kitchen and glances toward his wife. "I need to talk to her. It's urgent, Mama."

She holds the shirt and studies the blood soaked across it. After three seconds, she responds. "Yes. Of course you do."

He goes up the stairs, and I follow. Each step is an effort to keep the worn-down staircase from creaking.

We slip into his office, a simple room with a desk, a black leather chair, and a bookshelf. The walls are white. It's almost what I am used to.

"Bet you're comfortable here," Joe says, and I nod.

I do not know what comfortable feels like, but my body is not misbehaving. Is that comfortable?

Joe grins and shoves his shoulder against the white-painted bookshelf. It moves to reveal a small, dusty second room. In it is a large computer screen, textbooks with astronomical titles, technological equipment. A clay model of a Foxian male and one of a female sit on a desk.

Where did you get that? I need to stop asking so many questions in my mind. Even if I need to understand humans, it does not mean I should behave less perfectly.

"Room's soundproof." Joe shuts the door as I step inside. "So we don't have to worry about anyone listening in." He leans in toward me, and a loud breath moves through his lips. I remain quiet.

"So, your people are going to invade Earth, then?" he says. "I hope you have an astoundingly brilliant strategy to make that happen peacefully."

Chapter 6

AGS

"Oh stars in the galaxies."

Humans have a saying: "Walk a mile in someone else's shoes." This takes it to the extreme. I'm not in another's shoes. I'm in another body. And, with my first powerful breath, I'm certain it will be absolutely and completely different from my own.

My eyes blink open, and it's as if I've been almost blind and half deaf my whole life. A small particle of dust tumbles from the ceiling three feet away, thudding as it greets the ground. If only I had this body when I surveyed the Sahara desert or when I watched Kate and William's family celebrate Christmas. That would have been fabulous.

Here though, there's little to take in.

The room's pure white and completely seamless. The smooth air shifts around me in a constant wave of harmony. Who knew air made noise?

A few more dust particles dance around the room, and I find the distracting pattern irritating, which is odd. It's usually difficult to annoy me. Once, another student at the Academy poked the back of my head for five minutes, and it didn't phase me.

I slide off the machine, which isn't really white like I thought, but a light silver, and examine my body.

Wow. Oh wow.

I run my fingers over my translucent figure and giggle. My

conspicuous hearts pound in an exact rhythm in each arm. How freaky. How fun.

My lungs ease back and forth, slightly hidden by muscle and bone. Dark blood ebbs through my body. And I'm super buff. I touch my face, weirded out by the two noses. I'm strong and invulnerable, a mad combination of Superman and Capek's robot.

I can't think of a better way to learn about another group of people than to become them. Literally.

A gray hospital-like gown hangs from a hook on the wall, and I slip into the rigid fabric.

I begin to dance across the smooth floor, embracing how perfect my motions are. I spin in a circle over and over, but no dizziness comes. I pirouette and cabriole, leaping through the air on one leg, tossing the other upward at a perfect angle.

It's easy, but it shouldn't be. I love ballet, but I can only do a few moves.

How nice. My mind in this bizarre body. I stop instantly. *But, Foxian minds aren't like mine. They don't feel or understand. This is what humans are up against. These perfect...beasts?*

Perhaps. Or perhaps not. Hos could be wrong. I hope he's wrong. I shift to the door, thin lines cut into rock, probably invisible to non-Foxian eyes. My steps are noiseless instead of being awkward and clunky like usual.

I press the silver covered square button marked *open*. Time to find the Eldest One and figure out if Hos is right.

It opens to the weirdest view I've seen in my life. I'm on a mountain range, but every surface is level and uniform like someone took some kind of rock-smoothing machine across the entire mountainside to make it perfect. Carving up mountain terrain must have been harder than painting the Sistine Chapel upside down. Foliage exists, but only on the side facing away from the city. And the sky is grayish. Isn't there *any* color in this place? Even the city itself is a large white and gray mass of half-spherical buildings, looming like a giant graveyard.

Oh, and I have a major problem. I'm on the edge of a crevice-free, two-hundred-foot cliff. I dangle my toe over the threatening edge. The steady air stirs around me. It's not as if there's any surface to snatch onto. There's nothing to catch my fall.

I go back inside the hidden room. Nothing useful for climbing. I don't see any other solution: I've got to leap.

If I was good at math, I could probably calculate my survival odds in this body. I'd die if I jumped normally, but this body's insane. But what are the odds? I don't know. I'm brilliant at science, philosophy, art, writing, reading, and most everything else. But math and I have a mutinous relationship. *Els, did you forget to mention this little detail?*

She told me about the mountain range but not this. Probably did it on purpose. Knowing her, she's cracking up about my situation right now. I'd go back to the comfort of my own body to ask her if it's okay to jump, but I'm not sure how long it took for my mind to travel here.

I must be able to make the jump or else she'd say something. Give me some kind of solution. Right?

Okay, just do it. If you die, you die. At least it's an adventurous death.

I don't want to die. "Gods of the universe, send me pillows, please."

I check the ground, but nothing's there. I can't waste time. It's not like the results are going to be any different. I sprint and leap over the edge.

The rush of air encompasses me as I fall. It's me and the open sky.

My stomach should drop. My gut should clench in fury that its owner would be so insensible, but nothing happens in this Foxian frame. I'm terrified, screaming for my life, but it's only in my head. The surface and I close in on each other.

I land with my knees bent and feet on the ground like it was a simple task to jump from a cliff the size of a skyscraper.

Joy. I'm alive. I hug myself. Great, my own body won't be left as a mindless zombie in a machine back on Earth.

Even with my poor math skills, I can tell the city's far. It'll be a long walk.

Or will it?

I sprint. My metallic hair exudes behind me. My legs churn, free and fast, with no pain against my barefoot soles. Yet, my steps are so precise. And even though I'm going at least as fast as a cheetah (How do I know that?), I take in all the sights, smells, sounds that surround me.

Still almost nothing. The fresh-soil aroma lingers in the air as a few dust particles flutter past. Smooth rock stretches forward, and the pounding of my feet ring quietly. I don't even breathe heavily.

This is insane. What a body. A strong, invincible, awesome, scary body.

It only takes about an hour to approach the city. I check my clothes to be sure they are neat and kempt. Am I smiling? Can't smile today. I pace around a while and shift my arms up and down slowly like a Barbie doll. Am I doing it like Els suggested? I've got to blend in, or someone will suspect me. I might die if I can't pass myself off as a Foxian. That's going to be *easy* for me.

My feet move from rock to concrete. Bright lights radiate across the blanched street, and I'm lucky no one is around. I trod through the empty roads and pass half-sphered building after building, each with a single door and window on the front. They stretch forever. Where are the Foxians? Where are the animals? What is going on?

After hours speeding through the city, only the occasional Foxian has passed, but they never look my way. It's like they are ghosts. Wisps of something not quite real.

Finally, I get to the center of the city. Holy Stephen King book.

They swarm in mass lines like ants crawling toward an anthill. Hundreds of individuals move with equipment in their arms. Their plastered eyes stare forward, and their feet touch the ground simultaneously as they all move toward a giant piece of a finished spacecraft larger than a football field. It looks like a middle section as if other pieces are being assembled elsewhere.

They lift their arms up and down at the same time. Left. Right.

Each stride is one loud resounding beat as their feet pound against the ground. If my heart could pound in terror, it'd strum to their marching steps.

Els warned me that all the individuals on Foxia look exactly alike, move in preset ways, are robotic.

She wasn't right. They aren't exactly identical. One's neck is longer, one's fingers a little too fat. One's arm movement is a bit too jerky. But their actions are uncanny. It's hard to imagine these beings having any good intentions regarding humanity.

Okay. Don't panic. Don't panic. It's no big deal. Just a couple hundred invulnerable people who oppose Yadians. Nothing to worry about.

I lift a square metal piece of hardware and go to join them, but it tumbles from my fingers.

Their eyes shift, and hundreds of blank eyes turn toward me. Hundreds of pale jaws drop open as they give me instruction to lift it.

It's petrifying. Creepier than Planet Grex, a world full of cackling jack-o-lanterns. It's easy to imagine them thronging me at once and gracefully ripping apart my limbs.

Now or never, Ags. Now or never. I inhale and move away from them, ignoring my mind and giving in to the body. Now, I can easily copy their motions.

It's instinctual, natural. I move past the ship toward the center to where Els said the office was. No one calls me out, so my movements must be right.

The giant spaceship in the middle of town hurts my heart, if I had a heart that felt pain. Does it mean that Hos was right? Foxians are attacking Earth? Maybe or it could be for any number of purposes.

Hos, I hope you're wrong.
If I don't survive, will Earth?

KOKAB

"We can put you all in Antarctica. Nobody really cares about the continent anyway. But conditions there are harsh. Not easy to live in," Joe says, selecting from the options I have presented to him. We sit in his office, creating plans on his computer screen. The device whirs constantly, exact, emotionless.

Computers are like my people. Perfect. Obedient to every code given. Not unpredictable like mankind.

The Eldest One gave me some ideas for how we might acclimate to Earth, and he directed that I confer with Joe. But Joe has not been as open as he should be to ideas from an Elder One.

He rejected co-living in regions where only a few thousand individuals dwell, saying that "it will cause an uproar in the country, invoking fear in everybody's hearts." He also did not accept the idea that we move the humans to a specific safe space and perfect the overall planet ourselves. "That's crazy. And sick. And no, you will not make the planet a better place. You might improve pollution problems, but you will not make the planet a better place."

I did not say we would make the planet better, only that we would substantially decrease fatality rates for humans. I do not know why he would ignore this fact. Surviving is essential.

"That is more than is requisite," I respond. "We are accustomed to scarce resources. We each go for three days before eating, and our bodies can survive extreme temperatures. The continent of Antarctica is 5.4 million miles wide. This will give each individual over half an acre."

The white, barren location is more similar to my home than other places on Earth.

Joe fiddles with his glasses as they slide up and down his nose, causing an offbeat tapping. His fingers tremble.

"Your type has lofty goals, Kokab. Perhaps too lofty. Your Eldest One contacted me a few days ago and sent a communication device to the woods. It included the message that you were coming. He told me about your planet's dire situation and warned me that you needed help."

He hacks three times and licks his lips. Something is wrong with him. Is he sick?

"You know, my son saw the device from your planet. An advanced piece of technology. Incredible lighting and pure metal. And you know how he reacted? He got angry. And then, he pretended it was nothing. Chalked it up to a silly prank. That's what your people don't seem to understand. Human emotions are volatile. Hard to predict. How do you think people will react when they discover three billion of you are coming?"

"I do not know the answer to that."

"Neither do I. But I'm afraid there may be panic and chaos. Even if you don't harm anyone. Fear causes craziness."

"I am here to persuade humans to move peacefully. It is unnecessary to waste lives and resources."

"I'm aware," Joe sighs. "I want to help. I really care about Foxians. But you have to proceed carefully, intelligently. We can only discuss this with essential world leaders. No one else can know what you are. This is top secret. You understand?"

I will not tell anyone. I have already been given this order by the Eldest One, and I never disobey a command.

I nod and attempt to move my head straight up and down. In this body and environment, the movements are not like a Perfect or Almost. What am I now? I am not human, but I am not Foxian, either.

"And you've got to stop acting like that. Being so stiff. It'll be hard to persuade anyone if you act like a robot. I know there are a lot of emotions inside of you. I've seen it before in your kind. Give it your heart."

I look at my chest, ready to obey. With only one heart, I would die, but I will be obedient and do what is required of me to achieve this mission.

"What date will I be able to suggest this option to the leaders of the world?" I ask.

"Look," he says. "I can get you a meeting with the president, who can get you a meeting with a lot of other people, but it's going to be challenging. My reputation isn't what it used to be."

"What is the challenge?" I only have a few weeks before my people arrive. It is essential to act quickly.

"I have a moral conscience." He laughs, but it sounds somehow different than the young boy earlier who poked me, and he isn't smiling. "Seems to be a problem for people these days."

He lifts one of the Foxian models up, looks at it, then sets it down.

"I was working with the government for years, revolutionizing space technology and discovering new things about the universe. They loved me. I golfed with kings, won international awards, presented at the White House. And then, one day, my team met a real alien."

His hands writhe in his lap. Why?

"When they decided to imprison him, hurt him, and break him, hungry to get answers, so we could advance beyond our enemies, my conscience got the better of me. I was supposed to announce a new breakthrough in NASA technology, but instead, I told the world that aliens were real."

A small tear falls from his eye, perhaps undetectable to humans. It slides down his cheek and slips into the crevices of his brown striped shirt. This is the second time I have seen someone cry. What is the purpose of it?

"The government made sure my reputation was ruined. Made sure nobody believed me. Made sure the world knew I'd gone insane. To cover for themselves."

He shakes his head and smiles, but this smile is smaller than the times Carter and Mama smiled at me. "I'll try to get in contact with the president and get something set up. It will probably take a few meetings, and then maybe the president will schedule something with the UN."

He grabs my hands and peers at me. My stomach twists at being touched. "We have video cameras all around our property," he says and switches his screen to all the rolling film. "I like to take precautions since I was dragged off by the people who hired me. If anything looks suspicious, I'll let you know. Don't know why anyone would suspect you since they think I'm crazy anyway, but watch your own back."

I nod my head, running through options of how I might obey his order and watch it. I do not have eyes on the back of my head, but it must be possible if he asked me to do it.

I hesitate but then open my mouth. I do not often ask questions, but I must in order to receive clarification to achieve an order. "There is one other thing I am here to accomplish. The Eldest One said I must learn to embrace and experience human emotions, not just to help acclimate our people. I do not compute what he means entirely."

"As I said, you need to have heart. It'll only help your case. And if you can teach other Foxians how to feel, it will help your people thrive here."

I nod. Heart. That is what he meant when he suggested that I give it?

"Don't worry," he says. "Your Eldest One's message included how I might best help you make adjustments. According to him, the emotions are all there. Just let them out."

"How do you recommend I achieve this?" I ask. I have always obeyed every order, but understanding how humans work, think, exist? It will take all of my capacity. Even with this brief conversation, my head aches from trying to comprehend all his words. This time, I allow the throbbing to come. I must.

"You're here under the pretense of being a foreign exchange

student, so we need to keep up that lie. People love to come here and stick their noses in our business to see what crazy thing I'll do next." Joe grins. "They'll definitely notice you. Wonder why you're here. So it's probably best to hide you in plain sight, so no one gets too suspicious. Can't have anyone asking too many questions. Anyway, the most emotional place on the planet will also be a good place to learn," he says.

Then he folds his arms and leans in. "So, are you ready for high school?"

CARTER

Sputnik lounges on the homemade carousel curled up in a panting, black heap. When she sees me sitting lotus style on our back porch step, she leaps up and throws her just-washed body into my lap. She gnaws at my only pair of oxfords, so I smack her nose.

I want to sit here and chill with her for a little while, but every Saturday night, Mama drags me to visit Megan. I used to complain, but now I think Megan is hilarious. Though, I wish she hadn't asked me to wear a prince crown today. Antonio's definitely gonna have a joke up his sleeve if he sees me in it.

"You ready, pumpkin?" Mama says to me as she exits the house.

I make my way to my truck, rev up the engine, and straighten my tie. Megan's the daughter of my oldest cousin Patricia. Patricia used to babysit me growing up, so now I guess this is payback for all the crap she changed.

Whatever. After all this crazy chaos with Kokab and the possible prank in the woods, I need something to distract myself. Something normal and not weird at all. Dressing up like a prince should do the trick.

Mama and I check in with the bald man at the front desk once we arrive at the hospital. He sees me every Saturday night. I ride the elevator to the third floor, room 208.

I step into the room, and Megan starts squealing. Her usual pigtails are wrapped in a large black bun. Her poofy pink gown spreads across the hospital sheets, and glitter covers everything. "Oh yes, Carter, you remembered your prince costume. I was hoping you wouldn't forget. Tonight is Cinderella's ball, after all."

Good. At least someone's happy with it. My prince costume is my Sunday suit with a cardboard crown. It's the best I could do. She warned me about this "ball" when she called our house a few hours ago. Mama adds a get well soon card to the table and nudges me. I bow. "Yes, my princess. I am here to party."

Megan giggles, showing off the gaps in the front of her mouth. "No, it's not a party. It's a coronation ball. Patricia, get me my princess crown."

Patricia rolls her eyes. "Mom, you mean?" she says. "And you say please." She doesn't seem irritated, though. She pulls out a large plastic crown and sets it on Megan's head. Patricia smiles at me and whispers, "Thank you." She looks way more tired than Margi, even though Margi is super pregnant and handling three obnoxious kids. I get it. When bad stuff happens, it takes a toll on you.

"Good. Now, let's dance," Megan announces.

Megan lays in her bed. Her muscles are too weak to stand at this point, but I grab her fingers and rock back and forth beside her bed.

After a few minutes, I relax and sit beside her, and she chatters about glass shoes and her fire retardant castle. Mama chats with Patricia by the windows until Patricia says it's time for bed, receiving plenty of complaints from Megan. Sick or healthy, seriously every kid hates bedtime. I leave the room, and Patricia follows.

"How's she doing?" Mama asks. "Any diagnosis? Any signs of improvement?"

Patricia wraps her fingers around her wrist and sighs. "They're wanting to test for muscular dystrophy. But she's a girl and pretty young for it. No progress. Just worse."

Oh. Megan doesn't deserve this. Seriously, why do some people have such an easy time, and other people don't? It's rough that a kid has to deal with so much.

"How's Margi?" she asks.

"Good," I say. "For an angry pregnant person."

She chuckles and says I shouldn't make fun of pregnant people. It's hard, she tells me.

Mama gives me the "you're in trouble, mister," look, spends a few minutes chatting, then excuses herself to use the bathroom. I'm stuck in the hallway alone with Patricia.

"How's your dad?" she asks.

I hesitate. I don't want to talk about Dad.

"That bad, huh?" she whispers. "I'm sorry, Carter. He used to be such a great guy."

I shrug. The pity sucks. "Yeah, it's fine," I say. But it isn't.

When I leave the hospital, I can't shake her words. He *used* to be so great. Everyone looked up to him when I was young. I hang in the parking lot with the vehicle idling as I wait for Mama. It all comes back to me. All the reasons it hurts so bad to see an alien on a projection screen. The reasons I can't shake no matter how long it's been.

I was sitting at my desk like any ordinary nine year old, drenching glue on pennies.

"Hey, check it out," I told James, my best friend at the time. I spread some of the sticky mess on my fingers, dried it, and peeled it off.

Of course, he loved that, so I let him do it too. We poured glue on our hands. Some dribbled on the floor and on my hoodie since we hid under it.

We were in the middle of peeling thin layers off our skin when Mrs. Harrison made an announcement.

"Carter's dad's going to be on television. He'll be presenting at the International Space Conference. He said he's discovered an exciting breakthrough in science."

I grinned. *My dad is the coolest man in the world.*

We all settled in our chairs because watching TV is always better than schoolwork. My dad's face beamed larger than normal on the large screen. He lifted his massive chin.

That was my father on TV in front of the whole world. Again.

Dad straightened his tie. I can still remember the colors. Black and blue. Without any introduction, he told us his news.

"I've met an alien." I don't really know what else he said. Those words expanded in my head like a giant party balloon about to explode confetti. An alien? A real alien!? That's better than if my dad said he was best buddies with Santa, who I didn't believe in anymore, but I would've if my dad had made the announcement on national television.

But I guess others didn't agree with my thoughts. The next thing I noticed was the crowd on the screen. They laughed. The sound was loud and cruel, spreading through the arena.

No one should ever laugh at him. He was my dad.

But they weren't the only ones laughing. The kids in my class chuckled so hard a few fell off their chairs. James howled hardest and slammed his hands down against his thigh over and over.

"Stop it." I set my head on my desk to drown out the awful shrieks. "Stop it, you bullies. My dad is super smart. Aliens are real, and he met one."

But nobody listened. My teacher yelled at the class and rushed to turn off the screen, but I saw men in black suits with sunglasses drag him off stage. How could they be so mean? Why wouldn't they believe him?

After school, I went to the park. I only wanted to play. Like always.

But the big boys didn't want me to play. They shoved me to the ground, asking me if I believed my dad. I said yes. James threw the first punch.

I walked home, black and blue. Just like my dad's tie. My left eye sealed shut, blood spewing down my nose and dribbling down my Teenage Mutant Ninja Turtle shirt.

And there was dad, standing in the driveway. He already made it back, but a group of men dressed in suits stood behind him. "Dad!" I ran from down the block toward our house, wanting comfort, assistance.

But he didn't hear. Or maybe he didn't listen. He slipped into a limo, and it drove away.

I chased the car down the road with blood dripping down my knee caps, crying. "Dad! I believe you. Dad. I believe you. I believe you. Come back. I believe you."

But he just drove off, leaving me with gushing blood, hurting from more than my injuries in front of our house.

I didn't see him for six months. I thought I'd never see him again.

I push back the memories when Mama gets to the car. I shouldn't be thinking about this stuff anymore. I pull out of the hospital parking lot but can't shake the thoughts, driving into the same driveway from years ago. It's not really as helpful to think about the past as I hoped.

Mom goes inside, but I sit on the porch and chill with Sputnik.

Inside, I help the twins brush their teeth and force Jason to take a bath. I try not to think about how my dad left for months without saying goodbye. Mom said it was for rehab. If he left for rehab, then why isn't he better? Why is he still dwelling on aliens?

Dad, you can get better. You can be everything you always were.

I lie in bed.

Dad peers into my room, his tousled hair even less kempt than normal. He reaches into his brown jacket to retrieve a new, better-than-I-already-had phone. Once, technology like this would've been easy to afford for our family, but now it's a sacrifice. A huge one.

"Thanks," I mumble.

"I'm going to need your help. Kokab is not a normal American teenager. She's starting high school on Monday, and I need you to keep an eye on her. Can you help her adjust and everything? Make sure she's safe," he says.

I should've known it was a bribe.

I shrug, and he exhales. "Carter, I really am sorry. For everything."

I ignore the apology and instead agree to help out Kokab, and he disappears from the house like always, his truck engine revving as he pulls out of the driveway just like in the past. Who knows where he's going this time?

AGS

My heart pounds perhaps a hundredth of a second faster.
I continue walking until the large white building looms over me like a polished tombstone. Silver stripes coil around it and seem to point to the front door. It reminds me of Clotho's ball of thread, lines of life ready to be chopped.

Of course, the Eldest One couldn't be residing in a secluded hut. No, it had to be the most protected, important building around.

The solid concrete street isn't cold against my feet. How can they survive without the sensation bare toes bring, the earthy connection of body to ground? When will I be done? This was thrilling, but I want to get back to my more emotional, imperfect body. My emotions seem to be escaping me like a punctured balloon, and I know I should be more terrified.

Els made this task sound a lot easier.

The Foxians pass through the doors, all in white or gray, all silent. It shouldn't be hard to find who I'm looking for. According to Els, individuals' identities are checked when they are alone, but Younglings aren't put into the system until they are tested and assigned lifetime careers and separated into a status. They don't bronze-wear on a test day, a round piece of metal set against their chests and engraved with the Foxian letters for Youngling, and the best way to get access to the building is to follow the group inside. Individuals' identity is verified, but Younglings come and go as a large mass. In this stark place, the color brown of their clothes and metal will stick out like a rainbow sparkly dress would elsewhere.

After a few minutes, they come. They march in beat with a tiny circle of bronze metal on their chests. Time to act.

Don't be weirded out. It's not a scary movie. It's all real. Wait... that's worse.

I tap the shoulders of the boy in the back of the line. He turns toward me, still moving in the direction of the gaping entrance. "Step aside," I order. Els did say all Foxians obey direct commands.

He stops mid-step and moves beside me.

That was easy. I wonder what he'd do if I told him to jump up and down and cluck like a chicken. Not that he would know what a chicken is.

His behavior would usually seem funny to me, but it isn't. The longer I stay here, the more it seems like I'm stuck in a bad dystopian movie.

"Give me your bronze-wear and your attire, and don't go to the Office of the Elder Ones today. You've been reassigned to take the test tomorrow."

Without hesitation, he removes the bronze circle and his shirt and hands the clothing to me. Stark naked, he marches away from me as if nothing happened. Really? I expect some hesitation, a question, or at least an eyebrow raise. I get nothing. It is both great for my purposes and horrible.

Don't they think for themselves? At all? He's like a little computer program, happy to obey whatever code he's given, by whoever's giving it.

And these people are coming to Earth?

No. Be wrong, Hos. I think for the second time today.

The line's way ahead of me now, so I shift forward. I move my arms left and then right at the same time as the others until I catch up. The tomblike dark entrance swallows people one robotic stride at a time. The line of perfectly shaped heads blocks my view, so I'm oblivious to what's inside.

It's my turn. I move the door open meticulously because even in this strong body, it's heavy.

There is one desk in the twenty-foot (or so) high open room. A woman stands behind it, clothed in gray. Her black eyes peer into my Yadian soul and see my identity. At least, that's what I imagine.

She points down a narrow hall. "Proceed behind the others to be tested," she says. I nod but take a few steps in the opposite direction, toward the Eldest One's office.

"Proceed behind the others to be tested," she repeats. I glance toward the group, inwardly bawling.

Oh gods of the universe. How am I going to get out of this one?

Their perfect legs pump against the silver floor as we move closer and closer to a test of perfection and further and further from my goals.

My translucent arms sweep left and right in symmetry again. Every step forward is torture. Every step, I am less real. Less me.

Something, anything, human would be comforting. I crave the rough texture of my European leather jacket against my orange skin. A part of me wants to halt in the halls and start break dancing, just to see if I can get a reaction out of someone.

Of course, the rest of me wants to avoid getting caught. The white straight walls and bodies crowd me, my secret identity threatening to spill over with every smooth step forward. I can't keep this up, and I can't pass this test. I hardly know anything about Foxians except the little Els told me and the little I remember from the trip over.

I have to get away. As quickly as possible.

We turn down another white hall. More endless smooth walls welcome us. It's empty except for our large group. *Move. Now.*

I slip out of the line and turn in the direction I think the office is, but, after only a few steps, the woman from the front of the office stands in front of me. How'd she get here so fast?

"You have erred in directions," she says. "According to your bronze-wear, you are instructed to proceed with the rest of the group to your destination for testing."

I nod, because what else am I supposed to do? Say no? Not on this planet.

The halls continue, white and silver, beating steps amplified in my ears until we reach a corridor lined with doors. If I don't hurry, I'll be like the Tin Man in Oz, stuck as a machine without strong feelings. What can I do? Why didn't Els tell me it'd be so hard to get away from this group? Did she know?

A male opens a tall silver door. He buttons his red suit jacket and motions for our group to follow. "I am one of the Elder Ones. It is my job to send you commands while you are Younglings. After today, you will fall under another Elder's jurisdiction.

"It is a different opportunity to meet you instead of sending commands via your chips," he continues. "Today is your scheduled appointment for testing. Starting with the individual in the front of the line, you will each proceed into one of the side rooms. Your results are not alterable. We will decide your status, and you will be assigned a life career."

Everyone halts immediately after they are addressed. They turn their blank faces to him, but their eyes remain void. I'm not as fast as them, but usually, I'd tumble right over their bodies and end up sprawled on the floor. I copy them less than a second late. For me, this exactness is unimaginable.

A door swings open, and a Youngling marches in.

"Can I use the restroom before my test?" I ask, hoping I sound robotic enough to get away without suspicion.

The Foxian blinks. His flawless face shifts toward me. He stares. His black eyes drill into mine. He's identical to the others, but his eyes are different, deeper somehow. Do Elder Ones think for themselves more than others? Does he suspect me?

"No, Youngling. You must only relieve yourself in the evenings at 113:20. Proceed forward on your turn."

The air whistles around me as a white door twice as tall as me opens. I swallow. If I run, he'll catch me. If I take the test, I'll most likely fail and be discovered.

Most likely is better than definitely.

I'm stuck. I march forward, legs straight, mind racing, into the room. The automatic doors close, cutting me off from the rest of the group and freedom.

It's barren. More barren than before. There's nothing here but walls and air and strange lines across the floor. Two walls are white, and two are gray. It's silent, except for the pressured air and the beating of my two unfamiliar hearts. Panic writhes through me, only I can't express it. I don't sweat. My lips don't frown naturally. I'm trapped in this prison of a body.

Stupid body. What's wrong with you?

A loudspeaker resonates clearly through the room.

"Turn twenty degrees left," the voice dictates. The ground opens up, and a crackling fire appears on the floor. They want me to move into a fire? I turn. The flames barely heat my legs. Not sure what I've gotten myself into, but I'm certain it will be the most difficult test of my life.

KOKAB

I LIE IN BED. Noises keep me awake—the squeaks of mice running through the fields, the dog panting on the neighbor's porch, a couple speaking in increased tones down the street a few miles, Mama singing quite out of tune downstairs.

A few hours ago, dinner was so noisy. Children spoke over one another. Their high-pitched sounds scratched my ears. Mama handed me a plate, but no one told me to eat, and I did not need to. So, I did not eat.

I close my eyes and go into sleep mode.

A female's cry interrupts my sleep. "Help. Anyone? Hello? Come help me out."

The cry is more than a mile away, but I get out of my bed immediately.

She has asked for help, and no one responded. Does this mean it is I who should obey? It is hard to know who I must follow here.

I sprint down the dirt road, my motions meticulous and careful so as not to disrupt anyone. I am not in shoes. Pebbles and branches shatter and crumble under my feet, but I feel no pain.

The teenaged girl sits to the side of the trail beside a boulder with her legs sprawled out across the dirt, and her features visible beneath the full moon. Her black hair covers her eyes, but her face leaks.

Tears. I must get it right.

She clings to a bicycle. The front wheel twists across the rock. She presses her fingers against a large gash on her left leg. The wound is uneven, and blood flows to the ground, not ideal for maintaining a clean, sterile environment.

Humans are fragile.

"You requested help. How can I help?" I step next to her.

Her body jolts and her arms twist backward. She winces. "Seriously? You can't sneak up on injured people like that. I thought you were some guy about to attack me or something. Look, I'm bleeding." She gestures to the gash.

"I did not realize that my behavior was unacceptable. I apologize."

She stares at me and covers her mouth, and then she wraps her arms around her bare legs. The hairs raise where her shorts do not cover. "Can I just use your phone already? Probably shouldn't have gone biking in the middle of the night without a phone. But my mom took my phone soo..."

"I do not have a phone."

"Well, where's your car?" Her voice rises. "Can't you see I'm bleeding? Hurry and help me."

"I do not have a car, and I can see that." I do not understand her reaction. I am capable of running back and finding a phone for her, but she has not asked. *Do humans not ask when they desire something?* "How do you want me to assist you?"

She shakes her head, growling. "Why are you acting so odd? How'd you even get here with no car? We're miles from anywhere. You're no help."

She presses her thin shirt against her wound, stopping some of the blood. She starts crying again.

"I came from the Jamison's house. I am residing there. I ran when I heard you cry for help."

The girl's eyebrows raise. She tries to get up and fails. She talks speedier than humans usually do, words tumbling together, and her tone cracks. "Jamison's? As in Carter Jamison? Please don't tell me YOU'RE sleeping under Carter's roof." She glances at me, eyes scanning my body.

What is she thinking? Why has her voice changed? I am supposed to learn human emotions, but it will be challenging if I cannot identify what a human is feeling. She throws her head into her palm. Her dark hair dangles in the dirt, and her blood flows against the ground. "Oh, this is the worst day ever."

"That is correct. I am sleeping in the same house as Carter Jamison." I answer her question. She lifts up her head. Her eyes grow, and her voice changes as if her mood has changed as well.

"Hmmph. How did you get here so fast with no car?"

"I ran."

She glances down at the blood, rolling her eyes. She tucks her bangs out of her eyes, behind her dark ears. "Hey, not to be rude. But you don't look normal. Or act normal. And that's impossible to get here so fast. Are you an angel? I've been praying to meet one. There're some things I want to talk about." She laughs. "I'm joking. But I do want to meet an angel."

I shake my head. According to my chip, angels are fictional creatures with white fluffy wings and halos. However, she seems to believe otherwise. Foxians never make mistakes, so she must be misinformed about angels.

"Too bad. I was just about to order you to fix me. You'll just have to try to support me until we can limp slowly to someplace with a phone."

"Are you ordering me to fix you?" I ask.

She shrugs, shaking her head. "Sure. Whatever. Help me already."

I have always been taught to obey direct orders, so I will follow her command.

I lean over and touch her raw red leg. She jerks back, but I tighten my grip. I close my eyes and direct the nanobots to heal.

The raw skin threads together perfectly.

"Is there anything else I can help with?" I state with no fluctuation in my voice.

She leaps up. Her face, though dark, looks pale. Her eyes have a look I do not know. A bit quieter than I am used to hearing from humans, she says, "Thanks for the help."

Then, she turns and sprints down the street, leaving the bicycle behind. I could have fixed it as well, but she did not ask.

Humans are illogical. My brain spins as I try to gain information on the situation. Emotions are a challenge to interpret. This is my job, but I do not have a solution to how people think. For instance, when Jason thanked Mama for the cookies, he smiled. When this girl thanked me, she frowned. Doesn't frowning indicate sadness? But, I helped her solve her problem. Why would that make her sad? Or is it another emotion?

I shake my head, unfamiliar with my body's reactions, but I try to resist shoving the flickers away.

They commanded me to accept these. To access them.

I allow my stomach to churn, unable to identify what my own emotion is.

My duties complete, I turn and return back to the house. I slip the door open and lay in my bed, surrounded by cluttered structures and misshapen items. Nothing is plain, simple, like I am used to.

What was the look in her eyes? I must find the answers to how human emotions work on Monday in school.

Chapter 8

AGS

The gray boulder plummets from the ceiling toward my head as my test continues. "Catch it," the voice directs. How am I supposed to catch it? At a ninety-degree angle? With my arms straight out?

Thanks for all the help, Els. Next time, maybe give me a few hours to prepare before I leap into an unknown body.

I guess how a Foxian would do it, lifting my hands high before the rock smashes into my skull, its entire weight resting in my palms. What now? Do I set it down?

It's heavy, but I grip the boulder. I stand for five minutes with it in my hand. It's crazy that I'm not tired right now. Foxians obey all orders, right? And I haven't been told to put it down.

"Place the rock on the floor ten enes in front of you," the monotonous voice demands.

Right. Ten enes? I try to think like a Foxian, but it's still my mind, and I don't have a clue what that looks like. I try to let go. I try to feel it.

"Sit. Stand. Move five enes forward. Leap."

The commands come one second apart. It goes on for hours, over and over. I shift and move, letting go of my personal thoughts, detaching from myself to a numb Foxian. To move as a Foxian would. To obey.

The blank walls swallow me up. Achieving perfection becomes my goal. A narrow piece of metal shoots from a side wall toward my forehead. I dodge it, but not as gracefully as when I performed ballet by myself earlier.

"Lie down," the voice says. I blink. How do Foxians lay? I lay against the ground and cross my hands over my chest. I keep my eyelids wide open. Like a dead person. Because I feel dead.

This isn't working. I don't want to do this. I don't want to be this. I want wild, crazy Ags back. I'm commanded to stand, and I do.

"Recite the purposes for Abaddon's War."

"They are..." I'm smarter than this. I know this. I learned this a few hours ago, but it seems like a lifetime. "Conquest. Dissatisfaction with a ruler."

"Which is it?"

"Uhhh..." There has to be another way to find out if something's wrong on Earth. Maybe Mom already has. "I don't know."

"What?"

"I don't know," I repeat.

The voice goes silent, and another less monotonous one replaces it. Is it the red-cloaked Elder One from earlier? It's so weird that I can recognize his voice after only one encounter. Then again, anything unique on this planet stands out.

"Tell me why it's essential that no one chooses for themselves. Why is perfect obedience to every command necessary and not optional?"

I clench my fists. That has to be the worst question anyone has ever asked me. "It's not necessary. It's stupid."

I leap toward the door because I have to run, but the Elder One in the red robe steps inside.

"You are not a Foxian," he says, tilting his head. "You are a Yadian. Why are you here?"

I yank my perfect arms upward, ready to fight.

A voice comes over the speaker: "You are under arrest. You are under arrest."

A blaring alarm shrieks through the room and pounds in my ears. I shove past the Elder One and grasp the locked handle. I'm super strong. Can I break the door? I beat on the solid metal with my fists and then hurl myself against the frame. I don't even know if I'm trying to break it anymore or just trying to feel something. I pound my fists with all my effort, but no body parts break. Or bleed.

The handle flies off, and the door slides open. I fall down into several pasty hands.

They drag me down the plain white halls. I thrash, kicking them, trying to scream, but I can only whimper. They're as strong as me, but there are two of them.

Gods of the universe, is this the end? If so, please let my soul linger in the stars.

I didn't plan to die this way. I thought maybe I'd die nestled in the arms of a loved one. He'd set my body on the Panama River in a small canoe and twist lilies in my hair. Nobody thinks they'll die on a foreign planet in a body that isn't their own.

"Wait. Wait." A man with a slightly wrinkled face rushes toward us. His silver robe sweeps the ground. The two individuals dragging me halt. Immediately. "There's been a mistake. I order you to let her go."

They nod and release me.

"Oh, and don't tell anyone about this girl," he says. "You can go now."

They shift down the hall, perfect movements, identical to one another.

I examine the man. He's the Eldest One. It can't be anyone else. Els told me he looked old and different from others in this world. I finally found him. Or, really, he found me.

He grins at me and rubs his balding head. "What took you so long? I've been waiting for you for hours," he says.

CARTER

I TRY FOCUSING on Pastor James's video game analogy, but it's difficult. Two freaky things distract me. Freaky thing number one is Brian, an old coworker and high school buddy of Dad's. He leans against the back wall of the chapel in sunglasses with his beefy arms folded, possibly with a gun tucked away somewhere. Cheetos cover his fingers as he sneaks them from his overcoat. I haven't seen him since before the alien incident. The double doors swing open, and my dad walks through in the middle of the sermon, making eye contact with him. When was the last time Dad came to church? What's going on?

"Are you okay?" I whisper as Dad slides next to me on the wooden pew.

"Of course. Don't worry about Brian. I expected him here today."

He pats me on the hand, and I hope he's telling me the truth.

The second freaky thing is Anna. Of course, she's *always* freaky, but she came by herself to church. I haven't seen her here in at least two years. Plus, she's acting weirder than normal. She flips toward the back of the pew and waves wildly toward me with her arms in the air. Her orange purse flops around like a live fish trying to get away. A woman with a bun ducks her head to avoid getting hit in the face and mutters about Anna's outrageous behavior. I shift my attention to the black-bound Baptist hymnal in my lap, avoiding her attempts to get my attention. What now?

Last year we were *supposed* to go to prom together. I bought the tux, the tickets, a corsage. Everything. She got a fluffy pink gown. Then, a few weeks beforehand, she bailed on me.

She said the guy she really liked finally asked her. She said she was tired of all the jokes being directed toward her about my dad. She said my tie didn't match her dress properly. She said a lot of things.

Anyway, it's not that I'm mad. I just don't wanna deal with more of her drama, especially when I have plenty of my own to deal with. I glance at the man at the back of the chapel, and he waves to me.

"You sure you're okay?" I whisper, and Dad nods.

"So then Eve gave the fruit to Adam, and he ate it," Pastor Mike calls from the stand, pointing at his Bible. "All they had to do was obey that one simple commandment, and they could have lived in the Garden of Eden forever."

The pastor clears his throat as Anna waves toward me again, but he plows forward, probably because everyone thinks she's a troubled child, and they're praising Jesus that she came.

"That's it. Don't eat the fruit, and you can have eternal bliss," he says. "But did they listen? No! And what happened? The first man and woman were cast out of the Garden into our world. A world full of treachery and misery."

Kokab sits next to me with her back straight. She's got on one of Margi's old sweaters, navy with a sequined collar. Her long hair spirals down the front. It looks way better on her than it ever did on my sister.

Kokab's brave with whatever she's been through. A truck hit her, and she didn't even flinch. She's living with a bunch of strangers. She's away from everyone she used to know. Brian is here because of her, probably, but she doesn't look scared. She's still moving forward despite whatever crazy thing happened in her past. Now that's cool.

I smile at her, hoping she might smile back, hoping she's not in trouble right now. Brian's here to help her overcome all the difficulties she's facing. Fingers crossed.

Kokab doesn't smile and keeps staring forward.

Anna continues flailing her arms at me. The people next to her ask her if she'd mind settling down, so she finally stops.

But then Jason jabs Kokab, getting chastised by Dad, and Brian's probably staring at us underneath his glasses, so I miss the rest of the sermon. Sorry, Pastor, but there's a lot of chaos.

As Dad turns to leave, I get up, but Anna pushes her body over one pew, shoving aside a woman to lean into me.

"We need to talk. Right now," she says.

Dad puts his hand on my shoulder, and he motions toward Kokab as they go to meet Brian.

I hate getting left out, but, at the same time, if it's a top-secret government thing, what can I do?

I sigh and follow Anna out to the midsized parking lot of our brick church.

This is the second time in two days someone's wanted "to talk" with me. The first time ended with a bad car accident. I'm not too confident this'll end well either.

She's drama. Run away. Run away.

"What's up?" I say, trying to be nice even though I'm worried about Kokab. "Is everything okay?"

"Carter, I prayed to meet an angel. And I did. Maybe. Well, something's weird about Kokab." She grabs my wrists with her alternating pink-blue nails.

"Kokab? Yeah, she does look like an angel," I say, remembering how I thought she was ghostlike the first time I saw her.

Oops, that came out wrong. It's hard with so much going on right now. Anna glares at me and thrusts her bright fingernails into my skin. Ouch. I yank my hand away, so she reaches for my tie.

She leans in so far she reveals her plunging neckline. She's doing this on purpose. I know this nightmare's tactics. I keep my eyes focused on her forehead.

With her free hand, she pries her moist-from-Georgia-humidity bangs from her eyes and wrangles her fingers through her raven hair. *Why do you have to be SO hot?*

"Ugh, that's not what I mean," she says. "So, I went out the other night. 'Cause my mom was being stupid. Didn't bring my phone 'cause she took it, ya know?"

My eyes shift back to her. Now I'm the one who grips her, breath quickening. Is she okay? *Why do I let her do this to me?* "That's really dangerous. Do you want to get snatched?"

There's a difference between silly and reckless. I'm silly. Anna's reckless. *Remember that. She's not who she used to be. It's over between us.*

She used to sit behind me on my four-wheeler, laughing and

making up silly rap songs about her five fish. We'd sprawl out in front of a wild bonfire, and she'd set her head into my chest and chatter about life and school and the future.

A few years back, she used to be fun. I used to be crazy into her. *But no.*

Now, she pushes the limits. She sneaks backstage to concerts and goes to clubs for people over eighteen. She jumps fences and skinny-dips in strangers' pools. She goes on car rides and makes out with total strangers. She lies about her age to college boys and makes up stories of worse things that she never really did.

The girl's gone off the deep end since her parents divorced.

Anna laughs, and it's obvious she enjoys my reaction because her smile stretches to her perfect dimples.

Did she even go out? Or is she just trying to get my attention? It's hard to know if I can trust her, but I've always given her the benefit of the doubt. She does a lot of weird things, so her stories are real some of the time.

"Don't worry. I just ran into a rock and fell off my bike, got a gash. I got home fine."

I shake my head. If she did go out, where's the gash? What if she got stranded? Things could've ended badly. "Just don't do it again, Anna. Why are you telling me this?"

She's confusing, which is often the case with her. Anna wraps her arms around me and yanks me toward her. Her pink lipstick nearly touches my mouth. Fruit-scented perfume bombards me. *Get away. Get away quick before she rips you to shreds.*

"Because," she says, her voice lowering as a family of four passes us and climbs into their minivan. "Kokab came. She freakin' healed my leg, Carter. Like Jesus. She put her hands on me, and I was all better."

I yank away from her. What's she talking about? No, that's ridiculous. It can't be. Can it? Of course not. Anna's the source. "That's impossible."

"No," she grabs my only ironed shirt and twists her finger around one of the brown buttons. "It happened."

I don't understand how she could pull a stunt like this, make up a story so insane. Is this some space joke with Drew and the guys? Is this some kind of massive stunt to mess with me and my perceptions of reality?

No, she hates Drew. She wouldn't go in on a prank with him. Probably.

But this is too much, even for her. Is she okay?

"You aren't off your meds, are you?"

Anna shrugs, wrapping her fingers more tightly against my shirt. "Maybe. I wanted more freedom. But...I know what I saw. It's not like I ever hallucinated before. I'm not making things up. Not this time." She clenches her fists. Based on her reaction, it seems like she believes what she's saying, but I can't tell for sure. Miracles happen. Obviously, Moses parted the Red Sea and everything. But Anna wants pity or limelight, right? Like the dozens of other times. That's the only thing that makes sense. But her words bother me for some reason I can't explain.

My family exits the church, late like always 'cause Mama loves to say "hello" and "bless you" to everyone, shaking hands with the whole congregation. Lisa waves me over, and I pat Anna on the shoulders. *No, no. Don't let Anna mess with you.*

"Don't know what you're going through. But I hope you figure things out."

"Fine. Don't believe me. But she healed me, Carter. It was a miracle. On my Louis Vuitton handbag, I swear it," she mutters.

It's annoying, but her words buzz in my ear worse than bugs during gnat season. *She freakin' healed my leg.*

"It can't be," I say and stomp away.

KOKAB

"WELL, you aged thirty years in the last decade," the larger man says to Joe. I follow him to a white van in the church parking lot.

"Thanks, Brian. And *you* look as awkward as you did in high school." Joe grins as he fixes his crooked jacket. Brian chuckles and slaps Joe on the back. I need to understand their actions, but I do not. Why does a discussion of their appearances make them laugh?

"See? This is why you need to come back to work at the Pentagon," says Brian. "You're pleasant. I haven't had a good boss since...your public announcement."

With the last three words, Joe's lips tighten, and he nods.

"Sorry." Brian speaks quicker than before. "I didn't mean to bring up something sensitive. And I thought it was terrible what they did to the alien. I wish I had the grit to stand up for it too."

"It?" Joe frowns, and Brian shifts his focus to the van in the parking lot. I do not comprehend their interaction.

"What are you feeling, Joe?" I say. Joe's eyebrows raise. Was my question unusual?

Joe's mouth twists, but then he speaks. "Anger. At the US government. And...some sorrow."

I take note of how his shoulders tense up.

Brian opens the door to the van, and I peer inside. The air conditioner whirs heavy in my ear, the bright lights nearly blinding. Some dust lingers on a sink, and leather seats are tucked around a small bed table; various medical instruments and devices surround the room, including a mammogram and DNA PCR machine, indicating some type of medical work.

This is not as clean as a medical environment is in Foxia, but humans are never as thorough.

Brian gestures toward the van. "Get in," he tells me. However, Joe holds his palm up.

"You only have to do this if you want to. But we'd like to do a DNA test. The president doesn't trust me. Brian got my message to him. But apparently, the president thinks I'm crazy now, too," says

Joe, looking at me, one hand pressed against the back door. "The test will provide evidence that what I am saying is true."

"I do not know what I want. Will this help me accomplish the Elder Ones' orders to help us immigrate?" I ask Joe.

"Yes," Joe responds. "This will help you obey the Eldest One's orders."

I nod, getting inside. "Then, it is requisite."

Brian and Joe follow. Brian ducks his head as he moves inside, a dust particle drifting into his thick brown beard. He gestures toward the leather bed table, and I sit on it, back straight. Brian selects a cotton swab, wiping inside my cheek.

"This should be more than enough evidence for the big man," he says, placing the swab in a tube. He stares at me, eyes unmoving. Humans look at one another more frequently than Foxians, but Brian's stare makes my body itch. "She looks different than the other one. More human. Not so ugly. And where's the second nose? Are you sure she's the same species?" he says.

"Of course. I communicated with their planet shortly before she came." Joe leans toward Brian, speaking very clearly for a human. "Remember, this is top secret," he says. "No one in your lab can be allowed to see the results."

Brian smiles, but it's twisted. *A smirk?* The definition is in my chip, but I am not certain I am identifying it correctly. "Don't worry. You can trust me."

"Thanks," says Joe. "I owe you a lot. For standing up for me after I came clean about the alien. For finding my wife a decent job."

"Yeah, you do." Brian pauses. "I wonder what happened after that alien escaped anyway? I thought it'd never get out, but after your speech, it must've gotten up the strength. Ya think it ever got home?"

Joe runs his fingers over the dust on the sink. "Yes, I do."

His focus turns to me. "Brian'll be able to get the DNA results in two to three days to prove your identity. I'm going to fly to Washington, but I want you to prepare by learning as much as you can about how humans interact. Be ready to meet with the president in a few days to introduce yourself, just casually, so we can arrange a larger meeting with world leaders. I'll do most the talking, but try not to scare him at this point."

I nod, intent on obeying his order. We learn quickly as a kind, and my chip will assist me. This may be a challenge, but I have never disobeyed before.

I will successfully get Foxians to Antarctica and help them acclimate. I will also learn to feel because that is what the Eldest One demanded.

9

AGS

The Eldest One beams at me. His crinkled wrinkles imbue a sharp contrast to the sterile office room. He motions for me to sit down, and I do, sliding into the only chair besides his. The rest of the room is empty other than the desk and a small silver chest without engravings.

"Dreadful. I know," he says. "Such a boring workspace. It can't be helped, though. That's how the whole world works these days."

"Eldest One." I blink. My usual reaction would be to throw my arms around someone new and rub my nose against their cheeks, but I feel too empty for that. I reach out my hand to shake his, trying something touchy. "I'm Ags, a guardian of Earth. You were expecting me? That doesn't make sense. You didn't know I was coming?"

It comes out as a question. How could he know? I'm here to find answers, to find out if Earth is really in danger, but he couldn't know that. Right? And who is he? How is it that he's so normal? So *not* Foxian?

His grasp is firm. "Oh, my dear. Of course you're a guardian. With our Foxian ship headed toward Earth, we were bound to get some attention from Yadians. And I'm the only person open to contact, of course. Though I was hoping sweet Els would come. It's been so long since she's visited."

He sighs and winks at me. "How is she, by the way? Crazy as always?"

I shake my head, completely confused. I'd ask how and why they know each other, but more pressing things to discuss scream at me for their attention.

Can I ask him? I've spent all this time getting here, but now I'm afraid that the answer won't be what I'm hoping. I push forward. "Eldest One," I say. "There's a ship headed toward Earth. Do you know why? And the one outside, what is it for?"

"Eldest One. Everyone calls me that, but fiddlesticks. No one likes to be reminded about how old they are. Why can't someone call me Youthful One for once, hmm? Or All-Powerful One? I am a great leader," he says, ignoring my question.

I ignore his question too, because it's too awkward to call him young. "Please, tell me you aren't going to invade Earth."

The Eldest One leans back, and his smile disappears. "Fine, I won't tell you."

He pauses, running his fingers over his clear wrists. His head turns downward, avoiding my face. "Yes," he finally responds. "I'm sorry to tell you we're coming to Earth. Our world's dying, and we have to find a new home. She's helping us prepare."

I wait for more, but it doesn't come. I hoped he was wrong, but Hos was right.

His words repeat through my mind. Earth will be their home. These creepy, robotic people are coming to my beloved planet. And they are taking over?

I'd be sick again, but my body doesn't react. I internally beg for tears, but nothing happens. I'm stuck screaming in my own mind without being able to break free. These creatures are coming, and the only thing I know is that they are terrible.

Gods, why? Why would you do this? How could you let this happen to Earth? It's not right. Not fair.

"So, is it true, then?" I say, very quietly, but still certain he can hear. His ears are perfect. "You plan to conquer humans?"

"Oh no. No. No, dear. That's awful. We don't plan to do that. I've convinced the other Elder Ones that is insensible. A pointless waste of effort and energy. With proper planning, we can take up some of the unused space on Earth. It'll be an adjustment, but humans will get used to us."

"Get used to you?" I study my cold corpse-like fingers. "How can they get used to you? Three-billion robot-like people."

"No, we can change. We don't have to be like this. It's possible."

I remember their pale bodies, marching in place, so far from anything human. "No, I don't think so."

He grips his desk and scrubs his finger up and down the white cement. It must be his way of trying to feel something physically. "Then, what do you want of me?" he asks. "To let my people die? Is that what you want?"

Of course, I don't want anyone to die. That's terrible. But I don't want them on Earth, either.

I sigh. Finally, my body reacts. "And what if humans don't want you to come? What if they decide to fight you? What if they refuse to let you land?"

He shakes his head, looking sad. "Then, we will fight humans, and they will die. Unless you can come up with a better idea where everyone wins."

His words course through me, and something happens. My heart skips a beat. But it isn't enough. For the people I love most, for all that matters to me on Earth, all I get is a flimsy heartbeat? No. They deserve better.

He stands, frowning, concern in his eyes. "I'm so sorry," he whispers.

I turn toward the door, ready to leave this empty planet behind, so I can protect my humans. The Eldest One blocks my path. "You probably don't want to go back out that way. That other Elder One is still searching for you."

I raise an eyebrow. It's not like there is another way. He pushes his desk aside, a feat of ease for him despite his old body. There's a small line on the floor. "Not so easy to hide secret passages here as it would be on Earth," he says. "This goes straight to the room in the mountains."

What? There's an easy way?

"Did Els know about this?"

"Of course she did. She used it all the time."

Els...really?!? What were you thinking, messing with me like that? Didn't you know how important this mission was? How long it took?

He runs his finger along the line, and the floor opens. He chuckles. "She probably didn't tell you because she wanted you to learn a thing or two about this world," he adds. "Go straight. Turn right. And keep going straight. This is a strange and dangerous passageway. Do not take any detours."

I step down into the darkness and plod through the halls silently.

I'm ready to get out of the terrible body, leave this horrible place behind. I don't know what I'm going to do, but Earth needs help. Can these beings acclimate to humanity? I doubt it.

I continue climbing through the darkness. Walking through blackness isn't hard in this body, but I become more lost in fear of what's coming. All that I hoped was false is real.

So, what now?

Then I hear the creepy whispers.

CARTER

WHOEVER SAID DEALING with a brother-in-law is easier than dealing with your sister's boyfriends was wrong.

For instance, Cody's got Mama's special antique armchair shoved up against our ugly red floral wallpaper with the front two chair legs in the air. His hairy feet dangle down against the floor. Like a four year old would do.

"No way! Jason, you jumped from the barn roof onto pillows? Such a man," says Cody, giving his kid a high-five. "Did you fly in a UFO too?"

He laughs at his own joke, even though the only other person who laughs is Jason. We're all sick of alien jokes directed at my dad.

"Course not, Daddy," says Ellie, licking the chocolate off her fingers. "We never flyed in any UFOs."

I wince, and Margi shoves Cody's chair back down and scolds him under her breath. She rubs her pregnant belly. We're supposed to be doing Sunday night Bible study, but because of Cody, it hasn't started yet.

"What? I didn't mean anything. It was just a joke. A funny one," he says, then winks at me. "Besides, it's not like Joe's here. Who's it gonna hurt?"

Rather than return his wink, I yank a cookie from the coffee table and shove the whole thing into my mouth, so I won't say anything stupid. We've fought before over dumb things like this, and it always ends with Margi in tears.

But seriously, why does he always have to talk about Dad that way?

Cody and Dad never really got along, and now it's worse. It's a good thing Dad's gone off doing who-knows-what again.

Mama's face is scarlet, and her fingers wrangle a chocolate chip cookie. Crumbs fly across the sofa in her death grip. Swallowing the cookie in her mouth, she huffs at Cody, "I bet your vacation to Cancun was amazing."

"Yeah, hear you gain at least twenty pounds on cruises," I add. Mama elbows me, and I shrug like, *Expect something nice after that comment?* Punching Cody in the face is super tempting, but I picked the more generous alternative.

Cody laughs again, explaining how he'll be lifting when he gets home.

"So, Kokab, how do you like it here?" Margi asks, rolling her eyes at Cody and pulling open the Bible on her lap. Margi smiles at Kokab, who continues to stare forward.

Kokab's so quiet I almost forget she's here. She sits on our ripped blue couch. Her waist-length hair shifts as the breeze comes in from the open window. Goldenish brown strands float in her face even as she stays still.

Kokab's speech is slow and quiet. "It has met my expectations," she says.

"Weirdo," Cody mutters, getting a dirty look from Margi. I reach across the sofa to jab him in the ribs because now his jerkiness has gone too far. He howls, and I glance toward Kokab to make sure she's not hurt.

But she stays still like she's dead. Or an angel?

Carter, I prayed to meet an angel. And I did.

A gnat lands on my shoulder and tries to fly up my nose. And it reminds me again of my imaginary gnat. Anna. I swat it away. The buzzing in my ears starts up again, but not because of the bug.

She freakin' healed me, Carter.

Anna's annoying voice grows louder. If only I could swat it away like the gnat. Why is crazy, drama queen Anna so hard to ignore? It's obvious that Kokab's different, strange even. Of course she didn't heal Anna. That's crazy. Isn't it?

Mama clears her throat and thrusts open the word of God. "Shall we?" she says, starting in Numbers 21.

We all take turns reading, discussing as we go, and I help the girls get the words right. Lisa's struggling through a verse when Ellie starts screaming. She points to the front window, bottom lip quivering.

I turn.

He hangs from the open sill and gazes at me with his yellow cat eyes. Three feet long, he's one of the largest copperheads I've seen. His brown and white scales coil so tightly against the pot it might shatter. His jaw drops down, and his tongue tickles the moist air.

I shudder as I swallow my yelp, ready to act. I sprint toward my sturdy boots sitting a few feet away.

You aren't getting my family, you murderer.

He's frozen in midair with his eyes locked on mine.

"Kill it! Kill it!" chants Jason.

Mama snatches Lisa, who loves dangerous animals, gripping her tightly, "Stay here, baby. Stay here."

My boots dangle from my hands, but Kokab's there first, somehow moving from her chair to the window in seconds. The venomous snake loops around her bare arms.

Oh no, no. What are you doing? It's gonna bite. It opens its mouth. Fangs race toward her pale skin, and a cucumber stench floods the room. *No.*

I run to assist. It's gonna be too late. We're gonna have to rush to the hospital.

Kokab caresses the snake's head.

Its scaly skin slips open like it's being unzipped. Its bloody insides dangle down. The snake's long, two-pronged tongue drops out, and his solid brown head rips apart. His bloody innards spill all over the white vacuumed carpet.

What just happened? I shake my head, blinking. What just happened? Did she kill that thing with a touch of her finger?

"Holy—" Cody leans his chair too far back and crashes to the floor. "That was not human," he says. "Not human."

It's like my first day at swim practice when I got shoved and held under the water in a nasty prank by our team's captain Drew. My head spins from lack of oxygen. My lungs constrict.

Cody's right. That wasn't human.

"Let's get that cleaned up," Mama says to Kokab and wraps her arms around her like nothing happened.

I need to breathe.

I leap from the table and slam the door behind me as I step on the porch. The sweltering sun beats against my face and neck.

I grasp the loose railing of our home and try to force air back into my lungs.

Am I really so stupid? Was Anna telling the truth? Anna said she's an angel, but Dad said many times he met aliens. And there was a large flying object in the sky. Dad's argued with me about a communication device from space. About an *alien* from space. We ran into Kokab in the middle of nowhere with no vehicle to pick her up. And she was fine.

Nah, she can't be. She isn't. Right?

I've squelched the theory, buried it down, refused to trust its possibility. I hoped for too long that my dad was okay, only to realize he was wrong. My dad was not the hero I thought. He needed real help.

But what if? What if it's me who's been wrong? What if the whole *world* is wrong about Dad? How could I refuse to look and see what was right in front of me?

Because all the times I thought it could be true, I was wrong.

"I need to talk to Kokab." I slide my fingers through my fiery hair.

Almost as if she heard me, the creaky door opens, and she's next to me on our wraparound porch. She looks at me, waiting, obviously aware that I want to talk to her. But I don't do anything. I glance at her arm and realize her one wound is gone. No scars. How did I miss that?

I count the broken lines along the cracked driveway. I get to thirty and stop.

I shift over to the porch swing, which is old and weathered like most things at our house. With only socks on, I push off. The chain creaks as it slowly sweeps back and forth.

I gaze at her. Her face is solid like a rock, and her blue eyes seem drained. No one has a perfect figure like hers. She doesn't look like any person I know.

She peers at me as well, and I wonder what she is thinking. Is she curious? Scared? How did she even know I had a question for her?

We remain like that for a few minutes.

"Yes?" she finally asks.

"Kokab," I say. "We hit you with a truck, and you didn't seem to mind. You weren't too hurt, actually. And you destroyed that snake like it was nothing. I mean, that's okay. That's not what this is about. It's just my dad's a space guy. He studies the stars, learns about other planets. About...potential life on other planets. And I know this is a long shot, but I'm willing to consider it."

I exhale and allow the words to tumble out. "Kokab, are you human?"

She's going to be really offended if I'm wrong.

She turns toward me, and it's like somehow she's affected. Her lips twitch. She says nothing, but finally she shakes her head no.

"You aren't—Kokab, are you...are you an alien?"

"I am not allowed to answer that question," she says.

I take it as a yes. At least, I'm gonna have faith it's a yes. Maybe? I said I'd never believe in aliens, but things can change.

When I wanna believe it's not so hard.

I motion for Kokab to sit next to me, and she does. But, and I know it's selfish, I'd rather Dad be here instead of her, me asking him the same question. He'd sigh, put his thin arms around my shoulder, and tell me he's been hoping I'd believe him. We'd sit on this well-used porch swing together and watch the red-yellow sunset.

I'd tell him all the years of personal torture were worth it. For me. I hope for him too. He's not a mental case. He's a hero. A man who stood up for the truth despite ridicule.

I'd tell him I'm sorry. I'm really sorry.

I'm sorry for fighting with him. I'm sorry for causing him pain. Most of all, I'm sorry I ever doubted him. He'd smile, and everything would be okay in the world. But he isn't here. Like always, he's gone, and this isn't the sort of conversation I'd want to have by text.

And I'm not sure exactly what kind of trouble Kokab is in. But I owe it to my dad to help her. I gotta make things right with him.

KOKAB

"The DNA results are incredible," Brian says to me on the phone. His voice rises and cracks. Why? I need to comprehend his feelings. Based on information from my chip, he could be nervous or excited. He is too old to be going through pubescent changes. "The president wants to meet with Joe right away. And they'll have you come in two days or so, just to break the ice. No big announcements yet, got it, alien?"

I agree and hang up, though it is unclear why I will travel to Washington D.C. to break ice in August.

Carter's rusted, dented, and unsafe truck sits outside the house. He waits for me so we can depart for school. Country music blares out in between blasts of static, which shrieks in my ears. I climb inside, and he shifts in his sweat-smelling seat. His hands grip the steering wheel.

"Ready for the first day of school?" He grins at me.

I nod, and a twinge of pain shifts through me. Yesterday, when he asked me if I was not human, I said yes. Why? I committed to keeping my identity a secret, and I have. He does not know I am an alien, but he knows I am not human. I should not have revealed any information, and though the order was not specific regarding that, I did. I am not certain why.

He taps the wheel with his larger-than-the-average-human's fingers as he drives, slightly offbeat from the song. *Thud. Thud. Thud.*

"I think it'd be hard," he says, after a three-second pause. "To come to a new place. Figure out a totally different culture. To leave behind family or friends. Everybody you love. You must miss them."

I say nothing. I have not thought of anyone from my home planet. We do not love.

"Is it difficult?" he asks.

"No," I state.

His eyebrows furrow over his blue eyes. My heart speeds up to the beat of his tapping, and I wonder what that even means as far as emotions go. I grasp onto the change, attempting to feel.

It lasts three seconds.

"If you need anything, you can ask," he says. "I know you're in trouble. And Dad said to help you adjust, and I want to. I know I'd feel weird if I was on a new—well, if I was so far from home."

"I did not say I was from a far distance," I say.

"No, you didn't." He grows silent, and his eyes dart across the road. We pull into the school parking lot. He parks, and my car door squeaks as he opens it.

The sensations engulf me at Carter's home, but this mass of teenagers is far more encompassing. Hundreds of voices chatter in my ears, a blending cacophony of shrieks, laughter, yelling, and whispers.

Feet scuffle against floors, metallic doors slam shut, zippers open and close, and computers whir. Fruit-scented perfume and musky cologne fuse with heightened body odor, chicken nuggets, and dry erase markers. There are so many teenagers, flooding to the doors, tall and thin, dark and pale, hair in alternating styles, clothes created in a variety of fabrics and colors.

Each human is different from another.

My heart speeds up, and my stomach churns. It's the same sensation as when I was in the woods. I trip on the sidewalk, and my vision tunnels. Carter grabs my arm before I slam into the concrete.

"Are you alright?" He asks.

A short shock, like electric wires, shifts through my body at his touch. I usually can't feel touch, and yet his fingers are warm for .01 second. Then there is a dull pressure again.

I stare into the uneven crevices of his face. The warmth continues, only in my mind. I allow my body to embrace the feeling as it floods over me.

"Kokab?" he says.

"Yes?"

I pull away from him. Five seconds. This time the flickers lasted five seconds. I have never felt for so long before.

He scratches his head. "Are you okay? You didn't answer me."

"I apologize for the error," I say. I adjust my posture by pulling my back straight. "I am in normal condition."

He smiles. "Oh, good."

He grasps the strap of his plaid backpack as he turns toward the school.

"Carter," I say. I do not ask for help unless I need it. "I request your assistance in understanding emotions."

His eyebrows raise, voice lowering. Why did he react that way? This is why his help will be requisite. "Really? You don't feel emotions?"

I glance at my arm. The warmth from earlier is replaced with an emptiness. "I do at times. I need to understand what I am feeling in order to adjust, as you said. What are common emotions for a first day of school?"

"Excitement. Fear. Anticipation. Nerves."

"I do not know what I am feeling."

"Perhaps all of them," he says. He squeezes my hand, and the electric rush returns. A group of boys comes over to him.

"Aah, ready to kick Drew's butt in swimming this year?" A tall one with light brown skin and a buzzed head asks. Carter swats the boy's back. He waves to me and motions for me to join him inside. He helps me get to the office and introduces me to the various office employees.

I sit down with the vice-principal, Mr. Smith, and hand him my Alaskan transcript, created for me by Joe. It is not real, and I have never lied before, but Joe says it is necessary. Joe's in Washington, and I am here. We must achieve success in our goals quickly, and he says this is the best way. Mr. Smith tells me what classes I need to graduate. I allow him to create my schedule.

Next door, two women whisper about a male teacher and his attractive abs as they slurp some form of liquid. Throughout the school, others are expressing themselves, crying and being loud.

Joe is correct. School will be a place of learning for me, but I will not be learning math, science, or social studies. I will obey the Eldest One and fulfill my duty to my people. I will learn what it means to feel.

Chapter 10

AGS

The whispers crush me, rip past my veins, my muscles, my bones, and bound into the crevices of my soul.

I turn, almost like I've lost control of my body. The closer I get, the stronger the lure is. I can't understand what it says, and yet the voice pulls me in. It is male, cold and harsh, yet enticing and desirable like a nightmare I don't want to wake up from. A teenager who needs their next hit.

The Eldest One said to go straight, not to deviate, but I turn. I don't care anymore.

I follow the call through the hidden tunnels. The cold amplifies until it is no longer an internal imagination. I shiver and yank my gray robe toward me. Now, I thank the gods for this strange prison of a body. If I had my own body right now, I'd be frozen dead.

It's so dark I can no longer see anything, but I crave access to the voice. To find out what it is. To know what it can do for me. I speed toward it as I move over the dull surface. But I'm not quick enough. My hunger for its lures grows. I get to a center room. The shrieks heighten until it is roaring in my ears, but there is no visible person.

And then, I understand the words. They are lyrical, almost poetic and hip. Yet, they strike me like a supernova against the coldness of space. Promises.

"Worship me," it says. "And you can be a ruler on Earth. Favored and beloved by all men. You won't have to just watch humanity. You can own it."

My impenetrable knees quake. Through the dark, a sliver of light appears. A glass-like screen that could fit in my palm glistens against the ground.

When I lift up the glowing hardware, an illusion forms in my mind—bright and vibrant. I'm on Earth in the middle of a crowded room. People surround me in tuxedos and pricey gowns. They lift their wine flutes, cheering my name. The room fills with applause and tears. Humans hug each other. They love me. They are grateful to me.

But no. This isn't what I want. I want to help them, but I don't need glory. Do I?

Another vision courses through my soul. Thousands of Foxians pour from a spaceship, a white mass moving across Earth. They march over jagged mountain rocks and crush stone with bare feet. They swim through rivers and leap down waterfalls.

Their faces are blank. Everywhere they go, there is destruction. The Colosseum crumbles to dust. The Eiffel Tower topples onto roads and shatters across antique buildings. Bricks tumble off Buckingham Palace and roll onto the grass. A roar shrieks through the air, and then the masterpiece explodes. The sun blackens. Humans howl. An infant boy twists in the arms of a female Foxian, screaming.

I open my mouth to plead for it to stop. But I can't talk. My tongue is frozen. I collapse to the ground, trapped in absolute darkness.

"Get away!" another voice cries, and the shrieking flees instantly. The room is bright again. A person is hovering over me. A female Foxian?

I blink and realize it's the Eldest One. He stands over me. His white gown glows like a firefly. His wrinkled eyes meet mine, and he grasps my hand and yanks me up. He pries the device from my fingers.

"I warned you not to go off the path," he says and smiles, so I think he understands.

"I'm sorry," I say, not sure why I have to apologize but embarrassed all the same.

"No matter." He slips the thin glass screen into his pocket. "This device transmits precise estimates of the future to your mind based on the questions you have. But it's very dangerous, and we do not use it because it misses the details of the situation. What did you see?"

I stand. The gruesome vision courses through me. The future? I should not have hoped for anything else. Hos was right.

"Could Foxians destroy Earth if they wanted?" I ask him.

His lips purse, but he nods. "Yes, if they wanted. But we need to go to Earth to thrive."

I tear past him without waiting to hear more. The glow stays with him. I continue on in the darkness. Get to the small room and slide on the strange, rectangular machine. Finally, I can get back to my own body again. Finally, I can leave this imprisoned world. Not sure what I am going to do, but I'm certain of one thing.

Foxians are dangerous. If three billion of them come to Earth, the visions will come true. And I need to protect humans from such invincible monsters.

I will do everything I can to fight against them. I am a guardian of Earth, and I will protect it.

CARTER

I ONLY HAVE gym with Kokab, and it was somewhat normal. But all the stupid gossip about her has me so distracted it takes me a second to notice Anna parading across the cafeteria table in high heels. Her pink skirt tassels shift as she swings her legs back and forth. Students complain as they yank their trays away from getting stomped on.

"Cafeteria people, I need your votes. Is God real? Do angels exist?" She raises her hand high and yells. "Who believes in angels?"

Not good. At. All. I carry my tray toward Antonio, but my apple plunges from my tray as I switch directions. A teacher ducks around students to make a beeline for Anna at the same time as me, but a large crowd of kids blocks us. I dodge past them and ignore their complaints as I force my way through.

"Get down, please," I whisper, reaching the table. *Don't say anything about Kokab.* She whips around, almost plowing into my face with her butt. I jerk back.

"Why, Carter?" She bends until her eyes are closer to my head. "You don't believe me, but I know she's different. So, I'm getting a second opinion."

I have the same question as her: Why? Why did it have to be Anna? Why couldn't Kokab have healed a more practical person? Someone who knows how to keep their mouth shut?

I don't know what could happen to Kokab if people know what she is, but I don't think it'll be good. Would they drag her away? Experiment on her?

"Carter, maybe I was saved. Not just physically, but spiritually." She settles down on the table, and more students complain. "Shouldn't everyone know about a miracle?"

I grab her hand to pull her carefully off the table. She stumbles forward as her heels hit the floor. I catch her and then back off, but she keeps her thin arms wrapped around my waist. The teacher gets over to us, so Anna slips into the seat by Antonio.

"Sorry," she tells the teacher. "Please don't send me to the office. My dog died today, so I'm just having the worst day ever."

It works, and the poor teacher walks away with tears streaming down her face. *You're disgusting to lie about a dog. You've never had one.*

Antonio stares at Anna and scrubs his bald scalp. He picks up the apple I dropped and bites into it. "I believe in angels," he says. "But, if you were going to tell everyone you're angelic, you're not. If anything, you're the chupacabra."

Antonio's usually a really nice guy, but I'm not the only person who's heart's been stampeded on by Anna. Apparently, he secretly liked her when I asked her to prom. Nobody told me, but I guess he'd told her about his feelings, and she still said yes to me. So really, in the end, she bailed on both of us.

"Why won't you believe me?" Anna slides the bangles on her wrist up and down. She runs her fingers through her super messy hair. Her eye makeup smears across her forehead. She's usually gorgeous.

"Believe what?" Antonio tosses cucumbers out of his salad, nose wrinkled. "You do lie a lot. Like that one time, when you told us you were a professional hairdresser. And we were all, 'Really?' And then, Julie asked you to dye her hair platinum, and you turned it purple."

Anna glares at him and thrusts one of his cucumbers at his shirt. "Quiet, or I'll get you."

I glance at Antonio. He opens two milk cartons, ready for our daily chugging competition. Anna and I can't have this conversation in front of him, but what am I supposed to do? There's a cafeteria full of people, and I have to figure out how to get Anna to stay quiet. For Kokab and for my dad.

"Why don't you explain it to me again?" I say. "In private."

Her bright red lips twist into a smile on the words "private."

"Good luck," Antonio mouths.

Anna follows me out to the school parking lot.

"So, you believe me, now?" she asks.

How can I convince her not to tell everybody without telling her the truth? Her tangled hair lump is like the lump in my throat. I know what it feels like when people don't believe something. It's awful. But she's so hungry for attention she'd probably go to the news or something.

I thrust my hands into my jeans. "Nah," I say. "But you can't tell everyone you saw an angel."

"Why not?" She crosses her arms over the words "Rebel" on her shirt.

I shrug 'cause I'm still figuring out what to say.

"Why not?" She repeats louder.

"People will think you're crazy like my dad. They'll make fun of you. Do you want to get bullied?"

Her lips quiver and she fiddles with her bracelets again. "No, not really. But it actually happened. I was lying on the ground bleeding, and then she came up out of nowhere from a mile away in like a minute, she said. In all white. And ghostlike. I got to know I was right. I really need to know."

I hate this. It's my childhood replaying in the current day, only someone else's faith is being questioned. She twiddles her thumb, which is something she always used to do when we were dating. I can't do this to her. I'm the biggest jerk on the planet.

Before I know what I'm doing, I wrap my arms around her. "It's..." I say, "for the best."

I turn my head so she can't see my guilt oozing from my face. She grabs me by the chin and twists my face toward her. Her pink heels click against the cement as she trips backward. "You know something, don't you, Carter?"

I shake my head, but I'm not a good liar like her.

Her eyes brighten, and she claps her hand, her bangles jingling. "Oh, you do. You know what Kokab is?"

I shake my head, but apparently, I'm not convincing, because she beams. "I knew she was an angel. And I'm going to prove to the whole world that I'm right—because I am not a liar and I am *not* crazy!"

"No, you're not right. You saw nothing!"

I chase after her as she storms back into the cafeteria. She smacks Antonio on the back of his head with her wrist, probably just to get his attention, when she gets to the table, her tall heels clicking as she goes. He groans as she plops down into the seat next to him.

"Beat your chugging record by two seconds," Antonio says to me, wiping the chocolate residue from his face, licking off his fingers. "And it was glorious."

I sit down next to them and silently plead with Jesus to intervene. She can't do this. She can't.

"Don't look so bummed," she whispers to me. "I have to get proof first. Or else no one will believe me, like you said. But when I do..."

The lunch bell rings. She leaps from her seat and dashes from the room.

"Well, this is bad," I mutter to myself, chasing after her.

KOKAB

Sneakers squeak against the floor. Permeating body sweat lingers through the halls. I walk, erect and careful. Even though I must learn to embrace emotions, it does not mean I should alter the correctness of my physical behavior. A few dozen bodies shove against me as I march to my next class.

All day, I've listened to the whispers and loud exclamations of students regarding their feelings. Some of them talk about me and how strange and hot I am. I cannot say if they mean hot as in body temperature or attractiveness. My body temperature is low, and my appearance is far less perfect now than the average Foxian. Still, their interactions with each other have been informative, and I am beginning to distinguish what certain emotions might look like on another individual. However, I still do not know what things *feel* like.

I step into the classroom as the bell rings at the exact second it is supposed to start. I am not late. I am not early. The teacher chomps out of sync on gum instead of beginning on time.

A male in a *Swim Fast: Georgia State Champion* t-shirt with blonde curly hair that drips with water whispers to his friends about how good he is at getting girls, and he slides in the desk beside me. His jersey-wearing acquaintances stare at me. Why? I have noticed there are plenty of reasons people are stared at, which varies from having lettuce in their teeth to doing something deemed distracting to humans.

I align my desk straight with the front of the room to make sure there is nothing disturbing about my area. I pull out a sharpener and sharpen my pencil, setting it in the top left corner.

"Hi," the male says. "I'm Drew."

"Hello. I am Abedhakokab Trielldegerata, or Kokab for brevity. "

"What's up?" he says.

I look up.

"512 ceiling tiles," I say, though he should know already.

"Oh, haha, good one. I remember hearing that plenty of times in elementary." He rolls his eyes and elbows my shoulder. I pull away. I remember the way I reacted when Carter touched me this morning, but there is nothing now.

Why is that? What is different this time?

The teacher stands to address the class two minutes late. She explains that she is Mrs. Andrews and goes over some classroom rules. She lifts up a stack of papers. "So this is a pretest to see what you know. I want you to do the best you can, so I'm giving you all class period to do these calculus problems. This may be overwhelming. Don't worry. This is what we are going to learn over the course of the semester. I'll give the person with the highest score a candy bar as motivation to actually try since this isn't graded."

Drew flips his notebook open and scribbles with a pencil. "Don't care." He winks at me. "I've got better things to focus on."

The teacher approaches me. She chomps her gum, causing a loud thump inside my eardrums. I refrain from covering my ears to avoid the cacophony. She hands me the test. "I always hated being the new kid." Her lips twist. Is it pity? Or disappointment? "Let me know if this stuff is too challenging for you. Or if you need some help elsewhere."

Her eyes dart to Drew, and she shakes her head as she hands him the pages. "Stay on task," she orders him.

Drew keeps drawing, not obeying her. He hasn't even written his name on it. He doodles a picture of a GTA Spano. It's very inaccurate and not at all proportional. The wheels should be larger and the top smoother, but it's easy to recognize. "Beautiful car, huh?"

He gestures to his picture. "I'm gonna get it someday when I become a famous swimmer."

Then, he cups his hand to his mouth, moving slowly over to my ears until his lips are pressed against them. "But my ride's still pretty sweet if you wanna take a spin in it."

I turn away. I lift my pencil and start the test. My stomach churns this time. I do not know why it makes my insides sick.

He peers down at my sheet and whistles. "Done already?"

"Yes," I respond.

"Do you think you got the answers right?"

"Yes, all of them." I stand to turn the pretest in, moving toward Mrs. Andrews's desk.

"Do you need help with something?" she says, smiling.

I shake my head. "I finished the task as you directed."

"Hmm." She snatches my paper with her large fingers. It takes her 2.1 minutes to scan over my answers.

"Impossible to finish all this so quickly," she says, turning to the clock. "Class started only a few minutes ago."

I do not know why she said it was impossible. I have accomplished the task, meaning it is certainly possible. She hands me a new sheet with different problems. Her face twists upward. A smile, but it is somehow different than Carter or Joe's smiles. Can a smile be identified with a different emotion than happiness? Perhaps there is more than one type of happiness.

Emotions are not simple like math. As I learn more, things continue to be complicated.

"Do it with me watching," she says. She pulls out a different exam with similar math equations.

A student in a green blouse whispers to the girl beside her how I must be a cheater. The second time is easier because Drew is not distracting me. It takes thirty-three seconds. Mrs. Andrews lifts up the paper. She runs her fingers through her red hair and glances from me to the paper and back again three times. She goes over the answers, checking each one.

"Impossible," she says. "They're all right. Where...where's your calculator?"

"A calculator is not necessary for me."

Her hands shake. Her head bobs, causing the flab under her chin to wriggle in strange patterns. She pulls open her drawer and hands me a Hershey bar. "Bizarre," she says quietly.

Again, I do not understand her reactions. I completed the task as requested. Why is she shaking? I finished promptly and correctly. She said it was bizarre, but it was not bizarre at all.

I move back to my desk until Drew taps on my shoulder. The teacher said not to talk, but she is not watching. She stares at my paper, going through the problems again and again.

"You got to help out me and my friends," he whispers and hands me a large stack of papers. I complete the problems as commanded.

According to school policy, this might be cheating, but the teacher did not say we couldn't share answers with one another. I have never cheated before, but I have also never disobeyed a direct order either. I place the papers into his hands. A huge grin spreads across his dimpled cheeks. "You'll keep helping us, won't you?" He glances back toward his friends.

I nod, and his smile broadens. "Super hot. Smart. And chill. You're perfect, Koke. We should hang out more."

CARTER

I've been trying to handle Anna all day and assist Kokab any time I see her around, but things are getting out of hand. I hide behind my locker and pull out my phone.

Should I call Dad? Or not? I want to ask for his advice, and I want to tell him that I'm a believer in aliens. After all these years, I don't think he's crazy.

But, at the same time, I'm not sure I can open my mouth and say all those things in real life.

I go ahead and dial. For once, Dad picks up.

"Carter, is everything okay?"

His voice rises, and I can hear the hope in it.

"Err, yes...I..." I can't have this conversation on the phone. This is an in-person, face to face, kind of chat. One where we both hug it out. Besides, a couple girls gather by the locker next to me and gossip about how hot Charlie Heaton is. It's not like I want other kids hearing me tell my dad aliens are actually real. Or seeing me bawl my eyes out.

And as far as Anna and Kokab go, I can handle them. I shouldn't have called.

"Can we talk about something when you get back?" I say. "It should be in person."

"Are you sure?" He sounds worried. "We can talk about... whatever it is."

"Yeah."

There's an awkward silence, and Dad coughs. "I was going to ask you anyway...can you take Kokab to the Cherokee County Building at four o'clock? Brian's meeting her there to take her somewhere important. She'll be gone a few days. It's crucial. She can't be late."

"Okay. Will do," I say before the moment gets even more awkward. "I gotta go. Good luck with...whatever you're doing."

We hang up, and I go to meet Kokab at the front of her classroom. I overheard some people gossiping about how the principal met to talk to her about a special program for genius kids. I also saw her knock a boy out in gym class while playing dodgeball. He had a massive bruise on his face when he walked out of the nurse's office a few hours later.

I need to understand why she's being so obvious. Does she want someone to experiment on her or worse? Maybe she doesn't realize this behavior isn't normal? Dad asked me to keep her safe, and, after all these years of not believing him, it's the least I can do.

But when she steps out of the classroom, Drew follows her, his eyes wandering to all the wrong places. *Leave her alone, you creep.*

It's not just that he hassled me about the aliens. Right after he beats all of us by a couple laps, Drew likes to brag in the locker room about all the messed up things he does with girls.

She's gorgeous, and he's a reputable tool. It's trouble.

"I can't believe you aced that test in three minutes." Drew brushes her shoulder with his fingers. "So amazing. Wanna go out tonight?"

He continues to run his tanned fingers down her white sleeve, and she looks...uncomfortable? I can't say for sure, but she doesn't seem happy about it.

"Stop messing with her," I say, keeping a steady gaze on him, breathing in and out to keep from doing anything stupid. I glance at Kokab. "If that's what you want, I mean."

"I do not know," says Kokab, so I back off, still watching Drew.

I hope she knows soon. Kokab probably is out of my league, but she's *way* out of his. Even if he thinks he's top dog.

"I'm a perfect gentleman." Drew shrugs, and I walk down the old tiled halls, motioning toward Kokab. "Let's go."

She immediately and obediently follows, which is weird and seems like something she does a lot. Drew's well-maintained eyebrows raise, and I think he may have noticed too.

I get ready to give Kokab an uncomfortable lecture about keeping things on the D.L. as we exit the school door. But I'm out of luck. Anna's there. She's leaning against my truck door, sucking on a powdery bourbon ball.

The tangles in her hair are gone, replaced with a glitter headband and well-brushed hair. I'm not sure if it's a good sign or not, but by the way she hovers over my car like a wild animal claiming its territory, her revamped look is disastrous.

"Hey." She smiles at us as we approach. "I need a ride home."

"Anna, move." I grip my key. Students holler at friends as they rush past, on a natural high from first-day beginnings. People need my help, and Anna is an obstacle I don't feel like dealing with.

"Don't worry. Forget about everything I said. I'm over it. Let's just get some fries like old times." She fist-bumps my shoulder. She glances at Kokab and then turns to block her out. I don't buy her sincerity. But I need to figure out some way to get her to keep her mouth shut about what happened.

Maybe this is an opportunity. A messy, dangerous opportunity with a messy, dangerous girl.

"Fine," I say. Anna takes the front seat without being polite enough to ask Kokab if it's okay, and Kokab slides into the backseat. She flicks the dangling green-haired troll above the dashboard back and forth with one fingernail. She complains about the country music and changes the station to some heavy metal.

"Much better," she says, turning toward Kokab. "So, tell me. Where are you from?"

"I cannot say," says Kokab.

"Hmmm...interesting." Anna raises her eyebrow at me and purses her lips with an *I-know-something's-up* look. "You don't remember meeting me the other night, do you?"

"Tell her you don't." It's more of a breath than a whisper, but I hope Kokab can hear it like she seemed to be able to hear me out on the porch when I asked her to come out.

"I do not," Kokab responds immediately.

Anna growls, slouching in her seat. She hits the troll more vigorously.

I don't know what Anna's going through. I don't know why she went from being fun a few years back to psycho, but she needs to get over this. For our sake. And for her own.

She's never dealt with cruel kids who hate you for believing in the extraordinary before. She doesn't need to.

"See? She agrees nothing happened," I say. "Are you sure it wasn't just a weird dream?"

Anna slouches further down into her seat and examines her fingers. I try keeping my eyes on the road, but I notice her glancing at her arm and sitting up straighter.

"Yes, I'm sure," she says. "Positive."

I have a few hours before I have to drop off Kokab. If I can convince Anna not to say anything about Kokab, it'll be worth it. We drive up to Cheeseburger Bobby's. Grease and juicy beef shift through the warm August air. I can almost taste the massive double stacker.

Can I just tie her up and leave her in the woods? That'd solve the issues of her trying to figure out Kokab's secret. And a lot of my other life problems as well.

I mess with my junk of a seatbelt until it unbuckles and climb out. I get out to go open Anna's door, but it's locked.

"What?" I say. Did she just lock me out of *my* truck? "What are you doing?"

She swings into the driver's seat. "Sorry." Anna amps the heavy metal up and makes it hard to hear. "You should really stop being such a gentleman, Carter. Kokab and I need to take a little trip. I'm going to prove to everyone that I'm right about her!"

She slides the key into the ignition. She can't be serious right now.

I blink and then run for the truck bed, tossing my body toward it. The tires squeal against the pavement, and I miss. I fall flat on the road. My beautiful truck speeds past the parked cars.

I holler and sprint after it. "Gah! Wha-! Yo-! Sto-!" It's hard to form a real word. Children's eyes bug out with their cones of dipped ice cream dripping down their fingertips as they walk past me while I flail my arms in the air. Their mamas yank them away from me like *I'm* the dangerous one. I gesture toward the vehicle, but the words don't seem to come.

I try to wrap my head around what happened. Did Anna just steal my car? And kidnap Kokab? Really?! *Don't you dare hurt her.*

And nobody messes with a man's truck.

AGS

Els is the first thing I see when I open my eyes. I wriggle my nose, bouncing it up and down. It itches. *Oh you beautiful, wonderful nose with normal sensations, you.* I scratch it and beam at Els.

"Yes! It feels great to be back in my own body again. In case you were wondering."

Apparently, Els wasn't, because as soon as I sit up she jets out the door toward the front of the ship. I smash my fist against a wall, not hard, just enough to feel the pain. It works. Oooh, that hurt.

"Ouch," I say, still delighted by the fact that I can feel it. I love this cute, cuddly body. One heart. One nose. So much emotion and sensation. Just like a human body.

My excitement dulls when I remember the eerie voice, the

strange words from the Elder, and the truth of the Foxians. They're coming. Three billion empty people will flood Earth.

But in this body, with my soul intact, I allow myself to hope. Hope entwines itself through the crevices of my spirit, wriggling up and down within me like my nose bouncing a few seconds ago. Everything can work out. For humanity. For the Foxians.

I have a solution.

Somehow, as my mind downloaded to my body, probably because I could think hopeful thoughts with my own nice frame, I came up with a way for the Foxians to survive. Without coming to Earth. Praise the stars in the galaxy. I know it's a long shot, almost impossible. But, with the gods of the universe, all things are possible.

So, why not give it my all? Why not believe in the unbelievable? It can only help.

I move to the front of the ship and sit next Els. "The Foxians want to immigrate to Earth," I tell her. "I've got a different plan."

"Do they?" she responds. "Now, that's a curveball. Oh, it's going to be interesting to see humans' reactions when the Foxians come. So, dearie, what's your plan?"

It won't be interesting, but I understand that Els is loopy, and right now, I don't care. I smile. "You'll see."

We fly to Georgia to meet up with Mom with the spacecraft in invisible mode. I rush to my bedroom and change into American-style clothes, so I can fit in. My international wardrobe doesn't quite match, but I'll shop somewhere in town when I have time. I look out the window at the green foliage, thrilled that *my* heart can react. It soars along with the ship.

When we land on Earth, Els exits, but I remain inside. I toy with the sleeves on my sweater because the moment I've been waiting for my entire life is finally here. I've watched it for so long from above, but only guardians are trusted on the planet.

I get to be on Earth's surface. I've got to relish it, and I'm not going to worry about the Eldest One's ugly news.

I press the exit button, and the hatch doors slide open. There it is: grass.

Wow, it's *so* green. An open field dotted with maple trees stretches out and touches the massive blue sky overhead. A tinge of sweetness (honeysuckle?) wafts into the ship. It's not just a camera or a hologram. It's real.

I gaze at it for a few moments, mouth agape, and then shift forward and place my foot on Earth's surface, followed by my entire body.

"Oh my lanta. Freakin'. Goodness. Goat." I drop as many American expressions as I can, giggling.

I throw myself into the grass and tumble around. It's cold and wet and perfect.

My zebra-striped tennis shoes come off in order to truly touch the ground. I rub my toe back and forth in the soil to get it as dirty as possible. Els watches me as she leans against a large American beech tree. But I don't care if I'm acting odd.

I stand up and sprint barefoot through the field to touch everything. The dirt, an ant, a cluster of dandelions—all become the product of my enthusiasm. I arrive at the trees and shove my nose up against the bark, inhaling.

It's wonderful. I reach my arms skyward and soak in the light filtering through the woods.

Then, it's not wonderful anymore. A boy clinging to his mother as the Eiffel Tower falls flashes in memory. A darkness comes, a sort of stiffness as well, because this could be gone. Based on the vision I had before leaving Foxia, I might lose this. What I just gained.

Not now. Go away.

It's like a piece of Foxia, of that sterility, clings to me. *Go away. This is the moment I've been waiting for my whole life.*

I try to ignore the darkness. "Hello, little lizard," I say, as he scurries past me. He's adorable and incredible. For instance, if I accidentally stepped on his tail, it'd grow back. "Hello, woods. Hello, planet."

I'm here. The place I've always wanted to be, and I have a plan to save Earth, so there's no need to worry.

Go away.

Finally, I pull out the bright pink cell phone to call Mom. I've never used a cellular before. It's so human of me. It's hard for me to figure it out, but eventually, I get a hold of Mom, and she tells me where to meet her.

Els laughs her head off as I struggle to hang up. "You go meet your mom without me, child," she says. "I have things to work on." Her wrinkly blush-covered cheeks sag as she grins with mischief in her eyes. "You can take the moped."

She shuffles back to the spaceship without another word. Mom's planning on meeting me with the governor, so we can update each other on our findings, according to Els.

I get the moped from the back of the spaceship and examine the scuffs and rusted helmet. I've never driven a human vehicle, and I'm not the best driver. Do I dare try this broken-down contraption? Does it even run?

My heart beats as I drag the vehicle into the woods. I run my plan once more through my head to make sure it makes sense to me.

Ignore the vision from back on Foxia, the screams, the howling. Look around you, Ags. Things on this planet are beautiful now, and they will stay that way. They've got to.

I just have to persuade Mom and the whole government to buy into my crazy scheme. Then Earth will be left alone, and the Foxians will survive someplace else.

Should be easy to do, right?

I glance down at the moped and swing my left leg over to climb on. My skirt hangs low. Driving this has gotta be easier than a spaceship.

I press on the gas and the vehicle jerks forward. It grinds against a root in the ground, and I almost fall off. Oops. I try again, and this time I move.

Mom and Governor Ids want to know what I've learned. I sigh

because with Mom retiring, I question for the first time whether she's really as passionate about Earth as I once thought. Will she side with me even though my idea may be expensive and tricky?

I hope so because if I can't persuade her, I won't be able to persuade anyone.

KOKAB

THE TRUCK TIRES shriek against the ground, and I must refrain from covering my ears. Anna laughs as she pulls in front of an SUV. Its horn honks at us seven times.

"Isn't this fun?" She rolls down her window and shoves her head out. Her driving breaks many of the rules of the Georgia Driver's Manual, which I read thoroughly today in driver's ed.

"I do not know," I say. "Did you have permission to borrow Carter's vehicle?"

"Of course not. That's what makes it fun! Haven't you ever done anything stupid you weren't supposed to do? It's completely freeing." She yanks her hand off the driver's wheel and attempts to answer a text as she drives. This is also against state law.

I shift in my seat, examining the cars. Anna is not the only one breaking procedures in the book. A man down the street drives with only his left hand on the steering wheel. A teenage boy travels 7 miles per hour over the speed limit. Why do humans make errors? Does emotion affect their ability to reach perfection?

If so, will having emotions affect my ability to perform perfectly? This is the first time I have considered this.

"No. I always obey." I say. Anna says doing stupid things is freeing and fun, but I saw and heard students in school label things as stupid. Some had the same smile as Anna—or a comparable lift in their voice, but others were frowning or crying.

If this is fun, fun hurts my stomach.

"Of course you have. Everyone does stupid things sometimes." She giggles.

I shake my head, and Anna slams on the brakes two feet away from hitting a driver in a blue car in front of us. Her risk of getting into an accident is high.

"I don't believe you," she says.

"I never disobey a command." I check the phone in my hand. Joe has requested that I meet Brian at four p.m. He will take me to the airport. Tomorrow, I will meet with the president. This trip will need to be short in order to accomplish that.

"Really? So, you're perfect. Like an angel?" Her voice raises. Based on other students' reactions to various things today, this may indicate excitement. However, she could be angry.

"I am absolute in completing tasks."

Anna whistles and touches her arm with an unusually twisted smile on her face. She speeds through a red stop sign. "So, you *are* an angel, then?" she asks. She has already asked this question several times. Why does she keep asking? She will not get a different answer.

"I cannot say. I have been ordered not to."

"Hmmph." Anna pulls in front of a large, brick house. "Well, I'll just have to figure it out on my own then."

She loops her pink backpack in her arms and exits the vehicle, and I follow. We walk up a cobbled lane to the home. A granite cupid fountain sprays water. The gurgling continues, but it is much quieter here than the school. A few bugs crawl in the lawn, but I hear no voices inside. Only a breeze shifts through the well-trimmed trees.

"This is my dad's house. Stupid fancy. But who cares about that? He left my mom and me. He sucks." She shifts to the front door and pries a key from a large potted plant. "I've been wanting to do this for a few months but never had the balls. Carter knows something, but he refuses to tell me. But if you follow directions like you say, I bet I can make him tell me."

Anna steps inside. She rummages through her bag and flips open a small knife blade, moving to the large living room. Though there are some flaws, it is much cleaner and neater than Carter's house. A large satin sofa sits by a grand piano.

"Here." She pulls another knife from her bag. "If you're so obedient, cut up the couch."

"Is this your property?" I say to verify that I am not breaking a governmental law.

She nods. "Keep going until it's completely shredded."

She hands me the knife, and I begin making thin slices into the couch. She stands over me with a large grin on her face. I continue cutting the couch until the fabric is shredded into one-inch pieces.

I obeyed her order. I always do.

However, my stomach twists and my forehead begins to sweat. I never sweat. What does it mean? What am I feeling? If I cannot identify these emotions, I will not be able to use them to persuade humans to allow us onto this planet without war. I will not be able to teach my people either, as the Eldest One asked.

My meeting with the president is coming. Will I be ready?

Anna bites her lip, scratching her arm. She tugs on the sleeve of her *Rebel*-labeled t-shirt. She isn't smiling now. Did I do something incorrectly?

"Does this meet your expectation?" I ask. She gnaws on her lip until it starts bleeding.

"Right," she says, swallowing. "Of course. You really are obedient, aren't you?"

"Yes."

She asks a lot of repetitive questions. She pulls out her phone. Over her shoulders, I see her turn the camera to video mode.

"My dad didn't really care about this piano." She plunks a few white keys. The piano is so in tune that I can barely detect any off keys, even with my accurate hearing. "He bought it for my mom as an anniversary present years ago. She loved it, played it a few times every day. But, in the divorce, he took it. Just to be a jerk. Now, his new girlfriend plays chopsticks on it. It's super expensive."

She swings the camera toward me and squeezes her eyelids closed. "Destroy it," she orders.

Chapter 12

AGS

Mom winds her pink hair as she examines the menu. The woman at the cash register leans forward, forcing a smile on her face as she tells Mom her favorite is the double-decker for the third time.

"Sorry, are you sure there're no vegetarian options?" Mom asks.

"Not unless ya wanna do lettuce and tomato on a bun," says the employee. Her beam slips by the second.

She's a human—a real human. Another stands inches behind me. The teen wears a Kiss t-shirt and twists the chains on her neck. She rolls her eyes and complains to someone on her cell about how long we are taking.

I yearn to reach out and slide my fingers against her arm and see if it feels the same as mine. She makes me fan-girl as she brings her fingers to her mouth and yawns. Yadians don't yawn, and it's super awesome (as the humans would say) to get a whiff of her bacteria breath.

I've seen people before thousands of times via hologram video streams. But not for real. Oh, it would be so grand to touch her, but I'm aware that's weird, so I settle for touching everything else.

I slide my hand against the human counter, shake the human salt, poke the human cash register, and study the human menu until the employee starts giving me an annoyed look as well.

"Is that everything for you?" she asks Mom.

"Perfect," says Mom. They hand her a plastic number, and she gives it to me. Obviously, I can't keep it, but she knows I love these trinkets. We scoot into a booth to wait for Governor Ids, and I run my fingers over the red-engraved number 87.

Humans advance in some ways, but this type of thing is delightfully classic.

I study my surroundings. The old-school jukebox plays rock, beef sizzles on the griddle, kids smear ice cream across their faces. The scent of grease and juice permeates the room.

Yes. Classic.

I'm in a Burger Shack. Among humans. Living out the biggest dream I've ever had.

In every way, it's great, but it's not as great as I imagined it. I might jump around and shriek my head off. But there's a piece of me that's still stuck in a Foxian body unable to shake the stiffness. Also, there's a piece of me weighed down by the darkness of reality. Bad things could happen to mankind.

An employee shifts to our booth and places a tray full of food in front of us. I bite into the double-decker recommended by the employee as Governor Ids walks in.

As soon as he sidles in next to us, his fat bum takes up my spot on the booth, so I have to squash into the edges. Mom puts up an invisible sound shield to make people think we're talking about something normal. She pulls her pink hair into a ponytail and twists the strings on her sweatshirt. Time to get down to business. I'm nervous they won't listen. That's why I haven't told Mom about my plans yet. I'm hoping, praying that I can get the words right to explain that billions are coming and that I know we can stop them.

"Are you sure we look human enough?" The governor glances down at his baggy t-shirt. He stares at her in her slacks and heels and pearl necklace. I wish he would stop goggling over her.

"Yes. Definitely," Mom says.

Usually, guardians need more elaborate disguises, but on Earth, especially these days, we can pass as a human. They just don't realize my orange hair isn't a fantasy dye.

Mom offers some fries to Ids, and he takes a handful.

"I can't figure out why she's here," she says. "I scanned her at a distance when she first arrived, and there was no indication of a weapon of any sort on her body. I've been tracking her for the last few days, but she hasn't really revealed anything. The home she's staying at is cloaked with some advanced tracking blockers. Way too advanced for humans."

I munch on a few french fries, practicing how I'll tell them about my plan in my head.

"Then, I tried surveying her at school." She says. "She's causing quite a stir, but I didn't really learn anything new."

The governor dunks a fry into ketchup. He sticks it into his mouth and makes a face. He gazes at my mom's face but doesn't seem to hear a word she's saying. How is she missing this?

"Human food is awful." He swallows a half cup of water. "Being back in Fis City will be quite the upgrade."

"I hope you had better luck than me." Mom finally stops chattering and turns to me. She jerks her finger from her strings and taps the Coke with her long nails.

Now is the chance for me to get my idea out. If my mom will just listen. I know it will work, but a lot of Yadians will hate it. They don't have to love it, but I need them to go along with it.

Be smooth, Ags. And subtle. Really subtle.

"Three billion Foxians are invading Earth in a week."

Good job, Ags.

A man at the table next to me devours a burger. Ketchup slips down his chin into his scraggly beard. If he notices, he doesn't seem to mind. He chats with a girl, who's focused more on his beard than his eyes. She toys with her fluffy phone, which lies beside her on the red booth seat, out of his sight.

First date, perhaps? How entertaining. And hilarious. And tragic, if it is. But not as tragic as what may happen to them when the Foxians come.

That's why they can't come.

I grind my teeth together. Screams of dying people fill my head. I can't let it happen. The future of humanity is in my hands.

"So, they are invading?" Mom asks, her voice dropping. She begins tapping on her Coke hard enough that it tips, and ice tumbles off the table. I grab napkins and start dabbing the mess. The governor reacts by reaching his arms around Mom's shoulder. "I hoped Hos was wrong. I really hoped."

Sure, he did. He was just saying how Mom's new job will be an upgrade. He *hoped* for an opportunity to touch her. Mom's about to knock the ketchup over too, so I rush to explain myself.

"Not exactly. According to the Eldest One, they're going to try to cohabit with humans." I cross my arms, wiggling my nose to show how serious I am. I inhale, ready to explain my idea.

"Cohabit?" Mom sounds confused.

"Yes, listen—"

The governor cuts me off. "Doesn't sound so bad. They could really help this dump of a place out."

I narrow my eyes. "It won't work. We need to stop them, or they will ruin Earth as it currently is with their ideas of control. Earth's freedom and wildness make it beautiful."

I try again. This will work. It will work for everyone. We all win, right? "And the only way to do that is to help them."

"What?" Mom's eyebrows furrow, and I can tell I lost her.

"We need to help them instead. They don't have the resources to go anywhere but Earth. If we could just give them some giant ships, the resources to terraform another planet..."

"Do you know how much money that will cost?" The governor screeches. He raises his hand up like he's shutting me down. "We don't help Foxians, and most of the council doesn't care too much about humans. Foxians are awful, and I feel just as threatened because of their past as the rest of the committee. But it sounds like they just need a home. It's enough that we're currently paying for three guardians—"

"Not for long," I say, glancing at Mom, the soon-to-be-retiree.

"You don't get it. But humans are one of the greatest species around."
I glance at the bearded man beside me. He chows on greasy french
fries, so ignorant of the horrors that could come. In his relationship.
On his planet. He needs our help.

The governor frowns at my mom like trying to explain things to
me is hopeless. She knits her hand into mine and rubs her nose on my
cheek. "Ags," she says. "I know you love these people. I do too. But we
thought this was warfare on mankind. This is better news. Not great
news. But better. Even if we can persuade the council, after all we
did to Foxia, do you really think they'd want our help?"

I yank my hand away. "You taught me my whole life to love
humans. How could you side with *him*?" I glare at the governor and
then focus back on her. "You know the Foxians are dangerous. We
can do more. I saw Planet Foxia. They are a bunch of robots. They
can't survive with humans. It will end badly if we let them come. We
have to stop them."

My panic grows. The vision replays in my head. Mom tears apart
a french fry.

She bites her lip, looking at the governor. "It is true that having
them here could be much more dangerous for mankind than just
helping the Foxians ourselves. Perhaps her idea should be
considered?"

The governor's eyes dart to Mom's perfect hair. For once in my
life, I'm grateful he's attracted to her. "Fine." He turns to me. "You
talk to the council. Good luck convincing Hos."

I squeal, hugging the governor, and then remember I'm supposed
to be a professional. I clear my throat. "Right. Well, that's excellent."

We finish lunch, and I spend the car ride looking at all the old
buildings in downtown Canton. I roll down the windows, enjoying
the smell of barbecue restaurants.

Mom clears her throat. "I was really worried that this was going
to be a takeover. But I think you'll be able to handle this situation.
You've been very well trained."

"What do you mean?" My voice is on edge.

"I'm supposed to start training in a few days, and it takes longer than that to get to the location for my training. They understood the urgency of the situation, but now that warfare is out of the question, they'll be less concerned—"

"So you're leaving? When?" I interrupt her.

"Tomorrow." Mom sighs.

I shake my nose. "You spew all this nonsense about loving a species, and then turn your back on them in their time of need? I don't get it. You barely supported my idea at all."

"I'm not trying to abandon Earth. I just think a lot of good can be done for many planets if I can help make the rules. And it isn't that I don't support your idea. It's very clever. But I think it will be challenging to convince the Foxians to work together with Yadians."

"But you have to at least try." I grip the leather seat belt with my fingers and gaze at the dark star-speckled sky. How could she guard this place for years and then walk away so easily?

Mom glances at me. "Fine, if that's what you want to spend your time doing versus preparing to help them transition. This is your planet now. And I trust you to make the calls. You've got this, Ags." She wiggles her nose up and down, a sign of respect.

I don't respond because I don't really want her respect. I want her to help people.

We continue our drive in silence. Mom's booked a hotel. Tonight, we're supposed to swim in a pool, watch Netflix, and order room service. It would be fun, but now I know this is her way of trying to bribe me with an adequate goodbye.

This may not be how I imagined my first experience on Earth, but maybe someday, when the Foxians are no longer a concern, I can be carefree again.

CARTER

Anna. The drama queen of the century.

Anna. The psychopath of the high school.

Anna. The devil's adopted prized child.

Anna. Stole my truck and kidnapped Kokab.

After the truck pulled away, I paced around, screaming like a cow giving birth for several minutes, furious, annoyed, shocked, wild. All those things.

It finally happened. Anna did something psycho enough to land her in prison.

I'm supposed to get Kokab to the county building in about an hour, and Dad said it was important. But instead, I have to deal with more of her crazy. Our conversation from earlier devours me, and I hope she isn't planning some way to prove that Kokab's not human.

Oh, please, no. This is a mess. The worst scenario in so many ways.

Finally, I calm down enough to form a semi-intelligible plan, and I call Antonio. "Kokab kidnapped. Anna stole truck. Come now."

"What?" says Antonio. "Do you... Should you call the cops?"

Anna standing in youth court in front of a stern, large-nosed judge getting sentenced away sounds fantastic. In fact, right now, I'd love to be the person throwing her in jail, but I don't want Kokab to get tangled up with authorities. "No," I say through clenched teeth. "Let's try to find her first. She isn't answering my calls."

When Antonio pulls up in his mom's sedan, the phone finally buzzes. It's *her*.

"Whereareyou?" I say it all in one breath. I can't believe this moment in my life is actually happening.

"My dad's house," she says in a chipper voice. "Thanks for letting me borrow your truck. It was super helpful. You should come get it now. Kokab's great and waiting for you." She hangs up the phone right away, and I'm left with dozens of words unsaid.

"Mr. Chu's house," I say as Antonio throws open the door. "Let's go."

I took anger management classes after Dad's alien drama, so I try out the weird breaths. *In*. Anna is the Wicked Witch of the West. *Out*. But, she's been through a lot lately. She called me right away. She might feel bad. *In*. She's going to blow Kokab's secret. She's going to ruin everything. *Out*. Maybe not. The worst is over. She's giving me my truck back. Kokab's fine. *In*. She committed grand theft auto. She kidnapped a girl. And she's a terrible driver. I can't calm down. *Out*. Yes, I can.

We pull up to her dad's fancier-than-I'll-ever-live-in mansion. She's standing outside with an arm wrapped around Kokab and a bright pink smile.

Antonio gives me a knowing look. "Don't want me along for this conversation, do you? No problem. I hate drama and dealing with the devil. I'll ask Saint Cajetan to send you good fortune."

He fist-bumps my shoulder and winks. His way of telling me I got this. I step forward onto the manicured lawn and check my truck parked in the driveway.

"What did you do?" It's all I can say to the two girls in front of me. Kokab's shirt is covered in sawdust. She's stoic like normal.

But is that guilt in her eyes? In Anna's eyes too? What have they done?

"I have something to show you," Anna says. She grits her teeth, lifting her chin.

I follow her into the house to the living room. The place looks like our house after Jason demolished a piñata on his last birthday. Only this isn't a party.

The room's covered in splintered wood and red pieces of fabric. Did someone grind dust into the carpet? Piano keys are strewn everywhere. A soundboard lays on a destroyed couch, and the legs of a grand piano lay on the floor. One piece of the grand, what's still intact, is flipped sideways, the name "Kokab" carved across it.

I don't understand why she would go along with such a stupid thing.

"Did you take part in this?" I ask as Kokab stands in the middle of it all, silent and still gorgeous. I actually don't know how much she's capable of, so she's scary, too. "Why?"

"She commanded me to, so I obeyed," says Kokab. I turn from Anna to Kokab. Anna slumps onto the ripped couch and fiddles with her phone.

"And do you just obey everything?" I ask Kokab. "Whatever anyone tells you?"

"Yes, everything."

I know it's true. She's always done exactly as suggested or told. It's why she came out onto the porch. She heard me ask for her. It's why she went and healed Anna. Somehow, from our house, she heard the call. It's why she's hanging with stupid losers like Drew.

"Kokab." I grip her shoulders. "We have to be somewhere in thirty minutes. Can you please get into the car? I gotta talk to Anna, but I want it to be your choice to leave."

Kokab exits the house. I don't know how she feels, but her lips drop just a tiny bit.

Anna still sits and fidgets with her phone. She thrusts her fingers against the screen as dust particles swirl around her.

I try to stay calm. I try the breathing tactic again. But Anna is being Anna.

"What is your problem?" I lean in toward her and try not to holler. "Kokab is new to the US. She's still learning. You told her to destroy expensive property. What in the...errsh...were you *thinking*?"

"Kokab said she obeys everything, so I thought I'd put it to the test. I got it all on camera," Anna replies while texting on her phone. Her lip trembles, but she continues to justify herself. "She ripped it apart with her bare hands. Definitely freaky. And my dad's a lawyer. He'll sue Kokab if he thinks she did this. And then everyone will be watching *her*. I just need to know, okay? So tell me what Kokab is, and I'll take the blame."

"Look at me." My grip on Anna's sawdust-covered shoulders grows, and she shakes her head. My voice rises. "Look."

"I just want you to tell me what she is, Carter." Her voice cracks.

How am I supposed to get out of this mess?

"Please, Carter." Anna chokes. "I know what I did was awful."

Then, she starts full-on bawling. Gah. She did this to us, and now she's the one crying about it?

Tears drip down her face, mascara running. She sounds like a shot duck. "Can't you just tell me? I just. I need to know... I need to know if God is there."

Crying should be considered a superpower for girls. Despite all the stupid things she just did to me, she makes me want to tell her all I figured out just to get the tears to stop.

What's the big deal, anyway? Why is this so important to her?

I grumble as she throws herself onto the couch. I don't understand why she'd have a meltdown over this, but I hate being a jerk.

I pull her upright and wipe the tears from her face. "What is this about, Anna?"

She hiccups. "Ever since the divorce, it seemed like God didn't care. Bad things kept happening to my mom and me. And then, I started wondering if He was even there. And, if He isn't, if angels aren't real, I won't see Thomas ever again. I believed in that stuff before when I was a kid. But if God's there, why would he do this to me?"

Oh. I never met Anna's brother, Thomas. He committed suicide when Anna was five, years before I ever met her. But the pain would be fresh...if you had faith and lost it.

Kokab's not an angel, but I do believe in them. I just don't want to tell people to believe in something they can't see. I don't want to be bullied and harassed like I was for years. I got no proof. So, what do I tell her to fix the waterworks?

I need time to think this through. Would Anna act crazier than this if she knew the truth about Kokab? Or would it stop this disaster in the making?

Anna still sobs on the ground, so I sit by her. "If I don't leave in the next five minutes, Kokab will be late to something really important. But," I sigh, "can you hold off? Wait for me to get back? And we can talk."

She nods, and I hug her and get up.

Once outside, I give Antonio the thumbs up to let him know that it's going to be all right. He drives away. I climb into the seat by Kokab and start driving my truck. I'm happy enough to get the truck back with no damage that I want to kiss the steering wheel, but I don't since Kokab watches me.

"What are you feeling right now, Carter?" she asks.

I exhale. "Angry. Sad. Worried."

"Are those emotions directed toward me? What is it like to be angry? Sad?" she asks.

"Anger is like this terrible energy bottling up inside of you, and you want to act. To hurt someone. But you don't have to." I tell her I'm not up to talking about everything else right now. She nods, turning toward the road, her back straight.

Anna took advantage of her so easily. I'm not sure how I'll be able to protect her. Did Dad know the risk? Did he understand *exactly* how obedient she is?

"I don't know what life was like where you're from. But, here, it's up to you to decide what you want to do," I tell her. She needs to understand so that kids or adults don't end up harming or using her. "Good. Evil. You get to pick. Obedience isn't a bad thing. But you should only listen to the right voices, you know?"

"I do not understand," she says. "Who is the right voice?"

"You gotta figure that out. It's why emotions are so important," I say, realizing I'd never choose if I didn't feel either. What would be the purpose? "So, maybe study different religions' scriptures. Philosophers. Watch the consequences of people's actions. If you want. And then after all that, listen to *yourself*. You get to figure out what to do on your own. "

Kokab eyes widen. There seems to be more under the surface, needing to break free.

"I will consider your suggestion to make choices for myself," she says. She sets her fingers on my right hand, which is not on the steering wheel like it should be. Oh frack. Her fingers are smooth and warm, and I hope she doesn't move them. Kokab touched my hand.

Kokab's incredible, has superpowers, and is so pure. She's way out of my league, and a girl as cool as her may never touch me again.

KOKAB

The music in Brian's car is audible before I am in sight of the vehicle. Rap is much more rhythmic and hurts my ears less than what Carter listens to.

He's at the side of the county building in a white sedan, as Joe indicated he would be.

"Brian," says Carter as we exit the car. He crosses his arms when he sees him.

Brian jerks his head upward. "Carter, been awhile. Thanks for dropping her off."

Carter turns toward me. "Be careful. You have my number if you need it."

Carter drives away, and I am left alone with Brian. My heart quickens. Three seconds.

"Good news, alien," he says as I climb inside. He leaves the parking lot, and we travel on the highway. "The president's loaning us one of his private planes to get to him quickly and discreetly. Good thing he's got billions and plenty to spare. Airport security's a mess."

Even though I hear his words, the conversation with Carter rings in my ears as if he still speaks. Why would Carter tell me to choose for myself? Choice leads to pain and suffering.

But the Eldest One attempted to persuade me to choose once, and my mother often said unacceptable things about choice. I push those thoughts away. The Eldest One commanded me to feel. He did not say much about choice, and I have been taught that freedom to choose is incorrect. Why would a young teenager like Carter know better than the Elder Ones?

"Tell me all about your planet," says Brian. "I can't imagine being so strong and intelligent." He whistles. "All that capability."

Despite the questions in my head, I am quick to obey his demand. He is allowed to know about my identity, and obedience is instinctual.

"What information would you like to receive?" I ask.

"How are you all so powerful and exact in everything?" he asks. His face distorts. His grin is similar to Drew's. "And tell me about your body. Can nothing break or destroy you on this planet?"

I explain to him how a device was implanted years ago to stifle our emotions, and I tell him that I am invulnerable.

"Interesting... So nothing could kill you, then?"

"To die, a large bomb would need to drop on me, or water could kill me. My lungs are more human than they were. But drowning is still not likely with the current strength of my body. Additionally, I might still survive if someone was around to order the nanobots to restart my heart."

I am not sure why he wants to know these things, but the questions must be important to our mission, or he would not ask.

Brian parks in front of a large hangar. His vehicle engine idles. He glances at me, and his index finger hovers over the lock button for a second longer than is normal for humans. Why? He bites his lip and unlocks the door. I climb out and enter the large, well-lit hangar. The plane sits in the center of the concrete floor.

I have never ridden in a plane before, only a spaceship. Is it safe? My chip indicates that there are few accidents in planes. The pilot comes down the stairs and shakes our hands.

"You must be a pretty special girl to get to fly in one of the president's private jets," he says.

"I am not special," I say. "I am the way I am supposed to be."

"Huh, profound." He chuckles. "Let me show you the jet."

Inside, there are several leather seats, a cabin club, and maple wood veneer. The pilot shows us his seat and introduces us to the crew. They give us some snack options.

Brian whistles. "Own crew and plane. Sure beats coach," he says, sitting in one of the chairs and ordering wine. "Flight's about two hours. Entertain yourself, girlie."

He hands me an iPad. His demand is to entertain myself, but he does not say how. I consider Carter's suggestion to read scriptures from various religions. I do not know if I should choose like he recommended, but my chip tells me little beyond the basics of religion. Did the scientists who uploaded the information about Earth consider religion to be unimportant?

I am not sure, but, if it can help me learn emotions, I should do it. This meeting with the president is to introduce myself, but I must be ready. I must understand more about humans, or I will fail to achieve the Eldest One's request.

Two hours should be long enough to read several religious texts. I open up the beginning of the Koran, reading from my tablet:

In the name of God, the Gracious, the Merciful. Praise be to God, Lord of the Worlds. The Most Gracious, the Most Merciful. Master of the Day of Judgment. It is You we worship, and upon You we call for help. Guide us to the straight path. The path of those You have blessed, not of those against whom there is anger, nor of those who are misguided.

Chapter 13

CARTER

Isn't it weird how movies never deal with real consequences? A superhero flies in to save a city, knocking smoking skyscrapers into crowds of people. In the next film, everything's magically put back together again, and nobody got hurt. A hopeful high school graduate lies on her whole college application, but she only gets a light lecture instead of getting expelled. A couple sleeps together without forethought, but nobody gets heartbroken, herpes, or pregnant.

The thing is—movies are fake. But this is real.

I pace across Mr. Chu's yard and can't stop staring at the red Lamborghini parked in the driveway.

I got Kokab dropped off with Brian, went to work, and clocked out at Kroger's. I spent the whole time bagging groceries trying not to pummel any apples to death. But I came back. Still, I didn't expect Mr. Chu home before 10 p.m.

Anna and Kokab ruined a freakin' grand piano. Somebody will face charges.

What was Anna thinking? Does she want to ruin her future? And why should I care? It's not like being here will change anything. I walk up to the giant mansion and press the fancy cherubic doorbell. The bell rings, sweet and inviting. Not how I feel.

Mr. Chu answers the door with pursed lips. "Carter," he says. "Haven't seen you for a while. Sorry, Anna can't spend time with you. She...disappointed me," he says, rubbing his eyes.

"I know." I exhale again, remembering the sawdust-covered room. "I thought I'd come help clean it." I hold up my rag and cleaning supplies and point to my holey shirt. I stopped on the way home, thinking I might be able to help Anna make things better before he got back, and my help may persuade her to stop blackmailing me. Aika Chu usually gets home pretty late but not today. Apparently.

"Know what?" Mr. Chu's voice tightens. "Did you help do this? I thought she was acting alone—"

"No." I cut him off as his face grows red. I don't want to get in trouble for this. It wasn't me, but I did have some responsibility for Kokab. I should have known she needed very specific instructions. I should have known Anna would do something crazy. I could have done more to stop her. I could have told her the truth about Kokab. "I just thought I could help."

Mr. Chu drops his balled fists, his voice still tense. "Right. Of course that's why you're here, Carter. I'm sure she cried to you for help as soon as I scolded her. You always were such a good influence to my troubled...*child*."

That makes me feel awful. But I'm not to blame, right?

"Sure, yeah," I say. "Where do you want me to start?"

"Oh, no. Don't do that," he says.

"Mr. Chu, I need to help."

He nods, causing the dark lines under his eyes to be even more obvious. "She's just like her mom. Going psycho over this divorce. But it's not my fault, and I can't let Anna off easily. I've already done that. You may think this is strict, but it's my last resort. I don't know how else to help."

I swallow, and Mr. Chu lets me inside. Anna's in the living room, still bawling. Mr. Chu looks over at me, probably uncomfortable.

Sorry, Chu. I'm no good at this kinda thing, either.

He leans down and runs a finger over an intricately designed piano leg. "So many memories." He whispers it, pain in his eyes. Then, he straightens back up. "Right. Well, you need to clean this whole mess, Anna. Carter will help. But don't think that means I've changed my mind about pressing charges."

Anna whimpers, snot and mascara drenched across her face. Mr. Chu leaves, and I study her, still unsure what to do. I have to protect Kokab. But how? I can't let Kokab go to court. But I can't tell Anna she's an alien. Or maybe I should? Would it be much different than thinking she's an angel?

I start cleaning, trying to figure it out.

"She's not an angel, is she?" she asks, swirling sawdust around as I sweep up the mess alone.

"No, she's not."

Anna pulls out the video, watching whatever it is that Kokab is doing on screen. It incriminates her, and it proves something is weird about Kokab. "I don't want to go to court," Anna says, flicking a few wood pieces around instead of picking them up.

That's rough, and I wish I could do more for her. But, like I said, actions have consequences. She should have thought about this before deciding to destroy her dad's stuff.

I shift across the room, collecting splintered wood pieces and fabric. I need to convince Anna to delete the video.

"What is she?" Anna asks, staring at me with her dark brown eyes.

"I want to tell you, but I can't."

Anna nods, her body slumping to the ground. I pull her up, letting go of her fingers as quickly as possible. Together, we work. We pile wood into boxes, dust off the coffee table and high ceilings, carry items to my truck to haul to the dump. Anna smiles as I joke about the time we went camping with some friends, and she dominated in the paintball war and came out grinning until I nailed her.

She was fierce and free even then, and I used to like it. But she's gone too far now. There's a piece of me that misses that feeling of her perfume-filled, encompassing embrace.

When we finish, the room's back to its fancy self, except there is no couch or grand piano.

"Anna, the video of Kokab..." I say. "You need to delete it. Kokab wasn't responsible for what happened here. You were."

"You aren't going to tell me? Really, Carter?" Anna says.

"No."

She shrugs, handing me a large trash bag. "I guess if she isn't an angel...that's all I need to know. It wasn't a sign from God."

Anna yanks her cell from her back pocket. "I'm deleting it. She didn't know what she was doing," she says, finger sliding across the screen. "It wouldn't be right."

I pat her hand, amazed that she is being practical for once in her life. "Thank you."

Praise the Lord that's over. I hope Anna's done with her Kokab craze.

Anna glances over at me, chuckling. "So, grand theft auto. Bigger than vandalism. You're not pressing charges, right, Carter?"

I smirk. "Of course I am."

Anna's face drops.

"Just kidding," I say.

She smacks my arm, her bracelets jangling, and it almost feels like the way things used to be. Before she totally lost it.

She knows a lot more than she should about Kokab. She knows about some of her crazy physical abilities, and she knows that she obeys everything. But, at least, I understand better now too.

I don't know what Anna's knowledge will mean about the future, but I'm just going to keep trying. Whatever happens.

I collect my things, and Anna hugs me. "Thanks for putting up with me, Carter," she says, leaning in, and, just this once, I'm okay with it.

There's one thing I still need to do, though. I don't really like to tell people what to believe. It's caused a lot of torture in my past. But I can help out a friend.

"Kokab may not be an angel. But she did save you. So I guess that makes her your angel," I say and walk out the door.

KOKAB

Joe shoves his glasses toward the bridge of his nose as I finish my rehearsed speech. He sighs and then bites into a BLT from the Pentagon's Subway. There are 25,650 employees in the Pentagon, according to my chip. Sets of fingers click across the keyboards in their offices. Several whisper about government plans. Four or five individuals snore.

Brian lounges in the only chair in his office while we stand. He arranges framed photos of his dog. The left side of his mouth twists upward as Joe asks me to recite my lines one more time.

I do. I memorized the whole script Joe gave me in ten seconds, even with the distractions of several thousand employees working, and now I have been repeating over and over.

What is his purpose in the continued practice?

"You sound like a GPS." Brian moves the photo of his dog next to his computer screen. I do not know what such a muscular human would need a chihuahua for.

Joe bites his lip, giving me a smile that is smaller than his smiles normally are. "You're doing great. But, maybe, try a bit more emotion."

I try again, forcing my voice to inflect and fluctuate the way humans do. He did not tell me what emotion to use, and I do not know what emotion he wants me to select. If he did give me an emotion to use, would I know how to convey it?

When I first arrived on this planet, Joe set expectations that I would need to give my "heart" to the president to succeed. He defined this as learning to embrace human emotion.

I am not as far along as I expected. I understand some things about human emotion, and I feel more than I have in my life. Is it sufficient to complete what I was commanded to achieve? Will I be able to persuade world leaders when the time comes?

Joe asks me to try once more, so I do. Brian chuckles. "Oh, that's better. Now she sounds like a dying goose GPS."

Joe bites into his sub, offering me the other half. "Kokab, you're making progress," he says. "Just remember. You want to be likable. You want the president to feel for your people. He's a nice guy, but you're asking for a lot. We'll start by building relations, and then tell him your agenda after the first few meetings."

I nod, ready to obey. "I will accomplish what you ask," I say.

I have never failed to achieve a command before. I will achieve this goal of getting the president to find me likable by mastering Joe's recommended lines. I do not understand much about what it means to like someone, but I expect that Joe does.

After a few more tries, Brian and Joe agree that it will do. We head to the White House. The whole ride, I repeat the lines as Brian and Joe directed, raising and lowering my voice when asked to do so. I force my lips up, attempting a smile.

Does it work?

Brian glances toward me. "I know we suggested a smile. But maybe, don't do that face. You look like you're in some awful pain. Serious might be better."

Soon, the famous white building looms in front of us. The circular shape and color remind me of the Office of the Elder Ones. Will meeting with the president be similar to my experience meeting with the Elder Ones? What will the president want? Will I be able to give it to him?

The process of meeting with the president is complicated, according to Brian. Every minute of a president's schedule is booked, but knowing his special assistants can help since they run the schedule. It gives Brian an in, he says— half of them owe him favors. Besides, the president is a big pal of his, in Brian's words. According to him, once he shared the genetic tests he'd developed as proof with the president, it wasn't hard at all to get a meeting.

A group of security officers trails us as we walk through the West

Wing. They leave us alone when we get to the door of the office, an order from the president himself.

The president leaps from the ornate desk two and a half seconds after we enter. He leans toward me with a finger pressed against his lips and a slight grin across his worn face. "So, you're the visitor from another planet?"

"That is correct," I say.

"Well." He reaches out to shake my hand. I did not expect him to touch me, and my grip is too stiff for a human. "I was expecting someone a bit more ET, but welcome to Earth. Been looking forward to this all day. Imagine. Being the first US president to meet an alien."

"I will imagine if that is your desire," I say, and the president chuckles.

He gestures toward the leather chairs surrounding his engraved desk. I sit across from him and glance at the protestors outside the three large windows in the office. A large crowd shouts, ringing in my ears, demanding that the president be taken out of office. Joe told me that these types of protests happen with every election, but that would never happen on Foxia.

This is one of the reasons we are given for why we do not make choices on our planet. Choosing for oneself creates disunity. Everyone listens to those in charge on Foxia. They do not fight against them.

The president turns to Joe and clears his throat. "It seems I owe you an apology, old friend. Of course, I wasn't in office at the time. But when you gave that speech claiming to have met an alien, well, even those of us in the senate thought you'd lost it. Seems like you were right all along. Those DNA tests were incredible. Guess I should offer your job back, but, ya know, someone else has it..."

"It's fine." Joe's neck muscles protrude. His breathing accelerates, though I am not sure what caused it. Is it relevant to losing his job?

Also, I assumed the previous alien was under the supervision of the US government. How could a leader of America not know? Our

Elder Ones know everything. Perhaps the new president was not informed correctly by the previous president on the situation.

I run my lines over in my mind and evaluate the emotional shifts I must portray in my voice. I must get each word right. I focus on the president without smiling since Brian suggested against it and begin. "My name is Kokab. I am a young adult from Planet Foxia. We want to build positive relations with Earth. America is a beautiful country, and you are a splendid president..."

The president's eyebrows furrow as I continue. He jots notes down with a ballpoint pen. Almost halfway through my speech, he cuts me off.

"Flattery is great and all. But there's got to be a reason you'd travel all this way to Earth other than to introduce yourself? Are you a scientist doing research? Are you interested in intergalactic trade? What? Tell me."

My mouth pinches shut as his command runs through my head. I have not been given two opposing commands before, at least not any that were so direct. Joe said to wait. The president ordered me to explain myself.

Who do I follow? Carter said I could choose, but I cannot. I will not. I should not, correct?

I sit still for two seconds short of three minutes. The president lingers in silence. Then, out of the left edge of my eye, Brian nods.

They approve. I do not have to choose for myself based on what I think is best.

"Planet Foxia is expiring," I say. "Three billion Foxians will be without a residence. We desire to immigrate to Earth. Somewhere being unused like Antarctica."

The president grips his chair. He swears almost silently under his breath. "No, no, no, no." He repeats and slouches forward.

"Please." Joe rests his arm over the phone as the president reaches toward it. "Let us explain. It's not as bad as it seems."

"Now," the president frowns and focuses on Joe's position, "I like you, Joe. But, this is the end of my second term in office. I don't want

BECOMING HUMAN | 153

to be known as the president who let aliens invade the planet. So, please, if you'd be so kind. Remove. Your. Fingers. Or I will have you arrested for threatening the president."

Joe yanks his arm away, and the president lifts up the phone.

"As your old friend, trust me this time." Joe's focus bears down on the president.

"Can you send—" says the president.

"Please," Joe says. "Set up a meeting with United Nations. Give us a week. And then, let the leaders of the world consider it. Three billion—even of another species—don't deserve to just die. We're their last hope."

The president inhales. His heart rate slows by two beats per minute but still pounds. He shakes his head and drafts circles with his ballpoint pen. His phone remains against his shoulder. After thirty-four seconds, he nods.

"Never mind," says the president into the phone. He looks at each of us. "Two weeks. And if you don't show up for the meeting, consider it treason."

The president looks at me. "You need a substantially better proposal. Or your people are dead."

I blink, uncertain how things got so far from our plans.

AGS

I SUCK IN. The waves of the ocean literally move and crash in the Cassio painting on the opposite end of the room. It sits next to other paintings by some of the most famous artists in the universe, and the beauty of them give me a tiny bit of reassurance. It's an exact copy of the one on my ship. I flew all night, so I could come to the council meeting in person. Dozens of politicians lounge in lighted purple desks, and I stand alone up front. Mom is completing training a few galaxies away, but there was still a part of me that hoped, somehow, that she could make this meeting. She should be here.

I grasp the purple podium until my fingers turn pink. This room is much bigger in real life, and the council members look more bored. It reminds me of the last time I was in this situation.

My arguments meant little to them then. I was new. It was my first day. Now, I'm still new, but I've met the Foxians. I've transformed into one of them, so I'm not as ignorant as I was. This time I won't drown. I'll stand with my ship.

Hos smirks as I continue to stand there, mouth agape. The governor gives me a thumbs up and a weak smile. Does he believe in me, or is this all about getting in with Mom?

I cough, dazed, but then I lean into the microphone. "I've spoken to the ruler of Foxia, and he has admitted that three billion of their species are coming to Earth because their planet is dying—but not to wage war. To immigrate."

The politicians cheer. This is good news for them. They want to prevent attacks among planets, but immigration between worlds is not their concern.

I raise my hands, quieting them.

I hate the tactic I'm about to use, but they need to take me seriously this time. Fear motivates. I know because terror motivates me every day. "Now, I want you to consider what that means. Earth is a small planet with only seven billion people. Even if they don't take over now, the Foxians are much more powerful, stronger, and have superior technology. Once on Earth, they'll change their minds. They'll enslave humanity. It won't end well."

A politician with an extra long nose mutters to an older one with a painted rose across her cheekbone. *Hearsay. Pure hearsay.* Many shake their heads, saying that Foxians need to live somehow. Isn't it only fair if they seek refuge?

I tighten my grip on the helm. This time they'll listen. I hope. "Earth may not have many resources. But compared to Foxia? They'll have two hundred times the amount. And triple the bodies with human aid. Imagine what they could do. Who they could conquer—"

The voices pause. I'm sure they are considering the ramifications of fighting Foxians now.

But my plan isn't to fight Foxians. I just wanted to grab their attention. Now I have it.

"That's why we need to step in. Offer to help get them to an empty planet, one they can terraform, make their own. We can offer them some resources, but nothing like what they'll find on Earth. They'll be content that they don't have to adjust to humans and share a space. They'll owe us for helping, and they'll wind up with a lot less to cause problems."

This time I don't let the storm overwhelm me. I ignore their roars, pushing past the crashing waves of a distraught sea. The politicians don't scare me. Foxians taking over Earth scares me.

"We have no reason to help them. They're our enemies!"

"It's not in the budget."

"They're an advanced civilization. We only help those who really need it."

"Please, I had a vision..." I say, but their voices drown me out.

It's all a repeat of before, but Hos was right about Foxians invading. So it's worse.

"Listen!" I let out a massive scream, but they keep chattering. "If we help them, we build bonds. They won't be our enemies. They'll be our friends. And can you imagine how it would benefit us to rejoin positive ties with them? Two of the strongest planets in the universe?"

Whispers continue. Hos rises up, and I prepare to battle with him. If his voice is the one they follow, I've prepared for mutiny, and I'll toss him from the ship. He's not going to squelch my voice again.

"I agree with Ags," Hos says.

What? He agrees?

He agrees.

My nose drops. Politicians stop mid-yell. Their purple robes whoosh against the glittering floor as they halt.

"You-you do?" says the governor. He drops the gavel in his fingers, and it clatters against the podium. He scurries to pick it up.

"Yes," says Hos. The room is raptured by Hos. His purple cloak dances across the floor as he comes down to the front and sidles up next to me. "Humans are savages. Brutal monsters. What do you think would happen if they get a hold of such powerful beings like the Foxians. What damage could be welded to their galaxy, to the universe? And what about the group of Foxians with emotions? We have always been a threat since we sided with the king in Abaddon's War. Because of us, millions of them died. What do you think they could do to us if they had the same feelings as the rest of us? If humans rub off on them..."

"But they don't feel," mutters a portly man with a purple Afro. "They don't really feel anything."

Hos's rough words work. Politicians lean in. Concern shifts across their faces.

"And that is what makes them so dangerous. Some don't feel, but others do. And they are angry at us for what we did to them. They'll murder us."

Hos is a powerful figure, and, with his help, my plan stands a greater chance. I look over at him, and, for the first time ever, I give him a smile. Yes, it bothers me that he says humans would be the cause of Foxian issues, but he's still helping me.

"Needless to say," says the rose-decorated politician as she rises from her seat, "it is not in the budget. We prevent and aid massive wars. We collect knowledge. We can't afford to help an entire species immigrate if they already have a solution themselves. Then, other planets will want the same thing. We should step in once the threat becomes real."

"It already is. Waiting until the war starts will be too late!" says Hos.

Politicians dash across the room and collect opinions from one another. Their purple robes fly like flags as they go.

The governor's thick chin jiggles when the vote collector hands him an electronic disk with their decision. "They agree. It's not in the budget to terraform a planet. We are very tight this year and need the money to help fund some galaxy-threatening wars. They want you to focus on helping humans adjust to the immigration of the Foxians. I'm sorry, Ags."

My nose trembles. I force it to stay still because I'm not done trying. I can't *look* weak. "Please reconsider," I say. "Reconsider. You don't understand. This won't end well."

He gives me a pathetically fake sad smile, which I'm sure was more to build relations up with my family than because he cares about me or mankind.

"It's over," he tells me. "They've made a decision. Foxians immigrating to Earth won't be so bad, will it? A lot of the council indicated that it may be helpful to mankind's advancement to have such intellectual aid on Earth. Besides, Earth is such a minor concern anyway. Though I know it's major to you."

He winks at me as if that makes everything he stated much better. "Now, we have to move on to the next item of business..."

He gestures to the individual behind me who waits with some proposition or other to make. I grip the podium so tightly my forearms turn a brilliant purple. I twist my head back and forth, looking for some source of redemption for humans.

I'm not a quitter. I know how this will end, and I'm changing the ending. *Hos.*

His—what some call—dazzling eyes make contact with mine, and his eyebrows raise. Hos can help. Hos sided with me even when my own mother didn't.

I inhale and loosen my grip from the podium.

"Okay," I say, and exit the flooded room. They don't even notice me leaving.

I WAIT outside the doors of Fis City's government building; Dozens of grinning, colorfully gowned employees waltz through the doors of the stupendous pure diamond structure as their workday ends. Their chatty voices, arguing and enthusiastic, and the whole scene serves as such a contrast to the Foxian government building.

Hos comes out thirty-six minutes late, consistent in working overtime, unlike other Yadians. I slip in front of him, and he blinks at me and then grins. "I thought I might see you here." He smiles. "Your extreme passion reminds me of my own."

"Hos," I say. "This can't happen."

"I know." He tightens his grip on his purple robe. "Humans and Foxians should never mix. The council is so ignorant of many things. They should know by now when war is looming, but they never seem to figure it out until the last moment."

I nod my nose in eager agreement. "What can we do?"

"Well, Foxians are like North Koreans, aren't they?" he says. "Nobody cares what they do until there's evidence of warfare. You haven't given them that evidence. Only speculation. Use the girl. The *Foxian* girl."

He leans toward me as a few janitors leave the government building, locking things up. "Listen. The council knows a lot about Foxians, but they have no clue about how Foxians will interact with humans. Humanity is not a common species to know much about. Show the council how dangerous she is. Show them how easily humans manipulate her or how dangerous she becomes under their temperamental influence. Play more heavily to their fears. Send me what you find, and I'll show it. Then they will listen."

His robe sweeps across the bronze embossed spiral path as he moves away from me, apparently indicating that our conversation is over.

"You have what it takes. You know what's best as guardian of Earth," he calls over his shoulder as he leaves me.

I don't really like Hos talking about humans being manipulative or causing a negative influence, and I have no clue how he'd know the name of a country on a planet deemed as obscure as Earth.

And he's wrong. Humans aren't manipulative or wicked. They're the greatest species in the whole blinking universe. But I do know one thing. Whatever it takes, I'll do it. And if I have to slander humans and an alien I've never met to save mankind, it's worth it.

So why does a dark feeling lurch at my stomach as if I were a space pilot navigating through meteors blindly?

Chapter 14

KOKAB

My mother stands in a wheat field in a blue-streaked dress. When I was a Youngling, she often dyed her clothes as a way to separate herself from Almosts and Perfects.

She died, so I do not know how she is able to stand in front of me. I glance down, observing that I am in a dress identical to hers. Somehow, my body is as it used to be. Clear. Two hearts pump through me.

Am I dreaming? I have only dreamed once. Am I dead? This would mean that the scriptural accounts I have been reading are accurate, not fictional proverbs, as my chip indicates.

That cannot be. It must be a dream.

"Come, child," my mother says. She waves to me, and I follow. She wraps one arm around my shoulders and grasps my hand.

Her touch causes me to remember the days when she left my room, pressing her fingers to my arm without proper cause. Even then, the flickers came. Now, in this altered frame, with recent changes, they encompass me.

The feeling is bright, but it is not a brightness I can see.

We travel through the tall wheat, but our feet do not touch the ground. We glide.

"It is time, my child," she says.

The scenery changes. Our feet rest against the grass, and our clothes shift through many shades of the rainbow. I continue to follow her until we arrive at a path. A worn wooden gate blocks the way, but my mother opens the door. A thunderstorm crackles over the long dusty road.

My body begins to change, to alter. To become more human.

"Do you want to walk the path?" Mother asks, gesturing to a garden down the road. "It is very treacherous, but the treachery makes you appreciate the beauty on the road to the destination."

"Mother, I do not know if I desire that. I have never made a decision for myself."

"Why not?"

"It is incorrect."

"No, my child. Choice is the only way to really learn." She leans down, kissing my forehead. She never did that while she was alive.

"Remember the stories I told you as a child? Our world had choice once, but Abaddon took it away after the Great War."

"Yes, because it is incorrect."

"Princess Elsimmona does not believe that. She wants us to choose. Now, it is time to live again. She's coming to help you. Walk the path with her. Watch for her to come."

She waves and races down the dirt road, but the muddied ground doesn't leave any marks on her gown. She disappears, and I stand, staring at the open gate.

I open my eyes. I'm back at Joe's house, and I sit up in the creaky bed. What was that? Humans dream, but I have never heard of a Foxian dreaming of anything fictional before. Was it a dream?

Fully awake, the emotion from yesterday returns.

I do not want them, but I need to embrace the mood. Pain hits my stomach. What is it? Sadness? Anger? Guilt?

Six seconds.

A southern house spider weaves a web in a high corner of the room. Her eight eyes shift over the interconnected string, and her legs skitter across the wall, causing the fluttering of the web to whoosh in my ears as she leaps.

The pain goes away.

Carter let me borrow a copy of the King James Bible. I have read the New International and English Standard versions.

I finish the last verse:

The grace of our Lord Jesus Christ be with you all, amen.

Grace is a concept that allows for imperfections. We do not believe in imperfection on Foxia.

The scriptures are confusing, filled with many stories that are not possible on this planet, yet many people claim they are true. Words in one scripture account say an opposite thing as another, and each religion's interpretation of God varies. Does God have a body, or is He a spirit or energy that we become a part of? Does He slaughter millions of his children, or did He die for millions of them?

It should not matter if the words are not true, but what do these beliefs teach me about humans? How can I save 3.1 billion Foxians?

Carter discusses the difficulties of precalculus with his mom downstairs. She tells him that Mr. Chu called and was grateful he wanted to help clean up the mess Anna made.

Anna did not make the mess. I did. Why did Carter choose to help when no one asked? And, what did my mother mean when she said I cannot learn without choice? I have acquired plenty of information in my life.

Bacon crackles on the stovetop. I slip from the bed and tread against the floor. I dress into another of Margi's shirts.

I must admit the truth. I failed. I was given an order, but I did not achieve my goal. I did not please the president, and the statistical chances of completing the Eldest One's command have decreased.

I have never failed before.

Carter looks at me when I walk in. "Hey, good to have you home." He sticks several slices of bacon into his mouth.

I consider his conversation earlier with his mom and my own conversation with my mother. When do I choose? How do I make a choice?

"Carter, why did you choose to help Anna clean up her mess? No one commanded you to," I ask.

Carter chews on his upper lip, and I believe he is thinking. "It was a nice thing to do, I guess."

I nod. "But how did you know that?"

Mama opens her mouth but then hesitates. Why is she letting Carter speak if she has an idea on the matter?

"It's hard to explain." he shrugs. "You learn all this stuff from books. From people. Like I said before. That's how you get ideas on what to do, but their words can be conflicting. So you gotta decide. It's like there are two voices in your head. One is light, and the other is dark. And you should listen to the light one. Sorry, I dunno if that makes sense."

It does not. There is only one voice in my head, and I do not think my voice is on the light spectrum.

I do not understand humans at all.

AGS

THOSE STUPID FOXIANS terrorize me in my sleep. Last night, a bundled baby screamed as it was carried away by a stony-faced Foxian. A mountainside tumbled to pieces around the two of them.

I've had other dreams too. Good ones. For instance, I've dreamed at least a hundred times throughout my life of going to high school. And now I get to.

I pry my wooly blanket off and glance at the hotel alarm. It was supposed to beep, but I only have an hour before school starts. What did I do wrong?

"Ags, the American student," I say and inhale. I let Old Ags take over, the one who was never depressed or stressed, and I tell her again how enthused I am. It doesn't help anyone to have a negative attitude when trying to achieve success.

I loop my Hello Kitty backpack over my shoulder. I picked my favorite pair of red rubber boots and matched it with a Venezuelan liqui liqui. I wanted to include my Sushi coat, but I thought it'd be too much.

It's not an American wardrobe, I know. But it's what I like to wear, and I need it for confidence to get what I'm looking for. I tuck a few other outfits in the backpack too, just in case I want to make an outfit change throughout the day.

I glance at the credit card on the wardrobe. Good thing Mom has almost a few million dollars of American money saved up for emergencies. And good thing humans love rocks so much. It's one of the benefits of being from a planet where diamond is as common as graphite.

I settle into the seat and press the large touchscreen of the Tesla. I'm glad there are a few self-driving cars on Earth. I breathe in the new car scent: lemon and leather.

This is happening. Full immersion into the human experience. I won't just be watching. I'll be living it. And yes, going to high school will be the best way to stalk the Foxian, but it will also be amazing! Eeeh!

Of course, I won't forget what I'm here for. Hos gave me two options that might be convincing to the council. 1) Prove Kokab (Ugh, what a name. When mom told me, I gagged...) is so obedient, as is the natural Foxian way, she will do anything she is ordered, and I can show humans taking advantage of that. This will show how risky it is to have such powerful robots among humans. 2) Capture her doing awful things. If she is volatile, maybe they'll see how destructive the Foxians can be due to human influence.

They're opposite in a way, but I haven't seen any indicators of volatility, or any emotions at all really, so I have to capture her inclination to obey, as much as it hurts to portray humans like that. If I can get her to admit any likeliness of attack, that'd also probably help. Of course, if I find anything shocking, I'll record it for Hos.

I'm not really going to be a typical high school student, am I? I'm a secret stalker. That's what I was before, and that's what I will be. But I'm going to make the most of it.

It's funny, but after watching so many students on screen around the world—boarding schools in England, religious schools in Spain, military schools in Taiwan—I'm still terrified. Not only by the fact that I have the responsibility to convince a board of politicians to help a little planet out but because it's beautiful high school. Beautiful. But crazy.

I drive up to Sequoyah High, a square brick building with several trailers to the side. The wing car doors swoosh open as I pull into the parking lot. I'm sure a lot of kids will be impressed by my automobile. I meander over the worn-down pavement and enter the building.

Everything about the school is normal. There's nothing that makes it stand out from other high schools in the USA besides the mascot of a wildcat covering the wall of the main hall (it was an Indian Chief but since changed to be culturally sensitive, as it should), and that's what makes it so perfect.

The bell rings, and students flood the halls, diverse in style and culture. They rush past me without glancing my way. I slide two fingers across the wild beast's head in the mural.

I told Els that I was coming to high school to watch the Foxian girl so I could better help the Foxians immigrate, and she believed my lie and helped modify the school's computer systems, so I'm an official student. I'm in every class with the Foxian, including calculus. *Gah, torture.*

"Nice outfit," a tall boy mutters as he walks past me. He's being snarky, but I ignore it. I've seen enough high school shows to not be bothered by it. *Just an insecure boy, aren't you?*

I smile at him. "Thanks," I say, and he looks baffled as I lift my shoulders and chin. I stride into the gym for my first class. I head to the changing room two minutes before class begins, and I'm still only the second person to arrive. The girl's not here. One minute before, a large group of people pour in, screaming and hollering as they go.

The moment the bell rings, she steps inside.

Right. I should have known she'd be exact.

There's still so much Foxian about her, even though she looks more human. Her pasty skin contrasts the dark gym clothes, not as translucent as it should be but almost like printing paper. I've never seen a human quite so pasty. She glances toward me with empty, empty eyes. Not somber. Blank.

But she's beautiful. Her bronzeish hair drops down her back and reaches her muscular calves. Everything is toned in an unnatural superhuman type way.

I glance down at my overly orange skin and slide my fingers through my boring hair. I usually don't think about my looks, but I'm completely average. For a Yadian.

For a human, I'm a bit freakish.

The girl catches me staring at her, so she stares back. She doesn't blink. I look away, and she does too.

Everyone chatters as they change into a t-shirt and sweatpants, but I sit down and take some notes on the girl to send to the council. I'm one of the last ones out of the locker room, and Mrs. Bellows frowns when she sees me.

She blows the whistle. "Start jogging!" she orders.

The Foxian jogs next to a boy with red curly hair. What a hottie, as the American kids say. Yes, that hair is spectacular. His hair is like the male version of Anne of Green Gables. But he's talking to *her*. He looks familiar.

"You may not want to go too fast, Kokab," he whispers. "It could draw attention. Stay with me."

That's right. The boy's a member of her current residence. Mom showed me some 3D image renderings of the little she could figure out while tracking her, and that's where I know his face from. Such a shame. He's one of those people that are way more attractive in real life.

"Great job, Kokab!" says the coach as she sprints, exactly aligned with the boy, past.

She doesn't sweat. She lifts her rigid arms and legs at the same time. Kokab may look more human than other Foxians. But she is still just like them.

I shiver. What a mindless robot.

After class, I jot some notes down on an invisible screen and place them in a folder for Governor Ids.

As I get to the hall, I follow Kokab to see what she'll do. A boy with wet curls taps me on the shoulder.

"Hey, Cheeto-face," he says. "Maybe you should ask the tanning salon for your money back." He laughs and strolls to Kokab. I try to shake off his cruel words. As the humans say, words can never hurt me.

"Did the essays for us, right? Each different from the other?" he asks.

"Yes, Drew." Kokab nods. *Really?* Yes, Foxians obey, but this is a start to evidence I wanted. All it would require would be a simple command, and someone has gained their own army. I flip on an invisible video camera on my shirt and lean against the brick wall in the hall. Humans wouldn't notice it, but, even in her new human pretending body, I'm afraid she would.

I write a bit more, making sure to include these notes.

Kokab is going down.

Chapter 15

KOKAB

"I don't really have this lunch hour." Anna leans over. She pats my shoulder with her artificial nails. "But I had to tell you I was sorry. I was kind of a jerk, taking advantage of you like that. I mean, I had an awesome reason. But still."

I nod. Carter said he was angry earlier because I helped tear apart Anna's piano as requested. I am still trying to understand why, but it seems it was not her property after all.

She stares at her macaroni and takes a swallow of milk. "Do you ever wish there was a magical eraser that could just scrub away stupid life moments?"

"No," I say, but I remember the president. Magical erasers do not exist, so there is no reason to hypothesize.

I don't eat because no one has invited me to. I should be fine for another few days since Mama said I had to try some of her fried okra last night.

I listen for mentions of emotion in conversation. A boy talks about his dad and how angry he is at him for taking away his cell privileges. A girl explains to her friends that she's certain she's in love with a senior soccer player. Two teens say they hate a specific teacher who gives too much homework.

Drew sits on the opposite side of the lunchroom, but he whispers to his acquaintances regarding me. He says I am the hottest girl he's ever seen. The others agree.

From listening to many students, I now know it is likelier that he means I am physically attractive to him than that I am high in temperature.

He rises, swinging his arms back and forth as he strolls. He plops beside me. "Hey, Koke. You get my homework done like I asked?"

I nod and pass him the science worksheet. He nudges Anna. "Smart, right? Gave this to her five minutes ago. She's smart. And hotter than you'll ever be."

Anna snatches the paper from Drew's hand and rips it into small pieces. "Don't tell Kokab what to do." She rolls her eyes at Drew. "It's rude."

People always tell me what to do. Why not him? In my dream, my mother told me to choose for myself, but it cannot be appropriate to do so, correct?

"Why not? She likes doing my homework. Right, Kokab?"

"It does not cause pain or much extra time."

"See? She likes it. You should be more chill like her. Don't know why you'd want Carter over me." His eyes linger on her chest.

Anna leaps up, yanking up her low-cut tank top. She drenches Drew's striped v-neck in milk. Was she trying to make him colder since Drew suggested she should be more chill? But, he did not ask to be chill himself, so I think she was reacting to something he said. "I'm never giving you what you want. So get over yourself," she says.

Drew grabs napkins and rubs his shirt. It is not the most efficient method to clean himself. "What's wrong with you? You're crazy, girl. Though I imagine it'd be fun to—"

Anna roars like a beast, and Drew shuts his mouth. "Leave me alone," she says. "And don't mess with Kokab. If you try anything just because she obeys everything—"

Anna pauses, her eyes growing. She covers her mouth.

"What?" Drew asks.

"Nothing."

"She obeys everything?"

"No. She—I—I—I didn't say that."

Drew smiles. "Huh."

"Don't do anything stupid." Anna looks at me, and then at Drew. "I'm getting Carter." She sprints from the lunchroom.

Drew leans in. He pushes his face to my ear. He yanks a strand of my hair to his nose and inhales. "So, you're pretty obedient, huh?"

Carter warned me not to tell people. "I cannot say."

"Kiss me," he orders.

My arms tremble as he continues to touch me, something I have never experienced before, and my stomach squirms. Pain spreads through me, even though he cannot hurt me. I have never kissed anyone.

I lean in. It lasts less than a second.

"No, not like that," he says. "Long and hard."

His lips shift across mine. He bites my tongue, pushing against me more rapidly as we continue. What is this pain inside my head? "Wow," he murmurs after he stops. He strokes my cheek. "You're good at this. I wish more girls were so laid back like you. Can you kiss me again?"

I bring my lips back to his. As I start kissing him, my mother appears in the field of wheat, pointing at the path.

She says I must choose if I want to learn. Carter says the same thing.

Can I choose?

I do not know what is right, but this does not feel correct. I have never made a real choice before, but I stop.

He opens his eyes. "What's wrong?"

"No." I twist away. What am I doing? I have never done this before. "No...this is not...this is not correct," I say.

"What do you mean? I'm a lit kisser." He yanks my neck toward him. An emotion comes over me, fast and strong.

I grasp his hand and tear it off me. A roaring crack rings in the air. Drew screams, and I look down.

His fist. His forefinger twists two inches backward. Red marks stretch across his wrist.

It is likely his hand broke in multiple places. I am very strong, but I did not mean to break his hand.

He leaps up, screaming. "What is with all you crazy women?"

Carter dashes into the cafeteria, followed by Anna. "Leave her alone!" he says. "Leave her alone!"

A teacher notices after three seconds. "What is going on?" she asks.

"That psycho broke my hand." Drew points at me.

"I'll get her to the principal's office, Mrs. Sloane," Carter says. "He was trying to take advantage of her, though."

Mrs. Sloane's eyes narrow. "I'll take you to the nurse," she says to Drew, "and then, I'm taking you to the principal's as well, young man."

As we walk away, a girl with orange hair and skin studies me and takes notes on a digitalized screen with a crooked smile. The girl attends most of my classes. Is she human? Humans have unusual genetics, but I have never seen one with natural skin or hair so orange. Why is she here?

Carter walks through the hall with me. "Are you okay?" he asks.

"I am in good condition," I say. "He ordered me to kiss him."

"And did you?" Carter grips the strap of his backpack.

"Yes, but I did not continue the task. I refused to follow his requirement," I say. I consider the moment, and facts connect. I know. I can label my emotion. "Do you want to know what I was feeling?"

"Sure, what?"

I remember Carter's words perfectly. *This terrible energy bottling up inside of you, and you want to act. To hurt someone. But you don't have to.*

It is not the best emotion, according to him, but recognizing it is a qualification for helping my people. "Anger," I say.

Carter chuckles. "So, you didn't like kissing Drew. That might be a first for him."

I pause. I did not like it? He's right. I consider all the youth I've seen, the stories I've read where people are unhappy. I did *not* like it. What, then, do I like? And, was it that I didn't like kissing? Or that I didn't like kissing Drew?

I am not certain. There is still much to learn.

I think about how I feel when Carter touches me versus Drew. It is nice even though I generally have little touch sensation. Would I like kissing Carter?

I draw close to him. My heart speeds up by five beats per minute. I chose not to act, but I have never chosen *to* act. For some reason I do not understand, I want to. I want to choose.

I step toward Carter. His eyebrow raises. Confusion?

His body odor permeates, likely not noticeable to others, but pungent to me. But his other scents encompass me—bark from hiking in the woods, brown sugar from helping his mom cook, wax of crayons from playing with the twins. He grins at me with his flawed face. Those lines around his lips are from laughing too much. I have watched him get mud on his pants from working out in the yard. The scruff on his face is not from sleeping in but because he wakes up early and helps Mama get documents ready for work. He lacks time to shave.

There is a 90 percent chance Carter is a good man based on the things I have read and seen, at least, according to Earth standards.

I examine the blue of his eyes. The color of his iris shifts almost imperceptibly, my reflection visible in them. My own eyes stretch wide. I purse my dark lips, and a tiny drop of sweat slides down my hair.

I look almost human.

I tilt in, and I kiss him. Once more, the electricity ripples through me, and I do like it. At least, I am 76 percent confident I do. He kisses me back but then pulls off, blinking. "Whaa?" he says.

"I apologize. Did you not like it?" I ask. "I was collecting data to see if I find kissing unpleasant or Drew unpleasant."

"You don't kiss someone to collect data," says Carter. His cheeks brazen to almost the color of his hair.

"You don't? Why do you kiss someone?" I have seen and heard many people kissing in school, but they often don't explain themselves. Their kisses seem to be without much reason. Or they have a reason only they understand?

"Well, some people kiss 'cause they want to or they like each other or are in love, I guess."

"And do you not love me, Carter?"

Many religious texts discuss love. It is a commandment in almost every faith.

I pull words from the Buddhist Metta Sutta stored on my chip, reconsidering its meaning:

And with love for all the world. Reaching above, below, and all around, without any barriers, Freed from hatred and hostility, Cultivate a heart that knows no boundaries.

I have yet to comprehend love, but if most people believe in and are taught to love everyone in the world, and if Carter is a good man, why would he not love me?

"Not like that...no," he says. "But I do think you're really great."

I consider his words. Is there more than one kind of love?

"I see," I say, even though I may not. "I apologize for the choice then."

It seems I miscalculated. I may need more information before making a decision again. Perhaps I should not choose.

"No, don't apologize. I just—I don't want to take advantage of you." He chews on his lower lip, and the noise grinds in my ear. He runs his fingers over his wrinkled shirt. "But I do think you're special. In a good way. Ugh, I'm being awkward, aren't I?"

Is he? I am still working to identify behavior.

"Actually," he swallows, "if you felt like it, wanna go on a date with me? Antonio can bring someone too. No pressure or anything. Just for the experience. Want to?"

I am not certain. According to Wikipedia, there are multiple purposes for a date: socialization, companionship, courtship, among others. What are his motives? It may help me learn more about humans, but I do not know that it would.

"It is not what I am here for," I say.

He drives his fingers into the bottom of his pockets. His face goes maroon. "Right. Of course. You're busy. I'm sure you have insane things to worry about."

He halts in front of the principal's office. My destination.

"No, I will date you." I say it before I realize it has been said. I made another choice for myself. Was this a better one than kissing Carter?

I will find out.

AGS

I SPEED down the hall after Kokab. What happened? Drew left the cafeteria, screaming louder than angry protestors at a presidential rally, whatever it was. I picked the wrong time to go to the bathroom.

I open the office door and slide into the wing chair next to Kokab. "I'm in trouble for painting a mural of a vampire on the science teacher's wall," I say, making it up on the spot, running my rubber boots in circles on the carpet. I wave to the secretary, slightly excited to be roleplaying the infamous troubled teen high school scene. "Why are you here?" I ask Kokab. I turn on the invisible video feed to capture her words.

"I broke Drew's hand." She states her actions so matter-of-factly, no regret in her tone. That's terrifying and abusive behavior. The bell rings, meaning lunch is over, but I should stay here as long as possible to question Kokab. Perhaps I can get her to admit her people might attack if she fails. A confession from a Foxian of the possibility might be good evidence for the council.

"You are not human," she says.

I look up. "What?" *How does she know? I blend in so well.* "Of course I am."

"No, you are not human," she says. "I was not certain until you got this close. Your heart beats three times faster than a person's would. There was too much noise for me to hear it before. Why are *you* here?"

Oh drat. Gadzooks. Blood and thunder. I grasp the rounded collar of my liqui liqui as my fingers stiffen. I don't care if she knows why I'm here. She doesn't feel anyway. I want her to know she's unwanted.

A scene of a small baby crying hovers into my mind. His perfect face balls up in terror as a Foxian grasps him.

I throw up the invisibility shield in the office, so no one can hear. I shift past settings to make us completely invisible and block anything from getting in or out of the shield and select a mode to make it seem like we are having another conversation.

"I'm here because of you." I grind my teeth. "Your people don't belong on Earth. You'll harm humans. Have you thought of that?"

Kokab's mouth lifts. She says nothing. Of course she says nothing.

"Have you thought of that?" I ask again, glowering at her stark face. The office worker continues typing on her computer, and the burly principal exits his office and asks for some copies of an agenda.

This. All this. Could be gone.

"So stay out," I say. "I'm trying to convince Yadians to help you all terraform another planet. That's so nice of me, *huh?*" The huh comes out as a yelp.

"I understand," says Kokab more quietly. "I have heard of Yadians once in school. They are enemies to us, correct? Yadians will never offer aid, and, if they do, we will never accept it. We do not re-establish bonds with our enemies. I apologize for your efforts."

She says it all like she's reciting facts. But what does she know? She doesn't feel. Doesn't have hope or faith.

I do.

"No, you're wrong. You're...you're...wrong." My nose quivers. "This can work. It'll solve everything."

"I apologize, but the likelihood is very low," she whispers.

I cling to the vinyl seat. How dare she. Her words make me want to get a confession from her even more desperately. "You don't really think you'll convince humans to accept three billion immigrants?"

"Yes," she says, her voice clear, monotonous.

No.

"Admit that Foxians will conquer Earth if you fail," I shriek.

I cross my arms over my lace ruffles, and we stare at each other for what feels like ten minutes. I blink. Her blank black eyes never do.

"I do not know what they plan," she says. "It is a possibility."

I pirouette. The chair squeals as I leap away. The door clatters shut as I exit.

She finally said it.

CARTER

I RUMMAGE through the clothes pile on the floor and come up empty-handed. Nothing smells good enough. Everything's wrinkly.

Great, the biggest date of my life. If Kokab can hear Anna from a mile away, can she smell my B.O. from a mile away too? Hope not. I hope she just has super hearing and nothing else. Although, that's bad too. What if I need to fart? Even if she can't smell it, it'd still be embarrassing for her to hear.

After Drew's douchebag moves, I want Kokab to know that not all guys are losers.

I find a decent button up and throw it on. I run my fingers

through the hurricane on my head. I do a quick check in the mirror. It'll do. There's a rap at my door.

"Carter's got a crush." Jason's singsong voice melds through the door. "Carter's going on a da-ate."

"Dang straight, I am." I let him in. Margi must've dropped him off to get ice cream with Mama. It's a first week of school tradition of Mama's to take the grandkids out for ice cream, and Mama must've told him about my date. She gets really excited about things like this. For once, I'm glad Dad's not home. Would he be angry at me for dating an alien in danger? "And I'm not afraid to admit it. I'm lucky, my friend."

Jason rolls his eyes and starts rummaging through my old car collection. I stop him from yanking my 1958 Fury from the shelf, handing him one of the cheaper ones. "Eww, girls are disgusting. Ice cream's better," Jason says.

"Depends on the girl," I say. "How do I look?"

Jason rolls his eyes again and fiddles with one of the car wheels, so I know I lost him. "Get a supersized cone, and eat all of it," I suggest, leaving the room.

I got this. I stride down the hall with a few marigolds from our garden and knock. "I thought we could go off-roading," I say through the door. "It's bumpy but amazing."

There's no answer, so I knock again. Nothing. Is Kokab downstairs?

I glance in the kitchen and living room.

"Mama, do you know where Kokab is?" I ask. Mama's huddled over paperwork like always. She's probably trying to rush through it, so she can head out with the grandkids. "Hmm?" She glances up. "Oh hun, you look great. I think she's in her room."

"No, she's not," I say.

Mama looks puzzled, and she stands up, calling Kokab's name. Kokab would hear, but I don't tell Mama. Instead, I run outside, trying once more.

Where did she go? Did she decide to bail on our date? Or is something wrong?

I follow Mama back to Kokab's room. It's empty like I thought. Mama hunches down and slips her finger across the floorboard.

"What is it?" I say.

Mama opens her palm. Glowing purple slime drenches her fingertips. She smells it, nose wrinkling.

That look in her eyes is murder.

"I've smelled this before," she says. "I think Kokab's been taken."

Chapter 16

KOKAB

I wipe the purple formula off my arm and sniff the gel-like substance. Why do only a few of these chemical compounds exist on Earth?

The AC blows quietly against my leather seat. Brian's loud breaths come from up front. I have not forgotten much about my life, but I cannot recall how I got to be here in Brian's vehicle. Who brought me here? Him or someone else? Did I agree to come?

"Where is our end destination?" My hand slides toward the sleek handle. Rain pours outside my window, not common in the fall for Georgia. Eastern red cedars do not grow in Georgia either.

I forgot more than I realized.

Joe warned me that others may try to hurt me. Has Brian abducted me? If I have been abducted by Brian, this may be a situation where the correct procedure is to act for myself.

However, is it correct? I still struggle to know. Pain writhes through me. My stomach churns. Am I anxious? Confused? Perhaps both?

I can jog faster than the 82 mile-per-hour speed of the car. If I leaped from the moving vehicle now, my injuries would be minimal, and I would recover. I could get away if I chose to do so. Why is it so much more difficult to choose than to let others choose for me?

Brian glances at me. His shoulders tremble. "We're meeting Joe. We have another meeting with the president."

"Meeting. Joe," I state. If we are meeting Joe, then I must be safe.

Joe always protected me. This response makes logical sense. We need to prepare to meet with world leaders, and Joe informs me of his plans on short notice. It does look like we are headed toward DC based on the foliage outside. It does not explain how I lost memory.

"Absolutely," he says. "Don't worry. Everything's peachy, alien."

He smiles, but his heart pace accelerates. We drive for 255 miles after I wake up. Cars speed past us on the highway, and I can hear the voices of laughing families as they go by.

Thousands of tiny droplets fall from the dark sky and intermittently slam into the ground, shattering against the pavement. My ears burn from my first experience with rain. Thunder crashes like in my dream.

We roll into the parking lot of a dimly lit bar shoved against other dirt-encrusted stores. Brian steps out of the vehicle, motioning for me to follow. He holds an umbrella over us, but it does nothing for the ringing of my ears. The bar's neon sign flashes SIP FUZE, and its scent of fried fish and old sushi overwhelm me as we step inside. I blink.

Why would Joe want meet me at this location? The splintering rain fogs my mind.

"Brian, where is Joe located?" I ask.

"He's here somewhere," he says. "I'll find him. Just wait here."

He leaves me at the front. A woman demands my ID. "My ID indicates I am underage," I say. Joe falsified a driver's license in case I needed to drive somewhere in an emergency.

"Then, I'm sorry, hun. No partying for you tonight."

I slip outdoors, still close to the location where Brian said to wait. Where is Joe? I must ask him what is wrong. I do not know why we are here or why we would travel this way to get to the president.

The rain saturates my hair strands. Streams of liquid tumble through my eyelashes and dribble down my cheek like a human crying. The sound is deafening, but I hardly feel the rain.

The bar door flies open. The raw smell of alcohol passes me as a shivering lady stumbles by. She clings to her overcoat, muttering about the horrible chill, and her teeth chatter as she slips into a cab. The cold immediately affected her? Why is it so difficult for me to feel anything? Why can *I* not feel?

My shirt's soaked through, showing off the red bra I borrowed from Margi. Where is Joe?

The voices inside the bar blur together, but then Brian's whisper is loud amidst the sound of raindrops. "Where is he? He said I'd be paid today for getting her from the house to you."

"Patience," says the other voice.

His money? Why would he receive money for transporting me here?

Another voice responds. It is not Joe. It is not the president, either.

Humans do not always stick to their own rules. If Joe is not here, then it means Brian gave me false information.

Brian lied.

Lying is considered an evil in almost every religion and culture, but there are many stories of lying in history and the scriptures. Joe said people may attempt to hurt me, and he said to be careful. Brian might want to sell me or make a profit from me. I need to protect myself in order to accomplish my mission.

For the second time in one day, I disobey. I do not stay as Brian requested.

My foot slides from the pavement and clatters louder than the thrumming of the rain against the road. And then, I sprint.

I race into the parking lot and duck through the back alleys. Ants shift across the ground, scurrying to avoid my strong feet. I am like them, trying to escape.

I tear through dark alleys, slowing my pace as a truck passes me, and then an engine revs far behind.

It's Brian's car. How did he find me? I sprint faster and continue turning down alleyways, but the headlights follow, picking up pace as I do. My feet smack against the road like the rain splattering around me.

I cannot keep up this pace. Not in this body.

I turn into a dead-end alley. There's nowhere to go but toward the car.

I flip around and sprint at the vehicle, slamming with all my force. The front of the car bends, and glass lights shatter around us.

Blood drenches my hands. Brian rolls down his window and cocks a gun at me. I claw at the walls, but there is nowhere to go. Seven bullets fly toward me and smash into my stomach.

I fall into a pile of leaves, head spinning. The gunshot wound begins to evaporate as I heal myself.

"What is your objective with me?" I slur. I lay my head in the dirt, fighting the quick loss of blood.

A sharp pain rips through me as I try to maintain consciousness. Fear? Sadness? Blackness comes.

CARTER

Andromeda was my first dog, a fat beagle with huge ears. She was also my best and only friend when everyone thought I was the stupid kid with a UFO-crazed father. So when she went missing, I lost it. For three days, I walked all evening, searching through the woods and knocking on everybody's door in our sparse neighborhood, all five homes in the three-mile radius. They got used to me and told me, "No, I haven't seen her, just like the other seven times you asked." Then, they'd pat me on the back and wish me luck.

Finally, Mrs. Potter got the nerve to tell me the truth: she'd run over Andromeda with her minivan.

It was a cruel day. Mama said a prayer, and I marked the grave with a handcrafted dog sculpture made from a torn apart Pizza Hut box. Pizza had been Andromeda's favorite food to sneak under the dinner table.

But it's nothing like searching for Kokab. My stomach twists in bowline knots, and sweat drenches my wrists. I'm pretty sure I'm having a nervous breakdown.

My nine-year-old self never thought it would end badly until it did. My seventeen-year-old self? Not so confident.

Kokab's an alien. With superpowers. She's probably getting tortured. Kidnapped by Russians or terrorists. No. Don't think that. Maybe it's just Anna again. Anna, for once, I hope you're causing trouble.

I wind down the window and suck in air to try to calm down. Mama speeds, passing cars, scanning the streets.

"Call again," she says, her fingers clenching the steering wheel. We've tried the woods, the streets, with many people that Kokab has associated with. And nothing.

Dad's phone's off, and Brian won't answer his, but I try again for the twelfth time. "Dad, it's an emergency. Call back. Now. Whatever you're doing, this is more important. We can't find Kokab."

I scroll through Kokab's phone, which she left behind, also terrifying since she's so exact. I don't wanna infringe on her privacy, but I need a clue. Something. Anything.

The phone's empty. She hasn't sent any text messages. She hasn't downloaded any apps. There are only a few phone calls between her and my dad. There's no evidence that she owned it or possessed it. Almost like she really was a ghost after all.

Mom pulls into the parking lot at the police department, a small building on Marietta Street. I grab Kokab's falsified paperwork from the glove compartment and scrub the sweat off my hands.

This is risky. It will generate the attention we've been trying to avoid, but it's better than all the horrible things that could happen to her.

Of course, Mama doesn't know Kokab is an alien, so I'm just hoping I'm right to come here. My stomach clenches as a wave of nausea hits me.

"Try calling Dad again," Mama says, grimacing.

"Okay," I say.

In the building, a case officer with a tight bun assists us.

"We'd like to report a missing person," Mama says.

"Do you have any photos?" she asks, and Mama slides over images of Kokab we uploaded from Dad's video cameras.

That's the thing. Dad's always been big on security. There are cameras all around our house and through our acres of property. One second, Kokab steps into her bedroom, and then she's gone. The video goes blank for a few minutes, and then her room appears empty. It's not normal and makes this all as scary as a horror film. I hope that it's a weird glitch in the system and not evidence of some crazy mastermind behind this.

If the police get involved, the policewoman explains, they start by searching the home address, local hospitals, and areas close to where the individual was last seen. They'll check phones and social media accounts.

We've already done all this. There is so much information they need to know that they can't have. Kokab looks like a foreign exchange student interested in having an adventure or disinterested in her host family. She isn't super young. She doesn't have mental or physical health challenges. This makes it look less scary, especially since it's only been hours.

"She might be hanging out with some kids from school and have left behind her phone," suggests the cop. "Maybe we'll want to wait a little longer before going further with things. Unless you have evidence that there is a serious risk against her? That it isn't a normal night away from home?"

Mama shakes her head, and I wish I could tell the officer that she isn't a normal teenage girl. She's an alien with who-knows-what abilities, and I don't want her to get hurt.

AGS

I sit at the comfy human desk by the hotel bed, utilizing a lightbulb to record data. I could use a light rod, which would be more energy-efficient lighting, but using human tech is wildly fun.

I sent them the video with Kokab's confession halfway through the day. The rest of school was not as fun as I wanted, but I collected so much data about Kokab harming humans. After letting him bully me some, I convinced Drew to give me a detailed account of how Kokab "viciously attacked me after Anna threatened me." I talked to other students, too, and learned some weird rumors about her harming kids in a game of dodgeball as well.

Humans' behavior wavers from most, displaying lower morals and a greater tendency to take advantage of others for personal profit than many other planets. It is this tendency combined with Foxians' consistent obedience that demonstrates a great threat to the galaxy as a whole.

I cringe as I write the awful words, disgusted by my own condemnation of the people I love. And to top it off, I include videos Mom created throughout the decades of mankind's worst moments. Racism. War. Rape. Horrible records no one should see.

Most of the council won't know much about humans, and this makes people seem awful. It skips all the beautiful moments—the compassion, camaraderie, and friendship. The beautiful art. The captive music. The love.

But it will push the point. It will make it seem more dangerous to leave the Foxians here. And they *are* dangerous.

I rub my nose, exhausted from all the planning. Maybe I should take a break and get some ice cream. I've eaten it a few times but never in an ice cream parlor.

I leave the hotel room and make my way to my car. There, leaning against it, is one of the last people I'd expect to see: Hos.

"What are you doing here?" I say, glancing at his everyday jeans

188 | AMY MICHELLE CARPENTER

and designer-brand shirt. It's the wackiest thing to see *honorable* Hos in American street clothes. What's going on?

Before I have time to ask more questions, he gestures for me to open my car door, and he climbs inside. I do it because, though this is completely weird, I need his help. We drive for a few minutes. He overrides auto-drive and jerks the steering wheel, so we hurl off the freeway into a forest. We twist around maples. Mud splays across the new vehicle. He straightens the car as we collide into about a dozen maples.

The trees jiggle and evaporate as we hit them.

We're in a massive clearing. A hundred or so Yadian ships dot the landscape. Shadowing the rest, a glistening TurboShip rises over the entire forest. A red glow dances around its smooth surface.

A TurboShip is a ship of war.

"It took a lot of invisibility shields and work to get this area cleared and usable," He says.

"What?" I manage to utter. "But these are warships."

Why are they here? What can this mean?

"Your video and my persuasion methods helped convince the council to send them," Hos says. "The council is much more willing to have some employees sit it out than pay the trillions it'd cost to help the Foxians immigrate elsewhere. We'll be here prepared when they arrive, in case the Foxians decide they want war."

My gut sinks. That's not my goal. Did I make them too afraid? Why did *I* try that tactic?

"I don't want that."

"You should be happy," Hos declares. "It's a simple precaution. A lot of people think they'll immigrate peaceably. We think just letting them know we're here will be enough to keep them from warfare, if the situation demands us to send such a message."

"No," I say. I stare up at the giant warship. "I don't want the Foxians to come to Earth at all. The council was supposed to be convinced to help them terraform a different planet."

"And I'm sure you will convince them...after you get something more substantial."

"I sent some more information over," I say.

"I saw it. It's not enough."

I slump forward, and it's like my breath has been knocked from me. More substantial? This whole thing could lead to Foxians attacking *everyone*, not just humans.

"This is better than nothing, don't you think?" Hos says.

And I nod. At least now there's better protection. But it's not enough.

Hos urges me aboard the ship, insisting I must meet all the new temporary guardians who've been assigned to stay here until the Foxians come and all looks safe.

We climb the one-hundred-foot staircase into a gold-covered lobby (another more common rock of Yadia).

What now? Now, it's more urgent than ever I find some way to possibly persuade them. Yes, the humans need help, and this is better than nothing. But I don't want the humans to get in the middle of an intergalactic war at all, or the visions will come true.

I have to get Kokab to do something really bad...something that would prove terraforming is the only way for everyone to stay safe...or maybe there's some kind of financial loophole.

"Why do you look so glum?" says a familiar voice, tapping my shoulder. I whirl around, and Yas stands before me. His scruff's gone, and he's wearing an American button-up and cowboy boots. Still gangly and awkward, but more attractive than I've ever seen him.

My jaw drops. "You like?" He points to the studded boots. "I saw them at a store on my way in and thought of you."

"Yas," I squeal, grabbing his skinny arms. I almost speak to him in English, but then remember to speak Yadian. "I can't believe you're here. Oh. I'm sorry. They must've reassigned you from your favorite planet to this one. And it's all my fault."

My arms drop.

"It's okay." He shrugs his nose. "They gave me a really cool chemistry lab. Want to see?"

We make our way through the halls. Groups of Yadians sit at benches, munching on food from diverse planets—flaming rocks, spindly fruits, whistling bugs. It's hard to think about what they might be going through away from the planets they love and vowed to protect. None of them look at me. They don't blame this whole situation on me, do they?

Yas opens a door into a NASA-sized laboratory. The screen of the space engineering lab flashes as a formula spirals from the projection in 3D.

He slides on some gloves and mixes a flask of glowing chemicals. I slip onto a stool beside him. He creates a thick slime, which solidifies into a solid ball. It liquifies as Yas prods it with his finger.

"Wow," I say. "It looks like the little balls we saw at that one stand during graduation. Did you make it?"

"Yes," Yas shrugs. "They're ChemPods. This one's a histone deacetylase inhibitor. It makes you forget things. Hos asked me to make it for him."

Yas points to some of the other chemicals carefully sorted across the table.

Why did Hos want that?

"Well, I wish I could forget about the stupid Foxians," I say. "This teenage girl is like a robot, see?" I switch on a large hologram of her helping Drew cheat. "How she does everything she's told without any feeling."

"I don't know. I guess. She doesn't look too robotic to me, though," says Yas. "Something about her eyes."

Her eyes? They're dead. Absolute opposite of Steve McCurry's *Afghan Girl* photo.

"I'm glad that you're here." I set my head on Yas's shoulder, wishing we could go back to the moment on the hill when Earth was safe. But I can't go back. I can never go back. "My idea was to terraform another planet. It'll be the best. No one has to die. And it'll get the Foxians far away from anyone they can hurt. But I don't think the council really wants to be persuaded."

Yas chuckles. "Well, if anyone can persuade someone, it's you."

I change the topic. I ask him how he enjoys life on this giant ship. If he misses his old planet.

"Sure, that's why I became a guardian," he says. "But it's worth it to be here with you."

Yas wraps his arm around my shoulder and leans into me with his thin frame. He opens his mouth like he has more to say. But instead, he continues prodding the ball.

Yas is right. I'm not giving up yet.

Chapter 17

KOKAB

The room is white. White walls. White floor. Gray door. It's locked.

It reminds me of the first day I stepped into the Office of the Elder Ones. I did not know why I was there or my fate. Today is the same. My fate is undetermined. The room should be more comfortable for me since there are fewer sounds, smells, and textures. But the emotion I feel is not comfort. It is a rush like a computer being switched on and sparking problematically. Ten seconds. Twenty seconds. Thirty seconds.

The mood lasts without being pushed under or cut off. I cannot identify it—though I can eliminate many possibilities, it still is there. Dark and twisted.

Sorrow? It is different from anger but similar too. I believe it is fear.

I grasp my heart, not used to such rapid speed. Brian steps inside. The door locks behind him. He holds a glowing green globe. Where did he get it from? It is not human or Foxian either.

If they taught us more than what was necessary for our commanded tasks, I might know what the substance was.

How could I wish for something the Elder Ones did not choose to give? I take the thought back immediately because even though I am accessing my emotions in order to aid humans, it doesn't mean I should question my leaders' choices.

"Yadian tech can make you much more human than Foxian tech. You must swallow this." Brian orders.

"I will not," I state. Brian misled me before with his commands.

I have learned that humans are not controlled and perfect like Foxians. Their orders are not always correct. I do not know what his intentions are, but, based on kidnapping stories I've read about and watched on TV, he is disinterested in my well-being.

"Can't feel anything at all, can you, alien?" he says. "Well, this will make it so that you can feel. It alters the nanobots inside of you, reprograms the emotion blockers in your brain chip. Unfortunately, it also means you'll be more sensitive to death as well."

Brian yanks his arm back and grunts as he slaps me with enough force that he stumbles. It does not hurt. I stare at him.

I begin making plans for escape, calculating the weight of the door, the possibilities of unlocking it, when a hooded figure steps inside. The individual wears a brown and white cloak with intricate triangles weaved across it, almost like scales. Frays appear in the fabric, but the cloth is far superior to Earth's.

He or she hides their face.

"Here." The voice is male. "I believe I can persuade her."

He whispers some information into my ear. His hood creeps up one inch, enough for me to see his orange skin and a long nose.

I shudder, understanding now that I must obey. I am required to do this. I slide the ball into my mouth, and it disintegrates. Millions of nanobots pour through my veins into my bloodstream and mind. My lungs shrink inside of me. My skin loosens and softens.

I'll be more vulnerable to termination like he says. I can't see it, but if Brian is correct, I should have a thickening dermis associated with touch sensation beneath the layers of skin. I lift my hand to my face.

It stings.

"Your payment will be on your credit card in the morning," the figure says to Brian before disappearing through the doors.

"Don't worry. Your last memory will be when you were in your room, readying for the date." He shoves a plum ball into my mouth. "You won't remember any of this."

I spit the ball out, but his words encompass my mind. I try to cling to the memories, but I already begin forgetting. How did I get here? What am I doing here?

I fall to the floor .1 millisecond after I am inundated by a flood of emotions.

CARTER

I SPENT the whole evening pacing around and calling everyone I know at least five times.

She isn't Andromeda. She's stronger. More powerful than anyone I know. This could be different. Lots of stories end well.

Being positive isn't working well. Lots of stories exist of people getting raped or battered or stolen away.

I try Brian again, and he picks up. Finally. What took him forever?

His voice sounds pleasant. "Hi, I'm in the middle of a family thing. Is something wrong?"

I try not to get angry. It's not like it's Brian's fault Kokab is missing. "We thought you had GPS trackers on Kokab, but when my mom contacted my dad, he found nothing." I breathe out, slowly counting to ten in my head. "Can you tell us where she is? She's missing. We don't know what happened. She might be in trouble. Please, tell us you know where she is."

Brian chuckles, but it sounds off somehow. "Calm down," he says. "How long has it been?"

"Five hours," I say.

"That's nothing. I'm sure she's close by. Let me check."

Except it isn't. If he knew Kokab better, he'd know that. She's always responsible and always checks in. She'd never leave on her own.

His footsteps shift away from the phone, and I wait for an answer. Maybe things were glitchy when my dad tried to find her. Maybe it wasn't some genius person who hacked the system. I hope Brian has answers.

He returns, pleasant like before. "She's right outside your house. In the woods. Must've gone out with some friends for the evening or something. Not everyone is a homebody like you, Carter."

It doesn't make sense. Dad has a satellite surveying the woods. We scanned the woods, and no one was there. Anyway, Kokab wouldn't do that.

But still, I'm stoked. Kokab is all right.

Could it be true? Is she really home? My grin reaches to the stars and back.

"Are you sure?" I ask.

"Definitely," says Brian, and he hangs up the phone.

I rush downstairs.

"What? What is it?" Mama asks, her lips pursed open like a recent wound. She holds a cell phone to her mouth, making calls too.

"Brian says she's in the woods."

Her eyebrows furrow, but she hangs up mid-call, and we rush outside. We don't have to go far.

Kokab sits on the porch step. But something just doesn't feel right.

But she's home. She could have been dead. Maybe she did go out on her own for a while. I'm sure it's all overwhelming. She looks at me, and her head tilts.

"Where were you?" I ask. "Is everything okay?"

"I am not certain, " she says. "But I am in good physical condition."

She doesn't look hurt, just like she says. She's beautiful and put together like always—but something's different about her. It's not easy to figure out. She's wearing the same turquoise tunic as earlier. I can't explain it, but her irises are husky, and her posture seems...less straight, maybe? Her face pinches as if in pain. I've never seen her face show much expression.

I wait for her to respond to both questions like she always does, but it takes a moment. "I—I cannot remember where I was. I apologize, Mama. And Carter."

"Really?" I say. "You're safe. That's all that matters." I reach out my hand to offer to help her up, and she takes it. Her lips pop open, and she pulls away. "Is something wrong?" I ask.

"No." She shakes her head. "But you are very warm, Carter. You have never felt this warm before." She stands up and stretches her arms, also something I haven't seen her do.

"Are you sure you're okay, honey?" Mama wraps her arms around Kokab, and Kokab leans in. Normally, she's stiff.

"I do not know," says Kokab. "I feel strange."

"Oh, bless your heart, honey. Bless your heart," says Mama. She pats Kokab hard on the back, and Kokab winces. Kokab's never winced. She got hit by our truck and didn't seem to be in pain.

None of it makes sense. What happened? I hope it wasn't anything bad. But for now, I'm just glad she's home. And she's alive. That, for sure, is fantastic.

Kokab runs her fingers through her hair, almost like she's being shy. "Is our date on the itinerary still, Carter?"

"What? The date? I'm sure you need to relax and figure everything out," I say. "We should probably skip it."

"Carter," she says. "I'd like to go. I feel like I *need* it."

"Okay," I say, but it's weird. "We should do that after school tomorrow, though."

Mama rubs Kokab's fingers with her hands. "Oh, baby. You're cold. You don't have to go to school if you don't wanna," she says.

"I must go," Kokab says. "I must continue to learn."

The whole situation is weird. And suspicious.

But Kokab and I are going on a date. I'll pick more flowers, take a shower so I don't smell like Antonio after swim practice, and even have a wrinkle-free shirt this time. I'm going to make this the best date—okay, it's maybe the only date—Kokab's ever had.

She's here, so she must have just dozed off or something, right?

AGS

I GET to school and realize I forgot my swimsuit for gym class.

I slip into my sparkly leggings with a t-shirt because I don't have anything else and climb into the pool. The chlorine encompasses me, and I coax myself to the bottom. Feet wiggle over me. The giggles of flirting teens fade away.

In Asia, the Moken people hold their breath for twice as long as the rest of humanity. Their kids swim before they walk. I imagine I'm one of them and sit cross-legged on the bottom of the deep end, slowly letting bubbles out. The bubbles writhe through the water as if trying to survive. They climb to the surface.

I want to stay awhile and think. Alone, surrounded by water—the majority of Earth. If only my guardianship on Earth could be this simple. Like it was supposed to be.

It's only a few seconds before I have to come back up again, and I tread the pool in my leggings and gym shirt.

I giggle at a few girls whining about getting into the water. Cute.

"Hi, I'm Ags." I paddle over and greet them.

One with a fabulous drenched afro chuckles at me. Her eyes slip over my body. "What? Are you Mormon?'

I try again. "Actually, they wear swimsuits. I just forgot…"

But she's already gone. Making friends should have been easy for me. I've seen so many people interact, but nothing is like I imagined.

The bell rings, and I survey the pool for Kokab. Right on cue, Kokab enters the swimming area. But now what? I need one last thing to really prove how freakishly obedient Foxians are.

Command her to murder me, maybe? That would show how easy

she is to command, so even if there is no immediate war because of the Foxians, humans could really do a number on the universe if given the time.

Of course, I'd have to stop her before she actually killed me.

"Hey orange juice, why haven't you fixed that tan yet? It's bad. Seriously. Who you trying to impress?" I glance up and realize Drew is watching me stare at Kokab.

He hangs his feet over the pool and pats his new cast, which is covered in girls' signatures. Why does he have to be in three of my classes?

Drew's friends chuckle, and I remind myself it's him who's trying to impress someone. Why would I ever let him bother me? I've seen dozens of high school movies and read hundreds of books.

This is normal. Super normal. Kids want to show their dominance. Somebody has to be at the top of the food chain, and, since I'm new and haven't made friends yet, I'm an easy target. I've watched bullying happen to many people who didn't deserve it, and I've recorded their reactions. So why is it bothering me?

He shouts at Kokab when she climbs into the pool. "Well, I heard you got with Carter right after making out with me," he says. "What a slut."

Kokab grimaces, which is weird. But she doesn't do anything shocking during class. And I'm left with no ideas. The bell rings, and I head toward the locker room. Where are my clothes? I could swear I kept them in here.

"Might wanna check the hall," one girl giggles. I speed out the door.

"Catch." Drew thrusts my dress, followed by my bag, to one of his friends who takes off down the hall.

I ball my fists and start sprinting after them in my drenched leggings. Right now, I wish I had the ability to run like a Foxian. I could tear down the hall and get my backpack in no time. I, however, am a fairly slow runner.

"No running in the hall." A teacher chides me, glaring at the wet spots across the floor. I stop, panting. I've lost the kid and my bag.

I love humans, I remind myself. *Just not as easy to love humans like Drew.*

I remind myself of all the beautiful moments I've seen. The tender exchanges. I also know what causes these problems. Drew may come from a permissive, absent, or abusive home. Or this may just be a popularity struggle.

"Is everything all right?" I turn to a familiar voice. I've been watching him in gym class the past few days with Kokab. He's an adorable dork. Some of the guys tease him a bit. But he's really nice, and he's got gorgeous fire curls, and he's tall. It's too bad he's housing *her.*

"Not really," I say. "Drew and his friends stole my backpack."

The boy, Carter, I believe is his name, shakes his wet-from-swimming hair like he totally understands my problem. "Figures," he says and disappears.

I stay sprawled against the locker and fiddle with the sparkles on my human cellular device. I ignore the complaints from teenagers to move my legs out of their way.

A few minutes later, Carter appears in front of me and offers me a hand up. His fingers tug me off the ground, encompassing and warm.

"Thanks," I say. It's supposed to be lunch now, so I'm going to take some time to send things off and give a report. Who knows when my bag could go missing again?

"I had help," he tells me, and I wonder if the help was Kokab. She'd be able to get the bag fast. He hands it to me, smiling. "I'm Carter. I think I've seen you in gym class, right? You're pretty new, right?"

His drenched curls drop over his eyes. He pulls them away. Red hair on Earth is as uncommon as pink hair on Yadia. Only 2 percent of people have red hair.

It's spectacular, and I hunger to run my fingers through it.

"Drew's a jerk," he says. "Sometimes, at swim practice, I daydream about drowning him."

I laugh again. "This isn't how I expected my first week at school to go," I tell him, though I'm not sure why I decided to confide in him. "Obviously, I know kids are mean to each other, I've watched plenty of movies and such—but experiencing it is different. It's not so fun."

I think of all the things I've experienced vicariously. What would it have been like to be there? To actually step into a great or terrible moment? I thought I knew so much about mankind, but maybe I'm wrong.

Carter's laugh seems to flood from his soul like it's hilarious that anyone would find school to be fun. "Were you homeschooled or something?"

More or less, that's the truth. I nod. "I'm sorry it's not going like you wanted." He thrusts his hands into a gorgeous pair of well-used Wranglers.

"It's my lunch break," I say. "I don't really have anyone to eat with." I know it's his too. I've been watching Kokab from across the lunchroom.

"You want to eat lunch with my friends and me?" he asks.

I shake my head. Eat lunch with Kokab? Never.

"I don't do well with big groups." I lie, so he offers to eat with me.

I should watch Kokab, but just this once, I'd like to know what it feels like to eat lunch with a cute human boy. We go out to the hill by the tennis court with our lunch trays.

"There's something I've been wanting to try," I tell him. I lay on the ground and start rolling down the hill like I've seen in movies. It's not very steep, and I'm done after a few rolls. I leap up, beaming like I finished a wild roller coaster.

Carter blinks a few times, and his face looks weird, but then he starts howling in laughter.

He hops up and throws off his shoes and spirals down the hill. I laugh too, and he gets a big grin on his face. We keep rolling, and people walk past us like we're idiots.

"That was incredible," I say.

"Good. I'm glad you feel better," he says. "Don't worry about the haters."

I stand, admiring the grass stains on my skirt. Lunch is over, and Carter says he's running late to class, and he tries to only be tardy once or twice a day. He leaves, and I decide to take notes on weird things I saw with Kokab, in case.

Carter's so unique, and I love his hair. And he's *human*. It'd be so cool to be with a human boy.

My heart beats like crazy.

Chapter 18

KOKAB

I press one finger to my chest, unable to stop the rapid beating. My stomach churns. My lips tingle. Every nerve is sensitive. Every nerve is aware.

I grasp the bed frame, rough against my fingers. Touch has never been so real. My forehead sweats from the humidity outside. How has Carter been able to function adequately at this temperature?

This morning, Carter squeezed my hand with soft and sweaty fingers. And the electric sensation was stronger than before.

I do not understand how I am better able to experience touch sensations, but it must be because of whatever happened yesterday. I was in my room, and then I was on the porch. I do not ever forget. How did I forget?

It's not only my touch sensations that have changed. Inside, a sweet warmth courses through me at least 6.5 times stronger than any other emotion I have felt. It is the same emotion I had when Carter grabbed my fingers, but I do not have to force it to stay. It never stops. I am 92 percent certain it is comfort. Mama says her fried okra tastes like comfort. I feel like Mama's fried okra tastes.

But my stomach churns too, and I am not used to that. Mama enters the room, and I sit up.

"My stomach is sick," I tell Mama.

"Oh, first date nerves." Mama goes through the clothes in the closet. "It's a wonderful thing, honey. You're excited."

Am I? I believe it is true. I continue to try to remember what happened after I was standing in my bedroom. Carter said I was gone for about five hours. How could that be?

It makes me sick in a different way. Mama pulls out a cotton dress and places it on the bed beside three other options. The old mattress creaks as she sits down.

"Are you sure you don't remember what happened?" she asks. A type of pain stretches across her face. Concern? I am 84.2 percent confident. This is the way the calculus teacher looks when Drew does not answer a question correctly. "Are you okay, honey?"

I nod. "I do not recall, but I am acceptable."

But I do not know I am. Did I lie? Why?

Pain tugs at me. Why must emotions hurt so much? Guilt? I should not lie to the Turners. Lying is wrong. Or are there situations where it is right?

All the effort to access my emotions, and now it is easy. Guilt, excitement, and other emotions I struggle to identify roll against me. My heartbeat pumps inside my chest.

"Which dress do you like best?" says Mama, and I point to the blue one. The white one is more familiar because it is void like my planet. But the blue one appeals to me. I like blue, I believe. And it reminds me of the sky and Carter's eyes. My head still spins as I stroke the cotton fabric, long and flowing like my mother standing in the field. It was a dream, correct? My mother is dead. I wrap my arms around myself. I am going to break. The plethora of emotions are going to tear through my bloodstream, and I will explode.

This is not possible, but it seems logical based on how I feel.

I pull the dress over my head, and Mama styles my long hair into a crown braid.

She weaves in some sunflowers. "So beautiful," she says, stepping back and examining me.

Carter knocks on the door. He comes in with a bouquet in his hand from the yard.

"Ready for our date?" His tone drops, and I think he may be nervous. My gut plummets, so perhaps I am nervous, too?

"Yes," I say.

We exit the house and make our way to his truck. He squeezes my left fingers and opens the truck door for me. His touch is so warm.

CARTER

I TIGHTEN my grip on the steering wheel, scared as a baby deer during hunting season. I glance at Kokab. She looks incredible in the dress Mama gave her, which makes me more afraid because I don't wanna mess things up.

"So, we're going to downtown Atlanta. It's about an hour drive. There's something I think you wanna see," I say as we get on the I-75 freeway.

Usually, I do cheap dates. I'm a grocery bagger with hopes for college, so it's not like I have bills to spare. My best dates are getting fries and off-roading.

This date's $12.50 per person, but it'll be worth it.

"Sooo..." I try to think of something to say. Being alone with Kokab is nerve-racking and awkward.

What should I say?

Is she enjoying this?

Is it fun for her? Or is she bored out of her mind?

I can't tell.

She stares out at the open fields. Her fingers press against the passenger window. I'm next to the prettiest girl I know. A super strong, brilliant woman. And she's on a date with me. I need to say something to impress her.

I spend the next hour driving in silence.

Kokab shifts in the leather seat, and, again, she seems different. In a good way. Her back stays straight but more natural, maybe? She glances at me and tugs her hoodie off.

"Oh, are you—are you hot?" I ask. Gah, this is not a good start. But wow, her arms are so smooth and perfect.

"The blower resistor broke," I say as I gesture toward the AC. "I tried to fix it, but I think I need to get a new one. I'm really sorry."

"It is not an issue," Kokab says, and she slides her hand over the fan. It starts blowing better.

Some people might get freaked out by that because I'm pretty sure she did it somehow with her abilities like with Anna, but I think it's amazing. Kokab is smart, honest, beautiful, strong, and can do things I don't even understand.

Soon, Skyview, a twenty-story Ferris wheel with an epic view of Atlanta, hovers over us. The sun lowers across the city, and the sunflowers in Kokab's hair blend with the sunset. Wow. Just wow.

My planning is perfect. I'm the man.

Okay, so the line's super long, and it's the end of August, so we're both sweating out our eyelids by the time we get to our gondola.

Maybe not so perfect.

"Groupon deal comes with a free box of chocolates," says the employee at the front. I take the box of chocolates and motion for Kokab to step in first. We slip onto the benches, and I praise Jesus the compartment has AC.

"Enjoy the ride," the man says. The door closes, and we lift above the city. The brightness of Atlanta reaches for the stars, and it's pretty romantic. If only my brain hadn't transformed into a heaping bowl of sausage gravy.

Gah, say something ya idiot.

KOKAB

HE SEEMS to be unable to speak.

The skyscrapers are smooth compared to Joe's house, cleanly

designed with few errors. They stretch upward into the sunset, which blends three shades of red and numerous golds.

I see, hear, touch more than a human would. A couple strides through a crosswalk while arguing about financial debt. A street vendor cooks polish dogs. They sizzle as he lifts them off the grill. Cars maneuver through traffic, and a golden retriever sticks his tongue from the window of a Honda. I like the view, I believe.

I like what is inside the gondola more. I like sitting on the bench, the AC whirring in my hair, next to a boy who continuously chooses to serve others before himself.

Is that what makes me attracted to him?

A bubbling sensation fills my gut. It is warm and desirable. I have not felt this way before, so it is harder to identify. But I like it too.

I like to feel physically and emotionally, to be *able* to like things.

I glance at Carter. He tugs at his shirt, which is supposed to be a sign of nervousness? Does he need space to overcome it? Or does he need something else? I turn back to the window.

Carter hands me a chocolate but remains silent. I eat as I listen to his heart move at eighty-two beats per minute. After two minutes exactly, I decide to start the conversation. Humans like to talk about memories and their experiences, correct?

"How are you enjoying your life?" I ask.

Carter blinks a few times and then grins. His heart slows to sixty-two beats per minute. He chuckles. "Uhhh...life is great. Thanks for asking, Kokab. How are you enjoying life?"

He stops tugging at his shirt and carefully looks at me with his blue eyes. They match my dress. Perhaps that is another reason I like him as much as I do. His eyes.

"It is...different," I say.

He nods, still grinning. "I'll bet. Dealing with Anna and Drew. Going to a high-hollering Baptist service. All different from your old life, right?"

"Yes."

Now I have read more about religions, the pastor's services make more sense to me, but I do not understand everything. What the preacher says confused me.

"The preacher indicated that if Eve didn't take the fruit, she could have been happy in the garden forever. But what if she had to take the fruit in order to have the knowledge of good and evil she required? What if taking the fruit was the correct thing to do?" I say.

"What?" Carter asks. "Who? When?"

He does not remember?

"Two Sundays ago. Do you recall?" If the garden grew things for them and was perfect, would they have ever learned anything? Would they really be human?

In Foxia, we do not have to have knowledge of good and evil. We do not choose for ourselves.

I press my fingers against my seat, remembering my mother in the fields in a long, flowing dress like the one I am wearing. This is what my mother meant in the dream. Making choices puts a person on a path. But perhaps choosing is good for humans. Humans need to make choices to grow. But Foxians have been short on supplies for millennia. If we had agency, we might misuse the little we have. And we need to survive.

Then, what happens when we come to Earth and have ample supplies?

"Uhh..." Carter says. His face reddens, and I do not know why I find that attractive. But I am 78 percent certain I do because my hands sweat like Mama's when Joe comes home, and I cannot stop examining the tinge of his cheeks.

CARTER

AFTER KOKAB GETS the ball rolling, it's easier to talk.

"I'm glad I didn't kill you when I first ran into you with my truck," I say and laugh. Kokab's lips tweak sort of upward, so I think she likes my joke. "It's been good having you around."

"I appreciate your compliment, Carter." Kokab may not notice, but she scoots close to me. Her super toned, amazing calves almost touch my leg. I open the box of chocolates and nibble on one and focus on the window, so I don't get too nervous to speak again.

"Is it hard?" I ask. "To leave everyone behind? Your friends and family. And come somewhere new?"

"It is challenging to adjust," Kokab says.

"So, do you miss them all? I know I'd miss my family and friends. And Sputnik."

"I do not have any friends. Or family. My mother recently died."

Wow. I thought it was hard to not have my dad around, but to lose him? Or my mom? I couldn't imagine. Again, Kokab seems different. In a good way. Her eyes throb, if that's possible. She's a strong warrior like I always knew, but she's been through things I couldn't understand, I think. And she's more than that. She's vulnerable, for the first time ever.

"It seems like it'd be hard to know so much Earth stuff if you're from a different planet."

"I never said I was from a different planet." Kokab bites her lip.

I want to ask more, but it's a first date. So I don't pry like Margi might. I try something lighter.

"Are you really as smart as all the kids at school say?" I say.

"Yes," she says, after a second or so. "I know many facts."

"Hmmm," I say. "Prove it. Who was the eighth president of the USA?"

"Martin Van Buren."

"How long does a tortoise live?"

"150 years, depending."

"When did World War One end?"

"November 11, 1918."

"Well, you're either super brilliant, or you're a really good liar.

Would've helped if I asked you questions I actually knew the answer too," I say and laugh.

Kokab looks at me more serious than ever. "Yes, I know a lot of irrelevant facts. But knowing a fact does not make me intelligent."

I wonder what she means. She is pretty mysterious. A sunflower tumbles from her hair, and I reach for it to put it back in. I choke a little as my fingers slide into her hair.

I drop my hand but then hesitate. Now could be the perfect time to try to hold Kokab's hand. But then I get nervous. What if she doesn't want to?

I set my hand back on my lap, but I can't stop staring at her perfectly smooth fingers.

KOKAB

THE RIDE ENDS after twelve minutes and thirty-eight seconds. Carter leaps from the gondola and motions for me to follow.

We approach the Fountain of Rings right outside the carousel. The splash pad shoots water at intervals. Children ran in the fountain previously, but darkness made them leave. Lights sit under the water, turning it golden like the sky before sunset.

Carter slows and glances at me. He gulps and then grabs my hand.

His fingers tighten against mine as he pulls me toward the water. His hand makes my head buzz.

"Do you want to run through it?" he asks. When the children were playing in it, they screamed and giggled.

I nod. I want that. We sprint into the water. I can feel every line, bump, and crevice of his grip.

And it is like nuclear fusion.

I am a ball of energy, exploding, transforming into something new. The water engulfs my skin. It's cold, but I want to feel it. Every little drop cascades against me, drums at my hair, my face, my fingers. The water tinkles as the drops shatter beneath my toes.

Drenched from head to foot, I turn to Carter. But even though the liquid is cold, I feel warm. So warm. He slowly spins me in a circle. His lips turn up in the largest smile I have ever witnessed.

We dash out of the water. I press my fingers to my cheeks. I'm smiling, too. I have never smiled before. I look at Carter. His red curls stick against his forehead. Water drips down his chin, and a small giggle bursts from my lips.

Carter's eyebrows raise, and I think he is surprised by my laugh. Then, he starts laughing too.

Now I know what the bubbly sensation is that I have been feeling. For the first time in my life, I am happy.

AGS

THE WORDS on our personal ship's screen envelope me. *Ags project status: Rejected.*

It's one little word. One painful, little word.

REJECTED.

I curl into a ball, tuck my arms beneath my legs, and die a little. I'm not trying to be dramatic (though this makes me completely understand teenage angst), but this is everything I worked for tossed away, my failure to help mankind declared in massive red letters.

So yes. Dying feels like an appropriate definition.

I knew my data could've been stronger, but I was going to come up with another plan. Now no time exists. The painting of Cassio's ocean still hangs over the dashboard. The calm, rolling sea taunts me. Why can't I do my job and solve Earth's problems? Keep the oceans calm?

"I was supposed to have more time," I say.

Yas fixates his gaze on the starboard, explaining quickly, like hurrying through it might make it less painful somehow. "I guess war broke out in the Black Eye Galaxy, which needed a lot of funding, and they thought the added ships were solution enough for Earth. I'm sorry," he says, squeezing my shoulder.

I rush to our ship's mini library, and Yas follows me. The information screen blinks as I scan the search engine. Hos keeps talking about getting more evidence? But what if I need to address their concerns? If the problem is money, there's got to be a way to find the money.

Digibooks fly over my head with information about finances.

"What are you doing?" Yas says.

"Trying to find an answer," I mutter.

He nods and jumps into the only other seat. "I guess I can help. Not like I have much else to do right now. We may be able to finance your project through another planet. And then, the council will have nothing to complain about but personal labor."

We search for hours. My throat goes hoarse from shouting various demands at the info screen. A headache forms that seeps into my eyelids and dribbles to my nose.

But nothing. Yet.

"I need sugar," I mutter to Yas, and we climb out of our ship. I take him on my moped to the hotel. I'm not sure why he winces as I weave through traffic because I am a SPECTACULAR driver.

A few horns honk at us, but that's pretty common for humans. It has *nothing* to do with my driving skills. When we get to the hotel room, I dive into the mini-fridge to find eggs. Yas slips beside me and runs his fingers over the top and bottom of the fridge.

"Fascinating," he says and points to the gallon of milk. "What is that?"

"Milk. From a cow's udder."

"What!?"

I giggle at the expression of disgust on his face. The first time my mom brought milk back to our ship, it was goat's milk, but I was grossed out too. I was reluctant to try it, but I don't tell him that.

I hand him a measuring cup and set the bag of flour on the counter. "Get to work," I say and crack an egg across the pan.

Eggs. Milk. Water. Flour. The perfect recipe for crepes. I show Yas what to do.

"I don't seem to be very good at this." He swipes flour on his chin. He rubs it with his plaid sleeve (Is he picking out the country clothes because he knows I like them?) but accidentally gets it across the whole side of his face. He rolls his eyes but then smiles as I laugh at him.

I pour the mixture into the frying pan, then flip it on the small hotel stovetop.

Yas's mouth drops open as he bites into the crepe. "Wow. Human food. I could stay on this planet for years if everything tastes this good. How's school? Any better?"

"Much better." I sigh once I've drenched my crepes in chocolate syrup and whipped cream, happy to tell him that things are looking up. "I met a boy. An attractive boy."

Yas stiffens. His tongue pauses mid-lick. "A boy? A human boy?"

"Yes," I say. Did he not hear me right? What other kind of male would I meet on Earth? "And he was really whimsical. And funny."

"Oh," says Yas. He sets his spoon down. "And you're attracted to him in a romantic way?"

Obviously, didn't I just say that, Yas? "We rolled down a hill together," I say.

I want to tell him more about Carter's unmanageable curls and American Southern accent and manners. How he seems like a character from a classic novel I read.

But Yas is as stiff as a Foxian.

"What's wrong?" I ask. "Are you afraid crushing on this boy will affect my mission? It won't. I swear to you. I'm so focused that it's nice to be able to think about something else."

Yas shakes his head rapidly. The rest of him remains stiff.

"What is it, then?" I say. I don't understand why Yas reacts this way. I was excited to tell him all about my experience with Carter. I thought he would be excited for me too. After all, he is my best friend. Apparently, though, I was wrong.

His nose vibrates. "He's not good enough for you. No one is."

"You haven't even met him, Yas."

Yas sits in the chair, elbows propped up on the counter. He sets his head against its cool metallic surface and says nothing.

"I don't get it," I say. "What is this really about?"

Yas leans back. His hair drops into his purple eyes. "Don't you know?" He reaches for the milk, and his fingers linger against mine.

All the compliments. The kind gestures. Finally, it clicks. And I wish it didn't. He wasn't just being a friend. I wish I could take back my question because I don't want to hear him say the words. I glance around the hotel room, looking for some exciting human contraption to distract him with. Quickly. Quickly...

"Ags, I like you."

Too late. Everything is officially ruined. *You idiot.* And by idiot, I mean, me. Not Yas. The helpless victim.

"Oh."

Stupid. Stupid me. By the way he touches me and the way he acts, it should've been obvious. But I thought what we had was platonic. A perfect platonic relationship.

I'm not sure what to do. But I know leading someone on is rude. And painful for the individual.

"I'm sorry, Yas," I say. "But I don't feel that way about you."

I turn away because I don't want to see my best friend hurt.

Chapter 19

KOKAB

I tremble from the water and tighten the towel against me. Coldness bites my skin. I like it less than heat.

With all I have been able to experience through my senses, it is interesting I have never felt so alive until now. I roll down my window, glancing at the small white dots in the sky. The stars. I will not be able to see my home planet, but it is out there. I have never questioned how life is where I am from, but now I do. Are they ready to come?

I roll up my window to stop the nipping wind. My world has always been black and white, interspersed with a tweak of color. Now, not only are things around me vivid, intense, and bright, but they feel that way too.

"So, is this all it requires to have joy?" I ask Carter. "Doing activities that are pleasurable to you?"

I look over at him and smile again. It is more natural now. His blue eyes remind me of Earth's ocean and sky.

"Sort of," says Carter. "It can be. But sometimes doing the weirdest things can make you happy."

"What do you mean?" I ask.

"I can show you," Carter says. We pull up to the Northside Hospital, where Carter's cousin is residing, and he finds a parking stall after 10.5 minutes.

"You'll really like Megan," Carter says as we head inside. He shows the man at the front entrance his ID and the room number of the person we are visiting. They get my information and take my picture to give me an ID card as well, and we take an elevator to the third floor.

"Megan," says Carter as we enter. "I brought a friend." Doilies, rough paintings, and sketches of unicorns cover the room, while a mixture of crayon, body odor, and iodoform permeate it. An adult remains by Megan's bed. Her eyes droop, and thirty-two wrinkles spread across her face. Carter introduces me to Megan and the woman at the bedside, Patricia.

"She's my personal maid," says Megan, as Carter adds a plate of cookies and a glass of milk to Megan's random collection.

Patricia chuckles. "That's what they're calling moms these days?"

Megan rolls her eyes at me. She flips her pigtails behind her neck. Her mouth opens, and she whistles very quietly as she speaks because of her missing tooth. Humans might not hear it, but I do.

"This better not be your girlfriend, Carter," says Megan, pushing herself up on the bed. Megan's lungs do not sound pleasant. Her organs are much quieter than humans' usually are. "'Cause you know I found you a princess girlfriend, right?"

Carter grins. "That's what you keep saying. But I'm not sure how people would feel about me dating your six-year-old buddy in the next wing. She's a lil' young for me, don't you think?"

Megan sighs. "Well, then, I gotta meet the competition." She points to her side. "Get over here, you gorgeous freak."

I shift from behind Carter to the electric bed. Not because I have to be obedient, but because I want to. I move to Megan's side. She studies me, then grasps my hair and tugs on it. I do not expect it to hurt like it does. I almost like it because it reminds me I am real.

"Do you like unicorns?" she asks and thrusts a rainbow unicorn sticker on my forehead.

"The mythical creature with a horn on its head? They seem pleasant."

"Good. I approve." She leans back and pats the empty spot beside her on the bed. What does she want? I understand so much about humans now, but there is so much to learn.

"You don't have to climb up there," says Patricia after I pause. She rubs the back of her neck. She is embarrassed?

I *see*. Megan meant for me to take the spot. I climb into the bed, and she wraps her thin arms around me. It should be uncomfortable, empty. It always has been before, excluding when Carter touches me. Now though, her grasp becomes warm and soft. I do not know if that is because I have more touch sensations or because I have so much emotion, but it is nice. In a different way than touching Carter is nice.

Carter said helping makes him happy. I want that bubbly sensation again, and I want to be like him when he helped Anna clean her house.

"There was once a strong king," I say. "He ruled over his planet fairly. But then resources grew scarce, and his son and daughter disagreed on how to solve..." I tell her one of the only bedtime stories I know, the one my mother told me 127 times. She snuggles her head on my shoulders.

"I love you even though you're competition," she mumbles. After 2.4 minutes, she falls asleep against my arm. The strands of her pigtails tickle my neck.

No one has ever told me they loved me before. On Foxia, no one ever said they loved at all. Happiness overwhelms me, sweet and penetrating. This is what Carter meant regarding what makes him happy.

I understand now.

Patricia sets a tie quilt over her daughter's shoulder, kissing her cheek. "She was so strong only a few months ago," she says to us.

Carter and I sit down, and Patricia tells us stories about Megan. She tells us how she used to giggle at her own reflection in the mirror as a baby and how she loved riding her pink power wheels around the playground at their apartment complex. Sometimes, she repeats the same story again, but Carter does not seem bothered by it.

Megan sleeps, but I can tell she is hurting. I know because I can

218 | AMY MICHELLE CARPENTER

hear her body decomposing. Her lungs collapse. Her heart slows by a nanosecond as we speak.

"You love her, correct?" I say to Patricia.

"More than my own life," says Patricia. "I'd trade places with her if I could."

"You would?" I ask.

"Of course," she says. "People do wild things out of love."

Megan turns in her bed, dragging the IV hooked on her arm, still asleep. Patricia rearranges the cards on the side table, pulling the most colorful ones to the front.

The nanobots inside of me could fix Megan. Technically, she would still have the disease, but the nanobots would effectively repair her, so she could live like an average human being.

However, with new knowledge, I understand if I heal her, I could also give away my identity as an alien and threaten my mission to save all Foxians. I understand a lot more now that I can feel.

I do not know if I should heal her. The guilt is a new sensation to me too. When others control your choices, there is no need to worry about if it is the correct one. I focus on a *Get Well Soon* card with blue balloons.

I am not certain if I like feeling. It is much harder.

We stay for a few more minutes and then leave. Megan wakes up and thanks us for coming even though we did not do much.

In the elevator, a woman sits in a wheelchair, her hair matted, her body odor suffocating me. She clings to a baby in her arms. A man holds her hand. His clothes are at least two days worn, but he beams at the child.

Is this also love? As we get onto the freeway to go home, her words repeat in my mind. I think I understand what Carter means now about different kinds of happiness, but how does love play into it? Is that why Carter visits with Megan? Is that why he keeps assisting Anna, even though no one asks him to?

It seems a strange thought to have, but I wonder if I will ever love.

With all the vibrant emotions coursing through me, one could be love, but I do not know.

I asked Carter before if he loved me, and he said he did not love me in the way that would initiate a kiss. So, how does he love me? Are there different types of love? And is there anyone who has loved me as Patricia loves Megan?

My mother acted in a strange way with me. She tried to spend time with me for no productive reason.

She might have loved me.

If love is the greatest motivator, perhaps it is what I need to understand in order to bring my people safely to Earth.

CARTER

ON THE RIDE HOME, Kokab parks her hand against the center console. I know she's probably not trying to clue me in that SHE-FREAKING-WANTS-TO-HOLD-MY-HAND. She's still trying to understand social cues like that. But *I* still freakin' wanna hold it.

Dragging her through the water fountain gave me an excuse to touch her fingers, but I wanna know how she really feels about me. I don't know if she likes me, actually. I haven't asked.

So I man up. I subtly slide my right hand off the steering wheel. The bouncing troll bobble nods encouragingly to me, and I intertwine my fingers in hers.

She grins.

I come up with a clever way to ask her if she is into me without actually asking.

"Usually, people only hold hands if they are crushing on each other."

"I understand," she says.

Essssshaaa, her hand's in mine, and it's soft and warm, and I'm not on cloud nine. I'm on cloud ten plus plus. Actually, I'm higher than that. I'm on Jupiter. I'm on Kokab's planet. Wherever it is.

I'm the luckiest man in the universe.

I pull into our driveway. The living room light remains on. Mama likes to wait up to make sure everything is okay even though she's exhausted from working long hours. She trusts me, but she wants to be a responsible mom, I guess.

I open the door for Kokab but then grab her hand again. We stroll to our front porch and plop into the swing. "I had a good time tonight," I say.

Kokab leans toward me and lifts her red-like-velvet-cake lips. Unreal. I want to kiss her, but I'm not sure if that'd be fair to her with all that she is trying to figure out. Who's to say she really likes me *that way* with all she's trying to learn?

But maybe it'd be awesome?

In the distance, there's the humming of an engine, but I ignore it, too distracted by how pretty Kokab looks under the porch lights.

Kokab's eyebrows furrow and she jerks her hand away.

"What is it?" I say. Did I do something wrong?

"Drew is here."

It's a name that makes me instantly mad. I stop being so distracted and look at the road. Yep, Drew's muscle car is pulling into MY driveway.

We stand, and Drew steps on MY front lawn. Some guys from the swim team huddle behind him. For some reason, they stand pretty far back. What is he doing here? After the stunt he pulled, he's never welcome at MY house.

I'm sick of that bullying douche bag.

"What you think you're doing?" I say. "Aren't you suspended for what happened with the new girl? And for the proof they came up with that you sexually harassed Kokab? Shouldn't you be grounded or something?"

"Parents thought it was stupid she broke my hand and *I* got in trouble for it, so they gave me some money and told me to go out," says Drew. "Glad you're home. Swim team needed to show you something."

I tighten my fists. There may be a group of them, but they're dumber than a chicken if they think they can beat Kokab in a fight. She'll take them down in seconds. Her arms dangle by her side, face relaxed, as she surveys the group.

"Leave, Drew," she says.

"Oh, don't think I will," he replies. "Carter, so quick to judge me. I'm here because I care about you, man."

He pulls out his phone, and I'm ready to tell him off again. But then he shoves his fingers against the screen, playing a video, and I recognize the voice. Anna?

It's the video she promised me she deleted.

Drew places the phone in my hand, and I watch. I'm not sure why, maybe because I'm so shocked Anna lied to me (But why? I can't say since she always does.) or maybe because I'm afraid of what I'll see.

Kokab lifts a grand piano over her head like it's nothing and rips the leg off. Her expression stays empty as she shreds the expensive furniture to pieces. She looks like a beast.

"See, you're dating a monster. I had to warn you about the freak." Drew looks at how close we sit. "I'm just trying to help a brother out."

I wince, bothered I had thought about her looking monster-ish only seconds ago.

Kokab says nothing, just continues to watch herself rip wood apart.

"Don't know where you found that," I say, moving until my face is inches away from Drew's. "It's obviously fake."

Drew shrugs. "Guess Anna thought I was slut-shaming Kokab when I told people what she did to me. Making out with me and then dropping me seconds later. She said this video proves Kokab didn't have a choice. Kokab obeys everything."

I get in his face. "You need to leave."

"Just drop it," one of my teammates says. "Thought we were going out on the town with your parents' money."

What a bunch of great friends. At least Antonio's not here.

Drew draws closer to Kokab, and I grab the phone from his hands. "You *are* a freak, aren't you?" he says to her.

"I am not a freak," Kokab says. Her face intensifies as she views herself in the video, so I delete it. Her fists clench, which I've never seen happen. She lifts Drew up by his jacket. So much for my lie that the video's fake.

She throws him a few feet across the front lawn. Not too hard. Somehow she's good enough at throwing that he lands nicely on his feet. What a babe.

The rest of the team hustles to Drew's Mustang, telling him that they really oughta leave.

Drew growls and kicks one of Jason's soccer balls across the grass. He trudges to the car.

As he peels out of our driveway, he rolls down the window, shouting, "Doesn't matter that you deleted it. I already put it on YouTube. And it's viral!"

AGS

I REPLAY the video. 225 thousand views. And it's insane. Kokab lifts up a grand piano with one hand, and then she throws it down, and she pulls off one of the legs like it's one pound. She looks like a monster.

She *is* a monster. But I already know that. I've seen the future. And Foxians massacre humanity.

I'm changing that future. I send the video over to Hos in case it could be useful and then continue researching old bylaws and a dozen books hovering in front of me. *Carians 100 Oaths. The Guardy Galaxy Oath. Ondine Ancients Odes.*

Wait. Ondines?

I loved learning about Ondines, the best financial planners, in school. They could help.

I order the book open, and the text zooms over me. I request a page on financial assistance between Yadians and Ondines.

The page appears, and a few sentences are highlighted. I shriek. I read the words a few more times, reveling in the fact that they are real.

This is what I've been looking for. A solid chance at getting approved! The Ondine Attempt. How could I forget about this?

If the Expert Ondine can find a financial way to solve a problem and agrees it is an intelligent way to proceed, the Yadian Council will reconsider a previous verdict.

I GAZE out the window at the suburban homes interspersed among clusters of healthy foliage above Georgia. We hover about ten feet above the trees, but the invisibility shields block anyone from our view and allow any planes or birds to fly right through as if we aren't here. If humans only knew the universe hangs *literally* right over their heads.

The sunrise is like James Christopher Hill's *In the Beginning* painting, a warm blending of purple, blue, and red. Perhaps my luck is like the sun—a new hope, a fresh beginning peeking into view for Earth. I hope.

"I'm ready," I say to no one as I sprint from my spaceship into the TurboShip. A portly gentleman hurries past me in a color transforming vest, common on the planet Ostet. I make my way to the visiting office, a room for virtual trips across the galaxy, to put on the holographic gear.

"What're you doing here?" Hos says as I reach the right hallway. "This area's restricted."

He grabs my arm, but I twist it away and rush past him. He's a lot bigger than me. It should've been a lot harder. Does he know I'm trying to do something to convince the council still? Is this a sign of support?

Ondines live on Planet Oindi, and transporting physically to their galaxy is a bit dangerous with the Ondea Galaxy War IV going on. But this should be safe.

I throw open the doors and waltz in. "You don't have an appointment," says the office employee in Yadian. "You can't gear up."

She looks bored like she doesn't care either way.

I pull off my tank top and bell-bottoms. The grass stains on my pants remind me of rolling down the hill with Carter. That's what Earth is all about. Spontaneity. The unexpected. That's what I'm fighting for. Wonderful things like Carter. And bowling. And restaurant table numbers.

Dark things come, but the good outweighs them. Right? I push away the ugliness of Drew's bullying, not wanting to associate him with Earth.

I place contact lenses with small holographic screens into my eyelids and slide a few sliver-sized speakers into my clothing, and I change back into them. This would be easier if the office employee helped.

"I hope you know what you're doing," she says and soon closes her eyes. She snores as I finish gearing up.

Don't be nervous. Think of the Ondine.

I send out a call, which I believe is to the right Ondine, and then click the transport button on my wrist.

I appear on the streets of Critee city. It's nothing like standing in the middle of Foxia. A perfect sonata encompasses me, sung by the city walls. I'm not sure how the Ondines were able to blend so many medleys together.

I step onto a smooth and multicolored ground, made of crystal, but also covered in boxes of dirt and symmetrically placed flowers. Buildings stretch out in front of me like upside-down pyramids. Others ease upward from their side as if the architects wanted to prove their ability to perform geometry.

I've never been sold on math, but for the first time, I wonder if the Ondines' passion makes sense. Maybe math isn't so bad after all.

I wish I could smell the instis flowers draped along the street posts. I wish I could dig my fingers into the dirt boxes or order a spicy tamtilla from a street vendor. But I can't since it's virtual.

But it's still beautiful. Ondines wriggle through the towns. Their plump worm-like bodies leave a blueish line of slime. They wave to me with their six arms.

An Ondine exits a tall, thin skyscraper, which has strange gaps like a Jenga puzzle; it seems impossible to be standing. She makes her way toward me.

Is this the one I'm supposed to speak with? I turn my translation device on.

"So, you want old Ondine Teerr to give her approval on a financial matter," she says, referring to herself in the third person.

"Yes," I say. I hand her my screen with all the council's financial numbers and pieces of evidence I have collected against Kokab. She pulls out a long, rectangular device from her stomach. It resembles a modern abacus, and she lets go, allowing it to hover in front of her. She begins typing in it furiously with all of her hands. Numbers twist out of the screen and crowd the sky around her until she is encompassed by a myriad of equations and weird squiggles that make no sense to me and cause my head to writhe in confusion.

Are they good? I hope they're good.

Odine Teerr's elastic skin jiggles, emitting campfire-like smoke, and her stomach squeaks. "Pardon me. I haven't eaten all day and am getting a bit hungry. Financially, it could work. Your government may not be able to figure out how to fit it in, but I can. I tweaked the budget a bit here and there."

226 | AMY MICHELLE CARPENTER

She drags some numbers from the sky and shows them to me as if I could understand them.

"Plus, building relations with strong beings like the Foxians might pay off in the future," says Odine Teerr. She hands my screen back to me and crosses her middle two arms. "But I think it is a bad idea," she says.

"Why?" I ask. I try to say it as politely as possible, but my nose quivers. I have to persuade her. She's my last hope. "My plan helps everyone win," I whisper, urgency in my voice.

"Perhaps, but I'm not too sure about that. And I have a hunch things will work out with the Foxians."

A hunch? Yes, Ondines are emotionally sophisticated species as well as logical. But it is not her job to go off hunches; she needs to fix the budget, that's all.

She nicks my chin. "Besides, you're not being fair with your arguments. You're exploiting this girl. You're manipulating the info to make her seem like a monster."

"She is a monster."

"Is she?"

"Yes."

Odine Teerr steps right through me. It's weird that everything looks so real, but I can't actually feel anything on the planet. I rub my arms. Kokab *is* a monster, isn't she?

"And what about this girl filming the video? This boy whose hand was broken. What did he do to deserve it, hmm?"

I frown. I don't like her points very much. "I'm not sure. But they're humans, and I'm supposed to protect them. Please," I say. "You said it's in the budget. We're doing something nice, helping another species to survive. What could go wrong?"

The Ondine pulls out a golden tablet and begins making calculations.

"Yes," says Odine Teerr. "What could go wrong? I'll approve this with some suggestions to the council. But promise me you'll give the

Foxians a chance if your idea doesn't end up working out. Don't do anything too drastic, hmmm?"

I throw my arms across Teerr, kissing her wet, slimy body. Or at least that's how I imagine it, since I can't actually embrace her. Really, I waltz right through her.

Yes, thank you. Praise the millions and millions of stars in the sky.

"Thank you. Thank you."

"It's going to be hard to persuade the Foxians to go along with your plan."

I nod and order the sensors off. I reappear inside the office and dash out the door, blatantly ignoring the professional's request to slow down and drink some fluid.

An Ondine's approval means a lot when it comes to financial costs. We trust Ondines. According to the textbook, it's unlikely the council will turn me down now.

I send the verdict out to Governor Ids with all the calculations from Teerr. Her reworkings of finances will actually save us money. We'll be able to profit by terraforming multiple planets at once, and the Foxian planet will essentially be free.

Once done, I pace across the starboard floor. I jet through crowds of people. Is it really enough?

I hope. I hope.

Sure enough, the voting comes through. With the video and Ondine's approval, and Hos's talented persuasion, they're going to take the first step. They're going to reach out to Foxians to see if they want help.

Thank you, gods of the universe, for hearing my prayers.

I need to tell Yas. I dash to the science lab where he is and hurdle into his arms. It's a good thing he's so tall and I'm small because he's not that strong.

"They changed their minds." I rub my nose against his cheek. "They'll help the Foxians."

"Congratulations," says Yas, pulling me off him. He stalks out of the room, head bent. I didn't realize how mad he is at me, but I won't let him ruin the moment.

Though I'm surprised by how much I miss having him there for me.

But still. Earth is going to be saved from the Foxians. As long as I can convince them to accept our excellent gift.

Chapter 20

KOKAB

It's 4:03 a.m. when the downstairs door creaks open. Joe's clumsy footsteps move through the house. He sets something hard against the floor. His travel bags?

I check the computer, and the video of me is up to 540, 230 views. I see my face, void and expressionless. Wood shreds flutter around me.

When Drew showed me the video and called me a monster, it affected me. In the video, I am empty; it is clear on my face and through my actions. I did not feel, only obeyed. And I did not understand that I was destroying her father's property.

I was *hurting* her father.

How did I miss that?

I denied assisting Megan, ill in her hospital bed, to conceal my identity. I broke Drew's hand because he injured me first. I lied to almost all humans I have met about my identity and my purposes for being here.

I hurt them all.

A pain exudes from my stomach and masticates my soul. Is that what it is? My soul? Because a body part doesn't hurt, but it seems real.

540, 242. 12 views occurred in the last ten seconds. I play the video again. The empty face of a robotic-female meets mine.

Fear—I am 90 percent certain it is fear—gnashes within me, nourishing the guilt. If people know what I truly am, how will they react to me? Another idea comes too, slowly rattling in my mind, strong and unending.

What if I fail in my task?

Things were much simpler when there was less pain and no emotions.

I have always believed I would convince world leaders to accept our plan to immigrate to Earth. I have never failed at a task assigned by an Elder One before, and I never considered the consequences if I did.

But if I fail, the Eldest One said they will still come.

And what will my kind do? Wage war? If so, humans will likely die.

I play the video again and see what I truly am.

A monster like Drew said.

Joe comes up the stairs and stands outside of my room, and, this time, I do not wait for him to knock. I slip the door open. His weathered face greets mine.

"What will I do?" I say.

He seems to be aware I am referring to more than the video—humans are so good at picking up on these things.

I grasp the doorframe. If I were human, I might cry, but, despite all my growing, I am still a monster. "I am not ready to meet with the world leaders," I whisper. Joe still stands in my doorway. He has not yet spoken. "I do not understand humans perfectly yet."

I step into the hallway beside him, glancing at the old photo of Carter's family on the wall. They stand arm in arm, knee-deep in a lake, smiling. Is this the love that Patricia spoke of?

"Saying that means you understand more than you realize," says Joe, his hands thrust in his large coat pockets, dark shadows beneath his eyes. Perhaps from flying home tonight? Or from working toward a solution for the Foxians? Why does he care about my species so much?

"You won't be able to go back to school, you know. Too risky," he says. "Too many kids asking questions, trying to take advantage of you after this video. Hating you. Maybe attacking you. And it'll be hard to keep reporters away. Not to mention how Anna's dad will press charges and start looking into things."

I nod. School is an interesting experience. I will miss learning from youth. "I know," I say. "Where will we go?"

"We'll lay low in New York until the UN meeting." Joe pats my shoulder. "Mama said on the phone you and Carter were starting to... get along. I'm very sorry we have to leave."

He grips me, and again, I do not hate the touch. It does not assuage my fears, but it seems to reassure me incrementally. He trods down the hall and shuts the door to his bedroom. I can hear him greet Mama, kiss her lips, and tell her he missed her.

I left my species to locate to a new planet, but I did not miss any individual.

I step back into my bedroom and lay down on the queen-size mattress. The scratches and blemishes of the frame no longer seem so erroneous to me. Why is that the case?

I think of all that happened before Drew came, my date with Carter, his hand intertwined with mine. I liked it. From what I've seen between other teenage and adult couples, I like *him*. What if he knew I am here to help billions immigrate to his planet? Would he accept me like his father has?

I am not sure, but I hope he would. If I like him, it is right for me to tell him.

Correct?

I knock on Carter's door, and he opens it, rubbing his eyes. "Dad said you guys are leaving. Thanks for coming to say goodbye." He lingers there in superhero pajama bottoms but no shirt. For a human, he has very broad shoulders.

I open my mouth but say nothing. What is this? I try again, but fear makes it harder to speak.

Do this, I command myself, and it seems to be effective because I start talking.

"I apologize for disturbing you, but I cannot leave without telling you about my mission," I say. "I desire for you to know more about me."

Carter's face drops, not what I expected. Is that a sign of disappointment? However, he nods. We go to the kitchen and sit across from one another at the family table, Mama's paperwork neatly stacked on one end. I clench my fists, afraid.

I inhale, and my heart speeds up to a point where it is no longer steady. His heart races too. He is also nervous?

This is what it feels like to be human.

"Carter, I wish to indicate the truth regarding my purposes here. "To begin with," I say, "and I know you already know this, but I need to state the words... I am an alien."

AGS

I RUSH through the giant spaceship looking for Hos. The council has approved!

I ask around and find out he's in a meeting. The automatic door of a meeting room swings open as I step inside. Hos argues with some of the old guardians of other planets; they don't want to be here on Earth. Their home planet needs them, says an old guardian with yellowing hair.

Hos points at some strategic plans of Georgian territory. Forests dot a 3D map of everything below us. Hovering in the sky on the map, our ships spread across the area. "This is urgent for—"

"Hos!" I interrupt him mid-sentence. "I just got word from the council. We're going to work toward terraforming another planet."

"Actually, we're not." Hos smiles briefly, which seems weird considering the words. Maybe he's trying to be optimistic with others around.

"Let's talk." He waves toward the door, and the guardians get the message to leave.

"Your mom found a communication device out in the woods by the home Kokab is staying in," says Hos. "A Foxian leader was using it to communicate with a scientist in the household, Joe Turner. We contacted him with it, and he sent us a message. Would you like to see it?"

"Yes?" My voice drops. I cling to my bell bottoms where there is a grass stain, refraining from pacing around like Mom. What's wrong?

I wish Mom was here right now, even if she'd be fidgeting like a lunatic. Or Yas. Someone to hold my hand, reassure me like the first time I found out that Earth might be in trouble. But it's me. And I have to stay positive.

The Eldest One's face appears on the ship's screen. He wrinkles his forehead and his voice trembles. It's amazing a Foxian could be so emotional, but I guess he understands how terrifying this is for humans.

"Thank you for telling us about your plan to terraform our planet. How lovely of you," he says, and it's almost like he's looking directly at me even though it's a recording. "But I'm afraid my council said no. Yadians are our enemies, and they will not accept your help. Even now. I'm so sorry."

Hos swipes a long strand of orange hair behind his ears. His nose twitches and his frown deepens, but something in his eyes doesn't seem right. They're glistening. "There's nothing you can do, Ags." He pats my back. "I'm sorry. But there are millions of planets out there; you can't take care of them all." His hands hover over the 3D map of Earth, but then he shakes his head like he's thinking of something crazy.

What is it? What could I do to change their minds? What was Hos thinking? I stare at all the aspects of the screen, the woods, the house, the tiny people, and it dawns on me.

I shift toward the 3D map of Georgia, running my pinkie through the trees. It's awful, but I've tried to help my humans. I've tried and tried. I haven't lost hope, and so everything should work out as I want it.

But it isn't. It's not working. And I'm tired of all this craziness.

When I pledged to become a guardian, I said I'd do everything to protect my planet.

EVERYTHING.

I want the Foxians to accept my plan, but this is just crazy.

But sometimes, we have to do crazy things. I swallow.

"The ships," I say. "We can let them know we're here already. We can threaten the Foxians with our battleships. It will force them to accept our..."

I halt, realizing my words are so Foxian. Forcing them into my idea. But I don't care. The ends justify the means, right? I said I'd do anything for Earth. I stood before a council and fought. I stalked another girl. I traveled to a distant galaxy. I even betrayed humans by making them look bad. But it still ended with a no.

The Eldest One's words wrap around my head like a tight Sikh turban, squeezing me. *No. No. No.* So many nos.

It's better to threaten them than actually fight them. Then, the Eldest One will see how serious we are, and he'll convince the others.

"You want to go visible today?" says Hos, glancing as my finger hovers over our large ship. "You'd have to go up the chain for approval on the matter. I don't think there's time."

He exits the room and shakes his head, but he told me previously not to listen to anyone, only myself. And that means I don't even have to listen to him. Besides, there was something in his eyes that seemed to say *yes*.

I lift my fingers over the invisibility shield and hesitate. This is insane. I squeeze my eyes closed as I slide my finger against the screen and order the invisibility shields to be taken down.

It will only take a few minutes.

Our spacecraft are complex, majestic machines made from a soft metal that doesn't exist on Earth. Now the humans will know we're here.

Please, don't panic.

Chapter 21

KOKAB

Carter stoops over the table, covering his head with his hand. I did not expect this reaction. I do not know what I expected. Why is it every time I conclude I understand human emotions, I discover I am wrong?

"Serious?" he says. "That's the plan? Get humans to accept three billion aliens or what? They attack mankind?"

"That is possible," I say. "But I will persuade them to accept us. I do not want anyone to hurt humans."

"You don't?" He traces his thumb over and over on the cracks in the wood table. Finally, he glimpses at me. His red, tangled curls tumble over his eyes, but I can see the pain in them.

I have hurt him too.

"I thought you were here to save mankind. We have lots of issues. I figured your purpose was to help out somehow." His voice cracks, indicative of grief. I flinch.

"How could you do this to me?" He slams his fist against the table. Mama's papers flutter to the ground.

He breathes in, counting under his breath. His voice grows quiet, which seems much worse. "I trusted you. I trusted *him*. Why would my dad trust you? You don't care about us people, *do* you?"

His words twist inside me, more painful than being hit by Carter's truck. I try to show him I am learning to care by touching his hand. He yanks it away.

Maybe he is right. I never learned how to care until recently. I may not care as much as I should. I am a monster.

Perhaps I take too long to speak because Carter leaps up. His chair clatters to the floor. He stomps outside, slamming the mosquito screen behind him. I hear him pacing with Sputnik, murmuring about how I hurt his feelings and telling the dog I betrayed him.

Fifty-four leaves grind under Carter's boots. "Kokab, how could you. You're like superman. You could help people. Rather than hurt them. What're you thinking?"

It is possible he has forgotten I can hear him out there, insulting me.

His words sting. I grip my arms. His behavior verifies my fears.

I am a monster. I am a monster. I am a monster.

I quietly open the door and lock it behind me. Carter still stomps around, muttering, stepping on and squishing ants. I do not think he realizes they are under his feet. It is obvious he does not hear me slip past him as I run down the porch stairs, then sprint past the playground and tear through the woods. A car rushes down the highway with the music turned up. Some teens laugh as they make some remarks about a football team.

I will not turn back. Pain courses through me, and, for the first time, logic doesn't lead my choice.

I must prove I care, not simply for Carter but for myself.

I reach the hospital and show the employee my ID before I make my way to Megan's room.

She lies in her bed with some glitter on her cheeks. She inhales, her breathing broken.

"Hello, Megan," I say, and she doesn't stir. I place my hands over her and order the nanobots to heal her body. They cannot take away her autoimmune disease, but they can continue to fix her, so she will not be sick.

Megan opens her eyes and presses her fingers against my face. "I feel better," she says.

"Your body will function normally now," I say.

"I told my parents you were an angel, but they didn't believe me." She turns sideways and falls asleep again. Her breathing sounds normal. Her organs do too.

I step through the hall and make my way to the next room. I heal a small sleeping boy. But the patient in the bed next to him is awake. "What are you doing here?" he says. "You aren't family. I know all Mike's family."

"I can heal you. Would you like that?" I am 98 percent certain I sound scary, but how else should I proceed? I can help if they want it.

The boy shrieks, and a nurse appears. I repeat my words, and she tells me I must leave the hospital. I ignore her and sprint through the halls as quickly as I can, healing everyone who accepts it.

Soon, multiple humans dash after me. My identity will be found out, but maybe that is the answer to letting humans accept us. Maybe they need to know I care. Do I care?

You are a monster.

Either way, I decided to do something good for others, even if there is no benefit for myself, an illogical decision. I will follow through.

Because I do not want to be a monster anymore. I want to be more human.

I take the stairs, slipping out of the hospital, ignoring the joyful cries of people claiming to be healed. And the yelling of others that a lunatic is running loose.

It is done. I do not know if this will help humans to accept us or if they will fear us more.

I sprint through the woods and stop. I take 1.2 seconds to glance up at the sky. I look for the star, my star. My people are preparing to come, and for the first time, I worry about them and their travels and decisions.

As I examine the starry night sky, 122 alien spaceships appear over the Georgian woods.

AGS

THE HIGHWAY'S jammed with a long line of honking cars. So many headlights stream across roadways even out here in the country, it's hard to see the stars.

I tear across the woods on foot, hoping for peace, but I can't seem to find it. I pass a gathering of people praying as they gaze up at the ships, but they don't heed me.

Immediately after my decision to make the ships visible, news of them flooded the World Wide Web. It only took a few minutes for people to panic. Robbing stores for emergency supplies. Running out of town.

It might be worse, but even though the invisibility aspect of the shield is down, our Yadian ships still block anything from coming in and out. The Air Force is frantic, according to Mom's surveillance.

But it's better than being hunted by Foxians, so I had to do it. Right?

I lean against a tree and run my fingers in the damp moss. This was supposed to be beautiful, enjoying Earth like this, not painful. I stoop down and capture a firefly in my hand. It flits back and forth in my grasp, and then I let it free. How I yearn to be free like the creature.

Free of this Foxian problem.

I stand up, still lost, still unable to shake the darkness that isn't just around me.

I don't know what drives me to Kokab's home. Or maybe I do. Maybe I just don't want to admit that I'm desperate to know if our ships have threatened the Foxian.

The house is awake, lights on upstairs and downstairs, streaming over the worn playground.

Carter rocks back and forth in the porch swing and mutters. The light from the kitchen floods over his hair like its ablaze. He wraps his fingers in his dog's mane. "How could Kokab do this. How? How?" He moans to the dog.

What has *she* done to Carter?

I pull back into the maple trees to give Carter privacy. He's still going on about Kokab. Ridiculous how she doesn't even mind hurting those who care for her.

I turn, and there she is, sprinting through the woods. The beast.

"You," I say, and Kokab pauses, straightening. We stand an arm's length from each other, two females sharing the same space but never the same views.

"You. Hurt. Carter." I say it through clenched teeth.

She nods. "Yes, I know. But I did not mean—"

"Didn't mean to?" My voice rises. "Was breaking that boy's hand an accident, too? Can't you see your kind don't belong here?"

The spaceships in the sky. The rushed mobs. The robberies. The Foxians made me do it. It's their fault. *Her* fault.

"I apologi—" She starts but doesn't finish because I can't take it anymore. I lunge for her, and we both collide against the ground. Twigs shatter below us.

My breath grows frenzied. "Get off this planet! Leave my humans alone." I yank my palm back and slam her chest over and over.

I freeze, realizing what I have done. She could tear me apart limb by limb if she wanted. Instead, she lays beneath my grip and slowly breathes. She studies my face. I sob as I continue to hit her. She doesn't try to get up or stop me.

It doesn't hurt her. She can't feel my pain.

"I understand that you are scared," she says calmly.

Foolish, emotionless creature.

"No. No." I pant. I drop my face down until my nose almost touches hers. It quivers. My tears run onto her cheek. "No, you don't."

I'm going to stop the Foxians from coming. I've got to stop them. There's no other solution.

I reel back to strike her again, as hard as I can, and my fingers shatter as I slam against her. Broken. Like I'm hitting a stone wall.

"Get off, right now." I hear a voice behind me. It's Yas. He grabs me by the waist as I struggle against him. I try to pry his fingers off of me as he pulls me away.

"I'm sorry," he apologizes to Kokab, his arms wrapped around me. He apologizes to *her*?

"This won't do you any good. *Stop* being so stupid," he tells me as Kokab stands and wipes dirt from her face.

I flail against him and then go limp.

Stars. Blinking stars.

I know it's pointless. It won't help humans.

My arms shake as I wipe the snot from my nose. I inhale and exhale a few times. "Okay," I whisper, and he lets go. I hold my throbbing fingers with my right hand and glare at Kokab. Yes, it's pointless, but she makes a good punching bag.

"I understand," says Kokab. She moves toward me, touching my hand with her pale fingers. Now it's going to happen. She's going to attack. Kill. Maim. Like the Foxians in my vision.

I create a plan of defense, knowing I'll lose. But I'm still, almost wanting her to strike, so I have an excuse to continue. To let out all my fears.

She squeezes my fingers. Warmth spreads through me, and, in seconds, the pain's gone. And then, she sprints out of view at about 60 miles per hour.

I flex my fingers. My hand's okay.

Maybe I should be grateful. But for some reason, the fact I didn't phase her at all only makes me angrier.

Yas and I head back to my small ship in silence.

"How could you treat her like that? And Hos said it was your order to take down the invisibility shields? The governor's furious," Yas says after we enter the ship. "What were you thinking? Really, what were you thinking?"

Pink hair drapes the pilot's seat, remnants from Mom's bad habit. I'm really glad she's not here right now, or she'd probably be tearing her head to pieces.

"Oh right. You weren't thinking. You don't ever think, Ags."

Yas is not a yeller, but this is the closest to yelling I've seen him. After all the work I've done, how dare he?

He switches from Yadian to Xion, the most common language on the planet he guards. Though his volume stays the same, he speaks faster and faster.

Yas is wrong.

I think he's wrong. I hope he's wrong.

"Yas, listen to me." I grab his face, but he turns away from me. "This is the only way to convince the Foxians not to come. You'll see. Everyone will."

He shakes his head, so I open the hatch and sprint out. I can't keep listening because I don't have time. If he isn't wrong, then I'm causing worldwide panic for nothing. The spaceships *will* intimidate the Foxians, and they will accept our offer to terraform another planet. It's got to work.

I grab my scooter and leave.

I'm going back to Foxia to convince the Eldest One myself.

CARTER

THE SKY'S crowded with alien ships. I pull aside the blue curtains and hide behind the petunia in the window sill.

Dad left with Kokab this morning before I even got a chance to talk to him, though I half-remember him knocking on my door and telling me goodbye.

I don't even know what to think about *Kokab*. All the awesomeness of holding her hand and taking her on a date and then she had to go and tell me the truth.

The truth sucks. She didn't just drop a bomb. It was an atomic bomb.

Errgh. How could she not think about what would happen if she failed? How could she not care about mankind enough to wonder if we might die?

I thought she was invested in helping humans, invested in *me*, but I guess I was wrong.

It's *a lot* to process. What's even weirder to process is Dad. It makes no sense that he'd want to help billions of aliens immigrate to Earth. Yeah, it may be their only option to live. But did he consider what might happen if it doesn't work out? War. We die.

I guess I'm finding out my dad's a crazy all over again, not because aliens aren't real but because he trusted them. And it hurts like gunshot wounds through the brain.

I cling to my Remington rifle. It won't do any good against the aliens in the sky, but it might help with the reporters on the lawn.

The driveway crawls with the annoying pests. And I don't wanna talk to the entire world about any of this. Even though there are strange spaceships in the sky, I don't much feel like being on TV to defend Kokab.

Just got to do what you gotta do.

I grab my boots and throw open the rickety door. The reporters start yelling questions at me. "Your father claimed to meet an alien some years ago. Is your exchange student really an alien?"

"What can you tell us about the strange videos cropping up of your exchange student?" A guy with a mustache shouts before he accidentally steps into a pile of dog poo.

"How about all these theories involving the aircraft in the sky? Do you agree with those saying they're alien spaceships?"

I hoist my gun and give them my best tough-guy face. "This is private property," I say. "So, get."

They're still there after I slam the door in their faces and return to hiding behind the petunia, so they must not take the threat seriously. Fine. I put the rifle back and dash out the front door, head down. I shoulder through the crowd on my lawn as they all shoot questions at me.

"No," I say to the reporters. "No aliens. There aren't aliens. They're probably Russian."

The giant UFOs are more threatening in open daylight. Not one small controversial ship like I saw when lightning bug hunting. These can't be explained easily. Some small ones line the sky like the stars my dad studied. But a few are so massive, crazy colored and glowing, I can see them even from way down here.

Not human. I assume they belong to Kokab's species. They couldn't have been a little more subtle in their descent to Earth? This is gonna cause chaos. Total chaos. How could I have trusted Kokab?

I rev up my truck and speed away because I need some peace, and I'm not getting it with this crazy show in front of my house. Reporters jump out of the way to avoid being squashed. I pull onto the road. And since Mama was busy answering phone calls from panicked friends, no one said I *couldn't* leave. The movies have taught us that alien invasions are synonymous with end-of-the-world-apocalypse.

But that's not gonna happen. At least I'm gonna pretend it won't.

I turn on music to distract me from the spaceships looming above. The roads going out of town are clogged up. People honk at each other to get out of the way and scream from rolled down windows. But who can blame them?

Finally, after a few hours of heavy traffic, I get to Hickory Creek. Usually, a few runners travel on its trails, but now it's just me and the wild animals. Quieter than I was hoping. I pull my boots off and sit down at the edge of the stream. I roll my jeans up and plunge my bare feet into the water.

I check my phone when I get a text message from Antonio: *My selfie under the spaceships has almost a thousand comments on Insta.*

His next message is, *I think we're getting nuked by the North Koreans. Who do you know with a bomb shelter?*

"I thought I'd find you here," a familiar voice says behind me. Anna plops down next to me, tossing her stilettos off, and water gushes over my pants as she shoves her feet in the stream.

Still me and the wild animals.

She pulls her dark bangs from her eyes and slips on a leather headband. "Of course my mom wanted me to stay home during 'what could be the end of the world.' I snuck out early, hoping school was open, so I could see everyone's reactions to the spaceships. It sucks they announced the closings a few minutes after I got there."

"Never thought I'd hear you say that." I stand up, planning to leave because there's no way I'm ever gonna find *peace* with her here. I open my truck door and start climbing inside.

Anna follows me in her long metallic dress. I think her clothes are supposed to be some kind of end-of-the-world statement, but she looks pretty goofy, stumbling over rocks in her getup. "I told my friend you'd drive me home," she says. "She left me here."

I sigh, and she slithers into the truck behind me, but I can't deny the appeal of her fantastic but over sprayed perfume.

"Did you see the internet?" she asks me.

"The video you were supposed to delete?" I say. "Yeah, saw it."

I stick my keys in the ignition and start the vehicle, but she throws her feet up on top of my seat. Somehow, in the middle of an alien invasion, Anna still manages to be obnoxious.

"Not just that." She shoves her iPhone over with her search menu open.

Article after article speculates regarding the spaceships. I scroll down to one connecting Kokab to an incident at the hospital, which also shows the video of her ripping apart the piano. *Aliens Walk Among Us?* the title states. Megan grins on the front cover in her favorite PJs out of bed. She's glowing and looks...healthy? "I'm better now," a quote in the article claims. "All thanks to the alien girl."

Did Kokab *really* do this? Over forty people claimed someone came to their rooms, saying she could heal them and now they're recovered.

Kokab saved a bunch of people. My brain tries to process this in the middle of my anger at her.

She saved little Megan. Megan is okay because of Kokab. Why?

Because she actually does care? I could ask her, but I may never see her again. She'll live in Antarctica with a bunch of penguins if things turn out, right? Or we all die?

I don't know anymore.

"You know why the ships are here, don't you?" says Anna. I shrug and point to her feet. She pulls them down only to throw her stilettos over the seat next to me, almost beaming me in the head for the second time.

"No, I don't know what you're talking about," I say and get driving.

"Yes, you do." Anna climbs over the seat beside me as soon as I get on the highway. "Kokab's an alien."

"What?" I splutter. "No, she's not. That's stupid."

"She is." She says. When we drive up to Anna's place, a large crowd has gathered. Probably because she was the one who posted the video of Kokab. There are teams of reporters and people demanding answers. They must assume, since they saw a video at her home, the Chu's know stuff too. It makes me wonder if Anna was lying about the whole school thing. Maybe she just wanted to get away like me. Her dad stands outside demanding that people get off his perfect lawn or he'll sue, but no one seems to notice or care.

I climb out of the truck to help her get through this mess, and the news reporters swarm around us. I search for a possible escape. Anna points to a five-year-old looking girl who's bawling her eyes out. "Why don't you tell them that everything is going to be okay? The secret's blown anyway. If they know you trust Kokab, they won't be scared. At least, I wasn't when I saw the ships appear in the night."

I shake my head. No, I can't. I don't know if everything will be okay.

Memories of my dad announcing that aliens exist, me insisting that he wasn't crazy, encompass me. He *trusts* her.

I'm afraid to stand up. I want to help people. I thought Kokab was good. I thought my dad wasn't crazy after all. But I'm pretty sure I was wrong.

"Fine, then I'll tell them," she says and climbs up on her dad's fancy fountain, almost slipping and falling in, before getting a firm grip with her extra tall shoes. For someone who is so impossible to trust, she isn't afraid to take a stance when it matters to her. "Listen, everyone. Kokab, the strange foreign exchange student at the high school, she's really an alien. And Carter's dad, who we all thought was a nut job, he was right. Aliens are real. And they have a perfectly good reason for being here. Carter will tell you."

"No," I say. The reporters hold their mics out toward me; random strangers now stare at me like they want answers. Like I have them. I can't. I'm not even sure I believe in her. And I can't ask others to believe too. "I don't have a clue. I can't—"

My phone rings, the sound of a chicken bawking. It's Antonio, but I don't want to talk with him either. I swipe to ignore.

Anna grabs me by the collar and whispers loudly. "What's wrong with you, Carter? Think about all that Kokab has done. You know she's a good person. Look what she did by helping those people in the hospital? Why won't you tell everyone the aliens are nice?"

I back up, whispering to Anna because everyone is still looking at me. "I don't know if I can trust her. My dad's bought into some kind of crazy scheme."

"You know Kokab. She's a good person. And I wish my dad was like yours. Have faith, you idiot."

I shrug my shoulders and pivot as the reporters scoot in closer, waiting for a response. I inhale and then dash across Anna's perfect lawn, straight into my faithful truck. I can't help these people here.

Have faith, you idiot.

Anna's words ring in my ears, and I feel like a jerk because I can't stand up for Kokab or my dad. I didn't even hear them out, really. I didn't even get answers. But I seriously need answers.

I call Dad as soon as I'm away from the crowd, and he immediately answers.

"Dad," I say. "I'm coming to New York."

Chapter 22

AGS

As soon as I enter Els's ship, she flies at me with a fiery speed I wouldn't expect from an old lady. She pins me to the ground. "You dropped the shields," she says. Anger burns in her eyes. "Without my approval."

"You weren't there," I respond. " I had to do it to keep the Foxians away."

I try to pry her off, but she shoves all her thin weight against me. Oomph. I roll her over. Her sapphire dress twists against the ground.

"Stop," says Els, wheezing as she chases after me. "I might have been wrong about him."

I have no clue what she's talking about, and I feel somewhat bad about making an old lady run, but this mission is too important.

I can't give up now.

I switch the pulsing ball on and slip onto the machine and prepare for the horrible pain of transferring my mind to a Foxian body. My skin rips, and my muscles and bones shriek.

The world becomes crystal, but there's no way I'd admire things this time. I sprint. Thank the stars I know the shortcut, through the tunnels, and open the trap door.

Good thing I'm strong enough to push a desk over. I step out. The Eldest One settles over the opening with his mouth open.

"Ags!" His jaw snaps shut. His mouth twists into a smile. "Delightful to see you. To what do I owe this second visit?"

"Hi." I lift the desk and set it down where it was before. This time, I'm determined to feel. I will not let go of my passion for mankind. "I'm back. I really need you to accept this offer."

I sit in front of the Eldest One, explaining everything. I tell him how people are panicking and how people will panic more if the Foxians come. I explain this isn't what we want, but we will protect humans if the Foxians try anything. The idea of war against Earth usually causes chills to run through me, but now, in this frame, I can hardly feel any concern at all. But I grasp onto the memory, remembering why I cared. I try to express that in my voice, to get it out. Does it sound monotonous? I'm not sure.

The Eldest One bends over his pure white desk. His black irises widen.

I take the fact that his body actually reacts as a great sign, and I continue elaborating on why he needs this. I'm honest with him, and I share my fears of Earth with him. I even tell him of the vision I saw of the future. Finally, I stop, hoping for his acceptance.

Please, gods of the universe. Please let this work out.

"Wonderful job, Ags. Wonderful job." He presses his polished hands together in a tight clap. "I'm so proud of you for what you have accomplished."

"So, you'll accept the deal?" I ask.

"Mmmm." He taps my chin with hands as stiff as a corpse's. "You did so well, but I cannot, my dear."

"What? Why?" I say.

"Because, Ags, your people are a threat to humans, hovering in the sky. And fear is an excellent motivator, as you indicated."

What does he mean?

There's a knock at the door, quiet and in perfect rhythm. The Eldest One rises to open it. He's going to tell them to leave, so we can continue our conversation, isn't he?

Three guards step in. One's not wearing silver or gray, but white. His leg goes almost an inch longer than the other. His clothes tell me he isn't an Almost or Perfect, but I did not know there was any other classification.

I knit my eyebrows, confused, turning toward the Eldest One. His mouth twists in a crooked smile. It's the type of smile only the greatest movie villains achieve, the kind of smile that makes me excited about what actors are capable of. Only his is real.

"Arrest her."

Immediately, the three figures grasp me. If I wasn't in a Foxian body, I'd scream. I'd shout. But I feel numbness with a twinge of terror.

He rises. His long white robe wraps against him like a body being mummified. "You may have been trying to threaten us with your ships in the sky. But we don't get threatened easily. Humans do. They're terrified right now that all is lost. If only humans had something equally strong as the Yadians to sweep in and protect them. Good thing the Foxian ruler can protect them."

I don't have time to hear this. I have to get out.

I struggle against the others' grips, pulling free. Rush to the desk and shove it; it ricochets across the room in one thrust. I don't need to hear anymore. I need to get out.

Now. And never come back.

The Eldest One snatches my arm, and I struggle against him, twisting out of his grip. I'm strong enough to throw a desk across the room, but he's stronger. He wraps his arms around me, and I'm so revolted this body actually cringes.

"Think they'll listen to world-saving superheroes, Ags?" he asks. "Especially after they've lived with one who is pure, good, and has proven she helps humans? I think I'll be a fantastic ruler of Earth."

I spit on his face and thrust my knee as close to the groin as I can, but he only chuckles. "Little innocent Ags. So quick to form opinions. So passionate about following through. All it took was one measly vision."

He pulls a thin screen from out of his desk.

Cold air curls across my body and attacks me. I fall to the ground as I see a mother bawling over the limp body of a boy. His sister clings to his Hotwheels as a Foxian yanks the mother, tugging her away.

He gave the visions to me.

It was a transfer of falsified data. And I believed him. And now, because of me, the visions will come true.

All the panicking? Maybe coming true already.

It turns out *I* was the real monster.

"No. No." I sob internally, unable to cry real tears. The three guards grip me as I melt into the ground.

"Hos will stop you," I say, finding one more teaspoon of hope. "He's always good at politics. He'll straighten out the truth with the humans."

"Doubtful, seeing as how Hos is working with me." The Eldest One flips open the door, winking as if we shared a nice joke rather than him threatening an entire species. "I believe you left a body behind for me to borrow."

No. No. Never. Not mine.

I use all my energy to slam into the guards with my cold frame, but I topple to the ground. The visions were too much even for this body to handle.

This is my fault. My prejudice against another species, my inability to listen to everyone around me, led to this.

And now my beloved, good, beautiful Earth will fall.

I lay against the smooth floor, forcing my body to scream. The screech sounds barely startled rather than terrified and does not satisfy the dark fog coursing inside of me.

The Eldest One crouches down and strokes my face.

"Here, I am the Eldest One," he says, lifting me up and handing me to the different-looking guard. "Wise leader. But, I am also a warrior, conqueror, and prince of Foxia. Some people call me Abaddon."

He leaves me with those words, disappearing into the secret tunnel.

CARTER

MAMA WENT to stay with Margi and the grandkids, but I need to get to New York, even if the drive is thirty hours instead of the usual ten because of all the panicked traffic on the freeway.

If I can't believe in Kokab, at least I can be there for mankind. If I can't believe in my dad, maybe I can understand him.

He's been right before, and I haven't trusted him. Maybe, just maybe, he knows something I don't.

Believe. I tell myself. *Try to believe that things will be okay. TRUST.*

It's hard to trust when the world is falling apart around me.

My eyelids droop, and my arms slip from the steering wheel. The bright lights still flow through the freeway, but even frenzied people, loud country music, and a Monster Assault aren't enough to keep me awake at three a.m. Especially after fifteen hours of driving.

I pull over into an open patch by a 7-11. I yank the sleeping bag from the backseat and get the truck bed ready. I arrange myself so the metal curves in the bed won't poke into my back then finally give up on that.

I should've thought to bring a mattress, but, when the world is falling into panic, sometimes you forget things.

I should've thought of a lot of other things, too, like why Kokab might be on Earth.

Anna said Kokab's good.

If a war comes, will she support it?

Have faith that she won't.

Dad's helping his neighbors, friends in need, to survive. Even if they're friends from another planet. He wouldn't trust them without a good reason.

But what if he's wrong?

Have faith he isn't.

It's hard to believe in Dad. Harder than anyone else. Anna, I can excuse because of her rough childhood. Kokab, because she didn't understand how to feel until recently. Maybe because I expect more from him. He is, after all, my dad. Dads should never do anything to hurt their children.

HAVE FAITH.

I study the sky. September has some of my favorite constellations. Indus. Vulpecula. Dad taught me that stuff about stars before he got too busy, and I got angry at him for what I thought he was. A nut job. Maybe what he actually is. I'm not sure anymore, but I chew on Anna's words about having faith to keep myself positive. Of all the people to give me hope.

Here, I can't see the spaceships anymore. Here, it's easy to forget the world is falling apart.

I nestle deep into the bag to avoid the chills of early September nights. A car pulls up and parks beside me. A small, wimpy thing that'd get pummeled by my truck. The engine growls in death.

A girl steps out. Her car lights reflect against her nose.

Wait a sec. I know her. "Ags?" I sit up, and she moves next to the tailgate. It's hard to make out her face in the dark, but I think she's smiling.

"I have been looking for you," she says. "Aren't you headed to a meeting in New York?"

"What, how'd you—"

Her nose starts vibrating in a way that's definitely not normal, and it clicks. Oh. "You're an alien too, huh?" Her weird skin. Her freakish mannerism. Guess I always try to ignore what's right in front of me.

Still, that doesn't explain how she knows about the meeting. I dig for my flashlight, flipping the switch on, and point the beam at her. It's definitely Ags, but there's something different about the way she looks. I'm not sure what.

"Oh, my people do a great job watching you all via camera," she says. "We're researchers, and there was an unfortunate glitch in our invisibility shields. We didn't mean to be seen or to cause a panic. I need to come to the meeting to explain why our spaceships are in the sky. "

"What?" I say. I cling to my sleeping bag. The spaceships? I assumed they were Kokab's. This is better. Some curious researchers learning about mankind. Not Kokab's people to take over. They aren't the cause of the panic.

Hallelujah Jesus.

"Really?" I say. Her lips twist strangely, but only for a second. She frowns and sighs. "Yes, and I love Earth so much," she says. "I can't handle all the panic. There's only one way to save humanity now."

"How?"

She climbs up onto the truck bed and places her hand on my bare arm. Her fingers are clammier than I remember and give me chills. "I must get into that meeting with Joe and Kokab. And I must tell the leaders of the world the truth."

I unlock the truck and gesture toward the door. "Sure, I'll talk to my dad to try to get you in. If you're having car trouble, we can find a place to take it in the morning after we get some sleep. I have blankets if you need them."

"Thank you. I just hope things can return to the way they should be." She sidles into my truck.

The more I know, the more I realize I don't know. Ags being an alien, honestly, doesn't even freak me out at this point. And if Ags is an alien, who's to say there aren't more? Maybe there really is more that Dad knows about Kokab too. "You're real passionate about people, huh?" I say.

Her eyes gleam, a sort of fire, that freaks me out a little. "Oh, believe me, I'm very passionate about mankind."

KOKAB

144 PEOPLE LINE up outside Walmart before the store opens. Joe, Brian, and I speed past in one of the president's limos.

The closer we come to New York, the more noise crowds my ears. Yelling. Swearing. Whispers. If it was not for the vehicle we are in, it would take hours to get to our destination.

We drive past Central Park. Humans crowd outside the gate. Their sweat clings to my nose, and they mutter complaints and excitedly discuss. Two groups stand in separate locations on the lawn. Both are diverse, filled with men and women of different ages and nationalities. The main difference besides the distance is the signs they hold.

On one side, the signs read WELCOME TO EARTH, WE 🖤 ALIENS WITH CRAZY HEALING POWERS, IM UR BIGGEST FAN. HEAL ME.

But the other side is not so positive: KILL THE ALIENS, WE'RE WITH HOLLYWOOD. ALIEN INVASIONS END BAD. One holds a large poster with my face on it and has fifty-seven slashes across it.

This is why Brian had us hide out in his bunker for the last day before the meeting. People are afraid of me.

Humans' emotions are a strange thing. Both reactions come from the same inciting incident, yet are opposite.

I wouldn't have been able to understand how people could feel two different ways about an issue before, but now I do. Because I feel the same way about myself.

Torn. Am I a monster? Am I good?

I cling to my seatbelt, which grinds into my fingers.

What if I do fail? Then what will happen to humans? Humans have helped me. Will Foxians really attack? But my people do not deserve to die either.

Then I must succeed.

My hairs prickle and rise up from a flat position. It is such a human-like physical response.

I am 99.78 percent certain I am scared.

Joe glances toward the back seat with a sad smile. "Just ignore them," he says. "They don't know you or anything about you."

"Thank you for the compliment, Joe," I say, pushing aside my unpleasant feelings. It is necessary to focus on my task. "I give gratitude for all your aid."

The limo driver turns right at a red light, only to turn in to more people streaming the streets. A religious leader preaches about the end of the world.

"Course," Joe readjusts his glasses. "I would do anything to help you."

I glance at the sky. We are far away from the spaceships, but here, people are still mad. They have seen my inhumane face on video. They know Joe claimed to meet aliens. They saw the news story about the hospital. And the ships. They can connect the dots, even though they are wrong.

The spaceships do not belong to Foxians. "I do not know where those spaceships came from," I tell Joe.

"I know," he says. "Foxian ships look different."

I intend to ask him how he knows such a fact, but we drive up to a new crowd standing outside the hotel where we will be staying.

How did they know I would be here? Or is it a coincidence? I press against the door handle as fear overtakes me.

I must do this. I have been given an order, but there is much more to it than that.

I get out, and Brian moves in front of me, shielding me. I should be grateful for protection, but my heart pounds faster and faster like there's something horrible about Brian that I do not know. Or cannot remember? What could it be?

Two of the president's guards also follow. It is not that I need their protection, but I do not want to hurt people.

Brian blocks me from the crowd as we make our way to the door. A woman in a tie-dye shirt screams, rushing toward me. "Kill the alien! Kill the alien!" she says.

A security guard reaches for his pocket, but I block him from getting the gun. "Do not," I say. "It will only cause more panic." He nods and pulls his hand away. Brian plunges forward and tackles the woman to the ground, and we rush inside.

I can still hear their screams as we make it into our hotel room. The walls do not cover the sound from me, but I wish they could.

When the Elder Ones sent me to Earth, did they know there would be so much pain?

"Call me if anything seems off," says Joe, glancing at the guards at my door as I step into my room. I sit inside and ponder the words I must use. But then I hear familiar clunky footsteps in the hall.

"Carter?" I throw the door open. I take in his slightly blemished but beautiful face, and for a moment, I do not know what to do.

Carter hates me, I believe.

"I apologize," I say. "I should have told you my purpose for coming to Earth earlier. But I won't fail to persuade the council. I don't want to let humans down."

I stop talking because he wraps his arms around me. It is hesitant, and by the way his lips purse, I can tell he's torn.

"It's okay," he says. "I have faith in you."

His arms collapse, and his cheeks redden slightly enough that only I would notice, and I know he is not certain of his words.

But if Carter can try to accept things after all I've done, then there is hope that others will, too. And he, Joe, Mama, Megan, and others have taught me how it can be possible.

The elevator dings, and Ags walks through. What is *she* doing here?

She was under stress when she attacked. Be nice, I order myself.

"How is your hand?" I say.

I know it is fine, but it seems like a normal enough greeting.

"Hand?" She blinks. Why does she not understand my question?

"From two nights ago?" I prompt.

"Aaah, yes. It is well." There is something different about her. Her posture? Her diction? She notices my gaze and drops her shoulders. "I'm here to explain why my spaceships are in the sky. I want to help."

Good, that may benefit my case. "I am glad you are here."

Even Ags can get over her hatred of me.

"Where's my dad?" says Carter, "It's time I finally hear what he has to say about aliens."

Chapter 23

AGS

The white walls blend together in my windowless cell. There is nothing to surround or distract me from the cruel truth.

I focus on the smooth door, wishing for the security guard who comes every so often to feed me, wishing for something to pull me away as the Eldest One's words come crashing upon me.

All it took was one measly vision...

I'm the villain in this story.

It is because of me that Yadians got scared, and it was my persuasive arguments that pushed them to act when we failed. This is what the Eldest One wanted all along.

I still don't understand his plan completely, but I know one thing. I was played, and I fell for it. He wants to take over Earth, and if he's working with Hos, maybe Yadia too.

I suck in, inflating my lungs, attempting to scream. I want to scream like the man in Edvard Munch's painting, his face elongated, mouth dropping. My own Yadian mind is shrieking, and I need to break through the terror enveloping me. But it comes out as a little squeak. Again.

I thrash against the ground, beating it with my palms. At least I'm strong enough now to hit with power, the pounding almost as satisfying as a real scream would be.

Will I be stuck in this body forever? Probably. A Foxian I decided so quickly to hate.

I don't pray. I should prostrate across the ground I can't feel and plead for aid. But, would the gods want to hear from me? I have proven myself to be a terrible guardian.

A short beep rings outside my cell, the call of a visitor. Finally. A relief to distract me from my self-inflicted torment.

The security guard who locked me in here steps inside. The door closes behind him. He hands me the powder packet. The same nothing I've tasted earlier. Empty.

"This will provide sufficient nutrients for two days," he says, staring forward.

I grasp him by the ankle of his long leg, twisting him toward me. "Let me go. Please, release me." Maybe he will obey? "I need to go back to my body. The Eldest One stole it. I need to warn humans. I *need* to."

My voice raises. It surprises me how much I can actually feel in this body. That is one thing to be grateful for. Ags, weak and vulnerable *me*, would probably die from sorrow.

"What is your name?" I ask if only to distract myself.

"Brederion Ahgraama Hoxia. Or Bred to be convenient." He turns to leave.

"Wait," I say, an order he has not been commanded to refuse.

"What is your ranking?"

His face twitches as he responds. "I am Different."

He exits. A glimmer of light appears as he opens and then shuts the door, leaving me alone in the dark with nothing to preoccupy myself from this torture. I curl up into a ball, trying to escape from Dante's eighth layer of hell.

CARTER

THERE WAS a time when I had to look up to Dad when he was so tall, and I wondered if I'd ever grow to be as big as he was. Now, he has to look up to me, and he shoves his glasses up on the bridge of his nose, tilting his head upward.

I shut the hotel door, even though I get Kokab will still hear. Hallmark plays on the TV. Brian lingers at the table drinking a Coke, not even ashamed he's spying on us.

"Can you give us a sec?" I ask Brian, who gets up grumbling and leaves.

Dad slowly exhales. "I know it's a lot to take in. I assume you know everything...the aliens. Why they are here?"

Faith is a funny thing. I used to have so much faith in him. And then, because he said something others thought was crazy, I stopped. And I was wrong. I was way, way wrong. Aliens are real. They're all around us. But now I'm having doubts again about his sanity.

Life was simpler when I could believe everything he told me without thought, when I was a kid prying dried glue from my fingertips and daring my friends to eat worms.

I'm not sure how to talk about all this scary stuff, and I don't even know if I can trust him. But at this moment, as the world falls apart around me, I *need* to. Because I need my dad like I would as a nine-year-old kid.

"Dad." I groan and melt into his arms. He wheezes a little, probably because it's hard to hold up a guy fifty pounds larger than him. But then he wraps his arms around me.

It's funny. After I met Kokab, I dreamed of the moment I'd tell him I knew aliens were real. I imagined sitting on our porch swing, swapping feel-goods. But here we chill in a Marriott hotel room with Hallmark on, and telling him I know he's right would be pointless. I missed my chance.

So what can I say? That I'm proud of him for risking everything to help billions of aliens survive, at the possible cost of humanity?

I'm not there yet. Out of the window, a bunch of people with signs still stand. A woman wearing a green alien suit punches a man with a NOT OUR PEOPLE sign.

Things are too crazy though, so I gotta at least try to get somewhere closer.

"I don't get it," I say. "Why help them? Why not run screaming to the president that aliens are coming?"

"Don't they deserve a chance to live out their lives too?" Dad asks.

I shrug and turn off the TV because the lady in a billowing dress kissing the cowboy distracts me. Nobody deserves to die.

Dad takes a seat at the small table. He pushes away Brian's bag of chips and motions for me to sit next to him. Again, being in a hotel room with a pile of food on the table, unsure of Dad, isn't exactly how I thought this sharing moment would go. But real life isn't quite like the imagination, is it?

I plop down next to him and study my fingers. He clutches my face, maintaining eye contact. My dad's always been the one afraid to talk to me. Out of all the wild things in the world, I'm the only thing that can scare him.

Dad inhales. "When you were younger, Kokab's leader came to Earth to learn more about us. I'm not sure why. But I stood up for the Eldest One. That's his name. They..."

He trails off and grasps my arm, and I let him. His focus drifts to some red roses in the painting on the wall, but it's like he's looking somewhere else. "I'm sorry, Carter. They were torturing him."

He grimaces, and his voice crackles. "I figured telling the world would get them to stop."

I think he's ashamed. But he did what he could to save someone's life. And I hated him because of it.

"But it didn't," he says. "They tortured his body. Until one day, he just disappeared."

He reaches into the mini-fridge, grabs a bottled water, and takes a sip. Then he sucks down the whole thing and stares at me. He looks like he's seen a slaughtered bunny. "Want one?" he asks.

"Nahh, those things cost a million bucks," I say.

He sets his water bottle against the table and clings to the lid.

"Actually," he says, squinting like he wants to close his eyes to reality, "the worst thing was I might have let them do it. There was something about him that was so animalistic. But I knew he was an intelligent life form because I'd met a Foxian before. As a kid."

"You did?"

He finally looks up at me. "Yes, I believed she was my imaginary friend. But when I grew up, I realized she was real. She saved my life, Carter. And all of America. And after she died, I knew I owed it to her to help Kokab. Even if things fall through for the other aliens, I needed to help Kokab."

I can tell there's more to the story, but I let Dad pause. He shoves some potato chips into his mouth, and they erupt beneath his teeth.

"Because of how much she did to save the country, I'd die to protect Foxians if I had to. But I'm still sorry I made life so hard for you, Carter. I'm sorry I ruined your childhood."

I'm curious what he means, but it all seems like a conversation for another day. This moment is more important. I give Dad a little side hug, and he pats my back for about half a second. "I'm sorry too," I say. There's much more I want to say, but I think he knows what I mean.

I'm sorry for yelling. I'm sorry for calling you a crazy lunatic. I'm sorry for not believing. For even minutes ago, questioning your sanity. For even now, questioning.

We both know it means more. So much more.

"Who was she?" I ask when he starts looking a little less wounded.

"Oh." He blinks and then grins at me. "The Foxian? She was Kokab's mother."

KOKAB

PROTESTORS FLOCK the pavement outside the UN headquarters.

203 of them scream as I exit the limo. The guards circle our small group and point their guns outward as we make our way through the unruly crowd. A few people swear and continue their loud chant: "Not your place. Go back to space."

Again and again. One lady yells for me to die.

"Keep moving," Carter whispers urgently. A piece of me wants to travel through the crowd like a Foxian would, to walk straight and angle my arms robotically, to consider their cries as meaningless. However, I do not. Even if I chose to, it's unlikely that I could still block out the emotions. Pain is real for me. I bend my head and follow Ags, Brian, and Joe.

This crowd's hatred toward me is raw. No one has hated me like this before. But I understand.

A teenager spits on me, and a guard swivels toward him and thrusts his gun against the boy's chest. Joe steps in front of me, even though I should be the one protecting him. The spit dribbles down my cheek.

We make it through the doors of the skyscraper without an attack. My heart pounds in my chest, so strong it almost seems like the part of the body is, in fact, associated with emotions. Each beat is for someone. Carter. Carter. Carter. Joe. Joe. Joe. Mama. Jason. My mother.

Even Anna.

I may have been sent here to follow a direct order, and I have never disobeyed the Eldest Ones before. But now, it is not a simple matter of obedience. I choose to succeed because these people matter to me.

Carter stops outside of the general assembly hall since he is not invited. He toes the granite floor with his boots. "Look, Kokab. I do believe in you," he says, but I am still not certain if he does. "Do us humans a solid."

It is so simple, yet his words make me feel 63 percent better. I want to hug him or touch him, but what if he still hurts because of me?

We stand there, awkward for 2.6 seconds, and then he wraps his fingers in mine. He compliments my Peter Pan collar and braid. (I tried to copy Mama's styling.) His heart beats fast. I think he is afraid too. For humanity? For Foxians?

For *me?*

I want to lean in and allow the scent of woods and diesel to encompass me, but there is not time. There may never be a time to know if I might have had a relationship with him. My plans for success today probably mean I will not see him again.

The guards gesture to leave, and so I let go. I stride into the assembly hall, head high. Joe, Brian, and Ags all follow me. A line of reporters and security guards follow behind them.

The hall seats 1,800, but there are 2,002 here. Humans push against walls and jostle each other. Their whispered commentaries about me ring in my ears.

"It's her. She looks almost human."

"No, not human at all."

"Do you think they are telling the truth? That the Foxians will come and live in peace?"

"I doubt it."

"No, not human at all. A monster."

"Did you see the viral video? Almost predator-like."

They speak a variety of languages, but my chip interprets them all for me before the interpreters do.

People in thousands of skin tones, all ranges of brown and beige, fill every space of the room, dressed in various cultures' attire: suits, peplums, frocks, turbans, and even two muumuus.

We move to the seats reserved for my party on the front row. The prime minister of Great Britain, an obese man with an angular jaw, leans toward the USA president and whispers about how the world is doomed. Camera crews set up their gear. Reporters hunch over laptops, staring directly at me without shame.

These meetings are always scripted. Every line is written ahead of time, but today I will go off-script. I could not tell Joe about my plan because I was not sure if he would go along with it. The UN president calls the meeting to order. He is generally supposed to open the meeting, followed by the general secretary, and then Brazil, but today the floor is mine. It is not every day an emergency meeting is regarding an alien invasion.

I approach the mic. "I am Kokab. I am not of this world. I came here to save my people. That is my purpose."

I explain how our planet is dying, and I am acting as a scout.

"We do not wish for war, but without your aid, billions of us will die," I say. "We only need to survive. We will live in Antarctica. We reproduce at the same rate that we die. It should be ample room for us to survive. Even when the ice melts, there will be a quarter-acre remaining for each of us. We will sign contracts agreeing to stay away from humans unless they enter our gifted territory. You have no real use of Antarctica. To prove my sincerity as an ambassador to Foxia, I offer myself in exchange for safe passage to an unused territory of Earth. I will be your servant. You, as a council, can decide what you want from me. I can teach you advanced technologies, allow you to study the nanobots flowing through my blood. I can heal people. You can pull me apart for research if that is what you desire. I can help you improve the world. I will be yours forever, to use as you please."

In his plush seat, Joe presses his glasses against the bridge of his nose repeatedly. He whispers so only I can hear over the commotion: "You did not tell me about this."

"That is a generous offer," says the Barbados minister, a lady with an afro and pierced lips, nodding toward me.

"Use you?" the prime minister scoffs. "We could use you now if we wanted. Now, tell me, if we say no, what will your kind do? Leave us alone? Or will you attack us to get what you want?"

I swallow. The eyes of 1,997 people dwell on my face. Only a few turn toward each other to gauge others' reactions or continue taking notes.

Rescue us, or we will kill you. It is a tactic Brian suggested I use in the meeting, but I do not want to use it. At least not anymore.

It leaves humans with little choice but to comply. And I do not wish to instill fear. I have seen the consequences of fear on many faces. I saw it on the people in the streets shouting for me to die, on Drew when I broke his hand, and even on Carter when he watched the video of me destroying the piano. Fear caused the chaos.

Brian stands up, and eyes turn to him. I shake my head at him.

"You must realize it is likely that the aliens may attack if you do not comply with our requests," he says. "They are desperate for survival. They are far superior in technological abilities, and they will take Earth out of necessity for survival."

I am grateful Carter is not here for those words.

There are a few gasps, and the president glances over at the secretary general, who is swearing quietly, and whispers, "I told you."

I swallow again. "That is not our intention, however. We prefer peace. Please, we do not request your time, resources, or aid. We simply need permission to utilize unwanted land. Tax us if you must. Fight us if we do not keep our agreement. But provide us a chance to come quietly and peaceably. Help us."

"Why should we trust what *you* say as the truth?" says the prime minister of Barbados. Her eyes scrutinize mine, and I am 90 percent confident she desires to believe me.

"You should trust me," I say, contemplating the ragged mother in the hospital elevator, how she looked at her newborn infant and wanted to protect it. That is how I feel about mankind as well. I want to keep people safe, and I want to protect them.

"Because I love humans." It is sentimental and may not validate my trustworthiness to them. But to me, it is everything. "And I hope humans can come to love my kind as well."

I love humans.

I love eating Mama's grits and listening to Jason's confusing knock-knock jokes. I love Megan and her massive card collection. And I love Carter, not necessarily in a romantic way, because I am not sure yet how that would feel. But I love how he always opens my truck door and kisses his mama's cheeks. I love the way it felt when he pulled me into the fountain.

However things end up today, I will try to help humanity. Maybe Ags's idea to terraform another planet is not so bad after all. Can I convince the Eldest Ones of her plan if the humans do not agree today?

Please, humans, choose wisely.

The meeting goes on for minutes that feel like hours. Statements and speeches are made. Experts evaluate the issue til a diplomat finally thinks to ask the the most important question:

"But, if you do not want war, why are the spaceships hovering over Georgia?"

Ags raises her hand. No one follows the script anymore. "Those are not Kokab's species. They are a different species of aliens. Yadians. And the Yadians are here because they *do* want to start a war with you."

350 voices blend together, a painful cacophony in my eardrums. The guards redirect their guns toward her as if this second they realize she is here. War? Ags's kind protects Earth. Ags said it was an accident that the Yadian spaceships appeared in the sky. It cannot be true, but why would she lie?

My heart beats again, faster and faster. There cannot be war. I was supposed to stop it. I was not going to fail.

Ags glances at me, and her mouth twists a little on the left side. I know that smile.

You are not Ags.

Chapter 24

AGS

The blank walls surround me as I lay on the floor of my cell. There is no cold. No heat. No sound except my organs writhing inside of me. Only a pellucid whiteness encompasses all my senses until I am nowhere. Nothing.

It could be minutes, but it seems like years, and the torture continues.

I drag my legs to my chest, squeezing tighter until I get a slight tingly sensation. I cling to any good memories I have. But I spent most of my life examining people from a spaceship. My best memories don't belong to me. They never have, but they are still mine to love.

A kid received a Power Wheels truck, the present of his dreams for Christmas, and ran around screaming about how much he loved Santa. "He's real!" he'd said. "Santa even remembered the blue wheels." A Jewish girl celebrated her bat mitzvah. Music mingled with the cries of laughter in the backroads of Tel-Aviv-Yafo. Her mother squeezed her fingers, and her dad nodded his head. "You're a woman now," he told her. Princess Kate's wedding. (Everyone watched that.)

It's okay that they didn't belong to me because they belonged to the humans I loved. It's enough, isn't it?

It's a lie.

It isn't enough because I failed my humans when they needed me the most. I was supposed to protect them.

I squeeze my eyes shut. A swallowing blackness replaces the white.

A short knock at the door forces me to sit up. "Hi, Bredrion." I recognize him by the sound of his march. It's off for a Foxian.

"What do you need—" I don't finish the phrase because as the door slides open, light inundates the room, streaming over the walls, making even its perfect smoothness reflect minor cracks and blemishes. It's a radiance so extreme I have to squint. A woman glides inside, followed by Bredrion. She's familiar, but I can't place her.

She runs her fingers through her white hair. The wrinkles on her face waltz across her skin and almost seem to beam. She stands erect, and a light radiates from every particle of her as if it's bursting through her fingertips from within. Still old, but somehow she's breathtaking beyond any being I've seen. She gives me a goofy grin.

"Els?" I say. "Els..." I repeat the words because it's almost too hard to believe myself. "How'd you get here? What happened to you?"

Els winks and lifts me off the floor. "Finally remembered where I stored my body." She chuckles and does a perfect little chicken dance. She's as silly as ever. She has two noses, transparent skin, but only one heart: Foxian, but not the Foxian I know.

My eyebrows drop a centimeter, which in this body is basically the same thing as fainting or running around the room screaming.

"That saggy, orange body's not mine, sweetheart," she says. "I left mine when I journeyed to Earth, but it's been a few thousand years. I hid it in a spot so good I forgot where I put it."

What is she talking about? It's hard to process anything after being in a blank room for so long.

She continues. "The Yadians made that old Yadian body for me after Abaddon's War and let me hide as a protector of humans. It was kind of them. I'd lost everything in the war against my brother."

I stare at the person in front of me, this beautiful warrior woman bright enough to light up a room.

"Your *brother*? You mean...the Eldest One is your brother? Meaning you are...?"

"The princess in the popular Foxian war story I once told you. Yes, yes—" she says, pointing to herself. "I ran away from my brother to Earth when he won the war. But he traveled to the planet and thoroughly convinced me over the course of years that he'd changed his mind about feelings. About everything. Luckily, when he showed up on my spaceship today in your body and wrestled his way out the door, it joggled my memory about where I hid my body."

I inhale. My hearts skip the smallest beat. My fingers loosen. "You're a Foxian. A Foxian?"

"Yes, dear. You're very wrong about us, you know. We aren't evil. But not all of us had a chance to learn as you have. But even though you didn't give us a chance, I'm going to give you one."

She gyrates in a circle. The faint glow of her skin spirals around her, smothering her so I can no longer see her body. Els is light.

To my utter shock, Brederion's mouth lifts in something that resembles a smile. He shifts. His erect body drops to the floor as he bows his head in perfect symmetry with his body.

With all the light, it's easier to see the darkness in *me*.

He's not a monster, is he? And I didn't give him a chance. I was wrong. I was wrong about everyone. The Foxians. Their potential to feel. My fingers shake as Bred kisses Els's feet.

"My princess," Bred says. "There was a rumor among the Differents you would return. We have waited for you."

Els slips her fingers into mine. She grabs me and yanks me through the doorway. Her touch is lukewarm, but by the way her fingers radiate, I imagine it'd be the hottest thing ever in a normal body. "It's time to leave," she whispers. "You can redeem yourself yet."

KOKAB

At first, I assumed the Eldest One spoke truth. The Elder Ones are Perfect.

However, by the very fact that he claims to be Ags, he lies. It does not make sense. Elder Ones do not lie, yet he is lying.

Bodies rise and shout. Stressed adults' heartbeats pound in my ears. They sweat. They are afraid. I did not want fear. I was going to succeed. Everyone was supposed to be safe.

203 UN members stand. I wish I could comfort them. But there is nothing I can say to appeal to all 412 arguments.

"They will slaughter you." The Eldest One quivers in Ags's frame. He scrambles to the front of the room, gestures for me to move away from the microphone, and leans into it. I hesitate, but I still do not know his intentions. He is the Eldest One, so they should be correct. "You do not have the technology to stop them. I brought you this message because I care about humans. I don't want my people to hurt them. Foxians can fight them, though. Foxians can protect you. Just trust them. Let them direct you to conquer the Yadians. It's your only hope."

He glances at me as if he wants me to verify, and I have always obeyed an Elder One. I did think they were perfect.

Why is he doing this? Is it true? Is he inhabiting Ags's body as a means to protect humans? I would assume he is, but his tone crackles and screeches. A glint shivers in his eyes, something dark. It does not feel like love.

But how would I know? I am only beginning to understand emotion.

I shake my head. I am unclear what is happening. The crowd stirs among me. Their words grow more and more frenzied, distracted.

His lips twist upward into a scowl. Since he is in Ags's frame, his heart pounds quickly. *Buh. Bum. Buh. Bum. Buh-bum-bum-bum.* His eyebrows furrow in anger.

Some in our council do not agree that we should try to maintain peace. Those were his words. I had forgotten them. As I study his face, his darkening eyes, I realize he did not mean another council member. He was the one who argued for war.

This is wrong.

I reach toward him. He may be my leader, and he may have selected me because I was perfectly obedient. But now, I make choices for myself.

"You are lying," I say before I realize the words have come out. "You are lying."

The Eldest One's lip drops 1.2 centimeters. He sucks in.

"No," he says. "I came because I love humans and want to help."

I continue. "He's a Foxian. He's lying. The Yadians will not hurt you. They are protectors. You do not have to worry."

It does not matter. The humans aren't listening. They yell over one another, no longer willing to open their hearts to what I have to say.

"Take them both," the USA president says. He leaps from his seat, confusion still on his face. "Just take them both."

Guards speed toward us, but a color flashes across the room. The Eldest One tosses a small glowing ball right at the president. It explodes and instantly encompasses him. Purple dust writhes upward and spreads around his frame. He screams and collapses toward the floor. He stiffens, jaw dropped open as he lays sprawled out on the ground.

His breath slows. The president of the United States is going to die.

Diplomats scream and run from the room. Hundreds of chairs clatter across the floor as the dark curls away from the president and stretches across the auditorium.

I rush toward him to help. I can still revive him. But guards thrust their guns against the Eldest One and me. The Eldest One glances at the spreading smoke and disappears.

It must be Yadian technology with their devices to become invisible and block sound like I've seen Ags use. I hear the sound of dropping bodies and the absence of breath as I am dragged from the room.

Dead. Some are dead already. Where is Joe? I see Brian grab him and pull him out of the room as he tries to fight his way toward me.

The guards rush out the door, and I pull them off like they are small children now that I know the guards are safe from the gas. No one follows as I sprint back inside. No one wants to die.

I am strong. The poison from the ball will take longer to affect me. I get to the president and stoop over him. I press my hands to his still forehead, and his eyes open as I command the nanobots to heal. "Leave this room," I whisper, and the president jets away.

I continue. I start coughing, but I need to revive more people. They rush out until there is only me.

And the dead bodies I couldn't save.

"That's right." Ags' voice is close to the door, but I don't see anyone. "That's perfect, Kokab. Now all the world leaders will love you and respect you. And when I kill you, they will only believe the truth: that a Yadian tried to murder everyone and Foxians saved them. And humans will worship me."

I cough as I race to the door, but I cannot run faster than 6.4 miles per hour. The poison courses through my lungs. I hear no voice, no breathing, but mine.

I run out of the UN building onto the lawn. Helicopters hover around; people cry and scream. Their angry faces turn toward me.

Many wanted me to die before. Maybe now they will have their wish.

I stumble to the lawn and fall forward. A familiar hand squeezes my shoulder. I look up into his blue earth-sky eyes. "Kokab, don't give up," Carter says. "Run." I nod and force myself to my feet.

Angry mob voices scream and feet slap behind me as I rush forward.

I will find the Eldest One, and I will stop him.

AGS

BREDRION LEADS us through the halls of the office. They're going to catch us. Oh blinking stars, they're going to catch us. Els's radiation makes us obvious.

Her glow spreads to the blank white walls, and it's almost like we travel through light. We reach the Office of the Elder Ones. Someone is inside; I can hear his or her breathing.

"I apologize," says Els. "This is the only way to find information. The Eldest One stores it in his office. I'll get past...whoever it is."

She randomly cackles and shoves the door open.

An Elder One is on the other side of it. His red robe hangs carefully over his shoulders. He's settled into the Eldest One's white desk, and he scrolls over the contents on a thin screen.

I know him. He is the Foxian who dashed inside the doors when I was taking the Youngling test. He was going to arrest me, wasn't he?

"Majesty Elsimmona." His blank face gives nothing away, but he prostrates across the floor. His robe fans out around his body, deep scarlet against stark white. "You came at last."

Els grins like Mona Lisa, and her eyes soften. "Please don't bow to me, Adderrora," she says.

Adderrora rises, still perfect in his posture, but there's something about his eyes. It's like Yas said about Kokab; emotions are present.

Els softens. Her voice becomes pure and beautiful like her. "Please, tell me. What is my brother doing? Is he going to save our people? Or ruin them?"

Aderrora hands the thin screen to Els. She transfers an image of an asteroid to my mind. "Perfect Foxians don't make mistakes. I was suspicious when the scientists missed it."

It takes me 1.3 seconds to understand, but I am in a Foxian body. It doesn't take too long.

"It was a lie. It was a lie. It was a lie. A lie," I repeat to myself.

There never was an asteroid. The Eldest One lied. He

downloaded falsified information to Foxians' nanobots to make them see an asteroid coming. Just like he did to me.

My humans should have been safe. Everyone should have been safe. There. Was. No. Asteroid.

None. How could he?

That *monster*, I think. But then, I stop myself because that's the same thing I thought about Kokab. And I was wrong.

"Why?" I say. "Why would he do this? How could he do this?"

Els focuses on the screen as the asteroid hurtles toward Foxia; the sky darkens. Foxians scream. She flinches. "I think he's angry because Foxia's falling apart, and Earth's growing through my leadership. Maybe he believes I run the better planet."

Adderrora nods. I never knew what Els did to protect Earth, but she is the head guardian. Perhaps she does more than any of us realize.

"It appears he's been sending messages to a Yadian named Hos. And a human named Brian. Hos plans to murder the governor, take his seat, and allow the Foxians to defeat them. Abaddon wants Yadia, Foxia, and Earth."

"All of the ones I love," says Els. Her glow fades a little, and I grasp her right hand.

"I never should have hoped his goals were to help his people," says Els. "But he spent so much time convincing me when he came to Earth. He collected data on humans to learn how to be like them. He seemed different. I thought I could trust his sincerity. He's my brother, after all."

"No, that's what makes you so much better than him. You have faith," Adderrorra says. "And that's why I had faith and waited for you to stop all these awful nanobots that make our people emotionless."

I turn to Els. We have to fight. I never knew if I would be able to fight, if it was needed, but now I know I must. I must fight the Eldest One. And I must kill him. Even if that means destroying my own fragile, deeply feeling Yadian body to do so.

"Els, how are we getting off this planet? The only way I can leave is by transporting to my body, and the Eldest One stole it. Are there other bodies to do the mind transfer?"

Els shakes her head. "He only had the one hidden away for himself. He didn't know I was hiding my body too. But there can't be more. If they had enough resources to make more, they would have just shipped Kokab using that method."

Els taps her chin and then cackles again. Her white hair churns around her face and weaves across her shoulders. "There is a giant spaceship sitting outside with billions planning to board. It's simple, really. We just need to steal it."

CARTER

"Dad!" I rip past the masses of people who stream from the UN building to the streets of Roosevelt Island. I leap out of the way as an SUV skirts onto the sidewalk, followed by three black limos.

Their cries mingle together, but none are his.

"Aliens, aliens bombed us!"

"Run! Everyone, run! "

"Terrorists. Get out. Get out!"

The cars and fire engines scream and drown out my yells. So I holler louder. But so does everyone else.

Dad. Dad. *Dad.*

A kid stands frozen in place, sobbing as people rush around him. He's gonna get pummeled. I weave toward him, but I'm too far. A woman grasps his fingers and tugs him away. I sprint around the building with my cell in hand. I press dial until my thumb numbs.

But he doesn't answer. I stumble onto my knees as a diplomat knocks me down, and my rib cage crunches under his pressure. He keeps running, but I get back up and ignore the pain.

Maybe Dad didn't make it. Maybe he's still inside. "Dad!"

A guard staggers but manages to grasp me as I step toward the police officers who block the door. I recognize him. He went inside with Brian, Kokab, and Dad. He grabs my arm and drags me away. "Don't go in there, kid. The orange-nosed alien let off a bomb of some type. You'll die."

I'm almost as big as he is. I shove him down. "My dad. I got to find him."

"He's not in there. I saw him leave," he says. His posture melts, and he lifts his hand to his throat, hacking. The crowds thin. Where is my old man? Medical personnel carry injured people on gurneys. Injured or dead, I don't know. But he's not here. He's not okay—

"Carter."

I spin around, and there he is. His crooked glasses. He's got the serious look he always used to give me when I wasn't in trouble, but there was something he wanted me to know. Brian's next to him.

"We're not safe, Carter. If the crowd knew who *you* were connected to...in this mass terror... Well, you're lucky you're alive. We need to go."

He snatches my hand, and I'm a little kid trying to get across the street with oncoming traffic. Scared. Confused.

The streets are clogged. Police cars block the road to the UN building. Dad leads us to an underground parking lot about two blocks south of the UN building.

"What? This isn't where we parked."

Dad shifts past stalls until he gets to a normal gray door.

"No," says Dad. "There's a secret passage. It goes under the UN building too. That's how I got out. It can get us to safety. I've used it before. Brian too. We'll get you out of this commotion, and then figure out how to help Kokab."

Brian nods and pulls a key from his overcoat. We sprint inside.

Chapter 25

AGS

Els marches toward the sterile office doors behind Bredrion and the red-robed Foxian Adderrora. The entire building is empty. Only the air shifts quietly around us. We get to the entrance, and Els tugs her white hood down over her glowing face. She slides her fingers into her pockets.

I move in step with her. I've been in this body long enough, it's almost natural. Her heartbeat moves to the sound of our steps. It's beautiful, exact, but almost like a melodic chirping instead of a thrum. The beat of her heart gives me something similar to hope, if this body feels hope.

But when the door opens, the feeling dissipates.

Thousands of Foxians march through the one long street. Their feet drill against the ground like a rainstorm. A perfect, massive rainstorm.

"They're leaving," I whisper. My orange Yadian hands would get clammy, but these Foxian ones have a momentary tingle. How are we getting past *thousands* of Foxians to take this ship?

Els moves silently into the crowd, so we follow, making our way toward a group of Elder Ones on the deck of the ship. All at once, the Foxian steps halt. And we halt with them. They stand in a long line, evenly spaced. The smooth sound of the hatch opening thunders against the silence all around us.

Els slides past the Foxians, who do not react to her movements until she reaches the stairs. We follow slowly behind her as she starts to climb them.

"Boarding begins at 68:15," says an Elder One to her. "Remain in line until directed to move forward."

Els nods but continues to shuffle up to the top of the stairs. She lifts her hands to her hood and thrusts the fabric down, then turns to face the crowd. Light radiates from her and weaves through the clear skins of the Foxians, filling their bodies with brightness. We are swallowed in brilliant white light.

"It is I, your rightful ruler, Princess Elsimmona," she yells so the thousands can hear. "My people, I am afraid the Eldest One has lied to you. The asteroid is not real."

She places her fingers to her heart and pain etches in her dark Foxian eyes. It's real. As real as anyone's pain.

And suddenly it is not quiet. Most stand still, but a few murmured whispers spread through the mass. Three or four get on their knees. Bredrion, Adderrora, and I leap up six stairs at once and pin the other Elder Ones to the ground before any of them have a chance to give orders to stop us.

"This is the truth. He did lie. You are all safe to remain in your homes," Adderrora says. His hands clamp over the mouth of an Elder One. The Elder Ones struggle against our grip, and Adderrora points down at the crowd.

"You six, come arrest them," he orders, and dozens of bodies shift toward us to obey. "Their mouths must be covered until they are placed into a prison cell." Our hands cling to their mouths as they march up the stairs. I hold as tightly as I can as an Elder One in tan thrashes against me. If he breaks free, he can order them to arrest us instead. The Elder Ones are lifted and carried away. Probably shouldn't, but in this instance, I praise the gods that Foxians obey without question.

"By their walking speeds, they will place them in the cells at 68:12. That should give us enough time to exit before they give a command for them to get us," Adderrora tells Els.

I turn to slide into the hatch, but Els grabs my hand, and her glow engulfs it.

"Wait," she says. "There may not be an asteroid, but my people cannot truly live under these circumstances. They aren't all ready for Earth. But I think some of them are. Are you willing to let Foxians come?"

The question is so big. Opposite of what I wanted. But all I feared was a lie, fabricated by the Eldest One. Foxians don't deserve to remain in this prison. Maybe, perhaps possibly, Earth will benefit from them. I nod.

She turns to face the still crowd. But there are slight lifts of eyebrows, bare twitches in reaction to the princess, a few flushed faces, and some nodding heads.

"Are there any here who wish to come to Earth? Who want to discover what it's like to be free? Come if you desire. I'm giving you a choice."

It's silent at first. Then, Bredrion rises two steps and stares out at the crowd. "I am Different," he says simply. Then, he ducks through the ship doors. He's followed by not a few but dozens of individuals. Few compared to the thousands here and the billions of Foxians scheduled to board but so many more than I thought.

All quiet.

But they chose.

I enter the massive spaceship, and it lifts into the starry sky.

"Good luck, Els," I tell her. She grins at me and kisses my cheek.

She continues to visit with her people, and I make my way off the massive spaceship. I hop onto the scooter and drive at a quick speed toward the Yadian ship.

I need Yas's help to stop Hos. I hope he can forgive me.

I tear through the TurboShip almost noiselessly. It's different in this body. Through the overly bright walls, Yadians hunch over lunch and chatter about their day. Their laughs ring, and knives clatter against plates. One snorts as he mentions how much he hates Earth. So much noise.

I rush as fast as I can toward Yas. We don't have time. There's no stitch in my side, but my heart worries. The halls are bright, every beautiful detail of the paintings' movements leap at me.

But it's distracting. Now I understand why the Foxian world is so blank and sterile. It's hard to handle when every detail begs your attention and crowds your senses. Someone plods down the hall toward me, so I sidestep into a room to avoid discovery. What would people think if they found me in a Foxian body?

As I get close to the chem lab, I hear him breathing. It's hard to say exactly how I know it's him. But there's something awkward about the way he breathes. Almost nasally. But endearing.

I peek into the window and see him mixing bright blue compounds together. His eyebrows hunch downward, and orange pieces of hair twist behind his ears and stick out in various directions. His skin's so soft he reminds me of a French crescent roll.

I take in all the details in less than a second.

I shake my head. I've never seen my best friend like this before. It's...different. Is this what it's like for Kokab? So bright and vivid and overwhelming?

I push open the door and close it noiselessly.

I clear my throat, and Yas looks up. He leaps to his feet, the beaker rigid in his left hand. His orange skin goes yellow.

"Don't take a step closer, Foxian. I'll throw this at you. It-it's a deadly chemical." His voice squeaks. I step close, and his grip tightens. The muscles in his arm bulge. Who knew Yas actually had muscle? I guess in this body, I really can see every little detail.

"It's me...Ags," I breathe. My voice comes out calm compared to normal. I wonder if he will believe me.

"I'm sorry," I say. "You were right. About the Foxians. And I was stupid. Hos lied to me. He's going to try to kill the governor. He's making some kind of power deal with the Eldest One."

"Ags?" His grip releases barely and he peers at me. His eyes bore into mine. Does he see the same emptiness in me I saw in Kokab?

"Can you prove it?" he asks.

I bite my lip and slowly stand on one toe. I pirouette. It's much more perfect than I usually would do, but I'm still Ags. "I love my Mickey Mouse ears. And my favorite book is *The Scarlet Letter*."

"Okay."

"And on our first day at the Academy, I gave you a penny. You thought it was an expensive gift."

Yas yanks me in and wraps me into his arms. He sets his head on my shoulders, and his heavy breaths ring in my ears. But I can't feel any of it. He stares into my cold black eyes. I blink.

He must think I'm a monster.

"Ags, what happened to you?" he asks. "Why don't you have your body?"

I shake my head. "There's no time to explain. I need some of your ChemPods. Now."

He tears open cabinets and opens containers full of round, vibrant balls. He winces as one crashes toward the workbench. Balls clang together and leave a ringing in my ears. I rush to the cabinet and pull out four boxes at once. Yas's eyebrows raise. What does he think of me being so strong?

"Listen to me," I say as I lift the other nine boxes with one hand. "We have to stop Hos and the Eldest One. Can you help?" I study Yas. It's my word against Hos. "Do you believe me?" I ask him. These past few weeks, I've been nothing but cruel to him.

I rummage through the boxes until I find the ones Els told me to get. A minuscule red ball that reeks like a decomposing rat. And a glowing blue one.

Yas advises me on a few others that can help attack, and I tuck them into my pockets.

He grabs my shoulder, and I flinch. I'm not sure if I'll get used to not feeling anything. "I'm still angry at you," he says. "But I believe you. I'll help you. Lucky for you, the whole council's here trying to fix the trouble you caused. So I think we can get to the governor in time."

"The trouble I–" I'm interrupted when he wraps his arms around me again, and I love that his not-so-perfect Yadian heart races.

"I'm *really* sorry," I repeat.

I grab his hand and tug him out the door. "Now, let's go save three planets."

CARTER

I FOLLOW Dad through the tunnels. It's quiet, which is crap because it means I don't know what's going on outside. We turn left, and Dad halts.

"Mr. President?" Dad says. I halt before I step on the president with my boots. He's sprawled out facedown on the concrete. Is he *dead?*

The president groans, and Brian pulls him up against the tunnel wall and shines his phone's light into his eyes. "She saved me..." the president wheezes. "Your alien...resurrected me...magic... I couldn't get further... I need...help. I contacted... They're waiting outside the tunnel. Oh, good... It's my friend. Brian." He grins as his eyes swivel to Brian, and his head sags.

Brian lifts the president up over his shoulders and grunts. "Heavy guy," he says.

Dad and I travel behind him. Dad keeps glancing at me, probably to see how I'm handling an alien invasion. How I'm handling all of this.

People dropped like flies being attacked with bug spray. I'm not handling it. At all. At least Dad's fine. But is Mama safe?

Is Kokab? Last time I saw her, she was stumbling across the ground before she sprinted away. Is she alive, or did an angry mob attack her? No, she can hold her own. She has to be okay.

Please, Jesus, please.

Brian keeps swallowing like he's nervous. He's probably concerned about his family too.

We get to the light at the end of the tunnel and open the door to a tiny underground closet. Nothing fancy about it, but the room is filled with emergency supplies. Brian pulls an M-16 rifle from the wall.

"Left my gun behind for the UN meeting." He swallows. "But somebody needs to protect the president."

We unlock the exit to the closet and slip into a locked, shut-down laundromat that looks like it hasn't been in business for at least a decade. The place seems strange for a secret hideout but very subtle, not where I'd guess. The store stinks like dead critters, and when we make our way outside, the freezing cold grips me. I try to put on a tough guy face but inside I'm shaking in my boots. Cop cars holler in the distance. Brian stands with the president, extreme panic in his eyes. His head swivels, and his fingers shudder. What is wrong with him?

"You can do this," Brian says to himself.

He's a big guy, but he seems more scared than we are.

"The secret service knows where to find him, right?" I ask Dad.

"Should, yes."

He sets his arms on my shoulder, and I let him, even though I'm basically a grown man, because it's been one scary-as-death day.

"Glad you're okay," he says quietly. "And that we worked through our problems. Honestly, it's good to know you don't hate me."

I didn't realize how it must've seemed to him, all my hurting and whining all the time. The anger. I just let myself lose faith in him because all I could see was what the other kids said.

"Yeah," I say. "Hey, Dad, remember when we came to New York last? Not the city, I mean. The countryside?"

"Sure, and I let you use my twenty-thousand dollar telescope for the first time?"

"Yeah," I say. "That was a good day."

He nods, and we're quiet for a moment.

Down the block, a black limo drives toward us, and a group of well-dressed agents pile out and make their way over.

Brian pushes off the brick wall. "They're here already?" he whispers, and then he swears.

"Is everything—" I hear Dad say to Brian.

"Don't stop me," Brian says to Dad and points his gun down at the president's slumped body.

I turn toward Dad as he leaps away from the bricks and his feet pummel toward the president. A gunshot explodes in my ear. There's the thud of two bodies hitting the ground.

"No. No!" I hear Brian's voice. He turns to me, shock in his eyes. "I'm sorry, Carter. It wasn't supposed to be him."

My brain tries to grip what's happening. Killing the president is the worst kinda treason. This can't be real. I must be losing it with all the crazy going on.

"The president!" an agent says, and they dash toward us. They try to grab Brian, but he literally disappears into thin air. I can't process. Can't breathe. Can't think.

I look down, expecting the president to be dead on the sidewalk.

But the president isn't the one who's been shot.

AGS

I peer into the Ultra-Important Meeting Room, where the council stands, arguing about how to fix my issues. All the damage I've caused. Isn't that the truth?

In the middle of it all is my mother. She shoves her fingers firmly in her pockets, probably to refrain from twisting her hair, but she straightens her back and keeps her lips neutral. She stands in her sweeping robe and listens to each shrieking politician carefully. "She's just a kid," my mother says. "She's learning."

The governor paces on the opposite end of the room, avoiding eye contact with her, so I'm guessing Mom finally figured out his intentions and rejected him. At least I'm hoping that's the reason. The whispers and screams of council members speaking to the governor and with each other echo in my ear, loud enough that it's difficult for me to focus.

Where is Hos? He's not here. So does that mean we're here early enough to stop him? Or what if he's here invisibly? No, invisibility shields don't work inside war crafts. We're smarter than that.

Yas finally catches up to my Flash-like sprint and peers through the crack in the door as well. "He's not here," he states, which is obvious.

Maybe I was wrong? Maybe I misunderstood the Eldest One's words that Hos was involved in this? The conversation continues on, arguments rising until the council needs to call a break. They all exit (luckily through one of the five entrances to the room that isn't ours) until it's just the governor and my mom.

"Listen," says the governor. Ahh, his squeaky voice makes my now-perfect ears burn. How annoying. "I don't think you understood what I meant when I said I liked you. I—"

"I understood perfectly what you meant," Mom says coolly.

Hos waltzes inside.

I speed into the room, leaping in front of the governor to protect him. The governor shrieks as I realize my mistake. I'm a Foxian. Oh great...

"Help! Security!" He screams, not even thinking twice about kicking out his enemy.

He lifts his arms to cover his face and shoves himself behind Mom's body. What a coward.

"No, wait. It's me," I declare, but it's too late. He's made the call, and a plethora of guards tear through the door and pile on top of me. I toss most of them off, throwing one against the wall as gingerly as I can, but he lets out a colossal groan. I swipe the others onto the floor, and they tumble four or five feet in front of me before rushing at me again, grabbing at my arms. Some strike me, but those attempts stop as I hear the sound of bones shattering against my skin.

Yas runs inside, butting into a burly guard (I've never seen him act this brave before), but quickly gets tackled to the ground.

"Yas?" Mom looks toward him in confusion as he gets ripped from the room by the guard.

Hos's eyes grow wide like he realizes who I am, but then he smirks as he turns toward the governor. Dozens of guards pile on me now. I yank two off my shoulders and no longer bother to be careful as I toss them right toward Hos. But I can't stop one from throwing a silencing device over my mouth so I can't speak. I grasp the device, tugging at it, but super strength is no match for technology.

"I was rushing here to tell you that the Foxians are attacking," Hos says, as I try to pry myself free. They haven't gotten me out of the room yet, but as I get one off, two more quickly leap back on me.

Mom glances toward the door with a look of pure confusion in her eyes. Hos grabs the governor's arm. "It seems they sent an assassin here to take you down. Quick, governor, follow me. There's a hiding room in the back of the ship where no others will find you. Only a few have security clearance." I try to shriek as dozens of them drag me away, but, of course, my voice comes out muffled. I keep fighting them off, but they continue coming. They crowd together into one giant mesh of a mob, arms under me and over me, wrapped around every centimeter of my frame.

Don't follow Hos. Don't follow him. Mom! Mom! Look at me. It's me.

Mom's eyes stay focused on Hos as he leads her and the governor to the opposite side of the room toward what he says is a hiding room, but I'm pretty sure it's code for "death's door." As the guards reach the entrance to tow me out, a loud explosion booms through the ship, and pink smoke coils into the room. Yas dashes back in with the pink stuff coating his face. "I collected a few ChemPods too. Put my guard to sleep," he says, with the goofiest grin on his face. No time for this.

I twist through several guards' grips to gesture toward Hos. He opens his mouth like he's going to say something to stop Yas, and quickly, but he doesn't get a chance because Yas lets out a booming, "Stop everyone! Stop."

I blink. *Way to go, Yas.*

He swivels toward the governor and jerks his finger at me. "She's Ags. Hos is trying to kill you and take your seat."

Mom's face turns bright purple as she glances from me to Yas. She nods like she's figured it all out. Then, without hesitation, she runs to me. She plants herself in front of the guards, and raises her chin. "Stop," she demands. "It's Ags."

The guards' grips slacken, eyes filled with confusion, enough for me to break free. Mom squares her shoulders and nods to me. Simultaneously we dash toward Hos and plow into him. He gasps before I hit him hard enough to knock him out.

"I knew you could handle being a guardian." Mom smiles at me as she toes Hos's unconscious body.

"Yeah." I grin back. "And I guess you can handle being a councilor."

Mom pats Governor Ids's trembling back. Her hands are free, and instead of twisting her hair, she tucks it behind her shoulder. She clears her throat and points to Hos. "Arrest him," she says to a guard. "Arrest him."

KOKAB

THE STATUE OF LIBERTY sits on a 14.7-acre island, difficult to get to with all the frenzied traffic. Police vehicles race through the streets. Their screeching burns my ears and makes it harder for me to hear him. But I can hear Ags's, or rather, the Eldest One's, heartbeat nestled against Lady Liberty's torch.

I keep my face covered as I weave through the panic, unnoticed, uncertain if they are looking for me. If the people in the streets consider me guilty, though I am innocent. The poison writhes through my nervous system, and I struggle to focus.

The Eldest One could choose to block the sound of his heartbeat with his Yadian technology, which makes me 98.7 percent certain he wants me to hear him. No one else would be able to.

It does not matter what he wants with me because this is my best option to stop him from doing any more harm.

I plod down Morris Pesin Drive with my hood pulled up and let my ears guide me to his stolen heart. If he moves from his spot, I will sprint. Even if humans notice and attack me.

I have to do everything I can to stop him. If I do not, he will hurt everyone I know, all I have grown to care for.

It doesn't matter anymore that he is my ruler; I *will* fight him.

The water laps against the land's edge, and I leap into the harsh, unfamiliar cold.

Foxians can hold their breath for up to two weeks, but I find myself choking on it as I cut through the dense liquid. Why? I bob to the surface within two minutes and gasp for air. I can still hear his heart. I have to hurry.

But the poison and my inability to swim underwater slow me down.

A small raft suddenly appears in the water next to my head. It was not there before. And then, I see him standing on it.

A man—it's difficult to make out his face—wraps his fingers around my throat. He shoves me under the water.

I can't breathe. The combination of the poison and water tears through my liver and lungs, making it difficult to fight. Difficult to fear. I choke.

I kick against the boat and tear at his hands as bubbles burst through the water. My lungs ache in a way I have never experienced. My neck burns.

He yanks me back out. "Hi, Kokab," Brian says as I struggle for breath.

Something fuzzy comes to memory. A white room. A purple cloak.

Did *Brian* kidnap me? He was with someone. A Yadian.

Words come to me. *The Eldest One said to tell you that the only way to know how to save your people is if you allow yourself to feel.* Is this vision real?

He grins as I writhe against his grip. I claw at the raft. I should be able to fight easily, but I can't. I mentally shriek at the nanobots inside of me to heal, but they are doing their best. If I had 2.4 more minutes to recover from the poison, I might be strong enough. I do not have that time.

"I DIDN'T MEAN to kill Joe," Brian continues, while strangling me. "It was just an accident. Joe was always a good friend, but I needed the money I'd get for killing the president. Killing you, however, is personal. I wish you knew how much I've been looking forward to this."

Joe is dead? The words rush over me, far more painful than the pain of drowning.

My body goes limp, but *I* need to stop the Eldest One. *Carter needs you. Mama needs you.* I make a list of people. I let their faces fill my mind as I continue to writhe in his grasp.

I scream and tear his fingers off my throat, and my head bobs below the water. But he snatches me again.

Why? Why does Brian want to kill me? What did *I* ever do to him? And what happens if I die? Death is unknown. Death is terrifying. If I pass out, I can be resuscitated. Even if I die, the nanobots can restart my heart. But someone would need to be there to give the command if I cannot.

But there is no one to help me. No one knows where I am except Brian and the Eldest One.

And the Eldest One wants me to die. That is why he did not block out his beating heart. It was a trap.

The leader who was supposed to protect all the Foxians, keep us safe, who is supposed to be the most Perfect of us all, has ordered my death.

I am not ready for death. My life only started.

But I am going to die.

I command the nanobots to heal until I cannot think anymore. It's black for a moment, and I can no longer count the time.

There is warmth.

An encompassing light.

I lay in the arms of a radiant being on a brick path beneath the statue of a soldier carrying a wounded survivor, the Holocaust Memorial, not far from Lady Liberty.

The soldier stands erect and strong, and so is the woman holding me.

Her hair glows, and her face is free from any blemishes. She is Foxian. I am going to ask who she is, but by the way she is, she stands perfectly, erect and bright, and yet there is so much different about her—there is only one person she could be.

I do not know how to address Princess Elsimmona, so I stay quiet as she bends over me and drags my body to the statue of the heroic soldier. Her eyes sparkle, and she ducks her head into her arms as she does an American dab.

Cars honk and swerve only blocks away, but the Yadian invisibility field is like Joe's umbrella that blocks the rain. I am 98 percent confident I feel peace. From her or safety, I cannot say.

"Brian succeeded in killing you," she tells me. "Which is good for us because now the Eldest One thinks you're dead. Good thing I resuscitated you in the nick of time."

She sighs and shakes her radiating white hair. "I should never have trusted my brother. As it turns out, Foxia wasn't getting hit by an asteroid after all."

The news leads to a plethora of emotional reactions, only some of which I am able to identify.

She kisses my forehead, and I instantly feel the warmth of her superior nanobots running through me. "I'll be back soon with Ags. We need you to help us stand against him. Will you accept this calling?"

It is the same question the Eldest One asked me when I was going to leave Foxia, only this time, I do not answer out of a sense of obligation. I answer because I want it.

I choose it.

"Yes."

Chapter 26

AGS

I speed through streets on my broken bike and tighten my grip when a minivan swerves in front of me. Everyone is rushing to get out of New York. And I'm invisible.

It's not a good combo, but it has to be this way. I'm alien.

It's all over the news. Aliens. Aliens are attacking Earth. Not *just* aliens.

Me. Ags, a student at Sequoyah High, is a deranged alien, they say. A terrorist. A mass murderer.

Usually, the wind would lash against my hair. My breath would form clouds in this frozen fall chill. But it doesn't. And even without the shield, nothing would come. I close my eyes and focus on the sound of the wind.

Even if I can't feel as much as usual, this is too much for me.

I ride up to the edge of the bay and pedal to a stop. Els is in a tiny motorboat. "Stole this," she says, gesturing toward the boat and then points toward Lady Liberty. "The Eldest One's there."

I climb in. Lady Liberty greets the water. Her torch raises to the universe, the symbol of freedom. I've always wanted to visit her. But not like this. Not when everyone's freedom, all the beautiful Yadians and humans—and Foxians—is at stake.

We reach her Island. Everyone's gone. They've all evacuated from New York.

But the WE 🤍 ALIENS and GET OUT OF NY posters flutter

against the ground, left behind. An American flag small enough for a human child's grip rolls to my feet.

"Els?" I hear. I appear, except it isn't me.

It's like the 1930's short story, "The Thing on the Doorstep," where a man's body is possessed by something else. I stare into my own face, taken over by the Eldest One.

"You took my body," I snarl at him. My face stares at me, a look of fury and shock written across it.

The Eldest One shakes *my* head and turns to Els. He had no clue she could get to me via her former body, did he? He thought I'd be tucked away in a cell.

Well, too bad for him. He wriggles my nose. How dare he wriggle *my* beautiful nose.

In a flash, he yanks a ChemPod from his pocket. I'd shriek if I could. Els spins in front of me, and a light engulfs us and blocks his view. A sharp whistling cleaves the air. The ball spirals to the side of us, and flame shoots across the grass, singing it.

I cannot feel the heat.

Els's crystal voice cuts through the air. "I knew you couldn't resist reappearing when you saw me. Please, brother. We took your giant ship. You are without an army. Stop this nonsense."

"No," he says. His—*my*—voice crackles and crumbles. In his Foxian body, he always sounded cool and collected, but he's in my frame now.

His fingers shake as he claws at his pocket again. "When Hos takes over the Yadian government, he'll rig the war so I win. And I'll rule your precious humans."

Hearing those words come from *my* mouth causes my fists to clench. It doesn't matter what body I'm in. The idea of him hurting humans tortures me.

"I'll kill you," I whisper and disappear, using an invisibility shield as I dash toward him.

I sprint so quickly it's almost like I'm flying on air.

I'm stronger than him. I'll break my own neck with Foxian fingers if I have to. He laughs and disappears too. But neither of us can take the offensive position with the shields blocking the way in and out.

He reappears at the feet of Lady Liberty and weaves across the chains woven around her toes. "You can't do it. You love your own body too much."

The Eldest One turns around and tosses a glowing ball into my face. I dodge, grateful I can now move so quickly. My fingers find their target.

I yank the swirling orange ball from my pocket and pull back.

But it's too late. He throws one that explodes and encompasses the entire hill. Dirt and signs tear from the earth and spin into the water. The shattering noise beats against my eardrums, and I crumple to the ground.

Els falls too. I twitch my fingers and try to focus on my old face as I thrust the ball forward.

Goodbye. Goodbye me.

But, in my weakened state, my throw isn't as fast. He disappears and reappears over us.

He's going to kill us. This is it.

I failed.

"It's okay," Els whispers to me. "I didn't want you to do this to yourself. But I knew you needed to try."

She's so quiet only a Foxian could hear. Fortunately, the Eldest One is no longer Foxian.

KOKAB

Els got me here with her invisibility shield, and I hide in the walls of Lady Liberty's torch. The Eldest One would notice me if he was in a different body, but he is blinded by Ags's distracted nature as he fights below.

Els and Ags tumble to the ground as fire explodes around them.

With no time to hesitate, I clamor to the top and leap forty feet below me. The Eldest One tumbles backward as I land on him. He writhes and flails against me, but I'm much stronger than him.

Smoke curls around us as I grip him in a lock. His stare is cold, but he does not look away for 2.5 seconds.

"You were supposed to be dead," he whispers.

It is as if I can finally see his soul. His brows twist in fury. His eyes dance wildly like the fire around us. They explode and burn. How could I never see all the emotions teeming inside of him? He hid them so well behind the Foxian exterior.

And, for a moment, I wonder if it really is better to not feel if feelings could turn into him.

He whips his shoulders into my collar bone, and I grit my teeth. But I'm a lot stronger than he is. I shove him downward, and his permeating sweat drips across the sidewalk. His orange arms clam up.

I inhale and tighten my grip, fearful of what I must do.

"You have always been obedient to me. Do not harm me," he commands. His voice shakes. I ignore it as pain writhes through my gut and screams at me. Despite all he wants to do, all I heard him say as I listened from above, even the fact he tried to kill me himself, I do not want to hurt him. But it needs to be done.

I glance at Ags for her permission. It's her body, after all.

She barely nods and turns her head from the monster possessing her frame. Her eyes clasp shut, and it's amazing how much pain is displayed on her face. I've never seen a Foxian look so desperate before.

I stare down at the Eldest One, who still fights in my grip. "You did not save our people from death," I whisper. "You destroyed their opportunity to live. But I do hope, if there is a God or gods, you receive mercy."

I dig my fingers into his chest and order the nanobots to deconstruct. I could tear his body into two. I could unzip him from the head down and rip his organs to shreds. He deserves for his blood to stream over the singed grass as he screams in pain.

But I choose mercy. Still, I can hear the quiet unzipping of his heart as he gasps, and then there is silence.

His arms lay against the grass. His eyes turn as stony as the Lady Liberty statue itself.

A single tear drops from my eye. The warm water slowly slides down my cheek. It drips from my chin onto his silent chest. More tears pour down my face as I weep beside Lady Liberty's strong feet.

So this is why humans cry.

I bawl because of all that has been lost. For Ags, who relinquished something worse than her life: her identity. For Joe, who always helped me and died because of it. For Carter, who will now be fatherless. For the human politicians the Eldest One murdered. The Foxians he enslaved. And for the Eldest One himself.

And finally, I cry because my mother died in my arms on a bus, and I stood there stony-faced as they carried her away. No one ever allowed me to grieve her. No one ever allowed me to love her, either.

I glance at Lady Liberty's sign:

Give me your tired, your poor, your huddled masses yearning to breathe free.

I rub the water from my cheeks, more human than I have ever been.

Chapter 27

AGS

It's ironic, really.

With all the millions of stories, across all the thousands of galaxies, hundreds I know and cherish, this isn't the ending I imagined.

I'm stuck in a Foxian body leading a group of them to Earth. It's almost hilarious.

I watch through the windows of the ship as we near the deep oceans and greenery of the rich planet.

Yas grins at me as he chews some Artian rocks, which rings in my ears. But his lopsided grin is pretty endearing. I'm amazed that the guy was able to help take Hos down. Maybe he's not as wimpy as I thought.

Els waltzes over to me and places her arm over my shoulder. "You'll get used to the body," she says. "But I'm sorry. It's hard to lose yourself for a cause."

I shrug. "At least Earth is okay. Everything I caused is over."

When the ships disappeared, and the Yadian government explained everything, life went back to normal on Earth. What else could humans do without any trace of aliens' existence remaining? I mean, except for the tightened security protocols throughout the USA.

Now airport lines will probably be three hours.

We can't take the few thousand Foxians on this ship to Antarctica now. Not with humans watching for any possibility of alien life there.

Els says she has been watching a particular place for a while, and it's the perfect spot for seclusion and to learn human emotions.

We near the cascading peaks of the Himalayas and nestle into the white snow. Remnants of ash churn through the heavy winds.

Els lands in front of the small, beaten hut that belongs to the young couple I watched with her before my first trip to Foxia, if only for a few minutes. This will drastically alter their life.

"The Foxians will need us to translate," Mom says. I nod, and we step out into the snow.

"Good luck, my friends." Els bows her head and insists we introduce them alone. She waves as each Foxian steps from the ship.

They follow us. I no longer think they are creepy. They have the same potential as all of us to learn, grow, and become. At least, I hope it is the same since I am one of them now.

I'm not ready to accept this body yet, but maybe I will be someday.

The snow blows across the mountain. I always wanted to experience snow, but now I'll never know what it feels like.

Bredrion glances at me as I reach the little hut.

I tap the front door. No one answers. The couple never has guests. I rap again, and a woman flings the door open, surprise across her face, a tight red blanket draped over her shoulders. She shushes her baby as her eyebrows knit together in confusion.

"This is Bredrion," says Mom in Burman. "He is not from here. But he needs your help."

The woman holds out her arms, not hesitant to embrace the strange man. Nothing in her culture dictates anything but love. But I'm surprised when he hugs her back.

I look out at the scene, once more reminded of Dante's words on Hell:

> O'er all the sand-waste, with a gradual fall, were
> raining down dilated flakes of fire,
> as of the snow on Alp without a wind.

As they embrace, a wind stirs across the mountainside. The dilated flakes extinguish from the sky.

CARTER

MAMA CLINGS to Jason as he bawls with his little head shoved into her waist. For once in his life, he's not afraid that crying will make him less of a man.

Neither am I. I sob, face red, eyes swollen. My body shakes from how bad the pain is, and I tremble as the moment plays in my head all over again. The gunshot. Brian's shaking body. Dad's face frozen in time. The horror is fresh again.

Margi's baby was born a few hours after Dad died. He howls too as if he knows he's lost his grandpa. Margi stands next to him and whispers into his ear. Stories of who Joe Turner was. Cody wraps his arms around his wife, his own face damp from crying. He doesn't bother wiping away the snot. Megan, now recovered, stands strong, clinging to her mom.

The pastor says a few words on heaven and how Dad's in a better place. I understand now why Anna was so desperate to know whether she'd see her brother again. I wish I could have proof too, but if there's anything I've learned, it's that there's always more going on than we see.

Why? It's a question I've never asked God before, but I ask him now as the pastor prays over the large, brown coffin. The hot air rips through my grief. Why him? Why now?

I'm not ready to do this alone. But I must.

Dad needs me to.

We sing an old classic about a soldier boy who died too young. The rich words twist through the air. Mama's voice rings clear, big like always, even as her lips tremble. I step forward and set a painting of a star on the coffin. My talents are crude, but I know he'd appreciate a piece of heaven more than a rose.

Black crowds disperse. Lines of friends, coworkers, and science fans leaving until it is just the family.

"He really was a great man, wasn't he?" I say to no one in particular.

Mama grasps my shoulder. "Still is."

We drive home. David Bowie churns on the radio like the day I met Kokab. We all lost. I lost my dad. She lost everybody. At least now, because of her, my dad didn't die with a tarnished reputation. He died a hero.

Everyone walks inside, but I don't. I press my fingers against the walls of the home he repaired with me and breathe in the dust and peeled paint. Some people may hate our old home, but he always saw beauty in the flawed things of the universe. I go to the playground and sit in the swing he pushed me on as a child. My legs weave back and forth.

I remember him. Laughing. Looking up into space. Showing me the solar systems.

The stars spread across the sky, abnormally bright, even for the country, and I feel better knowing he's probably out there among them. He's not soaring around somewhere because that's not his style. He's hunched over, notebook in hand, studying a planet and asking God how He made it happen.

Dad wasn't afraid to lose everything, even his own life. I won't be either.

I go inside and hug Mama as she slices me a piece of brown butter cheesecake. It's up to me to look out for her now.

I step into my bedroom, closing the door. Fingers pressed against my cell phone screen, I pull up a photo of Kokab with my family when she first got here. It hurts to see Dad's smiling face, blue-framed glasses, and bright eyes.

His story needs to be heard from my perspective. The world needs to hear the truth. They need to know I believe him.

I post the picture online. "This is my dad, and this is my friend. Nobody believed my dad, but my best friend is an alien. She made the world a better place..."

I tell our story, inviting the world to accept her. Drew writes some stupid comment about how it's all a conspiracy, but I leave the status up anyway. Others may not accept the truth today or tomorrow.

But I'm going to keep fighting.

KOKAB

I LEAVE my bed and room in pristine condition.

I realize I am neat and tidy, and that will never change. I don't want it to. I'm only now starting to realize my identity as a feeling being.

Els let me use an invisibility shield to stay for the funeral, but I need to leave Earth before anyone learns I am here still. Humans aren't ready for more aliens now.

I jot down a note for Carter and the rest of my Earth family. *Thank you for everything. Thank you for life.* The message lacks content. I am still not verbose, not good at expressing my emotions or perfectly understanding them. There are some things I may never comprehend like why Brian would want to drown me. But I'm not sure anyone really understands how emotions work.

I slip out of the broken door. Carter stands outside, hands thrust into his pockets, pain etched into his face.

I pull him into the invisibility shield and wrap my arms tightly around his waist. His eyes widen, but he grasps me too. It's warm and familiar, though I've only hugged him once before. I'm not sure where our relationship could go, but I will figure it out. Someday. For now, I have other responsibilities to attend to.

"I have to go back to Foxia." The words choke in my throat, and I start to cry for the second time in my life. "They need to know the Eldest One is dead, and I have to try to help them return things to the way it was before he took away their emotions."

He inhales and tugs me closer, wiping the tears from my face. The smell of dirt, kids' toys, and woods encompasses me. It shouldn't be pleasant, but it is. It's *his* scent.

"I wish you didn't have to leave," he says. "With Dad gone, we need you."

But I know he realizes it isn't true. They don't need me. I smile at the world around me. The sun peeks through the trees, the wind rustles, and the morning dew forms on the many blades of grass. The world is waking, and so am I.

What a beautiful, painful planet.

A piece of me wishes I could stay. I do not know what I will face on Foxia, but I do know what I will find here: a loving family.

"Carter, they deserve a chance to find out what it means to be alive."

"At least let us say goodbye."

I shake my head. I can't handle it.

Lights come on upstairs. Jason awakes, crying about his grandpa. It is time for me to leave.

I step back and take in the weathered home, the crickets chirping in the woods, the scent of Mama's laundry and left-out-cherry pie. I linger as I enjoy this place for the last time. I once considered this house broken and lacking, but I now know it is beautiful. It is home.

I wave to Carter, then turn away from him as I sprint through the woods at 72 miles per hour.

Goodbye, I whisper, knowing Carter's ears aren't good enough to hear even without the shield, but hoping the message will get to him anyway. A red leaf spirals down from a tree, a sign of change, of death making way for new life.

It may be difficult, but I will find a way to return to my people and help them to become a little more human.

ACKNOWLEDGMENTS

It takes a community to create a book. Literally. The pages of this story were altered, edited, and published with the assistance of a bunch of my favorite people. Even during brainstorming phases, I had help.

Thank you first to Holli Anderson for acquiring my novel. Terri Baranowski, you are an incredible agent, and I really appreciated your help negotiating the contract. You did way more than I ever expected. You helped me better understand my goals, know if the company was a great fit, and you got me everything I wanted out of the contract. Thank you. Ashley Literski, you made a beautiful cover, and you really understood what I wanted. The cover said so much about the book and characters. Lindsay Flanagan, you are such a stellar editor. One of the reasons I signed with IW was because I knew I could count on people like you. You did a fabulous job, and I loved our brainstorms. So glad we made the changes we did! Thanks Staci Olsen for helping put together an ARC version of the book, and thanks to Pink Ivy Photography for such beautiful headshots.

A special thanks goes to my lovely writing group: you guys are some of the greatest writers I know, and it was the fate of God that we were all put together. Thank you Stephanie for catching all the teeniest details and asking all the hard questions. Thanks Cary and Lenore for begging for the emotions to be amped up and asking for more (much needed) description. Also, thank you Cary for recommending my book to the company. Thank you Quillen and Cheree. There were so many times I felt like ditching the story, and your positive compliments helped me keep going. I'm so glad I had everyone in the group to help me figure out my story, decide on antagonists, and fill in all my plot holes. And to those who helped with the finishing details: Kate, Sara, and Rebecca. You guys have been awesome additions!

I'm so grateful for my beta-readers: Nicole Taylor, Bernadette Cheatham, KR Cunningham, Chelsey Titus Long, Chris Keaton, and Mary Shanahan. Nicole, you were the first person to finish my book, and you helped me work out a lot of the details. I really appreciate that you allowed me to come back with more questions. Mary, thanks for working so hard to put in as much as you could. You had some really great suggestions. Bernadette, you helped point out a few really important details, and I also loved your positivity! Thank you! Chris, I'm so glad I had one male read my book before publication. Some of your critiques were hard to swallow, but they helped me push harder to make my book less mediocre.

Mckelle George, you are such a talented author. Thanks for editing my first chapter and my query letter. You really helped me polish up the things that needed to look pretty for submission.

And to those who may not know who I am or the impact they made on my book and life: E.B.

Wheeler, the first day I went to a writing group I was terrified to go. I stood in the front of the library debating whether or not I should enter, and without you ushering me in, I may never have started my journey toward publication. Thank you to the Cache Valley Writers of the Utah League of Writers who saw the very first draft, a terrible version in passive voice with no storyline. If you guys hadn't given me confidence, I might not have felt like I could write. It was what I needed while being a newbie writer. Thanks to the speakers at writing conferences who helped me hone my craft, Eschler Editing (because the best way to learn to write is to teach it), and Writing Excuses for teaching me every week.

To my Immortal Works family of authors, thanks for teaching me so much, so I could gain info to market my book. You guys are stellar at spreading the word about all of us. Thanks for teaching me about great programs, social media, how to get reviews, selling to bookstores, etc. etc. Thanks to Samantha Rose for being such a big cheerleader and for finding last minute revisions needed. You all are freaking fantastic, and I love you so much.

Finally, thank you to the ones who helped most of all in more indirect ways: my family. Thank you, Dad, for inspiring my creativity with your own made-up stories and pretending. Mom, thanks for always reading me quality literature. Dale, thanks for helping me see a pattern of hard work and how accomplishing dreams is possible. Colby, my hubby and best friend, I really appreciate that you read the first half of my book (even though you never read). I appreciate all the hours of babysitting you did so I could write, learn at conferences, edit, meet with my writing group, and more. Thank you for all your brilliant pieces of marketing advice. Thank you for helping me make changes that required your set of knowledge. Thanks for brainstorming with me and listening to me go on and on about my book for hours and years.

To everyone who helped, thank you again. You mean the world to me.

ABOUT THE AUTHOR

Pink Ivy Photography

Amy Michelle Carpenter is a developmental editor with Eschler Editing and a professional blogger. She's written hundreds of blogs and news articles for local and national companies. She also has a children's story in an anthology.

As the daughter of an Army officer, she grew up traveling the country and has lived by sandy beaches, southern woods, towering cities, and the rocky mountains. Now, she resides in the countryside of Tooele, UT with her husband and baby girls. She enjoys seeing what wildlife and farm animals dare venture into her yard only to be chased by her toddlers. Wherever family is is home.

This has been an
Immortal Production